Just Sex

SUSAN KAY LAW

BERKLEY BOOKS, NEW YORK

THE BERKLEY PUBLISHING GROUP
Published by the Penguin Group
Penguin Group (USA) Inc.
375 Hudson Street, New York, New York 10014, USA
Penguin Group (Canada), 90 Eglinton Avenue East, Suite 700, Toronto, Ontario M4P 2Y3, Canada
(a division of Pearson Penguin Canada Inc.)
Penguin Books Ltd., 80 Strand, London WC2R 0RL, England
Penguin Group Ireland, 25 St. Stephen's Green, Dublin 2, Ireland
(a division of Penguin Books Ltd.)
Penguin Group (Australia), 250 Camberwell Road, Camberwell, Victoria 3124, Australia
(a division of Pearson Australia Group Pty. Ltd.)
Penguin Books India Pvt. Ltd., 11 Community Centre, Panchsheel Park, New Delhi—110 017, India
Penguin Group (NZ), 67 Apollo Drive, Rosedale, North Shore 0745, Auckland, New Zealand
(a division of Pearson New Zealand Ltd.)
Penguin Books (South Africa) (Pty.) Ltd., 24 Sturdee Avenue, Rosebank, Johannesburg 2196,
South Africa

Penguin Books Ltd., Registered Offices: 80 Strand, London WC2R 0RL, England

This is an original publication of The Berkley Publishing Group.

This is a work of fiction. Names, characters, places, and incidents either are the product of the author's imagination or are used fictitiously, and any resemblance to actual persons, living or dead, business establishments, events, or locales is entirely coincidental. The publisher does not have any control over and does not assume any responsibility for author or third-party websites or their content.

First edition: June 2007

Library of Congress Cataloging-in-Publication Data

Law, Susan Kay.
    Just sex / Susan Kay Law.—1st ed.
        p.   cm.
    ISBN: 978-0-425-21523-4 (trade pbk.)
1. Adultery—Fiction.   2. Love stories. gsafd   I. Title.

PS3562.A8612J87   2007   2007004383
813'.6—dc22

PRINTED IN THE UNITED STATES OF AMERICA

10   9   8   7   6   5   4   3   2

Praise for the books of Susan Kay Law

"With her delightful sense of humor and ability to create real, likable characters, Susan Kay Law has a true charmer in *The Last Man in Town*, a romance with a big heart and feminist overtones. Just don't be the last one in your town to read Susan Kay Law's terrific, sexy tale." —*Romantic Times*

"Fans of historical romances by Jill Marie Landis and LaVyrle Spencer will find Law's latest their cup of escapist tea." —*Publishers Weekly*

"[*A Wedding Story*] definitely stands on its own and gives little away about the previous books—something that may tempt new fans into reading the earlier stories." —*Library Journal*

"Susan Kay Law renews our faith in human nature in this heartfelt love story . . . *Home Fires* will leave you with a warm glow long after the book is closed." —*Romantic Times*

Just Sex

1

The Order

"IT had nothing to do with you," he told her. "It was just sex."

That's when their fashionable, overpriced "marriage facilitator" had to pry Ellen Markham's hands from around her husband's neck.

"Nothing to do with me?" she shrieked as they wrestled her back into a caramel leather chair. Ellen *never* shrieked. But if there was ever a right time for shrieking, this was it. "Unless you wrapped her in latex from head to toe every single time you touched one of them, it has everything to do with me!"

"Of course I was safe." Tom smoothed his rumpled shirt, smoothed his rumpled expression, but it was far too late for that. They'd been married for twenty years. Did he think she didn't know his guilt when she saw it?

Which only made her wonder why she hadn't noticed it sooner. Because she hadn't wanted to: no other answer made sense. She'd wanted to go on living in the comfortable, content little world they'd built, truth be damned, until it smacked her in the face and she couldn't ignore it any longer.

And the fact that she'd become the kind of woman who'd ignore all the little clues bothered her almost most of all. She'd always felt superior to women willing to live like that, trading honesty and commitment for security. *She'd* never settle, she'd always believed. But she was discovering that dismantling a family was no simple thing.

"Tom." The energizing anger leeched out with the fear, leaving her as sweaty and weak as if she were coming off a three-day fever. She'd lost the ability to feel ordinary emotions, any shades of gray. Instead she swung madly between wild fury and trembling exhaustion, unable to settle into any livable place in between. "How could anything have any *more* to do with me?"

"Now then." Lauren—she'd told them to call her Lauren, rather than any of the formal titles the string of letters behind her name entitled her to—slid back into her own chair with a hiss of silk and whisper of expensive perfume, as polished and serene as always. Certainly she did not look as if she'd just forestalled a brawl. Maybe she was accustomed to such things; couples didn't come to her office because they were getting along just fine.

"Now then—" she began.

"If you ask me how I'm feeling," Ellen snarled, "I can't promise to stay in this chair."

Lauren smiled and reached for the cup of green tea on the low, Asian-style table. There were no couches in her office, no desk for her to sit behind. It was a good and undoubtedly expensive approximation of a downtown coffee bar, which was, Ellen supposed, the point. But no one paid $350 an hour to meet a friend over coffee, and it seemed silly to pretend anything else.

"Your emotions are certainly clear," Lauren said in the rich voice that could have made her a fortune in phone sex. "However, there is always a value in verbalizing them. Only then can one consider whether they are productive or not."

"I'm mad," Ellen said, which didn't seem to cover it. She was *mad* when someone stole her parking space at the mall, when her e-mail didn't work for the third time in two weeks, when the plumber didn't bother to show up. She was mad when the garage took four days longer than they promised to fix her minivan, when Tom forgot to record the $1,500 in instant cash he withdrew that month.

"I'm *fucking* mad," she said, the shock of it giving her a little thrill. What her mother used to call "bad language" was, like lawn maintenance and oil changes, Tom's niche in the marriage.

He swore freely and regularly and seemingly without any real emotion behind it; in some odd sort of cosmic balancing, she'd stopped almost completely.

But some things, she decided, called for really nasty words. Too bad she didn't know any worse ones.

"There." Lauren beamed at her as if she were a child who'd just tied her shoes all by herself for the first time. "What else?"

"I want to kill him," she said, warming to her topic. "Well, that's not completely true. I don't want to really *kill* him. I just want to make sure he's of no use to any woman ever again, and—"

"Christ!" Tom shifted in his chair and crossed his legs. "Do you really think this is productive?"

"You'll get your opportunity to speak shortly," Lauren told him. "And this time perhaps you'll be able to dig deeper than you have previously. For now consider this an excellent opportunity to utilize the active listening techniques—"

The thread of swirling, calming sounds—not really music, Ellen had decided the first day—that underlay their sessions smoothed into a bright tinkle.

"Time's up." Lauren stood, the slubbed silk of her skirt sliding around her excellent knees, and Ellen caught Tom's sidelong glance.

She never used to mind. It was an automatic response, she'd always figured. A man couldn't help noticing an attractive woman any more than he could keep from sneezing if pepper were blown into his face. They were just hardwired that way.

He can look all he wants, as long as he doesn't touch. How many times had she said that over the years, with the indulgent laugh of a secure wife? She'd been proud of herself for being mature enough not to be threatened by a bit of harmless admiration.

Had that been where it had started to go wrong? Maybe Tom assumed she'd be just as tolerant of a more physical form of admiration.

"But we're just—"

"Write it down in your journal," Lauren said, ushering them

out with the smooth skill of someone who nudged reluctant couples out of her office a half dozen times a day. "Use that emotion there, and we'll go through it all next week. You have been using your journal, haven't you?"

"Of course," Ellen lied with all the promptness she'd mastered in years of telling her dentist, "Yes, of course, I floss twice a day without fail." She'd tried writing about it, but it was one more duty, one that only seemed to spur her into a blind and useless fury every time, and she was tired of being the only one working on this marriage.

Another couple waited their turn in the tastefully neutral waiting room, leaping to their feet from the sage-colored couches where they'd perched awkwardly with a precise three feet between them.

Ellen knew that dance. Where to sit took on enormous importance while you waited for an appointment that you hoped would patch your life together. Not too far apart; that would imply there was no chance. And it seemed strange to sit carefully across from a man who'd seen you naked so many times he could probably pick out your cooch from a thousand naked crotches.

It had to be close enough to imply that there was still some connection between you. Some hope. Not so near, however, as to pretend that everything was fine.

The door to the inner office clicked softly shut, leaving them alone in the waiting room.

"Now," Ellen said, catching a second wind. "You—"

"Oh, no." Tom held up a hand to forestall her. "I'm not letting you start in without Lauren here to referee." He shoved a hand through his hair, leaving it—brown with a threading of gray—standing up in tufts.

She couldn't look at him without seeing the Tom she'd met all those years ago, at the beginning of her sophomore year, striding across the mall in a baggy intramural jersey and jeans that were ripped at the knee, a nerdy bookworm trying to pretend he was cool. He dressed better now, but that image was as clear as the one right in front of her, one superimposed on the other like double-exposed film. Thinner on top, thicker around the middle now. The same warm brown in his eyes, the same off-balance way of standing, his left shoulder held higher than the right. The same smile, though she hadn't seen much of it lately. She'd loved that smile first, missed it as much as she missed the warmth of him beside her in bed at night.

"Do you really think this is helping?" he asked, voice low and tired. "If this is not—if we're just going through the motions, tell me now."

"Tell you now so what? So you can stop having to *try* so hard? So you can stop *working* at it?" She felt the sharp slice of her nails against her palms. More pain, almost familiar now, better than nothing. "Our marriage is too much *trouble* for you?"

"Damn it." He shook his head. Helpless, hopeless. "What do you want, Ellen?"

Now there was the question: the only one that really mattered now. "I want my life back. I want *our* life back. The one I believed we had, the one where we were happily married." She wanted the impossible. "Not the one where you got to run around and have sex with anyone stupid enough to have you."

"I guess that makes you Queen Stupid then, doesn't it? You married me."

Tears flooded her eyes. Damn it, how could there possibly be any left?

"Oh, Ellen, I'm sorry. Shit, I didn't mean . . ." His shoulders slumped. "I never meant to hurt you."

Hysteria bubbled through the tears. "Well, you did a pretty good job of it." She swiped at her face. "What did you *think* was going to happen?"

"I didn't . . ."

"You didn't think," she said flatly.

"It's better than if I'd meant to hurt you, isn't it? Than if I'd *decided* to go out wreck it all? If I'd *thought*, then it would have been deliberate. And it wasn't. It was just . . ." His left shoulder lifted, fell.

"I don't know. At least that way you would have thought about me at some point, rather than the fact of my existence being so insignificant that it didn't affect your behavior in any way."

"Ellen." He said her name wearily, without any of the affection that used to warm his voice. "I didn't think you'd find out. And I wasn't sure you'd care if you did."

She gaped at him, as shocked as she'd been when she'd called his room at the Chicago Hyatt at 1 a.m. to report a late-night trip to the emergency vet, and a girl—the voice had definitely sounded like a girl, now that everyone under thirty seemed like a girl to Ellen—had answered, and all those small clues she'd ignored had all avalanched into place. *Click, click, click*, the puzzle suddenly solved, and the picture she hadn't wanted to face coming brutally clear. "I wouldn't care?" she repeated. She shook her head, unable to comprehend. Either he hadn't learned a darned thing about her in all those years, he was a lot more stupid than his summa cum laude indicated, or he had a remarkable ability to delude himself.

Maybe all three.

It did not speak well for her own delusions that she hadn't noticed it a long time ago.

"Are you implying," she said, careful to keep the anger tamped down, her tone even, "that this is somehow my fault? That I didn't make it clear enough to you that I cared whether you screwed somebody who wasn't me?"

His gaze fixed on the innocuous landscape over the couch, a bright and breezy picture of a windswept shore that was surely thousands of miles from here, as distant from a gloomy Minneapolis December as the truth of their marriage was from the image the world saw. "Be honest now, El. You can't say there is a whole lot of heat between us anymore."

"Heat?" she snarled. "You want *heat*?" Well, she wanted heat, too. Except *heat*, on her to-do list, came down somewhere below filling out yet another school form; fretting about their daughter's new boyfriend, who was clearly way too old for her for all that he was technically only seventeen; and catching one full, precious night's sleep.

Oh, she'd love heat. But mostly she'd like the time and energy for heat. "Aren't we too old for heat?" she asked, almost too tired to get the words out. But she didn't really mean too old. She meant too grown-up, too mature to put some quick flash of adolescent lust ahead of years of trust and companionship and commitment. And wasn't that supposed to be a good thing?

"No." He dropped onto the nearest love seat. He braced his elbows on his knees, his hands linked, his head bowed. She saw the thinning spot, right at the top of his head, that he covered up with a ball cap whenever he could. Because the sun was bad for you, he'd insisted, even as they'd both known that it was vanity that had him tugging on the headgear. But she was fond of that bald spot, found the bit of scalp peering through endearing, liked to run her fingers over it.

He lifted his head, looked directly at her, his eyes intense. He'd spent much of the last three months with his gaze flitting away from hers. Too guilty, she'd assumed. Or maybe he just didn't want to see her. *Look at me*, she'd wanted to scream at him. Now there was emotion there, but not remorse or shame or fear, none of the things it was her right to find. No, this was anger.

"Can you honestly say you don't miss it?" He grabbed her hand so he didn't have to look up at her, yanked her down on the settee next to him, and kept her there with a firm grip. It should have pissed her off, being hauled around like that. *Did*, she told herself, though he'd already done a thousand things worse to her.

But there was a small kick of excitement in it, a quiver of female response to a commanding man. He'd never been sexier to her than when she'd heard him on the phone, swinging a deal, giving orders, taking charge. It was sexist of her, archaic. There just the same.

And at least he cared enough to be angry. For three months, she wondered if he had cared at all. Oh, he'd gone through the motions of counseling, the routine attempts at salvaging their marriage, but she didn't believe he was doing it for *her*. He tried, or at least pretended to, because he'd finally realized what it all meant: angry kids, a bare and empty apartment, the division of the financial security they'd built so diligently, and the loss of someone to take care of the multitude of details Ellen attended to every day. That, she thought, was the loss he regretted. He missed his simple, neat, ordered life. But he didn't miss *her*.

"Can you honestly say you don't want that? You're trudging down the street, another day, another list of responsibilities, and you pass someone. There's a bit of smile, a little spark in a gray day, and you wonder."

"We're not here because you *wondered*, Tom."

"Tell me you remember," he said, with an urgency she hadn't heard from him in years. "You meet somebody, and you wonder. Wonder what it would be like if you kissed them. Wonder if they'd let you. What it would be like when you touched them for the first time. And so every second of that day you're *more* than you were before. Your life isn't gray anymore. You see everything, you *feel* everything. Damn it, El, how can you honestly tell me you're ready to give that up forever?" He still had her hand, still spoke to her. But he wasn't talking *about* her, the wife who'd propped him up when he'd nearly botched his first deal, who worked at a tedious accounting job to support them while he earned his MBA, and who carried his children.

He was talking about some random woman he passed on the street who somehow gave him more than she did. "If you're too old for heat, you're too old for *alive*."

And now he thought she was old. "Nice speech," she said. Flippant, dismissive, desperate to hide how much he'd wounded her.

Tom blew out a breath and let go of his wife's hand. He'd tried, hadn't he? She'd wanted him to explain, but she hadn't really cared about the real answer. She'd wanted her answer, of course, her way. That was Ellen, wasn't it? Wanting it her way.

"I don't know why you can't get past this," Tom said. "But I can't go back and change it, even if I wanted to."

Even if *he wanted to?* Ellen opened her mouth to pounce, but he was charging on.

"We could go bankrupt coming here, and it's not going to make any difference until you're ready to move on."

He was right, though Ellen couldn't bring herself to admit it. "You want to quit, then?" She flung out the words. He would have to be the one to give up. Not her, not ever her. Sometimes, though, it seemed like it would be so much easier just to have it *over*. To stop fighting and start getting on with her life.

But he had to be the one to finish it. He was the one at fault, and she wasn't going to let either one of them forget it.

"No, I don't want to quit," Tom said. "You'd like that, wouldn't you? One more thing to blame on me."

She had no answer for that. "I'll see you next week."

He tried one more time to explain. "It really wasn't about you. Wasn't even about *them*. It's just about the rush. About feeling alive. I didn't . . . care about them. It was just physical."

"Just like a golf game, huh? A nice, sweaty couple of hours where you didn't have to think about the job or the kids?"

"Yes, that's it exactly."

Before they'd married, she'd made sure they were compatible on so many levels. That they had the same views on finances, on children. Somehow she'd overlooked this completely. How could she not have known that vows were merely inconveniences to him, something that should not be allowed to spoil his fun?

"I just can't get past it," she said, her throat raw. It *was* the one thing he was right about: all the counseling in the world wouldn't do any good until she was able to let it go. But she was caught in it, spinning around and around in that same dark whirlpool: *He cheated on me. He cheated on me.* "I just can't."

He frowned. "So have one yourself."

"*What?*"

"If that's the only way to even things up. The only way to start with a clean slate. And maybe you'll finally understand that it really is just sex.

"Have an affair."

2

Juice

"So. Who are you gonna use your Get Out of Jail Free card on?"
Jill asked.

Ellen glanced over at her friend, flailing away on the stair-
stepper next to the one that was fast grinding Ellen into the
ground. Which one of them was it who decided fighting the inevitable was the right thing to do? Sliding peacefully into a
frumpy, chubby middle age was a whole lot more appealing
when she was sweating than it was when she was standing in
front of a mirror trying to find a something to wear that made
her look like she still had a waist.

Jill was her oldest friend, though hardly anyone who knew
them had figured out how that had happened. Jill played bad
girl to Ellen's good, short to her tall, her bombshell figure to
Ellen's . . . not. She'd had three piercings when nobody else in
St. Stephen's Junior High had even one; a tattoo long before
every soccer mom who was trying to prove she still had a wild
streak needled a flower into her shoulder; and kept her hair
flame red, short, and as messy as Sharon Stone's when she was
playing a bad girl.

They'd bonded in eighth grade when Joey Marcioni, the
dream of every Catholic schoolgirl, had the vast misjudgment to
flex his cocky thirteen-year-old attitude on them both in one
week. He'd asked Ellen—studious, wallflower Ellen, who'd
hardly been able to lift her eyes from the floor in his presence,
much less speak—if she'd wanted to go to the Harvest Dance

with him in front of his pack of hangers-on, and waited until she, her thrilled heart fluttering in her throat, had stammered out a "Yes" before he declared that that was too bad, because he'd never go out with a dog like her. And back then, *dawg* was anything but a term of affection.

Joey hadn't taken it so easy on Jill. No, he'd talked her out of her shirt, and her plain cotton bra, and was well on his way to third base when his friends piled into the gym storage closet precisely on what Jill had realized was a prearranged schedule. He'd left her standing in a pile of pink rubber balls, her arms jammed across her premature D cups, and refused to give back her shirt. Finally she dropped her arms. "Look your fill," she'd snarled. "God knows it's going to be years before any of you shit bags get this close to a girl's boobs again." Then she'd stalked by them and straight across the gym toward the locker room, refusing to run, bringing basketball practice to an abrupt halt and getting herself suspended for two weeks in the process.

What Joey hadn't counted on was that the two girls, who never would have spoken to each other otherwise, both had a vengeful streak. Ellen provided the brains, Jill the guts, and all the enthusiastic fans arriving at St. Stephen's seventy-fifth anniversary homecoming game had been greeted with the sight of Joey Marcioni, who looked a lot skinnier and paler and all around less studly wearing nothing but a pair of saggy, dingy, cotton briefs, enjoying the forty-five degree weather tied to the goalpost.

"My Get Out of Jail Free card?" Ellen managed, even though talking made the stitch in her side twist up tighter.

"Hon, you just got handed the dream of half of the wives in America. Your husband just *told* you to have an affair."

"I don't think that half of the wives want that."

"The ones that got any juice left in them do. Who cares about the other half? They're no fun."

"I'm not sure I have any juice." Ellen had no problem admitting she was by nature a conservative and careful woman, which she'd always considered more of an asset than a problem. She was still fun, she always thought. She just wasn't stupid about it.

But apparently Tom didn't agree with her.

"Of course you have," Jill said. "If you didn't, why would I still be hanging around with you?"

"Well, I'm still not going to do it."

Jill stopped chugging and rode the pedals to the ground. "You sure as hell are doing it!"

"I win," Ellen said, keeping the *thank-effing-God* to herself. She pumped through three more cycles, just to rub it in, before easing down herself. Luckily, her legs held up; it took the edge off the gloating if you collapsed when you stepped off.

It was a mark of just how fired up Jill was that she didn't even protest Ellen's claim to victory.

"And exactly why aren't you doing it?" She scooped up her water bottle and chugged down half.

Ellen shrugged. She couldn't just say, "It's wrong," because Jill'd destroy that argument in less time than it took for Ellen's heartbeat to slow from *You're going to die in two minutes* to just *When did you forget that you're over forty?* Jill hadn't become the youngest creative director that Young, Smiley, and Bartleman had ever had without being able to put a convincing spin on things.

"Oh, come on." Just because Jill was annoying her, Ellen moved to the nearest treadmill and ramped it up to 5.0. Barely a jog, but as much as she could handle. "Who'm I gonna use it on? The bag boy at Lunds?"

Jill dragged herself on the next treadmill, glanced at Ellen's display, and punched her own speed to 5.1. "Oh, what the hell. You'd make him a legend among the entire junior high. He'd never forget you."

Despite herself, Ellen smiled at the idea. "Sure. And poor Eric could never show his face at school again."

"So you'll have to pick a different Lunds."

Ellen would have laughed if she'd had the air for it. "Face it. I know no men."

"You know lots of men."

"I know no single men between the ages of thirty-five and fifty-five."

"So don't limit yourself so much."

"Okay, twenty-five and seventy-five. Better? I still don't know any." She considered. "Actually, I do. But if you discount my hairdresser, who hasn't looked at a woman since the late seventies when the drugs wore off and he noticed the difference between men and women and decided he liked men better, I know two. And they're both single for very, very good reasons." She made a face.

"You haven't exactly been looking," Ellen told her. "*I* manage to find them. At least I used to."

"*You* work, out there in the real world. My life is an endless round of PTO meetings, grocery stores, and playing corporate wife. And none of those places are exactly a gold mine of . . ." Of what? Potential lays? There wasn't a delicate term for it.

Delicate had never bothered Jill. "Fuckable men?"

"Yeah. Those."

"If there had been, you wouldn't have noticed. You just shut that part of yourself off and painted a big flashing Married sign on your forehead. If you open yourself up, who knows who you might find?"

"Uh-huh." Pain hitched up under her rib cage. "You know what I'm like. Some people are meant to walk on the wild side, and some people aren't. When we were in school you could skip class for weeks on end and get away with it. I'd do it *once*, and that would be the afternoon half of the faculty's wives were at the mall. I'd be hauled back before the final bell rang."

"You always did manage to get caught, didn't you?"

"It wasn't like I was *trying* to get caught." It had never failed, and the unfairness of it had never left her. The police cruised by the very instant she unfurled her first roll of toilet paper over the tree on Annette O'Neal's front lawn; her father's midnight trek to the bathroom always coincided precisely with her creeping in a minute after curfew; Mr. Hollinbeck would spring a pop quiz in Shakespeare the one day all term she hadn't done her reading the night before.

She'd have to have been an idiot not to realize that she was not supposed to nudge one toe off the straight and narrow.

"I'd probably catch something," she said glumly. "Do you know that a single kiss swaps as many as five hundred *different* bacteria? I'd end up in the *New England Journal of Medicine* as the poster child for a brand-new strain of VD. Not a deadly one. Just something ugly and painful and wildly embarrassing."

"You did get tested, didn't you?" Jill asked in the serious, grown-up tone she'd developed since her son Josh's birth. "You promised me you would."

Ellen swallowed hard and nodded. She'd never imagined having to walk into her doctor's office and get tested for STDs. She'd worried, pretty much weekly since Katie'd hit thirteen, about having to walk *her* into a clinic. But not herself. "Yeah. I'm fine. But I have to again, when the six months are up."

"Good." Jill nodded. "That's good. You'll let me know, right?"

"Sure. Sure, I'll let you know." And ask, if she needed her. Who would have thought it? That after everything—all those years, their families, Ellen's marriage, all the men who whirled in and out of Jill's life—the only person in Ellen's life who had always been there for her, no matter what, no questions asked, no secrets, was Jill?

She should find Joey Marcioni and thank him.

"And you'll be careful when you decide to go for it, right? I mean, honestly, they'll complain about it, they will—men are *such* babies about such things—but you're doing *them* a favor, too, and—"

"I'll be careful. I promise," Ellen said. "You sound just like me before that boy picks Katie up."

"I do *not* sound like you." Jill grimaced. For all that Jill was highly in favor of a liberated sex life, she had the same opinion as Ellen when it came to Katie's boyfriend. "Would you like me to talk to her? Sometimes . . . well, sometimes you can say something to someone else you can't say to your mother."

"No. You're the big gun. I'm saving you." Ellen slugged down room-temperature water. "Besides, even if I don't catch something, I'm bound to end up with a guy who's a stalker. Or, worse yet, married."

Jill scowled at the numbers on her treadmill. "Seventy-five calories. How can it only be seventy-five calories burned after all this work?" she muttered crossly and clicked the speed to 5.5. "Anyway. You can tell if they're married. You can always tell."

"You can?" Five point six. She was going to get thin or die sometime in the next ten minutes. Right now, either worked for her, as long as this torture ended. "How?"

"You just can."

It was a new notion to Ellen. She'd blamed Tom. Cursed him. A hundred times, a thousand times. But she figured those stupid women had been taken in by his lies, too, as much victims as she was. Slutty, sure, but not responsible.

But apparently they were. "Bitches!"

"Which ones now?" Jill said, while the exertion brightened her skin until the color rivaled her hair's.

"The ones who slept with Tom. They *knew* he was married? And they did it anyway? They're every bit as bad as he is."

"Not . . . quite that . . . simple," she said between gasps.

"What's not simple?" Ellen said, very fast, sharp spews of anger. "Some things are wrong. Sleeping with a married man is one of them. Okay, I give. I'm just not made for running. Don't know why I keep trying." She surrendered, dialing her speed back to a brisk walk. "The only people who believe things like that are complicated are those trying to excuse their own misbehavior."

"I could have run longer." Twin lines furrowed between Jill's brows, something that Ellen refrained from mentioning, because Jill would start talking again about needles and Botox and other scary things. "You don't always know the circumstances," she said. "Nothing's ever black and white."

"No circumstances that don't involve the CIA and saving the world are good enough." Ellen forced a smile, trying to soften her statement, knowing it did little good. Jill knew her too well not to realize when Ellen was angry or disapproving.

Jill had always had a much more . . . flexible idea of healthy and appropriate sexuality than Ellen. Most days she admired Jill's adventuresome spirit, understood her independence. Was even a little intrigued that she could manage her sex life like a man's, compartmentalized and uncomplicated and, well, *fun*. But no particular man ever seemed important. In the morning she went merrily on her way without attaching too much messy significance to the whole thing.

Jill handled her sex life like Tom wanted to, Ellen thought sourly. Except Jill had had the sense not to get married.

Ellen tried not to dwell on it too much. Sometimes it entertained her. Very seldom, she was envious. Every once in a while the fact surfaced that somewhere deep inside, as hard as she tried not to, she disapproved. Couldn't help but feel it was a bit sleazy.

Jill knew. She had to; she'd always been able to read Ellen cold. She ignored it, which only went to prove how good a friend she was.

"So. How're we going to find you a man?" Jill rubbed her hands together as if in anticipation. "This is going to be fun."

"Glad to amuse you," Ellen said dryly.

"Of course it's going to amuse me. Picking out lovers is my favorite thing."

She caught Ellen's grimace at the word and grinned. "Looovers. Ellen's going to have a *lover*."

"Look. I couldn't even bring myself to let Lars, over there—" She hooked her thumb in the direction of the blond god that manned the desk, a glorious specimen that she was pretty sure hadn't been born to that name. "—pinch my thigh to do that stupid body-fat test. How in the world could I ever let a stranger see me naked?"

"Lots of times it's easier if they're strangers."

"Jill!" Shocked, Ellen spun her head toward Jill. Just that quick, her foot hit the edge of the belt, and she went down. She grabbed wildly for the bars. It kept her from tumbling off completely but wasn't enough to save her. Her knees slammed to the spinning belt, legs churning just fast enough to keep her from flying off. Her shoulders were about to be pulled from their sockets, but as hard as she strained, she couldn't haul herself upright. But she didn't dare let go, either, afraid she'd go flying off like a character in a comedy sketch.

I'm gonna be stuck here forever, she thought. *Stuck in place, running as fast as I can on my knees, just managing to keep from falling completely, but never able to drag my way back up to my feet.*

"Ellen." Reflexively, Jill reached for her, had to double-step quickly to keep from tumbling off herself.

"Somebody hit the stop—"

Then there were strong arms around her, plucking her up as if she weighed no more than those annoying, tiny creatures who pranced around in sports bras and spandex shorts.

"You okay?" Lars asked in her ear. He kept one arm—rock-hard, very warm—around her waist to ensure she didn't fall.

Wish I hadn't had dessert last night, she thought, and sucked in her stomach.

"You can let go," she said. "I'm fine."

"Sure?" he asked softly.

She hadn't been this close to a man since she kicked Tom out. And she hadn't been this close to a man who wasn't Tom in years, not since Harold Merriman had too much to drink at the company Christmas party in '97 and decided that Ellen would respond to being pawed in the hallway on her way to the bathroom. And Harold Merriman was no Lars.

Neither was Tom, for that matter, not even when he was in his prime. She was pretty sure that back when she'd been in college there hadn't been any men like Lars around.

He released her, and her knees wobbled after all. From the adrenaline and the exhaustion, she told herself.

"Here." Lars reached around her and flicked the emergency clip dangling from the machinery. "These are here for a reason, ma'am. Next time, you put it on. I'll be watching."

Ma'am. Crap.

She watched him walk away. How could she not?

She'd seen Lars a hundred times. Admired him—a woman would have to be dead not to notice him—but always in the same clinical, detached way she'd appreciate any particularly well-done achievement. There certainly hadn't been any *juice* in it.

But somehow Tom's command had made Lars *possible*, as if a switch inside that had made all other men off-limits had gotten flipped back the other way.

And yeah, all of a sudden it was there, that heat that Tom had destroyed their lives for.

"Ellen!" Jill latched on to her wrist and dragged her across the floor to a quiet corner behind the leg press. "Why in heaven's name did you tell him you were fine? He might have carried you!"

Her knees burned. She glanced down, found them as raw and scraped as Katie's the first time she fell off her bike. Her cheeks burned, too.

She looked at Jill, whose hair stuck out even more wildly than usual, her hands on her hips as if she were ready to lecture. And Ellen burst out laughing.

Oh, heavens. She was going to go down in health club legend, the only adult besides Mrs. Lippman to fall off the treadmill. And Mrs. Lippman had the excuse of being on the far side of eighty.

"You missed your chance," she told Jill. "If you'd gone all the way down, he might have lifted you, too."

"Would've if I'd thought fast enough. Silly me, I was worrying about you instead."

"Hey, I didn't see *you* lifting me off the treadmill."

"Friendship only goes so far." She shook her head. "I can't believe you fell off the treadmill."

"Walking, no less." Ellen tugged at her shirt, at the hem of her baggy gym shorts, trying to gather the lost cause of her dignity. "Which only goes to prove why I shouldn't be allowed out. Can you imagine what might happen if I tried to have an affair? I'd end up in the *Tribune* for sure. If not jail."

Jill cast a longing glance at Lars, who'd taken up his throne behind the help desk again. "He'd be worth it."

Ellen let herself wallow in fantasy for a moment before she surrendered to reality and sighed. "Come on, Jill. You've seen the kind of women he goes out with."

Women with butts as tight as their workout clothes, all of whom were closer to Katie's age than Ellen's. The kind of women that Jill, in her glory days, might have had a chance against—but not Ellen. Never Ellen, even on her best days.

"You don't know that—" Jill began loyally. But even loyalty only went so far. "The sex gods owe you him, after all those years of being married to Tom."

"So tell me where to burn my incense, and I'll get started on that right away. Lars'd be worth a chicken or two." She looped her towel around her neck. "Come on. There's only one perfect male left in the world. Let's go get him."

3

The Pregame Show

ON her fortieth birthday Jill, who until then had evinced not one maternal cell in her body, who tolerated Ellen's children well enough because they were Ellen's and because they were—mostly—well-behaved, had gotten slammed with a galloping case of baby lust. Since Jill never lusted for anything halfway it was a world-class case.

By forty and a half, she was carrying around books of potential sperm donors the way Ellen had once lugged around textbooks. She read four thick tracts on genetics. Once, Ellen had even caught her drawing a Punnett square on a cocktail napkin.

She debated endlessly. Brains or brawn? Beautiful warm brown eyes or piercing blue? A well-built five foot ten or a lanky six foot five? An old-money ivy-leaguer or a pull-up-by-the-boot-straps Big Ten scholarship student?

It was, Ellen had teased her, a lot more consideration than she'd put into choosing the vast majority of her lovers.

She announced her pregnancy on her forty-first birthday. Josh came into the world screaming—Jill was doing a fair bit of that at the time as well—with a thatch of hair as blazing as his mother's. Ellen had been squeezing Jill's hand as the baby emerged, and both women promptly fell head over heels in love, an emotion that hadn't faded a bit since.

Today they fetched him from the health club nursery before they showered. Jill held him while Ellen rushed to scrub and change, then passed him reluctantly to Ellen when it was, finally, her turn.

Josh was four months old, as chubby and happy a baby as Ellen had ever seen, with eyes blue enough to put Paul Newman to shame and deep dimples that Ellen was convinced she saw more often than anyone else. Because of *course* he smiled more for her.

There in the locker room she slid down on the commercial carpet, her back against the royal blue metal lockers, laid him against her chest, and closed her eyes. He snuggled right up against her, warm and light, his downy head beneath her chin, and immediately she felt her blood pressure drop, her heartbeat ease.

Somebody could make a fortune renting out sleepy babies to stressed humans. Holding Josh was surely the only real peace she'd had in months.

It used to be so simple when her children were little. Oh, she wouldn't have called it *easy*. Katie had cried for a year every time Ellen tried to put her down, Eric had been born six weeks early, Tom had worked too much.

But everything had been so clear. The baby's crying: try to get the baby to stop crying. And she'd known all along that the challenges were temporary, and that she and Tom were united in a shared vision of their future. Her children, as difficult as infants could be, also held endless possibilities. There'd been no disappointments yet . . . only dreams.

"Back," Jill said, and Ellen reluctantly opened her eyes. Jill, unabashedly naked, scrubbed at her hair with a towel and smiled down at both of them with that new softness in her eyes that had shown up the same time as Josh.

"I know we pledged in eighth grade that no boy would ever come between us," Ellen said, "but I'm reneging on the deal. I'm keeping him."

"You go right ahead and try." Jill tossed her towel into a nearby hamper and rummaged in her bag for her underwear. She tugged on the tiny scrap of a thong she insisted was perfectly comfortable, a claim that had spurred Ellen to try one for two miserable days before giving up. What good was being panty line–free if you walked weird because there was fabric wedged in your butt? "You may be bigger than me, but you *know* I'm a lot meaner."

Ellen sighed. Josh stirred, and she propped him up against her knees so she could admire his perfect little face. "Funny. Wonder where he got those eyes. The sperm donor's you picked were dark brown."

Jill bent over to tug on her shoes. "Who knows? Genetic traits can stay hidden for a long time." She straightened, slung her bag over her shoulder, and held out her arms. "Gimme."

"Spoilsport."

"Nobody ever calls me that." She lifted her son, tucking him against her side. "Does he have the kids next weekend?" *He*. She'd stopped giving Tom the privilege of a name; he was just *he*, the hated one, the bastard husband. Jill had the luxury of having venomously uncomplicated emotions toward the man.

Ellen winced as she climbed to her feet. She'd stiffened up on the floor. This was what she was going to feel like all the time someday, she thought. And, considering how swiftly she'd gotten to *here*, that'd be a lot sooner than she'd like, too. How'd the time go so fast?

"Yes," she said, frowning. She hated the weekends that the kids went to Tom's. On weekdays she could almost pretend nothing had changed. The kids were at school, Tom on a business trip. Nothing new, all was right in her world.

But on weekends, when that big family house was stripped of its family, she couldn't pretend. Couldn't forget.

"What time's he supposed to pick them up on Friday?"

"I don't know. Six or seven, I suppose. I haven't talked to him. Why?"

"My mother's been nagging at me to let her have Josh for a night."

"You should." Jill, who'd once had a social life that would have made a gossip columnist drool, had been positively monklike since the day the stick turned pink. It wasn't natural. "We'll ease you into it. A quick movie, maybe, and then you can—"

"I wouldn't leave him for a movie," Jill dropped a kiss on Josh's head while he slurped happily on his fist. "It needs a better cause than that, but I just found one. Wear something sexy, will you?

"We're going to find you a fling."

* * *

ELLEN hadn't dressed to go trolling in over twenty years. Plus she was pretty sure what worked at one of the rare frat parties Jill had dragged her to their freshman year wasn't the sort of thing one wore to attract a mature and sophisticated man, which was the only kind she would . . .

Oh, who was she kidding? She wasn't going to attract anyone. Even if she did, she wouldn't have any idea what to do with him. But if she didn't pretend to give it a reasonable effort, Jill would keep dragging her out, weekend after weekend, until they'd worked their way down the list and the only clubs left in Minneapolis they hadn't tried were frequented by men with a penchant for leather. Biker or gay bars, she wasn't sure which—and Jill might not be put off by either.

Ellen didn't have any looking-for-a-man clothes. She had mom clothes. She had tastefully appropriate bank-director's-wife clothes. That was it.

Black pants, she decided. Couldn't go wrong with black pants. A medium heel, which she figured she *might* be able to tolerate for a couple of hours, and an emerald silk shirt that shimmered in the bathroom light.

Makeup. That was probably required. She did her best, tucked her smooth brown bob behind her ears, and went out to wait for Tom.

Katie was still closeted in her room. Ellen heard the thump of music through the door, hip-hop loud enough to make the floor tremble. She couldn't make out the words—small blessing, that. She supposed she should go listen at the door, then do the mom thing and confiscate whatever vile, misogynistic crap that it surely was.

But why was it always *her* problem? She was sick of being the bad guy, always the vigilant one, riding herd over homework and piano lessons and curfews while Tom flew off to another nice hotel, a "business dinner" that he pretended to dread. How bad could it be? Fancy waiters, great meals you didn't have to cook, all the overpriced wine you wanted. Even with less-than-scintillating companions it didn't sound half bad to Ellen.

But apparently it was bad enough that he'd had to reward himself with whatever dim-witted slut he picked up in the bar afterward.

It wasn't like it was going to get any better now. She knew how the divorced-dad thing worked. He'd buy his way into their children's affections. Weekends at Tom's would be jammed with fast-food meals, shopping trips, and ignored homework because he couldn't bear to "ruin" their time together with such unimportant frivolities as discipline and responsibility.

And it was going to fall on her to try to repair the damage.

So, just for tonight, she was going to let it go. Sunday night, she'd fight the good fight again.

She peeked into the family room that they'd added to the back of the house, open to the kitchen. Eric sat cross-legged on the floor, squinting at the screen, his thumbs flying over his game controller. *Beep, beep, beep,* backed by that brutally cheerful music she'd gotten heartily sick of months ago. Then came the sounds of an explosion, while Eric punched his fist in the air in triumph.

"Blow up something good?" she asked him.

"Hmm," he mumbled, his gaze never once leaving the screen.

Eric was thirteen but looked two years younger. She'd gotten him contacts before eighth grade started, but he hadn't quite adjusted to them yet, and his braces would be on for another six months. His hair stuck up on one side, lay flat on the other, an awkward jumble instead of the careless surfer-boy muss that had been the goal. She wondered again at the effortlessness of early adolescence for those few select golden children and the misery it was for the rest.

It seemed like he spent 90 percent of his waking hours with some sort of video game in his hands. It didn't take a degree in psychology to figure it out: it was the one world he could control, the one place where he was powerful.

"Kids who spend three hours a day playing video games are nearly four times as likely to be overweight as adults," she said, making the token, automatic protest.

"Oh, yeah," he said, whacking the hollow curve of his belly. "You might want to save that one for when I top one hundred and ten, 'kay?"

"I'll make a note," she said, smiling. He was the sweetest boy on the face of the earth. Unfortunately, sweetness wasn't a quality much appreciated in a junior high school, and she constantly battled a furious urge to go tie a few more obnoxious teens to goalposts.

"Hello!" She heard Tom's bellow, hurried to the front hall to head him off.

"If you don't start ringing the bell," she said, "I swear I'm changing the locks."

He paused halfway in the door and frowned at her. "Can I come in?" he said, very precisely, a clipped undercurrent of anger.

"I'm serious. You don't live here anymore."

"Still got my name on the mortgage, doesn't it?"

"We can take care of that easily enough."

He scowled at her, tucking his hands in the pockets of his pants. He was still in his business suit, the Jerry Garcia tie that was supposed to show he had personality despite being a "suit" loosened around his neck, the top button of his white shirt undone. She almost reached up to give him a peck, so automatic was her reaction: Tom, coming home after a long week, weary and rumpled, and her welcoming him. The same way she often turned her car on the road to school when she drove out of her cul-de-sac, even when she was headed somewhere else. She'd gone that way so many times her muscles wanted to make that action.

"Fine," she said. "You can come in any time you want as soon as you give me a key to your apartment and I can barge in whenever I feel like it, too."

He stepped in and closed the door behind him. "Not the same, Ellen, and you know it."

"Why? Because I might, uh, *interrupt* something, and you won't?"

He opened his mouth to say something, thought better of it. Instead, "Kids ready?"

"Eric is," she said. "He's just in the family room. Let me go—"

"Is he playing those games again?"

She sighed, knowing what was coming. She refrained from pointing out that Tom was the one who bought Eric the Game-Cube in the first place. "Yes."

"Shouldn't he be outside? Playing ball or something?"

"It's December, Tom."

"Hockey, then."

It'd be so easy to fall into the old quarrel. There was even a certain amount of satisfaction in it. It was an argument they'd had often over the years, long before their current problems. Tom wanted Eric to grow into the kind of all-American, athletic child he hadn't been. She even understood it: he wanted Eric's adolescence to be easier than his was, for Eric to be one of those kids who were automatically part of the group, who swung through their teenage years with few bumps and even fewer scars. He wanted to protect his son.

Except that that wasn't Eric, and all the prodding and pushing and wishing in the world wasn't going to change him.

"Fine," she said. "You've got him all weekend. Throw balls to your heart's content."

"I've got to work tomorrow. In fact, you need to—"

A car horn blared outside.

"That's for me!" They heard the thunder of quick steps on the upstairs hallway and then Katie threw herself down the stairs.

She stopped halfway down, her eyes on her father, and her face lit up.

"Oh. Hi, Daddy. I didn't know you were here." Even now, having watched her grow into *this*, Ellen still didn't know how it had happened. Surely this lovely creature, with her silky blond hair and the kind of body that gave parents nightmares, couldn't have sprung from her and Tom. There was nothing in the gene pool that portended this. Even less in the gawky thirteen-year-old she'd been what seemed like only days ago, all braces and glasses and bony legs. Now, two years later, she looked a decade older, and a sophisticated and gorgeous decade at that.

"You know it's my weekend. You packed?"

"Got a date," she said, her smile fading. "I'll have Caleb drop me off at your place later." She bounded down the rest of the stairs, pausing at the pewter-framed mirror that hung above the side table, and frowned at her reflection. "This green looks like puke." She unzipped her baggy hoodie, tugged it off, and tossed it toward the newel post.

Beneath it she wore only a thin, narrow-strapped tank in an electric shade of blue that made no secret of the fact that she didn't get her chest from her mother. It stopped a good four inches above the low waistband of her jeans, which were a size smaller than Ellen would have bought her.

Honk.

"Gotta go," she said, lifting one eyebrow toward her father as if daring him to comment, and headed for the door.

"You answer to that? He doesn't even have to come get you, he just honks and you run?"

"Yup." Cold air burst through when she opened the door, bringing with it the scent of pine.

"Take a coat," Ellen called.

"It's not that cold," Katie said and plunged into the evening. Not even six and already dark as sin. Welcome to December in the upper Midwest.

"Yes, it is." Ellen grabbed Katie's purple peacoat from the closet. "Here. Catch."

Katie merely tucked it under her arm and headed for Caleb's car, an ancient jeep, its army green color overtaken by rust years ago.

"That's it?" Tom asked in disbelief.

"That's it," Ellen said. Not that she didn't want to run after Katie, drag her back by her ear, and lock her in her room until her age caught up with her looks. But she'd known Jill as a teenager and remembered very well what happened when a boy was made forbidden fruit. It only turned him into a challenge.

Not to mention that over roast chicken at dinner she'd already snuck in reading aloud an article about how a girl who didn't use birth control had a 90 percent chance of getting pregnant in the first year she had sex.

"Damn!" Tom wheeled out, left the door gaping behind him, as he sprinted to the car. She saw him round the front end and lean down to the driver's window. Light from the streetlight scattered through the air, splintered by the moisture that hung there, waiting to turn to snow when the temperature dropped another three degrees. He stood, and the car jolted forward and down the street while Tom, hands in his pockets, stared after it. Then he turned and made his way back to the house. He looked tired, his shoulders hunched against the cold, his head low, and Ellen couldn't help but want to go to him. Six months ago she would have waited for him, arms wide open. How long would it be, she wondered, before those instincts finally faded? You couldn't spend so many years worrying over someone and have it go away in a snap. She wasn't even sure she wanted it to. When that was gone, would there be anything left?

Instead, she leaned against the doorway that led into the dining room. "What'd you say?"

He pulled the door shut behind him and shivered. "I told him that if he broke my daughter's heart, I'd rip his out."

"Think he bought it?"

"Probably not quite as much as I'd like him to."

"Did you enjoy it?"

His smile snuck up on them both. How long had it been? Since he'd smiled at her, since they'd been on the same side of anything, since she'd felt . . . not married to him, exactly, but at least like they were parents who were in this together, a united front against the storm of adolescence?

"Oh, yeah," he said. "A lot. And if it gives him just one second's pause, if it's the right second, it'll be worth it. I suppose I embarrassed her terribly."

"I figure it's our duty, once in a while."

"Yeah." He looked down at his feet, still on the entrance mat. He didn't usually bother to wipe them, just stood at the door while she hurried to gather up the kids and their things and send them all on their way. Any conversation they had was held there, like an awkward few phrases passed with an acquaintance.

He scuffed his shoes—black tied leather, polished to a high shine—on the mat and stepped in. His heels thudded on the gleaming oak of the entrance floor, a familiar sound that echoed strangely because it was one that she hadn't been sure she'd ever hear again.

"That outfit," he began. "Why'd you let her go out like that?"

"Why'd *I* let her?" she repeated. As if it were entirely her responsibility. The tiny bit of connection between them burst.

"If those pants were any lower, you'd see her pubic hair."

"Is that how you like them?" she asked. "Bet if it was anyone other than your daughter dressed like that, you'd be applauding her choice."

"Shush." He cast a glance toward the back of the house, where the muted electronic music and the sound of mock explosions still drifted down the hallway. "He'll hear."

She didn't know if she cared but dropped her voice anyway, always the cooperative wife.

"She didn't dress like that when I lived here," Tom pointed out.

"No," Ellen snapped, wondering if he were too obtuse to make the connection or if he simply refused to. "No, she didn't."

"Did you tell her?" he asked accusingly.

Katie had always been his little girl. When she turned thirteen, she'd decided her mother was simply too uncool to be borne. But that aversion hadn't extended to her father. Not once. He was still her hero, and she was still his princess.

Resentment burned, slicing hot as acid, every bit as damaging. "You think she didn't ask? She's not stupid."

His shocked expression nearly made her laugh. What did he think? That his fifteen-year-old daughter with the delinquent boyfriend didn't think about sex? Or that the little girl who'd always believed her daddy was perfect when her mother was *clearly* an idiot might, just might, suspect that he'd had a hand in their breakup?

"You *told* her?"

"You expect *me* to lie to cover up the fact that you can't keep your pants zipped?"

He took a step toward her, his hands flexing into fists. She almost wished he'd hit her. Because that'd be it. No more wondering, no more hoping, no more trying to pretend. It'd be over, she could hate him completely, and the simplicity of that seemed easier than the polluted muddle she lived in now.

But his hands relaxed, the calm businessman once more, and she realized how ridiculous that was. He was not a violent man, not even close. He'd spanked the kids only once when they were small: Katie, who, when she was three, had discovered that running out in front of cars was a fine game, because it made her parents shriek and start running to scoop her up, and all the time-outs in the world hadn't made any difference.

Katie'd recovered from the spanking in about ten minutes. It had taken Tom two days.

"We promised to keep the children out of it," he said, sounding perfectly reasonable, completely in the right. Of course they had to protect the children most of all. Especially when that necessity worked in his favor.

"Interesting how the thing I agreed to for the sake of the children is the thing that keeps them from hating you, isn't it?"

"So you didn't tell her," he said, his shoulders relaxing beneath the fine, dark wool of his conservative jacket.

"I told them it was complicated," she said. "And that some things were just between you and me."

"Good." He jingled his change in his pocket and looked down the hallway toward the family room. "That's good."

"I'm not going to have to be the one to tell her," Ellen said. "She—*they*—are going to figure it out sooner or later."

His expression tightened.

"They're smart kids. They have lots of friends whose parents have split. Other people were involved more often than not. They pay attention. They listen. Do you really think they're not going to guess?"

Anger flashed in his eyes. Easier to be mad at her for pointing out the obvious than to accept the truth of it.

So Tom was just as good at deluding himself as she was. She, in turning a blind eye to all the hints all those years, and he, in believing that he could keep that part of his life so separate from his children that they'd never know it existed.

"So then you'll tell her that's not what happened," he commanded.

"No, I won't—"

"I hope you're ready!" Jill breezed in the front door and slammed it shut behind her with her stiletto-clad foot. The instant she saw Tom, her smile vanished. "Wow. Looks like we're all having fun here."

"Haven't learned to ring the doorbell yet?" he asked her.

"No reason to now," she said and smiled, clearly pleased.

They'd never liked each other much. Early on in her marriage she and Tom had argued about whether Jill had too much influence on Ellen, too much of a claim on her time and energy. At the time Ellen had thought maybe Tom had been a bit jealous that there was someone else in her life with whom she shared such a strong bond. And Tom had never really approved of Jill's lifestyle . . . which was odd, now that Ellen considered it. Jill should have been just his type, shouldn't she? Not only blatantly sexy but perfectly comfortable enjoying that sexuality without worrying about monogamy. He should be holding her up to Ellen as an example.

Jill sashayed in, her black leather jacket open, wearing jeans that were only a fraction higher-cut and less tight than Katie's, heels that were a sprained ankle waiting to happen, and a bright lime sweater scooped low—really low—over a chest that was still her best asset.

Ellen narrowed her eyes, wondering. Tom was watching Jill, his brow furrowed, his mouth a set line.

Maybe he'd always been so prickly around Jill not because he didn't like her. Maybe he'd always liked her too well.

Jill paused in front of Ellen, weight on one precarious heel, and eyed her critically. "Damn. I *knew* you didn't know how to dress for this."

"Dress for what?" Tom asked.

Ellen frowned warningly at Jill. She'd rather Tom knew nothing about tonight.

"We're going out," Jill said, "after I fix her up." She jiggled the red duffel bag slung over her left shoulder. "But I came prepared. You've got a push-up bra around here somewhere, don't you?"

"So that's why you look so nice," Tom said.

Suddenly self-conscious, Ellen ran a hand through her hair, disordering her careful bob. Didn't matter; Jill'd be doing Lord only knew what to it soon enough.

Funny how he only noticed what she looked like after Jill had told him they were going out.

"Not nearly as good as she's going to look in half an hour," Jill tossed off and headed for the stairs. "Get your kids on their way, El. We've got serious work to do."

4

Battle Preparations

"WORK?" The corners of Tom's mouth lifted. "What kind of work would that be?"

Ellen shrugged, unable to meet his eyes. Where was this guilt coming from? Because she didn't intend to take his suggestion, or because she did? The vestiges of a Catholic girlhood could never be left fully behind. Though Jill had apparently managed to recover completely.

"You're going to do it, aren't you?" His smile veered into a smirk.

He looked far too pleased with himself, amused by the whole idea.

Shouldn't he be bothered by this, at least a little?

She still wasn't certain what he wanted out of the whole thing. Was it merely to get her to shoulder a share of the blame, albeit belatedly? Maybe he just figured she was destined for absolute disaster; heavens, it had taken a full three months after they'd become lovers for her to relax enough to find a whole lot of pleasure in it. Maybe he thought he'd look so good in comparison to what she'd find out there that she'd be willing to take what she could get from him and continue the marriage on his terms.

Or maybe he really didn't believe she'd actually go through with it. It had taken him weeks to talk her out of her pants, and she'd been in *love* with him.

"Maybe it has nothing to do with you," she told him. "Maybe I just need to get laid."

"Uh-huh," he said. He was going to laugh at her any second. "Sure you do."

"What's that supposed to mean?"

He'd once been a conservative man. An undergraduate degree in accounting; an MBA; the deliberate choice of an investment bank in Minneapolis rather than New York so that while the money was less, the competition was as well; a house in Edina; a classic wife. He still looked the part, with his safe gray suits and his beige sedan and his short-clipped hair. But somewhere along the way he'd abandoned any instinct toward self-preservation. "You've never been much of a . . . well, you're not exactly *driven* in that department, y'know?"

There was a heavy vase handy on the side table. And she'd been a pretty fair softball pitcher once. "Maybe there was a reason I wasn't all that interested."

"I haven't had any other complaints."

Her arms went rigid at her side, the muscles in her forearms knotting up. It was the only way she could keep from chucking the vase at him. Except she would have to be the one to clean it up.

"Come on, El!" Jill hollered from upstairs.

"Eric's ready," Ellen said in carefully measured tones. "I'll be here on Sunday at six. I expect you to be on time." She turned to the stairs, the dark red of the carpet runner bleeding into her vision.

"About that—" he called after her, "Saturday night, I've got to work, you need to—"

Sure you do, she thought. *Work*. It was his favorite excuse, his favorite lie. "Not my problem," she said and went to put herself in Jill's hands.

* * *

ELLEN hadn't gotten to keep a single thing on her body that she'd started out with—at least nothing that wasn't permanently attached. And she'd had to fight to keep some of those, threatening violence of her own when Jill started mumbling something about a Brazilian wax.

None of her jeans met Jill's standards, so Jill talked her into a short black skirt that ended three inches above her knees. It was much too cold outside, Ellen protested, but Jill was on a mission, absolutely sure of what was required, and it wasn't as if Ellen's life had been going along so well lately. Might as well try it somebody else's way for one night.

She drew the line at the thong—even though Jill *promised* it was brand-new—but traded that concession for the push-up bra buried in her dresser that she had worn just twice in only partially successful attempts to amp up her sex life. Ellen asked her what happened if she actually *did* meet a man. Wasn't that false advertising? "Hush," Jill said. "By that point, they're so happy to see naked breasts that it won't matter. Trust me."

"Naked." Ellen pressed a hand to her lingerie-enhanced chest, blowing out a breath that threatened to kick into hyperventilation. She just couldn't picture it. She hadn't been on a date, hadn't had "first sex" in over two decades. And even then, her previous sexual escapades barely counted. One stupid last-chance farewell to her high school boyfriend so he wouldn't forget her in college, which hadn't been all that much fun and kept him from forgetting her for all of three weeks. Two attempts at sexual liberation her freshman year that convinced her that she simply wasn't cut out for such things. And then Tom. It had been pretty darn good once they'd gotten the hang of things, but the first time . . . it had been memorable, all right, but not for the right reasons.

She was a good Catholic girl for all that she'd given thanks weekly for oral contraception all through her college years, and she'd planned on being married forever. Had hardly even regretted the prospect of never sleeping with another man, though the whole idea had made Jill weep into her margarita at Ellen's shower/bachelorette party.

"Here," Jill said, tossing her the bright red, thin-heeled sandals she'd unearthed from Katie's room when she'd decided none of Ellen's shoes passed muster. "These'll do. Mine are better, though. Don't know why you're so squeamish about a little pain."

"Yours are two sizes too small!"

"So? They're gorgeous. They make your legs look a mile long." She sighed. "Giraffe. I could wear *five*-inch heels, and my legs still aren't half as good as yours."

Ellen slid into the shoes and eyed herself critically in the full-length mirror. Say what you would about Victoria's Secret and the objectification of women as sex objects, the damned bras *worked*. "They are good, aren't they?" she said, and then pinched the roll at the side of her waist.

"Stop that." Jill slapped at her hand.

"But—"

"You can't maintain the proper attitude if you start focusing on insignificant little flaws. Confidence is everything. You have to *strut*, hon. You're one hot mama, and you have to remember that."

"Uh-huh," she said. "I've got the mama part down at least."

"I'm not done with you yet."

She dug through Ellen's closet and found a thin, sleeveless sweater, black shot with gold, that Ellen had never worn without the cardigan that matched it.

"I'm going to freeze," she complained again.

"All the more reason to find a man to heat you up." Jill shoved Ellen into a chair and hauled out her makeup case, an army green behemoth that she'd found in a sporting goods store and the only thing big enough to hold her entire collection of war paint. She considered it appropriate that it was intended to store fishing equipment. "Besides, it makes for good headlights."

Ellen's eyebrows shot nearly to her hairline and Jill laughed. "Stop that. I'm going to get the mascara in your eyes instead of on your lashes."

"*Headlights?*"

"I'm just teasing you. It'll be plenty warm in the clubs, believe me."

"Keep it up, and you're going alone. You're scaring me to death."

"That's half the fun of it." Jill scooped something out of a tin, rubbed her hands together, and started scrunching it into Ellen's hair. "Isn't it great? That shiver in the pit of your stomach. The wondering. Do you even hope yes? Or no?"

"Jill?"

"Hmm?" She stepped back, considering, and then tugged a swoop of hair across Ellen's right eye.

"Did Tom ever come on to you?"

Her hand stilled in mid-tug, then, ever so gently, she tucked a strand behind Ellen's ear. "I suppose so."

"You *suppose* so?" Ellen clamped down on the emotions that threatened to avalanche. Not yet. *Not yet.* Later, what was left of her life could fall apart. But not yet.

"Ellen." Jill crouched down where she could look up at her eyes without Ellen's bangs getting in the way. "I didn't know."

"You *knew*. All you would have to do was say one word. You could have saved me all this."

"Could I? El, you have to know that I would have if I could. You *have* to know that."

Ellen closed her eyes against the burn of it, against the look of guilt and pleading in Jill's. "You should have told me."

"Told you what? It was one of those stupid Fourth of July parties he always insisted on throwing."

Ellen had made Jill attend. She'd forced her to show up because Tom had decided years ago the Fourth was the right weekend for him to drag his way up the corporate ladder one more rung. He'd made it a tradition to have a blow-out party for everyone who affected his career even slightly, and then dumped the entire work of the annual affair in Ellen's lap. By the time the weekend arrived, she needed at least one ally present. Someone she didn't have to smile at; who'd drag her into the back bedroom, shove a gin and tonic in her hand when she desperately needed it, and let her bitch until she could go back out there and smile at everyone again.

"I wasn't sure if he even knew what he was doing. Wasn't sure he'd ever done it to anyone else, or it was just some stupid, one-time mistake. And hell, it wasn't all that much of a play. I figured even if he *did* try it on someone else, he wouldn't have had much luck."

Her hand found Ellen's and held on while her voice slid into desperation. "What was I supposed to do? Ruin your life over what might have been one drunken mistake? What if you never forgave me?"

"I would have forgiven you." Even more, she would have *believed* her. Until evidence she couldn't deny was slapped in front of her eyes, Jill would have been the only one she did believe.

"Then forgive me now." Her grip tightened. "If I'd known then what I know now, I would have shouted it right in front of that whole damned party the instant he so much as leered at me, I swear to God. But I didn't know. And I'm so sorry about that."

What would that have saved her? Ellen wondered. A few years, sure. But what else? Would it have been any easier to do this five years ago, seven? With the children smaller, the mortgage bigger?

Ellen had never been one to hurry the pain and get it out of the way. It wouldn't have hurt any less to have her heart shredded earlier rather than later.

She turned her hand in Jill's and gripped back. "If I'd really wanted to know sooner," she said, "I would have known."

"Okay." Jill blew out a breath. Her smile wobbled but held. "Okay. This calls for cosmos, I think. I'll go pick up that new Matthew McConaughey movie, too, and we'll have an old-fashioned—"

"No," Ellen said and stood, turning to face the mirror.

"I heard he takes his shirt off five times. My man Matthew bare-chested's bound to perk you right up."

"Nope." *I look different*, Ellen thought, appraising her reflection. Her hair was wavy and wild, purple smoked her lids, and she was flashing more leg than she'd shown in years.

But what was wrong with different? She'd had *different* forced on her, by God, but now she might as well run with it. "I don't look bad, do I?"

"You look *great*," Jill said emphatically. "*Hot.*"

"Hot," Ellen mused. She didn't usually worry about *hot*. Appropriate, elegant, conservative. *Nice*. Not hot.

What the hell, she thought. "Let's go get me laid."

5

Hunting

They tried Vodka first.

It seemed like a good place to start, a quiet bar perched high on the top of a downtown hotel, frequented by out-of-town businessmen and local professionals who preferred not to have their ears blasted while they were downing their very expensive drinks. An older crowd, Jill didn't say, but Ellen understood.

The place was fashionably dark, lit only by the glitter of the lights of Minneapolis far below; the gleam of what seemed like hundreds of bottles of its namesake behind the bar, glazed by a low row of spotlights; and the discreet edging of polished aluminum on the glass tables. The wood was dark, the leather black, the bartenders gorgeous.

"This looks promising," Jill said, appraising the place with a professional eye.

"How can you tell?" Ellen squinted, trying to make out shapes through the gloom. She could tell there were people clustered on the low banquettes, and—mostly—if they were male or female, but any details such as age or attractiveness were obscured by shadow.

"God, I hope I haven't lost it," Jill said. "I've been wondering." She gave a little shake. "Shoulders back," she whispered. "Chin up, boobs out. Go!"

"Jill!" Ellen grabbed her arm and hung on with a strength born of panic. "What do I do?"

"Look around. See if anybody looks interesting. Smile. Talk."

"I—" She gulped a breath while she wondered if terror could steal it from her completely. She'd have rather wandered into the tigers' den at the zoo than sashay into a bar with . . . what? Hooking up? On her mind. She hadn't liked it at twenty, had never been good at it, and the years hadn't improved things. "Maybe being married, even to Tom, isn't so bad after all."

"Yes, it is," Jill said sternly. "One step at a time. Can you come in and look around?"

She tried, she really did, but Ellen's feet refused to move. "I don't think so."

"Okay." Jill started to take a step toward the bar. "Ellen," she said, in the same tone Ellen had used on her when the transition stage of labor kicked in, "you're going to have to let go of me first."

"Okay." She didn't move.

Jill peeled off her fingers and steered her toward the bar. "Sit." She wagged a finger at her. "Stay here," she ordered and nodded at the bartender, bald and black and handsome enough to make Lars look ordinary. "Give her something."

"Yes, ma'am."

"Ma'am," Jill repeated, shaking her head sadly. "Just what we needed." Then she was gone, sliding expertly through a laughing, well-dressed crowd and disappearing into the murk.

"What would you like?" the bartender asked, leaning close, his voice low and lovely, and Ellen almost blurted out the obvious answer. *Jeez*. Her propriety apparently didn't run nearly as deep as she'd believed.

She stared at the gleaming ranks of bottles until her eyes crossed. "I don't know."

"Don't worry," he said. "I'm an expert. So. Sweet or hard?"

"What?"

"Sweet or hard?" He grinned, as dazzling as the display behind him, obviously aware of the implications of his words, two steps ahead of her in a dance she'd never learned.

"You must get *great* tips," she said, and he laughed, his practiced flirtation sliding into genuine amusement.

"That I do, ma—"

"But not if you keep calling us *ma'am*." She couldn't remember the last time someone had called her *miss*. Or the last time she'd been carded.

She was too *old* for this, which made the bottles behind him look a whole lot more appealing. "Sweet, I guess."

He slid something peach-colored in a martini glass the size of a soup bowl in front of her.

"What's this?"

"Trust me."

Her first sip was tentative. The second was not, and the whole thing disappeared before she could decipher what was in it. "How do you make that?"

"My secret."

Okay, so he got paid to flirt with her. It was good business to keep the customers happy. But she wasn't sure she cared. It was fun, and her stomach was starting to unknot.

Emboldened, she spun around to appraise the room. The possibilities, she reminded herself.

She still couldn't see Jill. But then it wasn't possible to see more than ten feet in front of her. The men—well, they all looked a little like Tom. Same power suits; same short, neat haircuts; same way of carrying themselves. Secure in their accomplishments, edging into smug. Her kind of men, mature and sensible.

Funny. She liked the bartender better.

But there was fantasy, and reality, and the drink hadn't been strong enough to blur that line yet, she realized with a little regret.

To her surprise the women were perceptibly younger, dressed in ways that made her own outfit look thoroughly conservative, all smiling brightly up at the men beside them. *On the prowl*, she thought distastefully. Kept women and trophy wives in the making.

She spun back to face the bar. "What's your name?"

"Mike."

"Mike." Worst-case scenario, she got to sit at the bar all night; drink those lovely things he kept mixing up, which really were delicious; and look at him. Which would still make it the best night she'd had in . . . well, she couldn't think how long. "I think I'm going to need another one of those."

"Whatever the lady wants."

Yeah, right.

Things started looking better as the second drink disappeared. Not a rosy-colored world, she thought woozily. Maybe mango-colored. And things looked better yet when a man paused at the stool next to hers.

"Is this seat taken?"

"Hmm?" She dragged her eyes up. Great suit, a smoky charcoal. It fit him well, almost hiding that little softness at his waist—but who was she to be judgmental about such things? He had nice, really broad shoulders, and he was tall, and his eyes, once she'd worked her way up that high, were clear and friendly. "You played football once, didn't you?"

He grinned. Good smile, too, she thought. Damned attractive, if you didn't compare him to Mike. And he'd come over to *her*, rescued her from feeling like a complete wallflower, and he deserved major points for that, didn't he? "Yup," he said. "How'd you know?"

"I know lots of things," she said, shocking herself by sounding downright flirtatious. What the heck had Mike put in that drink, anyway?

"Can I buy you another one of those?"

"Sure," she said.

He signaled for Mike. "Another one for the lady. And a Macallen, neat, for me."

Two *lady*s, she thought. Well, it was better than *ma'am*, which only sounded flattering when it came from someone Southern and under the age of twenty.

He lifted his drink, awaiting a toast.

"What are we drinking to?" Ellen asked, and raised her own.

"Why don't we wait and find out?"

"Come on," Jill said, popping out of the shadows with such suddenness that Ellen jumped. "We're leaving."

Leaving? Ellen was just starting to get the hang of things. "Now?"

"Now."

"But—" Ellen looked at Jill's empty hands. "Oh, there's the problem. Mike, will you get my friend one of these?"

"No, Mike, they look lovely—as do you, by the way—but I don't want one."

"Now whose juice's drying up?" Ellen asked.

Frowning, Jill put her hands on her hips. Then she shrugged, grabbed Ellen's new friend's left hand, and jerked it into the weak circle of light that sifted down from the nearest pendant lamp. "You should take your ring off when you golf, pal, if you don't want the tan line to give you away when you're cruising."

"I'm not—" At Jill's glare, he gave up. "It's none of your business, is it?"

"Nope," Jill said. "But she is."

"What's the matter with this place?" Ellen asked as Jill herded her toward the elevators. "Oh, I know what's the matter with *him*, but otherwise, I kind of liked it."

"You liked the bartender," Jill told her. "But he's gay, and all the rest of them are married."

"*All* of them?"

"All of them," Jill said firmly. "But that's okay. Because the next place we're going, none of them will be."

"Gay?" Ellen said regretfully, taking one last, wistful look at the beautiful bartender before the elevator doors eased shut, sighing for all the girls who would never have a shot at him. Not for herself, of course—despite the two fruity martinis, she was not that far gone, no matter how disoriented she was by the rush of hormones that had lain dormant for two decades. But she would have liked for some lovely young thing to enjoy him, a proxy for all members of her species. "How do you know?" Married, gay . . . clearly Jill was equipped with sensors that Ellen needed to develop.

"I don't."

"But why did you say—"

"It was the easiest way to get you to move." Jill punched the glowing red button for the lobby. "And while I'm all in favor of you having a little jog before you walk, even *I* know you're not ready for an Olympic sprint."

* * *

IT took Ellen all of about five seconds once they stepped into Paradise to figure out why Jill was certain that none of the men in the place were married. It was because every single person there, from the bouncers to the DJ to the bikini-clad bar girls standing beside the giant aluminum tubs holding chipped ice and bottled beer, was at least fifteen years younger than they were.

Real palm trees glowed with strings of fake fireflies. Sand piled into dunes in the corners the room, where more than one couple decided to try out a round of beach blanket bingo, which no one seemed to mind. Indeed, an especially enthusiastic pair often earned a cheering section. The ceiling was midnight blue, slung with enough twinkle lights to make your head spin if you stared up too long. A small, padded side room held a mechanical bull, which didn't seem to fit the theme and which Ellen had believed went out of fashion when *Urban Cowboy* put paid to the first phase of John Travolta's career. But all the kids—and they were *kids*, she couldn't think of them any other way— seemed fond of the thing, though she figured mostly the boys liked the way her boobs bounced whenever an overendowed and under-bra-ed girl took a ride.

The music was mostly the kind of throbbing pseudo-hip-hop that she tried to ignore when her daughter played it. The male bartenders were shirtless and looked damn fine that way.

"That *has* to be against the health code."

"Do you care?" Jill nudged Ellen in the ribs, nodding toward an especially fine specimen. "I haven't had a good goggle at something that looks like that anywhere except on my television for eleven months and counting. Don't ruin it for me."

Cheers erupted when a girl in a hot pink string bikini clambered on top of the concrete bar, holding two bottles high over her head.

"They won't want us here, Jill," Ellen shouted over the heavy thump of bass. "We're going to contaminate them all with over-forty cooties."

"Want to dance?"

Ellen turned to find a young man standing disconcertingly close to her. He was thin as a reed; his pants were going to slide off if he jammed his fists any deeper into the pockets of his artistically torn jeans. His glasses could have been swiped from Buddy Holly, and Ellen suspected, but wasn't quite sure, that there was no prescription in them. "What?"

"Wanna dance?"

She jammed a finger in her ear, joggled it around. The music *was* awfully loud. "Me?"

He nodded. The monotonous rumble of unintelligible lyrics suddenly segued into something vaguely familiar.

"The Beach Boys?" An overproduced, nearly unrecognizable remix of "Little Deuce Coupe," but the Beach Boys nonetheless.

He was still waiting on her answer, his head bobbing along in time to the beat. She opened her mouth to say no, like any good suburban mother would. But she'd been a wallflower too many times in her youth. Once, at a particularly painful mixer, when she'd watched Mary Ellen Sorenson turn down six unworthies in a row while she sat out endless songs, she'd even prayed about it. If God would only let someone ask her, she'd bargained, she'd never, ever be so ungrateful as to turn anyone down. Even that geeky Harold Olsen.

"Nice way to hold me to it," she mumbled at the artificial sky. Then she nodded and followed Buddy into the wriggling mass of young flesh that constituted the dance floor.

If nothing else, Paradise turned out to be darned good for her ego. She danced nonstop, except for the two times that she got talked into downing drinks with explicitly erotic names. To her initial shock you were apparently expected to glug from a glass tucked into the waistband of one of the shirtless bartender's denim shorts. But at that time it was too late to back out without looking like a spoilsport.

She'd half-expected to go out on the floor and have everyone turn, point to her, and shriek a horrified "Old!"—a reaction something like the one she'd once witnessed at a Viking game when a cheese-hatted Green Bay fan snuck into a purple cheering section. She was pretty sure that's what she would have done at twenty. This group seemed more accepting. As long as you didn't mess with their good time and appeared to be having one yourself, no one cared. It required Ellen to clamp down hard on her well-honed mothering/chaperone instincts, but it was worth it.

She liked to dance. She'd forgotten how much. Oh, the music still sounded about as good to her as a sledgehammer breaking concrete, but they mixed in another mutated Beach Boys song about every half an hour—it seemed to be a *thing*—and that helped. It also helped that the dancing didn't really seem to require a partner; it was more a vaguely pornographic group activity. Dancing had gotten a lot more . . . pelvis-centered since Sister Agnes hovered over the school dances, ever vigilant for forbidden contact. But hey, Ellen had seen *Dirty Dancing* at an impressionable age, and it had worked for Baby, hadn't it? And how was she ever supposed to have actual sex with a stranger if she couldn't bump decently covered hips with one? She must consider it an experiment, she decided.

And Jill was having a royally good post-baby time, shaking her butt between two guys who swore they were semipro hockey players. Maybe, maybe not, but they sure looked the part. *She's earned it*, Ellen thought. Jill'd done nothing but work and mommy for months. It had to be a shock to her system, poor girl.

"So." Her friend Buddy was back. He'd been faithful, breezing by to wiggle next to her and offer her a drink three or four times in the last hour before spinning off again. He was growing on her. Oh, he couldn't dance worth a lick, but his enthusiasm was kind of endearing, and his butt looked good in his jeans. She hadn't forgotten how to notice that. He had a nice smile, though the scruffy chin hair did nothing for it, and really good brown eyes: friendly, intelligent, and warm. If she'd been twenty years younger, she would have gone for him in a heartbeat.

He leaned toward her, close enough that she could feel the heat of his breath on her ear. "You want to get out of here?"

"What?" She froze. The lights spun overhead, and she figured those coconut-laced drinks had to have held a *lot* more liquor than she'd realized. But he was just grinning at her, hands in his pockets. "Is this a bet?" she blurted out.

He shook his head, not the least bit offended or discouraged. Maybe he had some sort of teacher or MILF fantasy to live out, maybe he just wanted a good story to tell. Either way he'd get laid, and that was probably good enough for him.

"But *why*?"

He shrugged. "Why not?"

And right there was the difference. Sex, to her, always had to have a *why*, and a pretty darned good one at that. For Jill, for most of the kids bumping and laughing around her, it was simply a *why not*? That's how it was for Tom, too, and she hadn't been a good enough *why not* to keep him faithful.

It was just that uncomplicated for Buddy. He kept waiting on her answer, smiling, but not particularly concerned, as if he'd just asked if she could give him a lift but knew he could score a ride home from somewhere if she turned him down.

For one brief moment she considered it. It'd serve Tom right for her to sleep with someone young enough to be his son.

The horror of it flashed through her. She had visions of Eric in a few years, reeling between one Mrs. Robinson clone after another, all of them murmuring *why not*.

Because if he was young enough to be Tom's kid, he was young enough to be hers. The fact that for one instant, no matter how brief, she'd thought about going home with him made the kamikaze mix of drinks in her stomach lurch toward freedom.

"You should go home," she said to him. "Your mom's probably worried about you."

"She's always worried about me. It's her thing."

"She can't help it. But hey, um . . . thanks?"

"Let me know if you change your mind," he said amiably and rambled off into the writhing masses.

She went in search of Jill, catching her as she jiggled across the floor, followed by a whole line of young men who seemed happily transfixed by the jiggling. "We have to go."

"But—"

"Now!" She towed her across the floor as determinedly as Jill had dragged her out of Vodka, gulping the blessedly bracing December air when they stumbled outside, the music muting to a distant thump as soon as the door shut behind them.

"Did he say something nasty to you?" Jill asked, eyes narrowing. "Because if he did—"

"Yes." There was a fine sift of snow in the air and she lifted her burning face to it. Wasn't she too young to be having a hot flash? Yeah, she wasn't too young for much, but she was pretty sure she was too young for that. She could have sworn this was what they'd feel like, though. "He asked me to go home with him."

"Well, thank God." Jill tugged her neckline up to safety; breast-feeding had taken her from *Playboy* to *Anna Nicole* territory, and her wardrobe hadn't adjusted. "I'd have been disappointed if you hadn't gotten at least one proposition out of that place. Why didn't you go?"

"Jill!" Now that she was out of the club, away from the seething youthful hormones that permeated the place, she was all the more appalled by her behavior. "Even you wouldn't've—"

"Why not? What's that statistic? About men reaching their sexual peak at, what, seventeen? Was he too old for you?"

Ellen started to sputter before catching the glint of humor in Jill's eyes. "I don't know about you, hon, but the ability to ejaculate and recover in seven point three seconds is *not* a desirable trait in a lover."

"At least they recover. And they're so . . . trainable."

"Your early years in the game must have been a lot better than mine," Ellen said. "As I recall, it wasn't all that great back then, and I'm not really interested in spending that much time training another one. Especially if he's going to go use it on someone else after all my hard work. If I'm getting one chance at this, I'm going to make sure I spend it on someone good." She slung her arm around Jill's shoulder. "Why don't you take me home?"

"Why, El!" She fluttered her eyelashes at her. "I had no idea. Not my usual thing, of course, but I'm willing to try anything once."

"Too bad we don't lean that way. Think how much easier it would be."

"Wouldn't it just?"

Ellen tugged her coat around her and turned in the direction of the parking garage.

"We can't give up yet," Jill protested.

"I'm not giving up." She wasn't committing to the plan—not even close—but she was closer than she'd ever been. Beyond not realizing that the guy in Vodka was married, beyond coming as close as she ever wanted to statutory rape in Paradise, it had really been sort of . . . fun. She was flushed and her heart was beating fast and she hadn't felt—well, anything but anger and hurt in a long time. "But give me a chance, will you? This was a big step for me. I've got to work my way up to the real thing." The neon palm trees blinked above her, turning the sputters of snow into a kaleidoscope. "Unless you're willing to go back to Vodka and let me take a run at Mike. For him I might be willing to ignore everything Sister Agnes ever taught me."

"Get in line, El, get in line." The door opened behind them, and a crowd of kids spilled out, carried on a wave of laughter and flashing lights and a shimmer of heat. "But I haven't been out in so long. I'd almost forgotten what it's like. Let me buy you one last drink before we go home. No more man-hunting." She held up her hands as to prove her good intentions. "Just a drink, I promise."

All the liquor she'd consumed sloshed in Ellen's stomach. "How about this? Just because I'm such a wild woman, I'll let you buy me a Diet Coke."

6

A Blast from the Past

THEY went to a bar. Not a club, not a pub, not even one of those places that became cool by being so resolutely uncool. Just a bar, a neighborhood joint with a sputtering neon sign and two small televisions mounted above the bar, a stone's throw from where Jill and Ellen had grown up and where then had run from as soon as they'd been handed their diplomas.

Back then the neighborhood, wedged hard on the northeast edge of downtown, had been made up of families, full of cops and nurses and small business owners with last names like Dziedec and Reilly. The boys played hockey and the girls cheered and learned to cook. In the last twenty years the neighborhood had slid down to the edge of seedy and was now headed the other way, on the verge of becoming fashionable. Jill's mother still lived in the snug brick bungalow where she'd raised her daughter. Ellen's parents, however, had sprinted for the north woods and the family cabin the instant her little brother had graduated.

Though the bar's name had changed—it had been O'Leary's back then, Ellen remembered, and the sign over the door now blinked Mac's—not much else had. There were mostly men inside, not nearly as well-dressed as those at Vodka, and not trying to hide the well-earned spare tires around their bellies, their bald spots fully exposed by the ruthlessly short cuts that had been done at the barbershop around the corner, if not their wives—no salons for this crowd.

A Hamm's Bear flickered over the cash register. Laughter erupted from the corner table where a bowling team divided their attention between SportsCenter on the nearest TV, three foamy pitchers of beer, and a heaping platter of chicken wings. In the summer the same group of men would still be at that table, Ellen figured, only in their softball uniforms.

A couple bent over a pool table, the man in an untucked denim shirt, the woman in a tight, overwashed T-shirt whose barely visible casino logo on the front did nothing to camouflage either her breasts or the roll of belly underneath. Smoke hazed the old fluorescent lights, spiraling up from the half-dozen people who blatantly ignored Minneapolis's clean air regulations.

Ellen relaxed. She understood this place, these people. Although there'd been a time when she would have rather strutted naked down Nicollet in January than claim any connection with the place, from a safe distance she'd learned to appreciate things like family ties and a hard day's work and forgive the lack of sophistication and the rigid insularity that had once felt like a prison.

Despite Jill's protestations to the contrary, she'd worried that she was taking her to another meat market after all. But Ellen couldn't be expected to meet a man here; they both knew places like this well enough to know that the vast majority of men in the place were not only married, but married to the kind of women who'd make sure they'd regret it if they stepped an inch over the line of fidelity. Plus they were drinking close enough to home to ensure that their wives would hear all about it if they did stray, probably before they got their pants off.

"There're two seats at the bar," Ellen said. They caught a couple of glances from the men as they wound their way through the close-crowded tables—women dressed like them didn't come here often, and if they did, they were in a group, usually with men, slumming. But the men quickly returned to their beers, their gazes fixed on the hockey highlights overhead. They came here to escape thinking about women, not wonder about ones they didn't know.

Jill fidgeted with her purse, checking her cell phone for the dozenth time.

"Go ahead," Ellen told her. "You've restrained yourself long enough. You should call."

Jill flipped open the lid, snapped it shut a second later. "It's late."

"Yeah, it's late. And you already proved you can go all of four hours without checking in."

Jill narrowed her eyes. "You and my mother bet on it, didn't you? What time did you take?"

"I didn't figure you'd last past ten, so I already owe your mother twenty. I underestimated the distraction value of the half-naked bartenders at Paradise. But I'd rather you weren't twitching the entire time we're here, and the only way that's going to happen is if you call."

"Well . . . he almost always wakes up about midnight, and—"

A cheer went up, causing them both to turn. The nearest TV screen was replaying a sliding goal that, according to the scroll, put the Wild up 3–2 on Calgary.

"You'd better take it outside." Ellen took her by the shoulders and gave her a nudge toward the door. "Or you're not going to hear a word."

Jill had her phone to her ear before she'd taken two steps.

"What do you want?" Ellen called after her. "My turn. I don't think anybody in here's going to buy them for us."

"You don't have to be so happy about that." Jill longingly considered the nearest pitcher of beer then sighed. "A Coke. The *real* thing. If I'm limited to one alcoholic drink a night, then I'm going straight for sugar the rest of the time."

The two empty stools were at the far end of the bar, with just one lone man beyond them, on the very last stool, hunched over his drink, his wide shoulders covered in threadbare blue. Family troubles, she decided. He was drinking alone and aiming to stay that way, or he wouldn't have picked that spot. Well, too bad. There was no place else to sit, and the shoes that had seemed bearable if not comfortable at the beginning of the night had turned excruciatingly painful about halfway through the second song at Paradise.

She plopped down and signaled the bartender, who was wrist deep in soapy water. "Two Cokes when you get a chance. One diet, one regular."

Hadn't been a horrible night, she thought. Not a great one, either, but not bad. She'd had a good time, in a strange sort of way, if only because the evening was so different from her usual life.

There was no denying she'd been in a rut. Heck, she *liked* her rut just fine. That didn't mean it wasn't good to bump out of it now and then, if only to check that you were there because you wanted to be and not just because you were bogged down in it.

Jill was going to be unhappy about tonight's outcome, though. She hated it when her plans didn't succeed. She'd set out to find Ellen a lover. She wasn't going to be satisfied until Ellen was.

But Ellen wasn't convinced she wanted a lover. What she *really* wanted was someone, someone a hundred times better than Tom, to flaunt in his face, to prove to him—and maybe to herself—that, while *he* might not want her anymore, someone else wonderful did.

The bartender set two glasses in front of her. "Two straws the diet."

She swallowed half of it in one long gulp.

"Ellen?" She swiveled to look at the guy next to her, who'd paused with his drink halfway to his mouth, apparently not quite as determined to be left alone as he'd seemed. "It's Ellen Miller, isn't it?"

The name took a minute to register; no one had called her by her maiden name in so long she no longer automatically answered to it.

He was about her age, she judged. Handsome, in the blunt and simple way of a man who didn't put much thought into his looks. His dark eyes were set deep, edged beneath with circles that betrayed too much worry and not enough sleep—an affliction she herself was familiar with, but he didn't have Lancôme's help to disguise it. There were nicks on his chin, almost hidden in the day's growth, like he'd shaved fast before barreling out in the morning.

He grinned, and there was something vaguely familiar in the dimples that suddenly creased his cheeks. "You have no clue, do you?"

"Sure I do," she said, cranking up memory neurons that hadn't been fired in years. One of her brother's friends, maybe, or someone from church. Probably not her class—he hadn't shown up at their twentieth reunion, anyway; she would have noticed if any of the guys she'd known back then had grown up this well.

He stood and ambled over to the nearest post, backing up against it, his arms behind his back as if tied there. "Now?"

"Oh my God." She scanned the room, searching for the best exit route. "Joey Marcioni?"

"Yup." He swung his leg back over his stool and curled his big hand around his glass. "Though mostly it's Joe now."

"Oh my God," she repeated. They'd studiously avoided each other for the rest of eighth grade. He'd transferred out the following summer, and she'd never heard from him again. "I'm so, so sorry, I—"

"Don't be." She kept a close eye on his hand around his glass, just in case he decided to toss it at her. "I was an asshole. Deserved everything I got."

"Well, yes, you were." She felt better when he drained his drink. He might have dumped the beer over her head, but she didn't *think* he'd actually whack her with the heavy mug. "But if you had to leave because of us, well . . . I still feel awful."

"No, it wasn't you. Not that I minded moving. Somehow I wasn't quite such the cool kid at school after everybody'd seen me in my shorts. But my dad got transferred to Chicago for two years, and when we came back, we moved to the suburbs." He made a face.

"A fate worse than death."

"Moved back to the city the day I graduated; haven't left since," he said. "Where do you live?"

"Edina."

"Oops," he said. "The suburb to end all suburbs."

"I've got kids."

"That'll do it."

He spun toward her, his legs wide, one fist resting on his thigh, giving her more concentrated attention than he had in an entire school year. Back then, if he'd looked at her that directly, she would have probably flipped right into an asthma attack. Even now there was a little jolt of awareness. Funny how your teenaged crushes never seemed to fade completely, as if your hormones imprinted on the first one who kicked them into gear, the way a baby bird fixes on its mother. "You haven't changed," he said.

"Thanks." *I think.* Was that, *You haven't gotten fat, you haven't wrinkled up, you're holding up okay, you haven't changed?* Or, *You're still as unsure and boring and stupid as you were at thirteen, you haven't changed?* It was a probably intended as a compliment, but it stung just the same. Somehow all those years should have made a difference. Should have made her better, inside and out, for how hard she'd worked during them. "You have," she said.

He chuckled and patted his stomach. "Yeah, it happens."

"No!" she said quickly, horrified he would take it that way, but then he grinned, obviously unoffended.

"More than you know," he said. "I'm a cop now."

"A *cop?*" He'd been a troublemaker in junior high—that had been part of his appeal, the boundless and fearless energy, the way he always danced on the edge of disaster.

"Yup," he said, with unmistakable pride. "Figured it was one side of the law or the other."

"Glad you chose the right one." She used the excuse of sipping her pop—flat, not enough ice—to study him over the rim of her glass. She didn't know any cops. They didn't live in her neighborhood. Couldn't afford her neighborhood, which was stuffed with doctors and lawyers and vice presidents. And the police never had much call to come there, either. The biggest crime was the Larsons' retriever's tendency take a dump in yards that weren't his own. "I don't know that I've talked to a cop since I graduated."

"Not even a traffic ticket?" His eyes took her in, top to bottom. "Oh, of course not. Forgot for a minute who I was talking to."

"Hey!" she protested, insulted. "I'm not *that* much of a geek."

"Uh-huh. Did you ever *not* set the curve in a single class?"

"I most certainly did."

"Hmm." Humor glinted in his eyes, and she remembered that instant of fluttering joy when she'd thought he'd liked her, too. "Gym, right?" he asked, chuckling when she refused to answer.

She dropped her gaze. His elbow rested on the bar, his thumb spinning the plain gold band on his third finger. "You're married?"

He spread his fingers, staring at the ring as if he'd forgotten he was wearing it. Then he curled his hand into a fist and dropped it to the bar, his laugh this time hollow and rueful. "No, actually, I'm not. I was, though, for years and years."

"I'm sorry. It's none of my business."

"No, it's okay. I've got to get used to saying it, don't I? We've been divorced for five months. This thing's stuck, though. Haven't gotten around to getting it cut off."

"I understand." She did, and knew perfectly well that not having enough time to attend to the task had nothing to do with why he hadn't taken off his ring. She held up her own hand and wiggled her fingers, the platinum and diamond winking dully in the cheap lights. Even after everything that had happened, she couldn't imagine taking it off. "Me, too. Not divorced, though. Separated. Three months."

"You, too?" He drummed his fingers on the scarred top of the bar. "Never would have thought it. Me, no real surprise I screwed it up. But you . . . figured you'd be the type who'd be married even longer than the 'death do us part' part."

"Yeah. I did, too."

They fell silent, the awkwardness of near strangers undercut by the comradeship of fellow sufferers.

"You never told anyone," she said at last. "That it was us, I mean, who did that to you. We would have been in so much trouble . . . I was too mad to thank you then, but you really did save our butts."

"My reputation'd taken enough of a hit as it was. You think I was going to tell everyone two *girls* tied me up?" He shrugged. "I said it was St. Basil's offensive line."

He tossed off her thanks, but she knew there was more to it than that. He'd protected them when he didn't have to, and who would have thought that Joey Marcioni had it in him?

Joe, on the other hand . . . Joe seemed to have rather a lot in him.

"Well," she said when she couldn't think of anything else. "I should—"

"There you are." Jill rushed up to her, her cheeks pink from the cold, droplets of melted snow glistening in her hair. "Mom said he's crying, and she swears he's okay, but—"

"Let's go."

"Do you mind if we go over there right away?" She had a death grip on her purse, and she was one second from bursting into tears. "I know it's late, and I hate to ask you to wait, but if I drive you all the way out to Edina before coming back here, it'll be ages before I get to him."

"You know it's fine." She reached for her coat, but Joe was already standing with it in his hands, ready for her to slip her arms in, a courtesy that seemed automatic to him.

"Thanks," Jill hurried on. "I know you think I'm over protective, but—"

"Yes, for I'm *such* a relaxed and hands-off kind of mother. I *never* worry unreasonably."

"I could give you a ride home," Joe offered.

Jill, who up until that moment hadn't noticed him, reverted to type, giving him a quick assessment.

"I . . ." It was a mere courtesy, Ellen told herself. No more important than his holding her coat. And yet it seemed so much bigger than that, taking her back to the days when an escort home implied a dozen heady and terrifying possibilities.

"I'll show you my shield if it makes you feel any better."

She would have grounded her daughter for a year for accepting a ride home from a man she'd met in a bar. But he wasn't a stranger; he was Joey Marcioni, for heaven's sake. And he was a policeman. What could possibly happen?

"Ellen?" Jill asked, one brow lifted in speculation.

"You go ahead," Ellen told her.

"You sure?"

"Sure. It's only a ride home," she said. But she couldn't shake the idea that it was no such thing.

Jill nodded and leaned forward to whisper in her ear. "Forget about the gym tomorrow morning."

* * *

"I suppose you know all the good spots."

The road, which plunged between a thicket of trees and curved high along the edge of the Mississippi, would have been impossible to find if you didn't know it was there. When he'd suggested stopping for a bit before going home, she'd nearly thrown up her Diet Coke. Parking? At their age? But there'd been such hesitancy in the suggestion, and he'd so carefully avoided looking directly at her, and she understood. He just didn't want to go home alone again. Not yet. And because she knew that feeling only too well, she'd said yes before she could think better of it.

"Yup," he said. "Early days on the force, I figure I prevented a good hundred pregnancies or so, roustin' kids out of here." His smile was nostalgic, maybe a little sad. "Legacy of a misspent youth. You know all the trouble spots."

"It's pretty, though," she commented while she tried to keep her stomach settled, her pulse calm. There was a break in the bare trees directly in front of them, giving her a good view of the river far below. A chunky crust of ice edged the shoreline. The water itself was deep and black, glistening in the moonlight.

"Yeah. I forget, sometimes. Too busy rushing over the thing to notice."

Is that what had happened in his marriage? She wondered. In hers? Just too busy rushing to notice until it was too late?

She shivered.

"Oh, hell, you're cold. I'm sorry." Before she could protest, he slid closer and looped an arm over her shoulder. "It was stupid of me to bring you here."

"No." Her voice stuttered, but that, too, she could blame on the cold. His motion brought the smell of him to her: the leather of his black jacket, the smoke his clothes had picked up in the bar, the spicy soap he used. Good smells, both familiar and totally strange. She stiffened, unwilling to pull away, not quite ready to curl in. "It's fine."

"We could go to my place," he suggested.

"I—" She stopped before she answered. She didn't *have* an answer. She'd never have another opportunity better than this. She knew it, but she still didn't know whether she *wanted* that opportunity.

"Not what you're thinking," he said quickly. He swallowed and there were shadows in his eyes that weren't from the moonlight. "I didn't mean . . . well, not unless you really want to, of course." His gaze met hers and skittered away, and his nervousness, the fact that he was as unsure as she was, tilted her decision in his direction. "I'm just so damned tired of being alone," he said, his voice as weary as if he hadn't slept since he'd walked away from her in the eighth grade.

And she put off the final decision a little longer. "That'd be okay."

* * *

SHE recognized his apartment the instant she walked into it, a prime example of the Recently Divorced Male style: sterile, boxy rooms; bare white walls. It held a couch and a chair, sagging, flowery things that had probably once been relegated to his basement and were the only pieces of furniture his wife let him take when he left. Newspapers piled at one end of the couch and a half-empty coffee cup balanced on a cardboard box beside it. The black hulk of a television as big as his SUV dominated the space across from the couch.

"Hmm," she said, contemplating the beast. "First thing you bought when you moved out?"

"Yeah," he said. "My wife'd never let me have one. Said it wouldn't 'go.'" He hadn't said her name yet, Ellen noted. She was always "my wife."

"It doesn't," she said, then let him off the hook. "Mine's a fifty-four-incher. Yours?"

"You have a fifty-four-inch television?"

"What can I say? I like movies."

They laughed together and then fell into one of those uncomfortable silences that Ellen had always found the worst thing about dating. Not that this was a date, she reminded herself quickly. But it recalled all those awkward times, when she'd known that it was always all her fault, that she was the one who wasn't interesting or skilled enough to keep the conversation flowing smoothly, who didn't know how to flirt and sparkle.

"Well," she said lamely, caught in a peculiar place between junior high and old age. She had been married forever, had had sex a million times, and yet she felt thirteen, here with Joey Marcioni, uncertain, waiting to find out what happened next.

But Joe Marcioni wasn't Joey, and he took care of things. He crossed the floor with its worn beige carpet and put his hands— big, rough ones, clearly a man's hands, harder and callused so they could never be mistaken for Tom's, and she was grateful for that—on either side of her head. Oh, she was always a sucker for that. He bent his head and kissed her, a sweet, shaky sigh of a kiss, a first kiss.

She'd forgotten how wonderful first kisses could be, all discovery mixed with terror while your heart raced and your brain started to fog. She fell into him because she'd missed it, far more than she realized, and her mouth opened and she heard him groan as his hands slid down her back and settled at her hips.

He let go and stepped back, and she was sorry. That surprised her. Shouldn't she be relieved? Better to have time to think this step over. Such things should not be decided in the heat of the moment. She'd warned her daughter about that a thousand times.

But she was damned tired of thinking about things.

"I—" His hands were shaking. She couldn't remember the last time a man had shaken because he wanted her so much. "I haven't done this. Not since my wife and I—"

"Oh," she murmured, touched. Here was a man so devoted to his marriage that he'd been divorced a full five months and hadn't been with another woman. Suddenly she was furious all over again at Tom, who hadn't even been able to be faithful when he was married, who'd hit on her best friend, who didn't understand why she thought that sex should matter.

Maybe she was the only one left in the world who thought it should. What was the point?

So she took her courage into her hands and put her hands on the hem of her skimpy tank. If she was going to do something so unlike her, might as well do it all the way.

Joe's gaze was glued to her chest while his own bellowed in and out.

Oh my God, what am I doing? Ellen preferred the lights off, her body cloaked in silk and shadows. At her age, things just looked better that way.

But she dragged her top over her head. The lights were full on—brutal, apartment-standard lights—and she stood in that sadly bare living room and she'd never felt so exposed.

Her hands went to the clasp at the back of her bra, and she had a horrible vision of what was going to happen when she released it. All that Victoria-created cleavage was going to vanish, and her breasts were going to drop a saggy three inches closer to her waist.

"By that point they're so happy to see naked breasts that it won't matter."

Jill knew a whole lot more about men than Ellen did. She was just going to have to trust her on this one. She popped the hooks and let the bra straps slide off her shoulders, fighting the urge to cover up, knowing there was nothing sexy about the way she stripped but that this was as close to *va-va-voom* as she could muster.

It was cold and uncomfortable, and she'd stopped feeling sexy when her sweater hit the floor. But Joe shuddered, his eyes still on her breasts, and she started believing things were going to be just fine after all.

Until Lieutenant Joe Marcioni burst out bawling.

7

The Morning After

It was four thirty by the time she got home. The temperature had plunged to near zero, and she was shivering from her quick trudge up the sidewalk. Next time, she was going to wear clothes that were appropriate for the weather, no matter what Jill said.

The house was pitch-dark—she'd forgotten to leave the front light on—and as soon as she flicked on the hall light, she wished she hadn't.

"Bad," she mumbled. "*Really* bad."

Her makeup was smeared from her forehead to her chin, and the circles under her eyes looked like they'd been permanently tattooed there.

So don't look, dummy, she told herself and wheeled away from the mirror. Amazing how forty-odd years of taking care of herself could get erased in one night.

She kicked off her shoes—*Thank God, thank God*—and headed for the stairs. Bed. All she had to do was climb the stairs, and she could sleep, blessed sleep, on her own comfortable mattress, in her own lovely sheets. For once she was glad the kids were gone. No nine a.m. trumpet lesson run for her tomorrow.

She flopped down on the bed. *Ahh*. Best thing in the world, ever.

She should go brush her teeth, wash her face. Would she wake up with rotten teeth and pimples dotting her face if she didn't do it for one lousy night?

Ah, what the hell. She'd gone out to be a bad girl for one

night, and she was pretty sure bad girls didn't always practice good hygiene before they zonked out from their wild nights.

Bad girls probably didn't check for calls from their kids, either. But some habits couldn't be broken. She lifted the receiver and winced at the insistent *beep beep beep* of waiting messages.

She squinted futilely at the numbers before she reached for the lamp, and had to close her eyes for a minute against the assault of the light when she flicked it on.

"You have four new—"

Crap. She punched double ones.

"Mrs. Markham, we're thrilled to inform you that you have been preapproved for a second mortgage—" She jabbed three twice, then seven.

"El! It's three thirty and you're not home yet. I'm taking that as good news. Or you've been kidnapped and turned into a sex slave. Hopefully not without your consent. Anyway, Josh's fine, I'm home, and you should call me with *every* detail the instant you get in. I'm serious, I don't care what time it is. I want to know."

Oh, yeah, she was calling Jill at this ungodly hour just to fill her in. Besides, she needed to get her story straight before she talked to Jill.

Tom's voice on the third message was shaky and angry and brought her bolt upright on the bed, instantly wide awake.

"El? It's me. It's three forty-five, and that arrogant little fucker hasn't brought Katie back yet. When can I call the police—"

The phone thudded on the carpet as she ran for Kate's room. And her heart, which had stopped beating, eased back to life when she saw the lump under the covers.

She tiptoed over to the bed. Katie lay on her side, curled up into a ball that seemed no bigger than the giant stuffed gorilla Tom had won for her at the state fair when she was four. The pink and purple quilt her grandmother had made her when she was eight, one of the few vestiges of childhood she hadn't thrown off, was tugged up over her ears. All that showed was a sweep of blond hair against the pillow, a curve of smooth forehead, a sweetly closed eye. Ellen reached out a hand that still shook with adrenaline and pushed back a swath of hair.

Like a little caterpillar, Ellen thought fondly, cuddled up in her cocoon. Except Kate had already turned into a butterfly, a fragile and vulnerable one.

No matter how hard Ellen's day was, how relentless her worries, during all the very worst moments of her life, those concerns always faded away as she watched her children sleep. She wondered how many times over the years she'd snuck in their rooms and kept vigil over them, letting her troubles smooth away. Sometimes, if she really couldn't sleep, she'd even slide into bed with them, and something about the warmth of them next to her, the even sighs of their breathing, would be enough for her to drift off as well.

"Sleep tight, my Katie," she murmured. Back in her own room, she plopped back down on the bed and wearily contemplated the phone she'd dropped when she ran.

She should call Tom, put him out of his misery. And he *was* miserable; the one thing she'd never doubted was that he loved his children.

But she was so tired. Not just tonight, but tired of it all, sick of all the nights' sleep she'd lost because of Tom.

Just a few hours, she thought, yawning. That'd be soon enough to call him, she decided, and pitched over into a well-earned sleep.

* * *

KATE listened to Mom pad back down the hall. She kept her eyes shut, counting off her breaths so they were slow and smooth, like she was really out, just in case Mom decided to come back. She was sneaky that way.

Not like Dad. Dad believed everything, grinned at her like she was the best daughter in the world no matter what she did. Mom—she was always looking for mistakes, always suspicious, always waiting for Kate to screw up. No wonder Dad couldn't stand to live with her.

When she was sure Mom was gone for good, she rolled over, feeling the tears leak out of the corners of her eyes, rolling down into the pillow that was already damp.

Shit. She swiped at the tears, mad that they kept coming. It wasn't worth crying about, was it? Wasn't worth even worrying about, Caleb had said. *"You're making too damn big a deal out of this, baby girl."* He'd told her, *"Once we do it, you'll wonder why you waited so damned long."*

And I'm not going to wait much longer. He hadn't said that out loud. Hadn't had to. She wasn't stupid.

Baby girl. She used to like when Caleb called her that. Made her feel safe, special, protected. Lately it'd had an edge to it, a little too much emphasis on the *baby*, like he thought she wasn't old enough for him.

She didn't know why she just didn't do it and get it over with. It was dumb to be so scared. But she didn't want to get pregnant, didn't want to catch something. He'd take care of it—he promised—but . . . she knew what Mom was doing, all those times she recited those awful statistics about AIDS and teen pregnancy. Damned if it hadn't worked, anyway. She'd almost given in tonight, and then it had popped into her head, Mom's latest lecture about a condom's 12 percent failure rate, and she'd shoved Caleb away.

He'd been mad. Well, you could hardly blame him, could you? She'd waited until kind of the last minute. And she wanted him to *want* to sleep with her. Her boyfriend was supposed to think she was hot. It would suck if he wasn't wild for her. But she didn't think he had to get so, well, sulky about it. She wasn't sure how much longer he'd wait. He was seventeen, and was used to getting some, and she'd seen the eye Heather Montrose had given him in the halls last week. Heather wouldn't be saying no at the last minute, that was for damn sure. She didn't say no at all, the slut.

Tonight, when Kate had stopped him, his voice had gotten all nasty and cold, and he'd dragged her out to the car to take her home. It wasn't how it was supposed to happen—they'd planned for her to stay the night, 'cause his folks had gone up north to go snowmobiling, and she was going to call her dad and say she was staying over at her friend Emily's.

But after she'd said no, he didn't want her to stay anymore. She'd looked forward to it. It would be so nice to sleep that way, all cuddled up and safe. But he couldn't stand to be close to her afterward. Didn't want to talk, didn't even kiss her when he dropped her off. She'd told him to bring her to Mom's, not Dad's, because she didn't want Dad to see her like that, all upset and puffy-eyed. Mom—she was used to putting Mom off, and Mom was used to her being "moody," as she called it.

Yeah, she couldn't blame Caleb. But knowing that didn't make her stomachache go away. It didn't make the sleep come easier, even though she was as tired as she could ever remember being.

So she just lay in her bed staring at the ceiling and at the glow-in-the-dark twinkle stars Dad had put up when she was a baby and never gotten around to taking down, wondering when her life had gotten all fucked up.

Oh, yeah—it was when her mom had kicked her dad out.

* * *

ELLEN only slept for an hour. She woke up to go to the bathroom, grimaced at herself in the mirror, with her smeared mascara and blotchy skin and hair that looked like someone had taken an eggbeater to it. Crap! Acting like you were still young could sure make a woman look old.

And then her guilt got the better of her.

She punched in Tom's new number, closed her eyes against the squeal of the ring in her ear, trying not to think of what happened the last time she'd called his number in the middle of the night.

If a woman answered this time, she was going to do a lot more than ask for a separation.

He picked up at the first ring, which only made her feel worse. He'd had to be waiting right by the phone.

"Katie? Where are you—"

"No, it's me. She's here."

"There?" He asked it like an accusation, as if it were somehow Ellen's fault that Kate had come home without telling him.
"Why's she there?"

"How should I know? She's sleeping. I didn't wake her."

"Why not?"

"Why? She's breathing. She's home, safe and sound in her
bed. It's five thirty in the morning. No reason I should have to
deal with all the snarling if I woke her up right now. You want
to talk to her, you come right on over here and wake her up. If
not, I'm going to sleep."

"Sleep? *Now?*" He was silent for a moment, sifting through
possibilities. "You just got home?"

She tamped down the slight surge of guilt. She had *nothing* to
feel guilty about. And, even if she had, well, that was what he
wanted, wasn't it? "Maybe."

"Where were you?"

"None of your business." She yawned and flopped back on
the bed. "Can I go to sleep now?"

"Have fun?" he asked.

Crap. Her eyelids slipped down. "Yes."

"Really?" he asked, sounding half disbelieving, half interested. She wasn't sure which one was worse. The disbelief was
insulting, but the interest was disturbing.

"I'm going to sleep," she told him. "If you want to yell at her
for not telling you where she was, you can come over and be my
guest. I'll even make an exception, and you can use your key. But
if you wake me up, I'm not liable for the consequences."

* * *

SHE got a full, blessed three hours of sleep before the phone rang
again. "What!" she snapped into the receiver.

"Oh. You're home." Jill sounded disappointed.

"Yup. I'm home." Ellen rolled over, squinting at the clock.
"Why are you calling me so early?"

"It's not early. Josh's been up for an hour and a half. You should thank me for restraining myself for so long."

"Times change, huh?" In fifteen years Ellen hadn't slept past seven thirty on a Saturday unless she could guilt Tom into taking the morning shift. She doubted that, before Josh's birth, Jill had ever seen the sun before ten on a weekend unless it was from the other side.

"Some things change. Not all of them. You still have to tell me all about it." She heard Josh's squall and Jill's answering murmur. "Wait a sec, we gotta change sides."

Ellen rolled to her back, the receiver against her ear. It seemed as if she'd spent half her teenage years like this, sprawled on her bed talking to Jill, dissecting the events of the night before.

"Okay, El. We're settled. Spill."

"What do you want to know?"

"Everything. Well, scratch that. Everything interesting. If you played cribbage in the back of Mac's and took a taxi home, I don't want to know."

"Well, then, I guess you don't want to know."

"Oh, hon. What am I going to do with you?" Jill sighed. "Okay, here's what we do. I'll call my mom about next weekend, you start looking for tickets. This calls for Vegas."

"Vegas?" Ellen grimaced. She'd barely survived one night of barhopping in Minneapolis. There was no way she was going to endure Vegas. "Do I seem like a Vegas kind of woman to you?"

"No, of course not. That's the point. "We'll—"

"You're breast-feeding, Jill."

"Oh. That's right." The phone was silent, though Ellen could almost hear the devious wheels of Jill's mind cranking. "I'll pump. This is an emergency. When Josh's old enough, he'll understand."

Crap. Clearly, the only way out of this was to tell the truth.

"He took me parking."

"That's better. Keep going."

"And then he took me to his place . . ." Ellen went on suggestively.

"Good, good." Jill waited. "And?"

"And I took off my shirt. And my bra."

"Really?" Her disbelief was only too clear.

"What's that supposed to mean?"

"I mean . . . well . . . it is *you*, El."

Ellen, who'd braved a whole ten minutes on the beach on their one "wild" college spring break trip before she'd tugged a T-shirt over her head and wrapped a towel around her hips, claiming an imminent sunburn. Ellen, who'd exchanged the G-string and garter belt she'd gotten at her wedding shower for a long, silky nightgown. Ellen, who, when roped into a game of strip poker her freshman year, had purposefully downed enough tequila shots to get sick, giving herself an out before she lost anything but her socks.

Shit. She really was boring.

"Well . . . you know," she said.

"No, I don't. That's why I'm listening."

"You don't really think I'm going to tell you more than that, do you?" she said. "You never tell me more."

"That's because you start blushing and giggling and won't *let* me go any further," Jill reminded her. "I'd be happy to share every single detail."

"You have no shame."

"Damn right," Jill said with more than a trace of pride. "And I've got no restraint, either, and you know I never give in. You're no match for me, El."

Which was true. She took one last stab at it anyway. "I thought we weren't supposed to kiss and tell."

"That's for the *guys*. Girls are supposed to tell their best friends everything. If we didn't get to compare, we'd believe all the bullshit the guys spew, and we'd never know what we were missing." She gave Ellen a long second to answer, and then sighed. "Okay, I'm coming over."

"No need," Ellen said, and hesitated.

She should just tell everyone she'd had an affair. Tell her

friend, tell her husband, tell everybody she could think of. Then maybe they'd all finally leave her alone.

But she was no better at lying than she was at doing the wild thing.

"And after the bra came off . . ." Jill prompted.

"He started crying."

And that one caught even "I've heard everything" Jill by surprise. "*What?*"

"You mean that doesn't happen to you?" Ellen asked. "I thought you were supposed to be good."

"Well, maybe once or twice, when it was all over, in gratitude, but not . . ." Her voice gentled. "El, what happened?"

"What can I say? The man's still completely in love with his wife." And so Ellen had gone into caretaker mode—that, at least, she was *really* good at—and held Joe while he sobbed all over her naked breasts, and let him tell her all about his wife, Cynthia. She'd tugged on her clothes and fed him coffee and cinnamon toast, and then hugged him good-bye after he drove her home. "Apparently the prospect of sleeping with me made him realize just how much."

The silence was so long that Ellen thought they'd lost the connection. Then Jill burst into laughter. "Only you, El. Only you."

"Yeah," Ellen agreed. "Only me."

8

The Christmas Spirit

CHRISTMAS was really, really going to suck.

Ellen knew it. She just didn't know how to change it.

It had taken a few years of negotiation early in their marriage to manage the families and holidays. Her parents wanted them at the cabin. His wanted them at the farm.

They'd solved it by having their own Christmas. The grandparents were invited, of course, and usually came. Ditto for their brothers and sisters and their associated significant others. Sometimes a dozen people stayed at their house, crammed into guest rooms and on sofas and the air mattress in the basement, another twenty dropping in or out as their schedules dictated. Ellen loved every second of it; where Christmas was concerned, she believed the more the better.

But this year . . . obviously, Tom's family was out. It would be just too awkward. And her parents were flying to Denver to be with her brother; his wife was too far along with their third child to travel. She'd wanted to go, too; she could take the kids skiing afterward, and it would be easier to be out of town, out of their house, away from Tom. It was going to be a peculiar holiday any way she tried to manage it; better to change it up completely.

Except Tom had adamantly opposed the plan. She'd already kicked him out of the house, he'd said; she would not take his children away from him for Christmas. And she'd had to admit he had a point. She could argue the "kicked him out" all she wanted, but there was no getting around the fact that having your kids gone for Christmas would be just plain awful.

So they'd agreed. The kids would stay home with her on Christmas Eve for dinner and church. And Christmas morning, for the stockings; he could come over early enough to watch them take them down if he chose. Tom would take the kids for brunch and get to keep them the rest of the day. She'd take them to the lake once her parents returned; he'd take them to his family's in South Dakota the weekend of Martin Luther King's birthday.

Crap, but separation was complicated. And lonely.

She'd tried to keep the weeks leading up to the holidays as normal as possible. The last thing she wanted was for the kids to suffer because of what Tom and she had done. Were doing.

But it wasn't the same, and now, as she pulled on a bright green sweater and threaded the hooks from a couple of dangling Christmas balls through her earlobes, she had to admit that she hadn't even come close.

Oh, the house smelled good as she came down the stairs. The turkey'd be ready in an hour, and nothing ever smelled as fabulous as roasting turkey. She never made one any other time but Christmas and Thanksgiving, even though the kids loved it, because she was afraid it wouldn't taste as good on the holidays if you got to eat it on ordinary days.

But she'd only put up half the decorations. She'd originally planned to do them all, every single one.

The outside lights defeated her almost from the start. Tom put them up early every year, before the snow fell, hundreds of them rimming the roof, around every window, wrapped around each bush in the yard. But she'd forgotten about it until after Thanksgiving, and by then it was already cold. So the lights remained piled in boxes, hopelessly tangled. She'd always wondered if Tom put them away like that on purpose, because then he could rope Eric into helping him untangle them. It was a challenge they'd spend an entire Sunday afternoon working on, on the floor in the family room in front of the Vikings game, and that kind of accord between father and son had grown rare.

But she knew her limitations, and so one lonely string blinked around the big bay window in the living room. It probably looked worse than nothing, but she couldn't stand driving down her street, seeing all the extravagant displays—even the big, blue-lighted menorah decorating the Adelmans'—and finding her house dark, when it had always shone the brightest of all. So every night at five she plugged in that forlorn strand of lights.

She'd tried to make up for it with the tree. It stood in the same corner of the room it always did, beside the fireplace where they'd moved the wing chair out of the way.

It was too damn big. She'd bought the biggest she could find; it had taken half the boy scout troop that staffed the lot, not to mention their fathers, to tie it on top of her van. She'd driven home at fifteen miles an hour, terrified it was going to slide right off.

She and Kate and Eric had dropped it twice as they'd tried to wrestle it into the house. She'd had to empty the vacuum cleaner bag three times just to suck up all the needles it shed along the way.

Now she stood in the entrance to the living room. The darned thing still wasn't straight. Who knew it required such a talent to get it to stay up? Or to wrap the lights around evenly? It seemed Tom was useful for a couple of things after all.

She'd put Christmas music on the stereo the Sunday they'd allotted for decorating it. She'd made hot chocolate and brought out a whole pile of Christmas cookies.

Kate had bailed in less than twenty minutes, when her cell phone rang, and she'd slipped out to answer it, a conversation that had apparently gone on for the next three hours. Eric, bless him, had hung in there longer, forcing a smile, even singing along to "Merry Christmas, Baby," but she'd been a mother long enough to recognize his misery. So she'd excused him to go next door to his friend Sam's house, where he didn't have to think about anything but the next warrior to cut down in *Warcraft*.

Okay, enough wallowing, Ellen told herself sternly. There were ropes of evergreens on the mantel, and both stockings. The angel perched on the top of the tree, even if she looked liked she'd climbed up there after downing a couple of shots of angelic cheer. They had a house, and a tree, and a turkey in the oven, and that was more than a whole lot of people had.

The doorbell dinged. She padded over in her stocking feet, peered out the paned sidelights, and tugged it open.

"Tom?" she asked. "I thought we'd worked this out. You're supposed to come tomorrow morning." She hadn't gotten that mixed up, had she? After all the arguing it had taken for them to settle on a plan?

Of course she hadn't. Maybe Tom had just conveniently "forgotten" another agreement.

He scuffled his feet in the thin coat of snow on the steps—she'd meant to send Eric out to scrape it off, but it was cold, and he'd been halfway through a battle he claimed he couldn't just leave, and well, who would be coming to their front door tonight anyway?

Tom's sedan was parked in the street, not the driveway. His gray coat was open, his cheeks almost burgundy with the cold, and a blue cashmere scarf was draped around his neck but unwrapped. She shook her head; she could provide him with plenty of warm clothes, but she couldn't ensure he bundled up sensibly.

"You're going to ruin your shoes." The black leather was already getting damp in the snow. "You forgot your rubbers again."

He looked down and seemed surprised that his shoes were getting wet. He had a big package in each arm, wrapped in shiny navy paper with squashed silver bows. "I know I'm not due 'til tomorrow." He seemed to lose his train of thought for a moment. He looked drawn, his cheekbones sharper, his eyes tired. "Anyway. I'm sorry I bothered you. I just—" He shoved the packages at her. "I wanted the kids to have . . . something from me tonight. I figured, even though you aren't at your folks, you'd still be opening some family gifts tonight."

She smiled. It had been another thing they'd had to work out early on. His family never unwrapped anything until Christmas morning, attacking the gifts after the stockings. Her family opened their presents on Christmas Eve. Her father claimed it was a Swedish tradition, but nobody she'd ever met had done the same, and a good chunk of them had a shot of Swedish in them—this was Minnesota, after all. So she figured her father, who had the patience of a four-year-old when it came to presents, had made it up. Since it got her gifts earlier when she was a kid, she kept her mouth shut. And once Tom had realized it meant a couple of extra hours of sleep on Christmas morning, he'd gone along with it as well.

"We will."

"Well. Then." He handed off the presents and stuck his hands deep in his coat pockets—no gloves, of course—and hunched over. "I guess I'd better go."

And suddenly she felt a small—very small—spurt of pity for him. He looked lost, standing on the step of the house that had been his for more than a dozen years, ready to go back to his barren apartment alone on Christmas Eve.

"You have plans, I suppose?" she asked hopefully. A hot date, preferably, which he would rub in her face so obviously that she'd stop feeling any sympathy and start hating him again.

"Oh, sure." He shrugged. It was nearly dark out, the sky a thick blue gray behind him. Along the street Christmas lights winked on, blinking merrily, picture-postcard houses holding picture-perfect families. They used to be one. "Lots to do. You know how it is."

"Hot date?"

"Of course. With a Stouffer's turkey dinner and a DVD of *White Christmas.*"

"Maybe you should go with *It's a Wonderful Life*," she told him. It was an old habit, needling him. Then he winced, and just when did she start feeling sorry for him, anyway?

But it was Christmas. "Why don't you stay?" she asked impulsively, and immediately she wished she hadn't.

Maybe he'd say no. Surely that crack about Stouffer's and a movie had been calculated to make her feel guilty. The hot date was a lot more likely.

"For dinner?" he asked.

"Sure. Dinner, and the gifts."

"Dad?" Eric was at the top of the stairs, a clean but untucked blue shirt over his khakis, his hair slicked down with water, the same hopeful smile on his face that his father had worn a moment before. "I thought you were coming tomorrow?"

Tom glanced at Ellen, then grinned up at Eric. "I am. But your mom invited me for dinner, too."

* * *

WHAT did they used to talk about? Ellen wondered, as another awkward silence fell in their dining room. Work, sure. The kids, yes. Plans for the future. But it seemed as if they'd all lost the thread of each others' lives, so careful tonight to avoid any topic that might explode their fragile truce that there was nothing left to say.

So they handed platters of food around the table—way too much, Ellen had never cooked for so few on a holiday before—and talked about innocuous things: football, the weather, movies. Nothing that mattered.

Tom was clearly on his best behavior. He didn't make one comment about Katie's boyfriend, nor did he take her side against Ellen when she told Katie she could not take a phone call in the middle of dinner. He didn't push Eric about hockey tryouts. He told Ellen how fabulous the food was and seemed to mean it, then he helped her clear the table and load the dishwasher without once checking his Treo for messages.

The living room looked beautiful, when they finally moved there, with the fire Tom'd started snapping away—Ellen had never been as good at it as he was—and the lights sparkling, even though the pile of presents was a third its usual size. Once he'd gotten the fire established, he'd nearly plopped into his accustomed spot on the couch next to Ellen. He stopped halfway down, shooting her an uncertain glance.

Was he waiting for her permission? Hoping for it? Was she supposed to tell him to go ahead, it was all right if he sat next to her? If he'd just sat down, she wouldn't have even noticed. But now she had to *think* about it, and she considered too long, until he moved back to the fireplace, poking unnecessarily at the flames with the poker before dropping into the nearest club chair.

They sorted out the gifts. There'd be more later, of course, when they saw their grandparents. But tonight there were only a few in front of each child, two in front of Ellen.

She fretted that the kids were disappointed by the skimpy haul. But they were of an age, past Legos and huge stuffed critters, where their piles would have been diminishing anyway. Gift certificates and CDs didn't take much room.

Eric's hand hovered over the package Tom had brought. He glanced uncertainly at Ellen.

"Go ahead," Ellen said. Eric shouldn't have to worry about picking one present before another, as if he were choosing sides. *What have we done to our children? What are we doing?*

"You should open yours at the same time," Tom said to Kate. "They're the same."

She raised her brow, so clearly skeptical of any gift that could possibly please both of them that Tom chuckled. Ellen felt herself relax for the first time since he'd rung the doorbell.

She and Tom had been a team once, a good one. And maybe she'd been trying harder than she needed to, to forget that.

"Kate, slow down!" She was tearing greedily into the paper while Eric carefully slit the tape with his thumbnail. "Give Eric a chance to catch up."

Kate's impatient sigh was both dramatic and expected, but she didn't argue and waited until Eric unfolded the paper and set it aside. The plain cardboard boxes the size of laundry baskets gave no hint.

"It's so light," Kate said as she lifted it and gave it an experimental shake.

They both yanked off the lids and pulled out twin iPods—white for Eric, black for Kate.

"Oh, Dad, thank you!"

Kate beat Eric to him, throwing her arms around her father in a quick, hard hug. Ellen saw Tom hesitate, then wrap his arms around Kate, his eyes closing as if he would freeze that moment, as if Kate had just given him the biggest present of the year. Ellen unexpectedly felt her eyes burn.

Married or not, they were always going to be a family, she realized suddenly. It was too late for them to be anything else. She didn't know the form yet, wasn't even sure what shape she wanted that family to take. But you couldn't make so many years, too many ties, disappear by wishing they weren't there. Unfortunately, she couldn't make his affairs vanish, either.

"Okay, one from Mom next." Kate, for all her I'm-all-grown-up ennui, couldn't resist the lure of presents. With her eyes shining, wearing the kind of open grin she rarely allowed herself anymore, she reminded Ellen of the way Katie was at six, at eight, when the world was one big adventure, full of joys just waiting for her to discover.

Ellen wasn't sure when she'd begun to lose that eagerness, when life had started to knock her around enough that she no longer awoke every day anticipating great things.

Ellen wondered if it was a path she herself followed. Somewhere along the line she'd started going through life with her head down, ready to flinch when it threw something cruel at her.

"Oh, don't worry about those right now," she said as Eric scrambled to pull out her gifts for the kids. "We'll save those for later. There's something from Great-Aunt Meredith, isn't there? She always sends something worth opening."

"Yeah, like socks," Eric said without enthusiasm. "Why not this one?" He waggled Ellen's gift.

"Well . . . uh . . ." She shot a quick glance at Tom while she willed her brain to spit out an excuse. She'd never been one for quick lies; she couldn't have lived a secret life for years.

"Don't want me to see?" he asked. "You caved and gave them something that you'd forbidden before, didn't you?"

"Yeah, that's it. I was tired of you getting to play Santa all the time. My turn."

His smile faded. "Shit. You got them iPods, too, didn't you?"

"No, just what you said. Forbidden. Got them ATVs. The keys are in there," she said flippantly.

"El, I'm sorry." He actually looked like he was. Funny. She would have thought he'd be crowing about getting there first. "I didn't know."

She shrugged. "Doesn't matter," she said and, surprisingly, it didn't. "Great minds think alike, hmm?" Eric was staring at his gift, refusing to lift his eyes, his head low, as if he were already getting out of the way of fireworks to come. Katie looked worriedly from Ellen to Tom, ready to step in if they started a battle. Ellen smiled reassuringly, though she was a little taken aback that Katie didn't think she and Tom were grown-up enough to behave, even on Christmas. Had they been *that* bad? "I'll take you guys back to the store. You can trade them in for—" What was it the guy behind the counter had tried to sell her? "—clocking stations or whatever else you want."

Eric rolled his eyes at her, his worry forgotten in the face of his mother's ignorance. "Docking stations, Mom. It's a docking station."

"Oh, that's right," she said, then caught Tom's amused look. He knew very well what she was doing, the kind of communication she thought they'd lost along the way, and he flashed a grateful smile. He inclined his head toward the kitchen.

"Excuse me a minute, kids." Ellen stood. "I've got to get one load out of the dishwasher and another in before it gets much later."

"Not *now*," Eric said, edging toward a whine.

Kate looked up, her fingers tracing the circle on her iPod. "Can't it wait?"

"You know the drill, guys." Tom rose and followed her toward the kitchen. "I'll help; it'll go faster."

"But—" Eric started.

"Hush," Katie said quickly. "Or they'll have us in there, too."

"No, it'll just get crowded," Ellen said. A flicker of suspicion creased Katie's brow.

"I'm sorry," Tom said, as soon as they crossed out of earshot.

"I know I'd said I'd leave the toys to you, and I was handling sporting gear, but I was standing there in the store, and I kept thinking, *They're not going to like this* and the only thing I could think of was—"

"It's all right," Ellen interrupted, afraid he was going to start tripping over his excuses, half-touched at his apparently genuine regret and that he'd tried so hard to please the kids, and half-angry that he seemed to regret this far more than his affairs. But it was Christmas, and, just for one night, she was going to let go of the anger. "Really, it's okay. I could have called and asked, right?" She chuckled. "And really, they were the only things I could think of, either. They're getting tough to buy for, aren't they?"

"Never thought I'd be nostalgic for Legos." He ran his hand over his hair. He was wearing it shorter, she noticed. It suited him. "It's really okay?" he asked, his surprise clear.

Had he really expected her to rain down the wrath of Ellen for this? Was she often that harsh? Well, yes, *lately* she was; he deserved that. But over something as small as presents and a little miscommunication?

The kitchen was warm, filled with the smells of dinner, turkey and cinnamon and yeast rolls. The air was humid from the dishwasher, the only light was the small one over the stove. This had always been her favorite room in the house, filled with memories of Katie laughing over decorating gingerbread men with tattoos and green hair, of Eric tearing through his math homework so he could run out and play with the dog. Even a rare candlelit dinner with Tom, on those scarce nights when both kids were sleeping over at friends and they'd preferred to eat at home, in half-dressed privacy, rather than go to the trouble of going out.

When they'd remodeled, she'd spent more than half her budget on the kitchen, and it was worth every penny.

"Well." He turned toward the dishwasher. "We'd better get going."

"Leave it," she said. "I'll finish cleaning up later."

"Later?" He craned his neck around the kitchen, as if searching for something. "Okay, what'd you do with my wife?"

My wife. The words brought them both up cold; so automatic, words that had come out of his mouth a million times, words he'd deliberately not used for months. Words she wasn't at all sure he had the right to, but that had seemed so natural.

"Oops." He winced. "Old habits."

She decided to let it go. Just for one night, she was going to let it all go, and see how it went. "No big deal. It's not exactly the first time."

"No, but—" He bit off the words, words she knew he'd wanted to say, another issue to dig through, but he, too, had decided to let things drop for once. "I don't mind helping with the dishes," he said, tiptoeing through their truce.

"No, let's leave it. It's not going anywhere. I'll clean after midnight mass." She hesitated. "Would you like to go with us?"

"To church?" He couldn't have sounded more surprised than if she'd asked him to swallow a toad. "Ahh . . ."

"Forget I asked," she said and turned away. "We'd better get moving, though. We're going, and the kids'll pout through the whole service if I don't let them tear through a few more packages before we leave."

"No, that's not what I—" She felt his hand on her arm—not a demand, but a gentle and tentative overture. "It's just—I mean, dinner *and* church, in one evening? I hardly know to what to say."

"I don't know what's come over me," she said, making light of it. "I'm just awash in the Christmas spirit."

"You are," he said in admiration, and it felt good.

"Or maybe I just figured church would be good for your soul."

"That's okay. My soul can use a little looking after." He drew his hand back, and she could still feel the spot where he'd rested it, as if her skin had to learn his touch all over again. "As long as you don't make me go to confession."

"Please! If there are any more secrets, don't confess them to me. I've had enough of secrets."

"I promise," he said. "No more secrets."

9

Overtures

THE storm started halfway through the candlelit mass, so when they came out they were disoriented by it, the darkness thick and deep as the snow that mounded over the cars in the parking lot. Their breath condensed immediately, and the worshipers drew their heads low, huddling into collars and scarves.

It took them nearly three times as long as usual to drive home, creeping through silent, unplowed streets, the only visual in the halo of their headlights a crowd of swirling white. The car was silent, both kids nodding off in the back, Tom hunched over the steering wheel—it was *her* car, sensibly so, because her all-wheel-drive minivan was better in the snow than his sedan, and they always took hers when there was the four of them—and he'd climbed behind the wheel. She hadn't even thought about it when he'd grabbed the keys off their hook by the back door, hadn't even considered protesting until they were all loaded up, and then it seemed too late to fuss about it.

Her life had so many tracks in it already, worn deep through years of daily traffic over familiar ground, and she kept sliding into them without even realizing it. It seemed a huge effort to avoid them, recognizing their presence and finding a way to pave them over to start gouging new ones. She hadn't consciously chosen any of those ruts; they'd just appeared on their own, well-worn before she'd even been aware they were being carved.

"Whew," he said, when they at last pulled into the attached

garage, the wheels leaving a deep impression on the pure white drift that clogged her driveway. "That was a trip."

Ellen took a moment to admire her children, sleeping in the back like they used to when they were small and the motion of the car put them out more reliably than a rocking chair. "A few years ago on a night like this they would have been worried about whether Santa would make it through the storm."

"Yep," Tom said. "Should I be insulted that they're not nearly as worried about *me* making it home?"

"Nope." She woke the children and nudged them toward the stairs, then pulled off her coat and hung it in the front closet. "Because that means they still think you're invincible. You don't want them to think you're mortal yet, do you?"

"No. Not yet." He stood in the gloomy hallway, his coat open, his shoulders tense, his expression thoughtful, shadowed with regret. The only light came from outside, where the fresh snow reflected the streetlights, making it far lighter than the hour indicated, the softened gleam coming through the diamond panes of the door's sidelights. Was he thinking of those days when she, too, had thought he could do no wrong? Regretting that they were gone?

"Here." He pulled out a small box, wrapped in the same paper that the children's had been, and thrust it at her.

"A present?" She was almost afraid to touch it, wondering what she'd accept if she did. "For me?"

"No, for your mother. Because I always shop for her." He chuckled. "Of course for you."

"I didn't get you anything." Guilt poked at her; it had never occurred to her to buy him anything, considering the way things were between them.

"Doesn't matter."

He'd obviously wrapped it himself; the corners were crooked, the strips of tape wrapping around the sides. He never wrapped presents. She'd done them all; he'd let the store wrap the ones he bought for her.

"Open it."

She broke the tape with her thumbnail, revealing a chocolate velvet box she recognized immediately—it was from the best jewelry store in town. Wary, she cracked open the lid.

"Oh." She touched the delicate white gold chain, the twin heart charms that each held a chip of a jewel—sapphire for Eric's September birthday, emerald for Katie's May. "It's beautiful."

"Yeah?" He looked pleased and relieved, as if he'd really been unsure of her response. He had to know she'd love it.

Had she become a challenge for him, then? She couldn't tell if he really wanted to get back together, or if he'd gotten caught up in the thrill of the chase, the thrill he'd been pursuing for years, trying to catch the woman he wasn't supposed to have.

"Yes," she said, closing the lid. "I do. Thank you."

He just stood there expectantly, as if awaiting some other response from her, while the silence deepened. "Well. I'd better get going." He opened the door, then slammed it shut again, slicing off a block of cold air. "Got a shovel?"

She peeked out the window at the mound where his car should have been. "Don't you have one in the trunk? What kind of Minnesotan are you?"

"One that's used to parking ramps."

"Yeah. I've got a shovel." If anything, it was coming down harder now, straight but thick. She couldn't even see the glow of the Nelsons' windows across the street. "You should stay."

"Stay?" He said the word as if he couldn't quite grasp the meaning of it. "Stay?"

"Sure." She would have made the offer to anyone, she reasoned. She'd only worry. Not because it was Tom, but about anyone she'd allow to drive in such weather. "Why risk it? No reason to go off in this if you don't have to, and you'd only have to drive back again in the morning. At this rate it might not be any better by then."

He took a step toward her, his hands in his pockets, the start of a smile on his lips. "Where would I stay?"

"In the guest room, of course." She took a half step back, then cursed herself for it. Why was she stepping away from her husband, like a girl who was afraid her date might come in for a kiss and she wasn't sure she wanted him to? Then she cursed herself even more for the way her heart sped up just like that girl's.

"Of course," he murmured, and his smiled broadened. He looked sexy, sure of himself. Tom on the chase; he hadn't used those moves on her in so long she almost hadn't recognized them. Even more, because he hadn't been all that good at it back then. Oh, he'd tried, and she'd found his awkward hopefulness, his attempts at cockiness, endearing. Back then smooth moves had frightened her to death.

But they were different people now. She wasn't nearly as easily scared off, and he'd learned a lot. She hated where he'd learned those moves, but she couldn't deny that they worked.

He pointed above him, where the bright sprig of mistletoe Kate had wired to the bronze and amber glass chandelier hung limply. "Mistletoe."

"Doesn't count."

"Why not?"

"Kate just wanted an excuse to kiss Caleb in front of me without me freaking out," Ellen told him.

"Did you?" he asked.

"Not so she could tell." She smiled unwillingly. "But I ate a whole pint of Ben & Jerry's Caramel Sutra just after they left."

"That's my girl," he said approvingly and cocked his head. "So. Shall we?"

"Ahh . . ." It just didn't seem like a good idea, but for the life of her she couldn't articulate why. Any more than she could figure out how she felt about the "my girl." All she knew was that she was all churned up inside, worried and unsettled. But not angry, not right at this minute, and the absence of it was both a huge relief and . . . odd, like trying to walk after you'd taken your ski boots off after a long day on the slopes.

"I know you always respect tradition."

Tradition. Right. She respected tradition.

"You're thinking too much, El," he said softly. One of his regular accusations, but there was no bite to it tonight.

What the hell, she thought. It was Christmas, and if she couldn't even *kiss* him, there was no hope for them. She'd consider it an experiment.

She turned her cheek up in his direction. Maybe he'd be satisfied with a peck. And if she were disappointed by that, well, that would tell her something, too.

But he wasn't. He put his finger under her chin, tipped her head back to him, and put his mouth on hers, a quick, smooth move that was unfamiliar to her. Oh, he'd kissed her fast before, but there was thoughtlessness in it then, an automatic gesture. There was nothing the least bit thoughtless about this.

Strange, she thought distantly, beneath the low kick of pleasure. His mouth was so familiar, but the touch of it was suddenly different, the pressure new. Had she forgotten he could kiss like this, or had he never done so before, at least not with her?

He moved a step closer, his body coming up against hers—careful, gentle, but there—and she automatically sank into it, into him.

His hand went to her breast, and she shivered. He was so smooth, all easy confidence, as if he knew exactly what she'd like. Which of course he did. But this heat was stronger than it had been in years, a heavy, persistent ache of need, the kind that drove otherwise sensible people to do really stupid things.

She put her arms around him, let her tongue respond to his.

Stupid, maybe. But wonderful, yes, to let her body take over, to feel instead of think.

Was it simply because he was suddenly forbidden, sending her back to the days when sex was all tangled up with danger, the sensations sharpened by the knowledge that the consequences could be anything but simple?

Or just that she was primed? She'd spent much of the last months thinking about sex, far more than she usually did. His affairs, her potentials . . . they were always at the forefront of her mind, when they had spent so many years in the back, crowded out by more pressing demands. Even more, in all these months of *thinking* about it, she wasn't actually having it, by far the longest dry spell she'd had since she'd met him. Obviously she'd missed it far more than she'd expected.

His mouth cruised beneath her ear, his breath hot and moist and becoming labored. He still wanted her.

It would be so easy. She could take him upstairs, and to her bed, and pretend the last few months had never happened. They could go on with their lives, his stupidity forgotten, back to the smooth and easy rhythm of the future she'd always expected, the two of them working together, growing old together, all the pain and mess behind them.

"Merry Christmas," he whispered. "I've missed you."

She'd missed him, too. Oh, she'd missed him, too.

All she'd have to do was say yes. And it would all be the same.

Except it wouldn't be the same. Because never before had she worried about him. Worried, every time he worked late, every time he traveled, about what he was doing, whether he had another woman with him. It would drive her mad.

And he hadn't promised—not once, not yet—that he'd never cheat again. She hadn't asked, as if she thought it wouldn't count if she'd had to plant the idea.

"Tom?" she murmured as she let her hands trace his back, straight and smooth and wonderfully familiar. Her hands knew what to do, where to go. "Are you sure?"

"Of course I'm sure," he mumbled automatically. He pressed his hips against hers, so she could feel just how much he wanted her. "Can't you tell?"

He was sure. He was sure about sex. But he obviously wasn't thinking about anything else, and it had been silly of her to believe that it might mean more.

She pushed him away. "I'm sorry," she said. "Sorry," she repeated before turning to flee for the safety of her bedroom.

"El?"

Her hand on the banister, she turned to face him. He looked adorably rumpled, his hair disheveled, his shirt wrinkled.

She should explain. She probably owed him that much. Except they'd had a nice Christmas, and she didn't want to mess it up with a discussion that was likely to go bad fast. "The guest room," she said. "You know where it is."

"But—"

"Merry Christmas, Tom."

* * *

THE plows came through at seven, and Jill showed up on the dot of seven thirty, wheeling into the driveway in her little red Audi, sending chunks of the snow dam the plow had left flying.

She wore a big puffy jacket the color of a fake suntan. Her narrow jeans tucked into boots that seemed to have been made from a skinned yeti.

"Oh! There's my handsome boy." Ellen snatched Josh the minute they came through the door. His fuzzy blue hat sported teddy bear ears, and his snowsuit was yellow and blue and thick enough to keep him warm through an arctic winter.

"He's been up for two hours, and fussy for every minute of it. I'm running out of ways to keep him quiet, and you know what Mom's like if someone pries her out of bed before ten. I'd prefer a happy Christmas, thank you very much."

"So you figured to share the joy?"

"You don't growl as much as Mom," Jill told her. "It's safer here."

"Well, he's not fussing now, is he?" She got down on the living room rug with him, working the zipper all the way down to his toes. "You don't fuss for Auntie El, do you, sweetheart? Only Mom. Because you know I love you best." He gurgled as she peeled off the layers, exposing a bright red stretch suit with *Baby's First Christmas* embroidered across the chest in glittering gold thread. "And because you know your mom has abandoned any pretense of taste since she had you."

"I'm too tired to protest right now. As long as he's happy for a good ten minutes, you go right ahead and think it's because he loves you best." She flopped onto the couch and let her head loll over the back. The blazing red of her tight, scoop-necked sweater clashed violently with the hairy, snot-green scarf wound around her neck, she didn't have on so much as a swipe of lip gloss, and Ellen didn't even want to guess when was the last time Jill'd run a brush through her hair.

"I thought he's been sleeping through the night," she said.

"Until he decided he was going to be efficient and get four teeth at once. I don't suppose you've broken open the vodka yet, have you? Screwdriver, Bloody Mary, mimosa, whatever. Anything alcoholic and vaguely breakfasty."

"Nope." Ellen blew a raspberry on Josh's round, terry-clad belly, earning a happy gurgle, then lifted him up for a cuddle. "There might be a little wine left over from last night, though. Is the breakfasty a requirement?"

"No. Of course not." She yawned. "I was trying to sound like a responsible grown-up who wouldn't drink something before noon unless there was a fruit or vegetable serving involved."

"How healthy of you."

"Yeah. I don't know what I was thinking."

"So . . . is it for you, or for him?"

"El!" It might have been the only thing she could have said that would have brought Jill's head off the sofa back.

"It's an old wives' remedy for teething," Ellen said, grinning at Jill's shock. "Kidding, Jill, kidding."

"You'd better be." Her head sagged back again, her eyes closing as it fell. "I'll take that wine now."

"If I give you so much as a teaspoon of alcohol, you're going to be sleeping right there for the rest of the day."

"That's my plan," she mumbled. "If Josh gets hungry, just lift up my shirt and stick him on. You'd do that for me, wouldn't you?"

"Anything for a friend. But are you really going to sleep through his first Christmas?"

She sighed and dragged her eyes open. Then she bolted upright, as alert as if a soldier carrying an AK-47 had just come through the door. "What the hell is he doing here?"

Tom wandered into the living room, as comfortable in the house as if he'd never left. He was in his stocking feet, the pants of the day before were on but wrinkled, his hair was in no better shape than Jill's, and he was shrugging into his shirt, open over his bare torso.

He'd lost some weight, Ellen noted; that little belly she was fond of patting was gone. She'd like to think he was wasting away for missing her, but it was more likely he was missing her cooking. Or he was getting himself in shape for his imminent return to the dating pool.

Either way, he looked pretty darn good for an old married man.

"Merry Christmas to you, too, Jill," he said, cheerful, more than a shade snide.

"El?" Jill sprang out of her chair and rounded on Ellen, as much accusation on her face as if she were a wronged wife herself. "What's he doing here?"

"Hush," Ellen said when Josh stirred against her and let out a short wail of complaint. "Play nice, children."

"What"—Jill bit out the words, an angry whisper—"is he doing here?"

"He brought presents by last night," Ellen said, feeling like a fifteen-year-old trying to explain away damaging evidence to a suspicious mother. And, just like when she was fifteen, she hadn't earned this, either. "You saw the storm. It would have been stupid to send someone out in that."

"Yeah, I guess it would have been kind of dangerous." Jill grinned with malicious glee at the prospect. "He might have slid right into the Mississippi."

"And that would have been a tragedy," Tom said. He still hadn't bothered to button his shirt. Ellen doubted he'd forgotten. He was taunting Jill with it, and with his place here, lounging back in his favorite chair. "Would you have missed me?"

"I tell you what," Jill said through gritted teeth. "Why don't we try it and see?"

Tom opened his mouth to reply but yawned instead, as if he were suddenly bored with their verbal sparring. He slapped his hands on his knees and rose. "Love to stay and chat. But, well, places to go, people to see."

"Tom?" Ellen put Josh to her shoulder, patting his sturdy little back. "You're not staying? I've already put muffins in the oven. I thought I'd make omelets."

"Sorry, hon." His tone was light, his excuses practiced. "We're supposed to be at Ben and Sarah's by ten thirty. She'll be insulted if we eat first."

"But the kids aren't even up," she protested as a thread of panic curled in her stomach. She couldn't care less about brunch. But he really was taking her children away on Christmas Day. Somehow she'd allowed herself to forget that. Believed that, because she'd asked him to say, ensuring he didn't have to spend Christmas Eve alone, he'd extend the same courtesy to her and not whisk them off to his sister's house.

But apparently not. "Katie's going to pout all day if you wake her before nine."

"Naw. I put something extra special in her stocking. She'll get over it."

Had that been what the necklace had been? A little dazzle to distract her? He really couldn't think she'd be as easy to placate as Kate. He had to know her better than that.

He'd crossed to her and chucked her companionably beneath the chin. "She always does."

Yes, she did, because Katie had put her father up on a pedestal from day one and preferred to leave him there. Tom liked being first with her, adored her back with a blind and simple faith that didn't allow for the messy complications of real life or the missteps of teenaged girls. It was Mom, annoying and embarrassing Mom, who mucked about in the darker undersides. And Ellen couldn't even regret their relationship; she envied it, but as much as it irritated her, she wished that she'd had a father who thought she'd not only hung the moon but created it, too.

But right now his confidence annoyed her, the swagger that said that he knew that it was only a matter of time before Ellen forgave him, too. He simply couldn't conceive of anything else. He'd always gotten everything he wanted eventually.

He bounded up the stairs, all cheerful energy, while she wondered if he felt that good in truth or if it were merely show, and whether that display was intended to impress her or Jill.

"*What* is he doing here?" Jill hissed.

Ellen sighed. Her life used to be so simple. She was getting tired of surprises, exhausted from the drama. "It's Christmas, Jill. That's all."

"Hmm." Jill narrowed her eyes suspiciously, and Ellen contrived to look innocent. Then Jill's mouth dropped open.

"You slept with him, didn't you?"

10

Itsy-Bitsy Teeny-Weeny

"I did not!" Then she tried to deflect the conversation away from touchy areas, at least until she got the time to plan the right words. "Well, actually, I have. I know it's a shock to you, and my sainthood notwithstanding, but the children weren't conceived immaculately. We *have* slept together a few times over the years. Not lately, though."

Jill, however, wasn't so easily waylaid and didn't even smile. "Yes, you did. You won't look me in the eye, and you're blushing. You did something you don't want me to know about."

"You should have had a daughter. She'd never get away with lying to you."

"God forbid," Jill said. "That's exactly why. Can you imagine how terrible it would be if your mother knew *everything*?"

"I didn't sleep with him, Jill. Really, I didn't." Then she gave in, merely to short-circuit the badgering to come. Jill had her bulldog look on, and the odds of her giving up on the topic were nil. "Okay, I thought about it. Just for a minute or two."

"Oh, El." Disappointed, Jill flopped back down on the couch. "For God's sake, *why*?"

"I don't know." She turned Josh around in her lap and gave him a ball of wrapping paper. He promptly dropped it, and she bent over to pick it up. "Don't you ever get tired, Jill?"

"Me?" Her eyes widened in mock shock. "No, I'm never tired. I haven't had six straight hours of sleep since I was three weeks pregnant, but I don't get tired. I just *love* getting up every night."

"Not tired like that." Josh crumpled the paper and blew a happy raspberry. "I just wanted it to be like it was before. I don't want to be mad anymore. I don't want to fight anymore. I want my life back, Jill."

"I want a villa in Barbados and three outrageously hot pool boys at my beck and call, but I don't think that's happening, either." She smiled to soften her words. "Most unfair, isn't it? Who could possibly appreciate a life of luxury and boy toys better than me?" She reached for Josh, her eyes going soft and sweet at his wide, gummy grin. "You can't go back. You can forgive and go on, if that's what you really want. But forget?" She shook her head. "It ain't gonna happen, hon."

"Yeah, I know."

"Good. Because I've got a present for you."

"Mom?" Kate stumbled into the room, still wearing the oversize *The Killers* T-shirt she slept in, but she'd tugged on a baggy pair of bright pink track pants. Her feet were bare, the chipped polish on her toes a bright and sparkling purple. "Do we really have to go to Aunt Sarah's? Her turkey's as dry as sand, and there's not another thing on the entire table that's not a simple carb."

Tempting. Oh, it would be so easy to say no. They could stay here all day, eat and watch old holiday movies that would have the kids rolling their eyes but they'd watch anyway because it was Christmas and they were supposed to. Eric would make Josh giggle—he was really good at that—and Katie might even decide to pretend that she enjoyed spending time with her family. It was a lot to ask, but it *was* Christmas Day. "Not my call, hon."

"So if Dad lets me off, then I don't have to go?"

"Sure."

"Tight." She grinned and headed for the stairs, no doubt on her way to wheedle freedom from her father, who was probably still trying to drag Eric out of bed.

"While you're up there," Ellen put in, "make sure your dad knows I want to talk to him before you guys head out."

Her back to them, Kate paused with her hand on the banister, one foot on the bottom step. Her hair had tangled in a long twist down her back, which she'd looped over into a loose knot, and her pants sagged at the butt like she was a two-year-old with a full diaper. "Talk to him?"

"Well, sure. To thank him for being *so* understanding of your feelings as to let you stay home."

Kate spun and jammed her arms across her chest, glaring, caught before she could even try her wiles.

"What was your story gonna be?" Ellen asked conversationally. "That you had a stomachache?"

"Oh, that's a good one. Especially if you blame it on your period," Jill suggested. "Freaks guys out enough that they end the conversation right there."

"*Mom!*" Kate tried to look offended, then gave up. "I was going to say how *lonely* you'd be without me. And how *much* I wanted to see Aunt Sarah and Uncle Ben, and I would be devastated to miss it, but I couldn't bear to leave you alone. Given your fragile emotional state and all."

"That's good, too." Jill put her hands over her son's ears, as if he were old enough to understand. "If you mentioned that she'd be alone with a full bottle of tequila and *me*, it would have worked for sure. Since I'm such a horrible influence on her, who knows what ideas she'd get."

"You think?" Kate beamed at Jill's praise, until she remembered she was supposed to be angry and scowled. "How'd you know that I wasn't just going to ask him?" she asked Ellen.

"I've known *her*"—she nodded in Jill's direction—"for darn near twenty years."

"You'll catch up someday." Jill gave a royal wave. "After all, you can learn from the master."

"I'm going dressed like this," Kate warned.

"See, you're learning already." Jill leaned over and dropped three quick kisses on Josh's fuzzy head. "*Never* give up when there's something left to try."

"Go right ahead and wear whatever you want." Ellen settled back in her chair.

Katie stomped up the stairs.

"One thing, though," Jill called after her. "Your mother doesn't understand these things. But take it from someone else who's, ah, mammarily blessed. You're going to want to put on a bra. If you let gravity start doing its thing when you're fifteen, it's going to be a sorry picture by the time you're forty."

* * *

TOM hustled them out not ten minutes later—a world record in getting the kids out of the house, considering they had to stop and dump out their stockings first. Eric was still half-asleep, though he managed to give her a quick hug on the way—she didn't know what she was going to do if he ever got the stage where it was uncool to hug his mother. Katie followed, scowling but moving. She'd changed her clothes, Ellen noted, though she would have preferred the giant T-shirt and baggy sweats to the skimpy sweater and low riders. There was a bra, though— she shot a glance at Jill, who grinned and winked. Would that parenting would always seem so easy to her, Ellen thought. She'd no idea of the dangers ahead.

"There're shovels in the garage," she told Tom. "Happy digging."

He grimaced and headed out.

As soon as the door shut behind them, Ellen felt tears threaten. Stupid. Did she think she was always going to get to spend every minute of every holiday with them? She knew that privilege would end sooner or later. She grabbed Josh from Jill, cuddled him up, and smiled into his round face until her heart eased.

"It's going to be an awful long wait for grandchildren," she murmured.

"*Grandchildren?* Are you nuts?" Jill felt Ellen's forehead. "You're heading into your prime. How are you going to do the wild thing if you're a grandmother?"

"I don't care." What did it matter? It was useless to pretend she was young and fresh and the world held endless possibilities for her. But grandchildren . . . they had to be fate's recompense for all that the years had taken.

"Well, *theoretically* . . . I thought you were terrified Kate was going to have sex with that boy. I suppose you could manage to leave her alone one weekend and bingo! Grandchildren."

"Shut your mouth!" Josh pulled the two fingers he was chewing on out of his mouth, trailing a long strand of drool. "Okay, I take it back. I don't want to be a grandmother for a long, long time. Maybe never, since that would mean one of my children has to have sex one day, and I'm pretending that that's never going to happen."

"Just thought you needed a dose of reality."

"Forget reality." If only she could. But Josh and Jill were real, too, and that wasn't all bad. "Thanks for having him, Jill. Really."

"Anything for you, hon." She pawed through the battered, black leather tote that served as her diaper bag. "Speaking of which. Here."

Ellen traded Josh for a small, flat box, neatly wrapped in shocking pink.

"Oh, you shouldn't have," Ellen said, then snatched it with the greed of a four-year-old. "Very Christmasy," she said, flicking the loopy violet ribbon.

"Looks Christmasy to me."

"I'm getting worried about opening this." Jill looked far too pleased with herself, mischief glinting in her eyes, as if she'd just gotten a new man in her sights. But she knew that wasn't the case; Jill had been whining about it too much for her to have found herself a playmate. "There's not something in here the kids shouldn't see, is there?"

"Your kids are gone."

"Josh isn't." He was snuggling down comfortably in his mother's lap, perfectly content, exactly where he wanted to be without a single doubt that his every wish would be fulfilled. When did you start to doubt that? Ellen wondered. The first time you take a step and fall flat on your butt? "You don't want to scar him for life, do you? If there's a giant, plastic piece of male anatomy in there, he might never feel the same about his own."

"Don't be silly." Jill waved away her concerns. "That package's way too small to hold anything worthwhile in that department."

"Okay, you're scaring me." But she dug in anyway, revealing a silver box. She wriggled off the top. "Umm . . ." She held the little scrap of hot orange fabric up by its strings. "A bikini? You bought me a bikini?" Okay, she knew Jill had a tendency to buy her things that nudged her in the direction she thought Ellen should go, but still . . . Ellen hadn't worn a bikini since 1982, she'd been uncomfortable even then, and sworn off completely until she magically woke up with Heidi Klum's body.

"That's only part of the present. Keep looking."

"Okay." Suspicious now, she peeled back tissue paper the color of limes. Underneath lay a square envelope in bright turquoise.

"Open it," Jill urged.

"Does it go with the bikini?"

"Yup."

"Great. Just great." She worked the flap free. "If it's a gift certificate for a bikini wax, you can just forget it. Nothing's getting ripped off down there, *ever*."

"We'll talk about that later," Jill said in a voice that indicated she'd far from given up on that topic. "Come on, come on!"

The more excited Jill got, the more worried Ellen got. There was just no way this was going to be good.

She pulled out a glossy brochure that pictured a dazzling beach, a string of palm trees, a glittering ocean in a blue that couldn't possibly be real. A man rose from the waves, the water lapping so low that if it moved down another fraction, it would show whether he was as well-favored below the waves as above. And he was plenty blessed above, bronzed and buff and glistening.

"Sizzle Island?"

"It's a trip." Jill scooted over and opened the brochure to point out a photo of a bunch of gorgeous, barely dressed people shaking it on a dance floor. "The third week in January. The whole island is one giant resort, all-inclusive, singles only. It's perfect."

"Perfect." The only thing perfect about it was the bodies on the models. Everything about it reminded Ellen of what she wasn't. She didn't do beaches, she didn't do skimpy clothes, she didn't do wild parties with other singles.

"It's too much," Ellen said. "You can't spend that much on a present for me."

"Pshaw." She waved her hand, dismissing the argument. "Don't I get to be generous once in a while?"

"No." For all her flamboyance, Jill was downright careful with her money.

"Okay, fine. I didn't pay for it. They're a client, and they were thrilled with our campaign ideas and gave several of us trips for a reward. I think they figured it would inspire us even further."

"Well, then! I *can't* take the trip. It's yours. Your client would be downright insulted."

"Oh, I cleared it with them, of course. They understood perfectly."

Ellen groaned. "Do I want to know what story you gave them?"

"Nope," Jill said cheerily.

Ellen felt doom in the guise of rum-soaked decadence and sex-crazed vacationers hovering. But she no longer surrendered quite so easily, not even to Jill. "So lots of your coworkers are going to be there. I don't think I could be properly . . . uninhibited if I knew your spies were hovering around, waiting to report."

"I understand perfectly." Ellen would have sighed in relief, but Jill looked far too pleased with herself. "Except we're all scheduled for different weeks. I believe they thought that we couldn't experience the sizzle of Sizzle to its fullest if there was a chance of running into our boss on the nude beach."

"So what happens on Sizzle, stays on Sizzle?"

"Yeah," she said regretfully. "We couldn't use that one, though. Las Vegas got it first."

"There's a nude beach?"

Jill shrugged with complete unconcern. "I got the impression that, sooner or later, *all* the beaches are nude beaches."

"You know, this is just sounding more and more like my kind of place all the time."

"I'm so glad you're seeing the possibilities."

Oh, she saw the possibilities all right. In fact, she saw the probabilities: the very high probability that, if she went to that horrid island, she'd hide in her room the entire time. Or, if she ventured out, in her khakis and her polo shirt, that she'd be ignored by every man in the place in favor of women wrapped up in strings and scarves and little else. And maybe, just maybe, if she worked up her courage to venture out on that beach in a swimsuit, that she'd flee in mortification when people recoiled at the sight of her Minnesota-pale cellulite, but not before parts of her that hadn't seen the sun in twenty years turned the color of Josh's Christmas stretchie.

"It's your trip." Ellen carefully folded the bikini back into the box. "I do appreciate the thought, I really do. But I . . . I wouldn't make good use of it. You've earned a break, and you'd enjoy it so much more than I would."

"No I wouldn't."

"Oh, come on," Ellen wheedled. "You could have *sex*."

"I can't go." Jill looked down at her son. He'd nodded off, and his mouth worked in his sleep, as if he were dreaming of lunch, and his skin looked like cream. "I thought I could, El. But I can't leave him, not yet."

Ellen almost argued the point. But she saw the look on Jill's face as she stared at Josh. Jill had waited a long time to feel that, and she couldn't blame her for not wanting to leave him, even for a second. That simple, pure adoration would get complicated soon enough.

"Please?" Jill looked up, still smiling. "The client really would be unhappy if *nobody* used it. I figure you'd appreciate it more than my mother."

"I don't know," Ellen mused. "I'm pretty sure I've seen Ruth eyeing the boys who are always playing ball shirtless at the park."

"Don't even say that!" Jill pulled a face. "I suppose I could offer it to Katie. They'd never guess she was underage."

"If I have a heart attack and die, Tom'll get everything."

"All right, no Katie," Jill said. "Please, El? You might have fun."

Yeah, she might have fun. If she stayed in her room the whole time with a pile of books.

Come to think of it, that might work. No one said she had to dive right into the singles scene, or even the ocean. She could eat pineapple, open her window to the ocean breezes, and read to her heart's content. Go to sleep early, float around in the ocean in the morning before anyone else was up to bother her. And she would *not* be bullied into having an affair, drinking too many piña coladas, or doing anything else that everybody else thought was a good ol' time but made her stomach hurt just thinking about it.

"Okay, I'll go. *If* I can get the kids covered."

Jill brightened. "The kids'll get covered. Hell, *I'll* move in if I have to."

"Great." As much as she loved Jill, a year or two ago she might have had a few twinges at the idea of Jill spending too much time alone with the kids—not that Jill would ever offer. Now, however, it seemed perfectly natural.

"Though I think it would be better if *he* has to take care of them for a whole week." Evil anticipation lit up her smile. "Bet that's not quite as much fun as just stuffing them with pizza every other weekend."

"I bet not." With any luck, Katie'd have a date or two during that time, and he could do the worrying, the lying wide awake in bed, listening for the crunch of tires in the driveway.

She lifted the bikini and waved it in the air, marveling that any designer thought that a grown woman would be willing to stretch that over her body. "But I'm not wearing this."

"We'll see," Jill said lightly. "I've got almost a month to work on you."

"You're really a pain in the ass, you know that?"

"You know that's what you love about me."

11

Auld Lang Syne

"So? What do you think?"

Joe descended the staircase, his face as uncertain as a girl's coming down for her first prom.

"It's good that you're not too cool to show you're nervous," Ellen told him.

He put on his cop face, a menacing scowl that would have a suspect dropping to the ground long before he'd drawn his gun, but he couldn't hold it. "Only for you, hon. Only you get to see the real me." He stopped at the third step, tugging uncertainly at the bottom of his jacket. "But if you tell anyone, you know I'll have to shoot you."

"Duly noted."

He'd gone upstairs to change after she'd fed him dinner—she did that at least once a week, for she'd discovered early on that every cliché about a cop's poor diet held true in his regard, and his mother had given up cooking when the last of the Marcioni boys moved out. He protested the first time she'd invited him over, saying he didn't want to take advantage of her kind nature, but she'd told him that she simply didn't have enough people to feed anymore, anyway, which was the truth. And besides, she appreciated the shape he was in too much to watch him blimp out on doughnuts and drive-through burritos.

This was the first time she'd seen him in full uniform, all pressed and shiny. And proud; anyone could see that the clothes, and the job, meant something to him.

She whistled, low and admiring. "What is it about a man in uniform?"

He tucked his hat under his arm and ran his free hand self-consciously over the messy waves of his hair. It was damp, threaded with comb lines, and not even close to being under control. She figured he'd stop fussing if he knew just how attractive that disorder was, but that hint of insecurity in a man who otherwise was anything but held its own appeal. "So I look okay?"

"You look fabulous." She reached up and smoothed down a collar that had flipped up. "Good enough that it's a damn shame that you wear that thing only for funerals and dress balls."

She stepped back to give him an admiring once-over. The department held one big formal a year, between Christmas and New Year's, which accounted for the uniform tonight. "Good enough that females of the world lost out when you went plain-clothes. Sure you don't want to get busted back down to uniform? We'd all be grateful."

He tugged at his collar where a flush of red was creeping up. Blushing. Who'da thunkit? Joe Marcioni, who could handle any bad guy in Minneapolis, couldn't handle a bit of flattery.

"Good enough that sometimes I'm really sad that you're so much in love with your ex-wife."

Joe relaxed and grinned down at her. "That's half of what you like about me."

"True," Ellen admitted. She'd always been a sucker for a man who knew how to love well and right.

Joe shifted, moving his cap from hand to hand as if he couldn't quite settle. "You think it's going to go all right?"

Joe and his ex-wife—Cindy was her name, Ellen had learned, a nurse who he'd met when he'd brought a shooting victim, also a suspect—the other guy hadn't made it—into the emergency room at HCMC—had been dating, irregularly and cautiously, since two weeks after Ellen had found him in the bar.

But this would be the first night that Joe and Cindy were to appear in public together, a statement that they were trying to work things out. And considering that Joe's job was a good part of the reason that they'd split up in the first place, going to a department event was a huge step.

It had to go well for him. It just had to. If it didn't, well, Cindy was simply not as smart a woman as Joe made her out to be. Because any woman who would pass up Joe Marcioni had to be a world-class fool.

"It's going to go great." Ellen knew she was too invested in Joe's love life, but she couldn't seem to help it. The romantic in her—and it was there, underneath her practical outside, always had been—really, really needed to know that some marriages, even ones that had rocky spots here and there, could work out.

"I didn't mean just tonight," Joe said gravely.

"I know." And then, because he was looking too serious, she said, "Just wear the uniform more often. How can she resist?"

"I can't wear it on duty, and we don't have—"

"Joe," Ellen said. "I wasn't suggesting you wear it out of the *house*."

"Happy New Year," Ellen told herself as she plopped down on her couch alone.

Every year, Ellen tried to get out of the New Year's parties. They just weren't her style. Too much booze, too many random kisses, too much calculated *fun*, which really wasn't all that much fun. She wasn't crazy about going out when it was utterly freezing, and you always ended up wearing an outfit that was not only a shade tacky and not nearly compatible with said frigidness but was somehow the only thing that was considered appropriately festive New Year attire. Not to mention that she really didn't like the idea of driving around when there were so many idiots, who'd done a little too much celebrating, out there on the road with you.

"*Let's stay home*," she always suggested. Curl up in front of a fire, wearing comfy clothes—her favorite old jeans and a nice roomy fleece, maybe—with a bottle of champagne and something mindless on the television. The only people she'd kiss at midnight were her family. *Start the year as you want it to go on . . .* that was how she wanted it to go on. At home, everybody safe and sound and together. But she'd always been overruled.

Be careful what you wish for . . .

Her robe was even better than the jeans, she decided, an old velour one that covered her from her chin to her thick shearling slippers. She had a stack of DVDs on the table in front of her, all her favorites, everything from *The Pirates of the Caribbean* to *Major League*, from *To Catch a Thief* to *Simply Ballroom*. Snacks: homemade caramelized onion dip, turtle brownies, a massive bowl of Doritos. Had to have Doritos. The fridge was full of Diet Coke. Her recipe for a perfect New Year's.

Except she was alone. Alone, damn it, and none too happy about it.

Eric was sleeping over at his friend Adam's. He'd gone off with a case of Mountain Dew; every piece of electronic equipment he owned, including his computer; and a boxful of cords, mumbling something about hooking up a network for a LAN party.

Kate's dance line was having a sleepover at their coach's house—a young woman who'd been part of the team herself only five years ago—so Katie would be there for the night. Ellen had checked it out thoroughly. Though Ms. Wilson was young, her disciplinary style was a lot closer to a drill sergeant than a fellow dancer's. Ellen figured it was because she remembered only too well what it was like to be a fifteen-year-old girl and so was determined to head trouble off before it began. Ellen was almost scared of her herself and figured Caleb would have more trouble getting through Ms. Wilson tonight than he would through either Ellen or Tom, so Katie was safe for the duration.

It wasn't like Ellen didn't have friends. Okay, not quite as many as she thought. She had acquaintances, dozens, her children's friends' mothers and the wives of some of Tom's colleagues and the other women on the school fund-raising committee. But while they were certainly friendly, and she enjoyed seeing them socially now and then, they weren't *friends*, not the kind you counted on to get you through your first miserable, single New Year's Eve.

She sifted through the stack of movies, but none of them appealed, not when there was no one to laugh at them with her. And wasn't she turning into a pitiful creature, feeling all sorry for herself?

She counted Joe as a friend now. Had she ever had a male friend? Just a friend, with maybe a hint of flirtation here and there, just for some spice, but no real undercurrents of romance? Not that she could recall. It wasn't so common back when she was growing up as it appeared now. Katie certainly had male friends that were nothing more, and it seemed a natural thing. It was good, in Ellen's opinion, to know the opposite sex in a more natural way, without all the trappings and facades of courtship.

Ellen was certainly enjoying it now, but Joe was on duty tonight—one of the trials of police work; they needed more cops working on holidays, not fewer. And he was headed for Cindy's the instant he got off duty, bless him. Ellen wondered how long he was going to be able to wait before he started trying to talk his ex-wife into dropping the *ex* part. Not long, if Ellen read him right.

And there was Jill. Always Jill. Except Josh had been running a slight fever since yesterday afternoon, and so Jill was staying in. Ellen offered to go to their condo, but Jill had said they were both cranky, running on too little sleep. "Have fun," Jill had told her. "We won't be fun. Trust me. It's New Year's!"

Jill was a mother now, and her first priority was Josh. Had to be. Ellen understood that, admired that, considered it a more than even trade for the opportunity to play auntie. But still . . .

"Fun," Ellen murmured. "Oh yeah, we're having fun now." She dragged a chip through onion dip and popped it in her mouth. But that wasn't what she wanted, either.

She should have been content. She wasn't the sort of person who always needed others around. The opposite, in fact; when she was forced to interact with too many people, too often, she craved solitude. She found parties, no matter how enjoyable, draining.

But that was when there were lots of people regularly in her life. Soon enough, this would be the usual state of affairs. And not just the kids grown up and gone; that would mean that all their friends, the crowds of noisy, hungry young ones that she was used to dashing in and out of her house, plopping on her sofas, and emptying out her fridge would move on as well.

And Tom. Yeah, Tom. Who'd been knit into her life for so long that she couldn't remember what it was like without him. Her life was shaped by his, their social life propelled by the friends they had as a couple, by the demands of his job. Though he traveled a lot, and worked even more, in many ways his presence had always been there even if he was physically absent—in the anticipation of his return, in the wait for the touch-base phone call at the end of the night, in the planning and rearranging of her schedule to accommodate his.

Alone. That's what she would be if she went through with the divorce. She would have thought she'd be okay with alone. Maybe even craved it a little. But alone as a choice, a once-in-a-while stage in the midst of a busy and full life, was one thing.

Lonely was quite another.

Begin the year as you want it to continue.

This wasn't how she wanted to spend her year, alone in front of the TV plowing through a bag of Doritos.

"No," she said. "Just no."

She moved before she could talk herself out of it. She'd been thinking for four months—for her whole life, if it came right down to it—and it hadn't done her a whole lot of good.

Sometimes you just had to take a leap. Hadn't that been what she'd told Joe? But she'd never been able to do it herself.

But she knew what she wanted. She wasn't ever going to get it until she just went ahead and took a leap.

She ran up the stairs and threw on the first clothes she saw.

She grabbed her keys, her navy blue parka, and headed for the garage.

Time to leap.

* * *

LEAP, she told herself. *Just leap.*

The thirty-minute drive through Minneapolis had given her just enough time for her courage to waver. Cars jammed streets slicked with a dusting of snow, the sky was dark, and nobody was driving well. Which meant by the time she found the apartment building her hands were frozen in a clench around the steering wheel and her armpits were damp.

Now she stood in front of the door to Apartment 1812, one white door in a long, bland hallway of identical doors, and tried to summon her determination. She must have had it. She'd gotten this far, hadn't she? But until this moment it hadn't been too late. There'd still been time to turn around. Once she knocked, she'd be committed. Fixed in a course of action that she still wasn't at all certain was the right one. But doing nothing wasn't working, either.

She wanted the life she wanted, she reminded herself. Time to start getting it.

So she knocked. *Thump thump*, too quiet, the sound muffled by her gloves. It was quiet within, no music, no footsteps.

He probably wasn't even home. It was New Year's, wasn't it? What kind of pitiful person spent New Year's Eve at home, unless they were throwing a party? If there was a party going on inside, it was the quietest one ever.

That could be a sign, she decided. She hadn't ever been one for signs, though her mother swore by them. She suddenly remembered how Tom had lost his wedding band two days before the ceremony, when Ellen had assumed it was tucked safely away in his sock drawer. They'd had to rush to a jewelry store and take the only thing in his size, a plain gold band that looked too thin on Tom's large hands. Her mother had nearly had apoplexy.

Maybe she should have started listening to the signs a long

time ago. If he were here, that meant she was supposed to be with him. And if he were gone . . . well, she'd go home, none the worse for the wear.

She pulled off her glove, jabbed at the doorbell, and heard footsteps inside.

"Ellen?" Well, he wasn't going out. Instead, he wore only a green velour robe, tightening the loose belt after he opened the door. "What are you doing here?"

She felt the smile on her face fix in place. "I just—" Behind him there was an open bottle of champagne on the ugly oak coffee table next to two half-empty flutes. A fluffy white fur coat that looked like someone had skinned the Easter Bunny was thrown over the pea green chair. There was music after all, from the bedroom, something low and sultry.

"Are the kids okay?"

"Ah—yeah, sure. They're fine."

"Then why are you here?"

"I—" Hell. What was she supposed to say now? He was the one adept with lies and alibis, spinning them on the spur of the moment.

Platform sandals with clear acrylic heels had been abandoned on the way to the bedroom, and she couldn't stop looking at them.

They hadn't discussed whether he was allowed to see other women during their separation. She'd just assumed that, while they were in counseling, while they were actively trying to salvage their marriage, he wouldn't be dating.

She'd *assumed*. That's what had gotten her into this mess in the first place, hadn't it? She'd assumed he would respect his marriage vows, assumed she meant the same to him as he did to her. What a slow learner she was.

"I just needed to talk to you," she said.

Tom glanced over his shoulder, then raised one eyebrow at her. "Do you want to come in?"

Tom had moved into the place the day she'd kicked him out, a tall building of furnished apartments primarily rented by the month to businessmen in town on a project. It was comfortable enough, stocked from towels to silverware, though everything in it, from the white walls to the beige furniture to the forgettable landscapes on the walls, was so determinedly inoffensive as to be without a shred of personality. But it was convenient, close to the office, Tom had said, though it was anything but convenient for the children. Not near their schools, and Katie hated that she had to share the second bedroom with her brother.

"I—no," she said quickly. "I'm on my way to a party."

"A party?" He took in Ellen's bulky ski jacket, open in front, and the baggy purple fleece pullover beneath.

"It's very casual. *Very.* Invitation said to wear the most comfortable thing you own," Ellen reeled off, all the while thinking: *Stupid, stupid, stupid.*

"Well, I guess you're going to be the best-dressed person there, aren't you?"

"That's the plan," she said, finally finding her balance. Signs. She'd been looking for a sign. *This was a sign, all right.* "This was on my way, and I thought I'd take the chance that you hadn't left yet. I really wanted this settled, you see. Anyway, I'm going on vacation, and I need to give you the dates, so you can make arrangements. You're going to have to be in charge of the kids."

"But—" He frowned, puzzled. "I don't understand."

"I'm leaving," she said. "The Bahamas. For a week. You need to take over."

"I can't," he said automatically. He hadn't checked his calendar, Ellen thought sourly. Hadn't asked her when she was leaving. Just, "I can't."

"Sure you can," she said. "It's not like they're infants, Tom. They can manage most everything themselves. Though getting to school might be a problem if you move them in here," she mused, glancing around the apartment. "You'd have to drive them every morning, pick them up every afternoon. Maybe it's best if you just came and stayed with them, so they can take the school bus. This place really isn't set up for kids, Tom."

"But—" He was still frowning, too confused to be angry. "I have work, I have obligations. I can't just—"

"Come now, Tom. How many times have you dumped a last-minute trip into my lap, no matter what other things I had planned, and left it to me to rearrange my schedule? Heck, I had to reschedule my wisdom teeth removal when you suddenly got called to Charlotte."

"That was *work*."

Work. As if that always made it acceptable. As if work excused everything.

"Well, this isn't work, but I'm going anyway. I leave three weeks from tomorrow, and you're just going to have to manage." She zipped her coat up to her chin and yanked her gloves on.

"You owe me, Tom."

12

Complications

KATE scanned the lunchroom, looking for Caleb. She'd skipped the line today, as usual. She was hungry, but she was feeling bloated. And anyway, if she took the time to wait in line, she wasn't going to have long to spend with him. Their lunch hours only overlapped by fifteen minutes.

There were at least a hundred more kids there than the place could comfortably hold, and all of them were shrieking, laughing, shouting, letting off steam from being cooped up in class all morning. The basketball cheerleaders were selling popcorn balls on a table in the far corner, the drama club was in full costume at another, trying to drum up interest in their weekend production of *Guys and Dolls*. Three boys were dancing in the center of a group of appreciative girls, their joints popping like they were pulled by strings, and a kid was plunking away on a guitar near the door.

There were days when she loved it, all the noise, all the activity, friends everywhere she looked.

And there were days, like today, when she just wanted to crawl into a locker to get a little peace and quiet.

Caleb was always near the left wall, the first table he found free when he came in. Hopefully he'd saved half a sandwich for her.

There he was. She started to smile. He had on her favorite black T-shirt today, the one he'd swiped from his Dad's old concert shirt collection, and the gray in the striped shirt he wore over it made his eyes look almost silver.

She headed over that way, her smile fading when she saw who'd claimed the spot right next to him, crowding him against the wall.

"Shit!" She stopped walking and turned to her friend, Jackie, who had Spanish with her last hour and had a wild, futile crush on Caleb's friend Adam.

"Quick. You got any gloss?"

"What?"

"Look at me!" Why did it have to be today when she'd woken up late, tired, and crampy. She'd felt too lousy to do anything but pull on a pair of old yoga pants and a big, bulky school sweatshirt. "Heather's practically sprawled all over him, and I look like crap."

She pulled the elastic from her hair, bent over, and rubbed at her scalp, trying to force a little volume into it. Then she flipped it back and greased her lips with the tube of watermelon-flavored gel Jackie thrust at her, as fast as she could, because she knew every second she took now was one more second that Heather could whisper Lord only knew what into Caleb's ear.

"What do you think?" she asked.

"Well." Jackie eyed her critically. Which was the best thing about her; she listened, and she could be counted on to tell the truth, even if it wasn't what you wanted to hear. "What do you have on under that shirt?"

"Nothing."

"Hmm." Jackie winced. "Well, that'll get a reaction, all right."

"Never mind." She couldn't waste any more time. She took a deep breath, threw back her shoulders, and made herself slow down as she made her way across the lunchroom so it didn't look like she was worried.

She swung into Caleb's lap and planted a good one on him, with a lot of tongue and some strategic wiggling. He got into it quick, kissing her back, his hand finding a spot on her rear and squeezing.

She pulled back and smiled at him. "Sorry," she said, and wiped the smear of shiny pink gloss off his lips with her fingers.

"S'okay," he said, grinning. "You taste good."

Feeling better, Katie turned to face the group. Bottles of Gatorade and cans of Mountain Dew littered the table with crumpled plastic wrap and the peel of an orange. She nodded at Caleb's friends, told Adam how hot he looked that day—she liked Adam, he was always nice to her, even if he wasn't nearly as sexy as Caleb, and he didn't have the sense to appreciate Jackie—making sure that Heather was the last one she turned turned to.

"Oh, hey, Heather. Didn't see you there."

"Uh-huh." She'd expected Heather's smirk. What she didn't get, though, was why Heather looked kind of amused instead of pissed. Like she knew something Katie didn't.

Kate shrugged and wrapped her arm around Caleb's neck. He smelled like smoke—damn, he told her he'd stop, but obviously he'd snuck out before lunch again. "You save me anything, baby?"

"Oh. Sorry." He shrugged. "I was hungry."

"That's okay."

"You hardly ever eat anything, anyway."

"I said it's okay." It was true; she did almost always skip lunch. But it would have been nice, wouldn't it, if he'd saved some, just in case?

"Heather's got a brownie left," he suggested.

"Well—" she glanced at Heather, who was just biting into the bar "—I guess not."

Heather shrugged in apology. As if she hadn't started eating it the minute Caleb suggested she share. Not that she would've eaten so much sugar, anyway. Heather'd better stuff herself with brownies; maybe then she could have a figure that looked more like a girl's than Eric's.

Heather swallowed and washed it down with a swig of Cherry Coke. "You're almost choking him, Markham. Worried he's going somewhere?"

"Oh, he's not going anywhere, are you, babe?" She tugged Caleb's head closer, until it was resting on her boobs, reminding both him and Heather that she had some.

Caleb's grin broadened. Well, why wouldn't it? Any guy'd like to have girls fighting over him, whether he was interested or not. And having Kate reminded that there were other girls out there interested only made her more determined to make him happy. She couldn't be mad at him for that.

Heather—now, that was something else entirely.

"I suppose, though," Heather said thoughtfully, "that you really can't help it. Given that you know all about men who, ah, wander a bit."

Kate felt her teeth grind together at the back. "What's that supposed to mean?"

Heather shrugged, too casually. "You should ask your mother."

Kate went stiff, hanging on to Caleb to keep from launching herself at Heather.

A year ago Angie Morton, Heather's partner in bitchdom, had bopped over to Kate's table with a big smile on her face and cheerfully "mentioned" how she'd seen Katie's dad the night before at Manny's, where her folks had taken her for her birthday, and, by the way, who was the pretty blond her dad was so friendly with?

It hadn't been Dad, though. Kate knew it hadn't been, no matter how much Angie swore she was telling the truth, because Dad was in New York. He'd called her from the airport.

"Now, ladies." Caleb's hand had worked its way beneath her sweatshirt, rough and bare against her lower back, and Kate shivered. She loved how slow his hands moved, the same way he walked, the same way he talked. "Kate knows she doesn't have to worry about me, don't you, baby girl?"

Didn't she? It was good to hear him say it, out loud, right in front of Heather. But somehow she always seemed to worry all the time, anyway.

Everybody around the table suddenly went quiet, looking over Kate's head.

Uh-oh. She twisted around to find Miss Holy-Water-stone, who should have been a nun instead of a vice principal, for all that she walked around with her hair pinned back and her high white collars and ugly navy suits, looking down on all of them like she knew exactly what kind of sinners they all were, frowning down her beak nose at them.

"Oh. Hi, Miss Waterstone," Kate ventured.

"Caleb. Kate." She nodded, her lips going so thin it didn't look as if she had any. "I believe we've had discussions about inappropriate displays of affection before."

"I guess that depends upon your definition of inappropriate," Caleb said, and Kate snickered. Miss Waterstone probably only made such a fuss because *she'd* never had a boyfriend who couldn't keep his hands off her. Didn't she have better things to do, anyway?

Miss Waterstone's small oval glasses slid down on her nose until Kate wondered if they were going to slide right off. "My office," she said sharply. "Now."

Kate sighed and climbed to her feet. Why was it always her who got caught?

Miss Waterstone was calling her mother for sure.

* * *

THE doorbell rang just as Ellen stuck her toothbrush in her mouth. It had been a long day, capped off by Kate, who had not appreciated being grounded for the next week, slamming her door so hard Ellen grabbed for the framed family pictures on the wall in the hallway, afraid they were going to come crashing down.

She had nothing to wear to Sizzle, Tom was still complaining about the kids moving in for a week—when he really should be in Saint Louis that week, he kept reminding her—and yet refusing to consider that he could move in there, despite the fact that he lobbied regularly to move back in permanently. And despite the fact that he seemed both amused and satisfied that she was heading south; he apparently thought it gave him a free pass on New Year's Eve, if she was going off to have a fling herself. She was too tired of the topic to fight with him about it.

So Ellen was more than ready to curl up in bed. She considered ignoring it, but the bell rang again, and it was no doubt

Caleb, coming to try to talk her into letting him see Kate, and she'd just as soon get rid of him right now.

She pulled on her old red velour robe, shuffled slowly down the stairs—let the brat wait—before sighing and pulling open the door.

"You should check who it is before you open the door," Joe told her, "even if it is Edina."

His black leather jacket was open, over a faded *Murphy's Pub* T-shirt and a pair of Levi's that should have been retired, for all they fit him really, really well. He leaned against the doorjamb, his cheeks red from the cold, and his smile was weary.

"Then I wouldn't have the fun of opening my door and finding a handsome man on the other side, would I?" She stepped back, pulling the door wider, feeling the air seep through her thin socks. "Would you get in here? It's cold out there."

"Is it?" He looked around as if noticing the temperature for the first time. "Yeah, guess so."

She shook her head. What was it about men, that they were all too macho—too stupid—to bundle up? No gloves, no hat . . . lucky he'd survived walking a beat with his toes and fingers intact.

He let out a long, heavy breath as he stepped inside, as if he were relaxing for the first time that day.

"Rough day at work?" she asked him.

"No. No, actually," he said in some surprise. "It was a good day. We caught the guy who shot up the coffeehouse on the South Side."

"That's great!" The gunman had taken out a teenager and a grandmother in the process, and the entire city had been screaming for an arrest for the last week. But closing the case certainly hadn't given Joe a rush; red rimmed his eyes, and his shoulders sagged.

"I shouldn't have come," he said, looking at her robe, as if he'd just realized she'd been getting ready for bed. "It's late; I'm sorry."

"Don't be stupid," she said and headed down the hallway, expecting him to follow. He knew better; after she'd cried on Jill's shoulder New Year's Eve, she'd used his New Year's morning, dragging him out of bed to take her out for pancakes a good three hours earlier than she expected he'd have gotten up otherwise. She'd figured they were past worrying about things like imposing. "I'll make coffee."

"Cocoa?" he asked hopefully.

"Can't be too bad," she said. "At least your sweet tooth's intact." The only thing that numbed it, she'd learned, was a particularly gruesome murder scene, and then only temporarily.

"No," he said, but he wasn't the least bit convincing.

She stationed him on the family room couch with a remote in his hand while she made hot chocolate with real whipped cream. She debated with herself a moment before plopping a healthy scoop in her cup, too, just to be companionable, hushing the nasty little voice in her head that reminded her she was going to a *beach* resort soon.

"Here you go." He'd found a basketball game, on late because the Spurs were playing in L.A. She sat down beside him and curled up, her head against his sturdy shoulder. "So what's up?"

He slung his arm around her and pulled her close. "Maybe I just wanted to see you."

"Uh-huh." She wished she could believe that was true.

But obviously he wasn't ready to talk yet, so she settled in, surprised just how comfortable she was there. An ember of heat underlay the friendly warmth, buried way deep. It was nice to have it there, appreciate that it could flare to life if given the opportunity, enjoy the fact that it existed. But the warmth was darned good, too. She'd almost forgotten how good it felt just to be tucked safely up against someone you liked.

There was a certain kind of comfort, she reflected, in hanging out with someone who knew you at thirteen, at your gawky, geeky worst, a kind of comfort that could never be earned any other way.

The Lakers were going down big by the time he got around to talking.

"I had dinner with Cindy tonight."

"That's nice," she said neutrally. He and Cindy dated cautiously but regularly now, and it did not generally propel him to show up, weary and hollow-eyed, at her door.

"She wants me to quit the force."

"What?" That brought her up straight.

"Get back here," he said, and tucked her back against his side.

"Do you *want* to quit?" she asked carefully. As much as, back in junior high, she could never imagine him as a cop, now she simply could not imagine him as anything else. He could quit the force, but it wouldn't make any difference. Joe Marcioni was a cop, and that was it.

"God, I don't know," he said roughly. "What the hell would I do?"

"How, exactly, did this come up?"

"Oh, there were shots fired when we picked up the suspect this afternoon," he said as casually as he would have said, "I stopped and got gas on the way over."

Her heart clutched. The fact that there were guns involved in his job was something she avoided thinking about when at all possible.

"Did anyone get hurt?"

"Nope," he said. "But Cindy heard about it, and it—well, she said she just didn't think she could go through that every day."

"It must be difficult."

"I was a cop when she met me."

"She didn't love you then," Ellen reminded him, trying to take a careful line. Way down inside, a wicked little voice mentioned that, if Cindy and Joe broke up for good, maybe she and Joe . . .

"Yeah." His head tipped back against the high curve of the couch.

"I don't know if I can *not* be a cop," he said. "But I'm not doing so hot at living without her, either."

"It's hard."

"Damn right, it's hard." He rolled his head toward her, his eyes dark and brown, and she could have kissed him if she'd leaned forward three inches. "Maybe I should just give up. There's been so much . . . we tried to have a baby, did I tell you that? For a year. We'd just started the testing, and it was really tough for her."

"That's a tough one," she said. "But there are other ways to get babies, if it comes to that."

"You could do that? Love one that you didn't grow as much as one you did?"

"Oh, absolutely," she said with feeling. "I used to wonder, before I had them. But once they were here—I would have loved them any way I got them. Hell, I'd take Josh from Jill in a heartbeat if I didn't know you'd wind up having to arrest her for my murder."

A smile. She'd gotten him to smile.

"I love her," he said simply.

"I know," she said with just a twinge of regret.

"Shouldn't that be enough?"

"Yes, it should." There should be a way. A way that two people who really and truly loved each other could navigate all the storms along the way. It *had* to be enough, damn it.

"Sometimes I wish I didn't," he said.

"I know that, too."

13

Coming in for a Landing

ELLEN had never realized she was terrified of flying.

She flew pretty regularly, of course. Twice a year on family trips: Disney or skiing or Mexico. London once. All in big shiny planes with distinguished, briskly confident pilots in crisp uniforms and efficient attendants. Planes like the nice, smooth one that she'd taken to Nassau—first class, no less; she liked Jill's client more all the time.

Not like this one. Not like the one they'd walked to at the Nassau airport, not through a cool and shiny concourse but outside, swimming to the plane through thick, humid air that had her peeling off layers and digging through her bag for her sunglasses.

Not a plane that seemed hardly bigger than her van, slapped with paint, orange, green, purple, trailing jungle vines that looked like they'd been done by a third-grader, a big wavering parrot on the tail. Not flown by a pilot who swaggered up in a backward baseball cap, in a white tank with a splotch of ketchup on the front and fraying cutoffs. A pilot who didn't look much older than Eric and who'd grinned and told them to buckle in, that the ride would be almost as much fun as Six Flags.

She'd rather have had Eric behind the . . . not a wheel. What was it? At the controls. At least she knew Eric had logged thousands of hours on his flight simulator program.

There were six of them on the plane, packed so tightly into the private shuttle to Sizzle that her knees bumped the back of the seat in front of her, even though she had them drawn nearly up to her chest.

When her stomach lurched along with the plane, she clutched her bag and wondered if she could bring herself to throw up into it, if it came to that. Her glasses were in there, and her wallet, and some underwear in case the airlines lost her luggage.

It'd be one way she could get away without wearing the bikini Jill'd insisted she bring, though. That was in there, too, and it'd almost be worth the mortification of tossing her cookies in front of everybody to make it unwearable.

The box of condoms Jill had also insisted upon were packed in her suitcase, and so she was half-hoping the airlines really *would* lose her luggage on that account.

She tried to focus her blurring vision on the back of the seat in front of her, a loose, dirty orange weave with flecks of unnatural blue. The plane lifted and dropped again, and she felt acid burn at the base of her throat.

"Are you doing that on purpose?" she shouted to the pilot, then bit her tongue when every other person in the plane turned to look at her.

The boy laughed. "Only sometimes." He jerked a thumb over his shoulder at the blue drink cooler on the floor in front of the first seats, round with a spigot, the kind the nuns used to serve lemonade out of at church picnics. "There's rum punch in there. You can break it out if you want to start the party."

"Great. Just great," Ellen mumbled.

The guy across the aisle—well, it was barely an aisle; Ellen was pretty sure she couldn't have gotten her butt down between her seat and the one opposite—leaned over to her.

"Don't like flyin'?"

"I like flying just fine." The left wing dipped, and she crossed herself, falling back on old reflexes. "It's having my life in the hands of a kid who probably thinks bungee-jumping's relaxing that bothers me."

The man chuckled. He was big. Had to be six three, six four, and on the top side of two fifty. She'd noticed him checking in, wondered if he was going to put them over weight—and didn't that inspire confidence in an airplane, when they asked you your weight when you checked in so they could add them all up to make sure it wasn't too much? Probably why they picked that pilot. He didn't add much to the total.

"Statistically speaking, it's more dangerous in your bathroom than on a plane," he told her.

"Not *my* bathroom," she said.

"You can hold my hand, if it helps."

He held it out. Great big hands, went with the rest of him. He was ready for the tropics already, decked out in baggy khaki cargo shorts and a Tommy Bahamas shirt splashed with blue and yellow flowers. His cowboy hat was ivory, and the crown brushed the roof of the plane.

"Maybe later," she said.

"Rum punch?"

Her stomach revolted at the suggestion. "God, no."

"I'm not getting too far here, am I?"

Ellen considered the man. He was in his forties, certainly, with a broad, round face and cheerful eyes. As big as he was, he wasn't all that soft. "Maybe when I'm not on the verge of death, you'll do better."

His grin broadened. "Bobby Tucker. Dallas."

"Is that, Bobby Tucker Dallas? Or, Bobby Tucker, from Dallas."

"Second one."

He was taking her needling well enough, Ellen thought. Nice when a guy didn't take himself too seriously. "Ellen Markham. Minneapolis." She shook his hand across the aisle, and he released her the minute she loosened her grip. Manners were good, too.

"Minneapolis? Whee, it's a might frosty up there these days, ain't it?"

"You might say that."

"Well, Sizzle'll warm your toes, that's for damn—pardon—sure."

"I hope so." She wouldn't mind warm toes.

"You never been before?"

"No. You?"

"Oh, sure." He shifted in his seat, trying to fit his bulk comfortably in a chair designed from someone the size of a champion gymnast. "Fifth time, I think. Go every January, ever since my divorce. It's a nice place." He nodded. "Show you the ropes, if you want."

She searched for a hint of a leer but didn't find one. "Maybe. That'd be nice. Thank you, Bobby."

"How about you?"

She whistled through her teeth when the plane tilted abruptly to the right. But it wasn't quite as bad as before. The distraction was helping, and she was grateful to Bobby for making the effort. "How about me what?"

"Divorced?" He gestured to her left hand. She'd debated that morning, the entire time she was packing, on whether she would leave her rings on or take them off. But then the taxi had started honking, and she'd forgotten until she got on the plane. Too late then, and she refused to believe there was anything Freudian in it. She could decide when she got there if she wanted their protection or not. When she decided just how much she wanted to sizzle. "Not divorced, no."

"Oh. No?" Bobby raised his brows in question. But it was too long a story, too complicated, to dump on a near stranger. And not something she really wanted to spend all that much time dwelling on for the next few days.

What the heck, she thought. She was never seeing any of these people again, anyway. "Widowed."

"That explains it," he said gravely. "Long time?"

He was going to start patting her sympathetically on the shoulder any second, and she was already starting to feel guilty about the lie. The nuns had done *way* too good a job instilling a conscience all those years ago.

"Long enough," she said quickly. "Long enough that my friends started to get worried about me and sent me on this trip as a present. Said it was time for me to get back out there."

"Good friends."

"Yes. Yes, they are."

He nodded, then glanced out the window. "Can never get over how beautiful this place is. Every time I go back home, I start to thinking how it really couldn't look like that. Nothing could. But then I come back, and there it is. We don't have that color in Texas."

She hadn't looked out the window since they'd taken off. She hadn't actually screamed out loud yet, which she was damned proud of, and she didn't figure she should tempt it by seeing how close they were to crashing into the drink.

But she was curious about what would get a guy like Bobby, who seemed like he'd wax poetic only about beer or his shotgun, dreamy over some scenery.

She sucked in a breath. Water shimmered below, endless rolling stretches of it. Blue, green, aqua, turquoise . . . they didn't have that color in Minnesota, either, and she didn't think there was a term for it. Intense, the sun glinting off it so strongly as to hurt the eyes, but clear enough to see straight to the bottom most places, to pale sand broken by ragged, dark curves of coral. If they dipped lower, she wondered, would she see fish? Kelp? What'd they have in the Bahamas, anyway? Sharks, yes—she'd looked it up. Caribbean reef sharks, mostly. Lots of blacktips, and nurse. But also bull and tiger and even hammerheads.

Islands dotted the gorgeous sweep of blue, small green and beige humps of land that barely looked big enough to bother with. But people did—she could see houses on some of them, toy-house-sized wooden structures, occasionally huge, white shining things that stood on top of one of those spits of land like a castle.

Boats cruised over the water. Small dark fishing boats bobbed in groups of two or three. Big powerboats zoomed along the horizon, leaving a spray of white in their wake. There was one lone sailboat, a big one, anchored in the curve of a small, narrow island.

Beautiful, all of it, a dazzling kind of beauty that kicked you in the gut, clear and sharp and shiny. Bobby was right. It didn't seem real.

Ellen was suddenly glad she'd decided to go. Not because of Tom, or that tramp he'd spent New Year's with, or even because Jill had pushed so hard that it had been easier to agree.

But because it had been years since Ellen had been on the front end of an adventure. Decades since she'd had more possibilities than plans. The little kick of excitement and anticipation and, yes, fear—it wasn't all bad.

"It really is amazing," she agreed.

"Wait'll you see what's under that water."

"Under?"

"You're going snorkeling, aren't you? You gotta go snorkeling."

Snorkeling. Under the water with the sharks. Sharks that attacked fifty to seventy people in the world every year.

"Maybe you'll even go with me," he suggested.

The plane waggled as the water gleamed beneath them. Sharks. Surely they'd go for Tommy first, Ellen thought. She'd scarcely be a snack next to him. "Maybe."

"Welcome to Sizzle," the kid at the controls shouted back to the passengers. "We're coming in to land. Your life'll be heating up in no time."

Ellen squinted at the strip of green that floated just ahead of them. They weren't landing on that, were they? It was hardly wider than the plane. And she couldn't see an airport. It was a thick tangle of green, edged with a broad, pale strip she assumed was beach.

The nose of the plane sheared down at a steep angle, and sound roared in her ears.

She groped for Tommy's hand, which was right there waiting for her, and hung on.

* * *

SHE agreed to have supper with him. It was the least she could do, considering she'd nearly pulverized his fingers on the way in.

They bumped down on a thin, short strip of asphalt that split the thick vegetation that ran down the middle of the island. It hadn't been fun, but she'd been so elated when they landed she'd nearly run up and kissed that silly pilot.

She really hadn't understood how small the island was, how isolated. An out island of the Bahamas, it was one of dozens that scattered east of Abaco, all of them small and flat and sparsely settled. There was nothing on Sizzle but the resort—no roads, no town, nothing but the cluster of cottages that ran along the beach and tucked back into the coconut palms. She figured there had to be more buildings somewhere, places for the workers to live, some semblance of civilization, but they were well-hidden from the guests, who were halfway to playing out desert-island fantasies or pirate and wench games before they'd ever landed. The combination of the rum punch and being so far away from their normal lives was making them all downright giddy. Ellen suspected silly, ridiculous, and smashed weren't far behind.

There weren't even satellite dishes, said the lovely, dark-skinned young woman who showed Ellen to her room. Her name, Melody, was printed on the name tag pinned to her flowered halter. No television, she said, and only a few ever managed a brief and wavering cell phone connection now and then. There were phones in the rooms, but all calls had to go through the front desk.

"Why does anyone ever *come* here?" Ellen asked.

"Oh, they seem to adjust quickly enough," the clerk said. "Truthfully, we have to shove most of our guests on the plane at the end of the week to get them to leave."

"That's just because they don't want to get back on that toy plane," Ellen grumbled.

"You didn't like the trip over?" she asked, surprised. "We used to have a boat shuttle. That was fun, too, but it took three hours. Everyone's usually in a hurry to get here and start sizzling."

"How many times did you have to practice to say that with a straight face?"

The professional smile on Melody's face widened into a genuine grin. "It took a few." She stopped in front of a cottage that was no more than twenty steps from the beach. It was tiny—looked barely big enough to hold a bed—and fine-grained sand spread right up to the base of the front veranda. Palms arched behind it, with a rope hammock slung between two convenient ones, swaying in the constant ocean breeze. The air held that salty marine tang, and the scent of flowers, and, from somewhere she couldn't see, a fire.

"Here you go," Melody said. "It's one of our best. Word came down that you're to be treated especially well. Not that we don't treat *all* our guests specially."

"What do we do if there's an emergency?" Ellen asked. It was occurring to her that being away from everything meant being *away* from everything, and that anything approaching civilization was far across that surf that rolled in so picturesquely, and that she was going to be able to walk back and forth across this island in under an hour. "Say, a shark attack?"

Melody laughed. "No shark attacks. Management wouldn't allow it. Wouldn't be good for business." She slipped a key, an old-fashioned brass one, into the lock and turned it before pushing the door open. "But if there's really a problem, we've got radios. Airplanes, boats. A helicopter can get here in twenty minutes, if need be."

"Don't you go stir-crazy?" It was, Ellen thought, a decided possibility.

"Oh, hardly any of us *live* here. There are at least seven cays within a half-hour boat ride. Most of us live on one of them. A trip can be arranged, if you'd like. There's a small market on Bonefish Cay, and the fishing's good off Spit. But very few of our guests choose to leave once they're here."

She gestured for Ellen to enter the room before her.

The bed *did* barely fit, but it was a big one. The room was spare, very simple and clean compared to the Technicolor lushness of the island. The walls were bright white, the floor tiles the color of sand, and the bedspread a pale and watery blue. A ceiling fan spun lazily above it.

"Bathroom's through there." Melody indicated one of two doors that flanked the white-painted headboard. "The other one's the closet. It's very simple. But guests tend not to spend that much time in their rooms, anyway. And when they do, well, it's not really the décor they're interested in."

"Great. Just great." She tried, for Melody's sake, to work up some enthusiasm.

"If you don't find the room meets your standards—"

"Oh, no. The room is lovely." It was. Who wouldn't like a dollhouse of a cottage on a perfect Bahamian island? It wasn't Melody's fault that the whole idea of the place put her teeth on edge. It seemed . . . artificial, a singles bar dressed up in pretty trappings.

Nobody's making you do anything, she reminded herself.

"Good." Melody handed her a folder with a photo of a gorgeous, sun-bronzed couple running down a beach on the front of it. She'd been relieved to discover that none of the people on the plane looked anything close to the models. Took some of the pressure off. Though she figured it was a disappointment to some of the guests.

But in regards to the island itself, the brochures hadn't oversold the place a bit.

"All the information you need is in there," Melody informed her. "Classes, mixers, spa treatments. Coed intramural water polo and beach yoga are very popular."

Heaven forbid.

Melody was starting to look concerned. "Ms. Markham, you don't seem pleased. My instructions were quite specific. If there's anything you wish to change, anything at all I can do to make you more comfortable, *please* let me know."

"No, it's nothing. I just got a little airsick on the plane over." *Terrified out of my mind, that counts as airsick, doesn't it?* "My stomach hasn't quite settled yet."

Melody's expression cleared. "Of course. Maybe you want to take a nap? I'll open the windows for you; the breeze is quite restorative. You'll feel better in no time."

"That sounds lovely." *And if everyone just leaves me alone in my cute little cottage, it'll be even better.*

"It's open seating for dinner. Most of the guests start gathering for drinks at Heat, the open-air bar on the beach, around seven."

"Actually, I'm meeting someone then."

"Oh, how wonderful!" Melody beamed at her. "You're making friends already. That's the Sizzle spirit."

"Yeah, I'm just brimming with Sizzle spirit."

"The dress code is—well, there really isn't one. Most people don't bother with too many clothes. There's not much point in it." She moved toward the door, her legs long and bronze below her tiny white shorts. "You could come naked, and nobody'd care."

"No health department here, huh?"

"There aren't a whole lot of rules here, period." She opened the door, and the ocean breeze billowed through. "Since you had such a bumpy flight over, I'm sure the management would like to make it up to you. When you get to Heat tonight, you look for Jake. He's the bartender, you can't miss him. Everybody knows Jake. He'll take good care of you."

14

Heat

SHE almost missed her date, and she didn't even have the rum punch for an excuse.

She'd made a quick, hideously expensive phone call to Tom's to report that she'd arrived safely. Katie'd answered the phone, which spared her from having to talk to him.

Putting her clothes away was the next logical step. She never felt comfortable in a new place until her clothes were tucked neatly away, her face-repair potions lined up in the bathroom. Then she could relax.

Except putting her stuff away proved to be a challenge. The closet was the size of a gym locker. They must only have thin guests, because anybody of any size—Bobby Tucker, for example—was going to have a heck of a time turning around in the bathroom, and the pedestal sink wasn't wide enough to hold but one tube of moisturizer.

The brochure had claimed the only thing you needed at Sizzle was sunscreen. Apparently they hadn't been kidding.

So she wedged her suitcase into the closet, leaving the door open and a corner of the case hanging out, and lay down to try out the bed. She always had a hard time sleeping in a bed that was not her own.

Except if Sizzle had one thing right, it was the beds. She woke up to the screech of sea birds, the rhythmic surge of the waves, believing she'd only closed her eyes for a moment and hazily thinking how pleasant it was not to have to hurry.

Sizzle didn't believe in clocks. There were no alarms on the small rattan beside table, only a plain beige phone. She rolled over to squint at her watch, wondering if it was a good time to call Jill and whine yet, and yelped.

Six forty-five. Crap. The first date she'd had in over two decades, and she was going to be late.

No time for any of the primping and curling and clothing trial and discard that should comprise the preparations for a first date, which took half the fun out of it. But it left no time for nerves, which was probably good.

But she couldn't go as she was. She'd been sweating pretty much nonstop since she arrived in Nassau. Even though she had no plans to get *too* close to Bobby Tucker, leaving the option open was kind of the whole point, wasn't it?

Though he looked like the kind of guy who had a regular acquaintance with sweat.

She peeled off her travel clothes and tossed them in a corner. Good thing her kids weren't around; she'd never hear the end of it. She ran a washcloth under the faucet, cursing when it took forever to warm up before she gave up and used it cold. She scrubbed frantically at all the important parts: her pits, her stomach, her neck and, after some reflection and with Jill's voice in her ears, between her legs.

She swiped deodorant under her arms; thank goodness she'd shaved before she left home, though another scrape for insurance wouldn't have hurt. A plain bra, simple beige cotton panties—here she shut out Jill's voice. She wasn't dressing for sex when she had no intention—well, *almost* no intention—of having it. If it happened, well, if he wasn't the sort to overlook uninspiring underthings, he wasn't the guy for her first voyage over to the wild side, anyway.

She dropped a long, sleeveless linen shift the color of ripe peaches over her head, slid her feet into flat metallic sandals. No time for makeup, and it was too hot for it to stay, anyway. One quick slick of melony lip gloss would have to do. Her hair— well, it didn't bear thinking about, so she plopped a straw hat on her head and carefully avoided the mirror. "You look good," she told herself, though she didn't believe it. Jill had great faith in telling yourself what you want to believe, though Ellen didn't see how something so simple could work. There were too many dissenting voices in her head. But what the heck; she was determined to try all sorts of new things this week.

No need for purses on Sizzle, she'd been told. Nothing to buy. But there was no place in her dress for a room key, so she grabbed her purse anyway, and headed out the door at 7:05.

It wasn't hard to find Heat. The music throbbed through the tropical air, making it pulse around her, an island beat heavy on tin drums that made it almost impossible to stay still. She hurried along the crushed shell path and careened around the corner, coming to a stop when the bar came in sight.

The floor was concrete, the corrugated tin roof held up with simple wood posts. Ropes of colored lights looped from the overhead beams, palms arched above the roof, and small wooden tables painted a bright and glossy blue clustered around a wide-open dance floor.

And she was way, way overdressed, she realized immediately.

Not overdressed as in "too fancy." Overdressed as in wearing more clothes than any three other women in the place put together.

She stopped uncertainly just under the overhang of the roof. At the nearest table, a balding man who looked about fifty had a bikini-clad woman on each knee. A cluster of women at the next table raced each other to the bottoms of their drinks, tall, pastel-colored things with flowers hung on their rims. The dance floor was full of people rolling through the same kind of bump-and-grind gyrations she'd seen at Paradise, with far less proficiency but even more enthusiasm.

Bikini tops and sarongs seemed to be the unofficial female dress code. Sometimes a halter top and a skirt that barely covered their asses—and, in one case, didn't fully do the job. Ellen nearly turned and fled. She was totally out of place, certain everyone would decide at a glance that she was a prude who didn't belong.

She selected her clothes to be appropriate and inoffensive

first, flattering second. Standing out was not in the plan, and now she was doing just that by being all covered up.

No running away, she told herself. She'd promised. She wasn't going to stand up Bobby just because she hadn't dressed properly. She'd been stood up a couple times, a long time ago, but she could still acutely recall what it felt like.

Through the screen of wriggling bodies she could see the bar on the far side of the room, a long, curving surface like an up-turned boat. Glass floats hung from fishing nets above, along with a blown-up plastic shark wearing a straw hat, big yellow sunglasses, and a toothy grin.

She squeezed through the crowds, dropping with relief onto the nearest metal barstool when she managed to navigate the dance floor without bumping anything . . . fleshy. The men, it seemed, had at least started fully dressed, in shorts and swim-suits mostly, but more than a few shirts hung unbuttoned, and quite a few more had been surrendered, hanging around the necks of the women who'd stripped them off like trophies. Two brave, or stupid, men wore nothing but flip-flops, Speedos, and thick gold chains around their neck. Neither of them should've.

The bartender had his back to her, dropping chunks of mango into a blender. A nice back, she noted, far better than most of what she'd passed in the bar, deeply bronzed, and he was wear-ing a low-slung pair of surfer shorts.

The bartender spun and caught sight of her. He held up a fin-ger, signaling her to wait, and grabbed a big bottle of rum. The liquid streamed into the blender. Either he was making several drinks at once, or any one would be strong enough to put Ellen under the table in one sip. Which probably explained a good share of both the behavior and the clothing—or lack of it—around her. The bartender punched a button on the blender, bopping to the music while the bright-colored liquid spun.

Wow, Ellen thought. *Just wow.*

Was there some universal rule that said all bartenders had to be gorgeous? She hadn't had much experience in bars until re-cently, but really, didn't all the male customers object to the women they were trying to meet being unable to get their eyes off the men servings the drinks?

He wasn't her type at all. She'd never had a thing for that slacker, surfer-boy look. Oh, the lean, ropy muscles were nice enough, the messy hair, a deep brown streaked bronze by the sun, that looked like he'd just climbed out of the ocean and come to work without bothering to hop in a shower. Didn't look like he'd bothered to change his clothes, either. He was younger than she—at least ten years, maybe a lot more, though he had wrinkles around his eyes when he grinned at her, creases along his mouth, the kind you got from spending too much time squinting into the sun.

Maybe she didn't really know her type after all.

But nice as he was to look at, she wasn't here to admire the bartender. She twisted on her chair, searching the crowds for Bobby. With his height he should have been easy enough to find, even if he'd given up the cowboy hat.

Now that the shock had worn off, Ellen noticed in relief that not all those bodies gyrating—not too expertly, but vigorously— on the dance floor were beautiful. Oh, some of them were, but far from all. And the women who didn't belong on the cover of *Cosmo* appeared to be having just as much fun as those who did. She envied their freedom, their bravery. The woman in the tangerine bikini with the big Cesarean scar and a belly that jiggled every time she shimmied had her hands above her head, dancing between two men who didn't seem to mind at all that she'd left her hard-bodied days behind long ago, if she'd ever had them. A redhead, pretty enough to remind her fondly of Jill, wore a tropical print tankini cut nearly to her hipbones, which didn't do a darn thing to disguise thighs that were broader than her hips and sported skin as rippled as an orange peel.

Ellen appeared to be right smack-dab in the middle as far as age, too. The music, and the general air of celebration, was infectious; her toes were wiggling in her sandals, her fingers drumming against her thighs.

"Here you go." She turned at the voice in her ear, felt her

mouth come open at the shock of eyes the color of the water she'd flown over. Her stomach dropped abruptly, as if she was back on that plane and it had just taken another dip.

"You must be Ellen, right?" the bartender said. "They told me to look out for you."

"Yes." Ellen gave herself a mental shake. No good. She closed her eyes briefly, figuring when she opened them again the shock would have worn off.

Nope, they really were that brilliant. But at least half of her brain was starting to work again. The other half was still occupied by admiring, but how could you not? "You must be Jake."

He grinned at her as if she'd just won the lottery. "Ah, my legend precedes me."

She caught herself before *I'll bet* popped out. "Melody mentioned you."

"Ah, Mel. She's a good one, that." He lifted two empty glasses from the bar and dropped them into a tub of soapy water. "Hope she said good things."

"Do women ever say bad things about you?"

"I hope not." Sunglasses hung around his neck on a strap, alone with a shark tooth and a Chinese character carved from jade. "Drink up."

He'd put a glass at her elbow, a margarita glass the size of a bowling ball. The outside was frosty, the rim coated with big sugar crystals that sparkled like diamonds. Bright wheels of sliced orange, ruby cherries, and a thick slab of pineapple dangled from the edge. The orange peach concoction he'd been mixing up was swirled with something deep and red.

She eyed it doubtfully. She'd seen just how much liquor had gone in there. "How much do you think I can drink of that before I start feeling it?"

"Depends." He spun an amber-colored bottle in one hand while grabbing a chunky, low glass with his other. "How much of a lightweight are you?"

"Very," she said, admiring how he managed to keep his hands flashing while he carried on a conversation with her. He didn't even look while he scooped a couple of ice cubes and clinked them into the glass, following it with a steady pour of liquid that stopped just shy of the rim.

"About three swallows, then." He grinned and put the drink on a tray shaped like a seashell that already held two bottles of beer with wedges of lime hooked onto their necks. "What does it matter? You're on Sizzle now. Live it up."

"See, now, about that living it up thing . . ." A server expertly scooped up the tray, air-kissed in Jake's direction, and sashayed off. Now there was a woman made for her outfit, a top that appeared no more than two lime-green postage stamps strung together with floss. The floral-print sarong around her hips was no bigger than a scarf and a lot more sheer, and a big purple flower was tucked in the waterfall of her hair. "I've really not had all that much luck with that."

"All the more reason to try it," Jake said.

She gave the drink an experimental sniff and reeled at the alcohol fumes. "I don't think I'll have to drink it. All I have to do is smell it."

"I made it just for you."

Laughter burst from the dance floor. A man had climbed up on top of one of the tables and held two coconut shells over his chest, his hips spasming like a seizure victim's.

"Do you suppose," she asked, "he's trying to dance?"

Jake glanced up from slicing oranges. "One way or another, Ellen, they're all trying to dance." He pointed with the knife. "You haven't touched your drink yet. You want something else? I can do something without alcohol. Nobody mentioned that you didn't drink."

"It's not that." She tried a sip. It wasn't as sweet as she expected, cold and creamy, sliding down a lot easier than something with that much rum in it should. "It's good."

"Of course it's good." He poured three bottles at once in a clear glass fishbowl, filling it with deep blue liquid.

"What is it?"

"I call it *crave*."

Ellen figured she'd better find out if she'd been stood up or not before she decided whether to down the rest. "Have you seen a man?"

He chuckled. "There're plenty around here," he said. "Though I can't say that I noticed any one in particular. Not really my style."

"No . . . I . . ." *Shoot.* "I was supposed to meet him here."

"Ahhh." He dropped a couple of gummi fish into the drink and perched a plastic, bare-breasted—and extremely *breasted*, at that—mermaid on the edge of the bowl. "Got a date already, do you? Fast work."

"Don't call it that."

"Don't call it what? A date?"

"Yeah. That." It was bad enough to think about spending an evening with a man. Worse to think about it as a date.

Even if it was one.

"What is it, then?"

"Just a friendly meal with a new acquaintance."

"A new acquaintance who happens to be of the opposite sex."

"Yeah."

"And who, like you, is single."

She hesitated long enough for Jake to glance her way. "Of course. Of course, single." Single. That's what she would be if she went through with the divorce. Damn. She'd never wanted to be single.

"On a romantic tropical isle, on a beautiful evening."

She took another sip of the drink, hoping it would calm her stomach. Or at least numb it. "Yeah."

"That's a date, Ellen," he said kindly. He started lining tall glasses up on the bar, two at a time.

"Yeah." She pressed her hand to her stomach. "Maybe he's not coming."

He had three blenders going now, and the smell of pineapple and coconut filled the air. "You sound awfully hopeful."

"No. Of course not." That wouldn't be very nice of her, would it? Ellen tried really hard to be nice.

He gave her an appraising look, up and down, and his eyes gleamed. "He's not standing you up."

"Oh. Thanks." He didn't mean it. He couldn't. He'd been told to keep her happy.

But she appreciated it anyway. "Well. Anyway. He's pretty tall. Maybe three, four inches more than you? Big. He had a hat on the last time I saw him but I don't know—"

"Ah." He filled the glasses, and people started filing by, grabbing them as quickly as he poured them. "The cowboy. He was looking for you. Well, I didn't know it was *you*, but he was looking for his date." He smiled on the *date*, waiting a beat as if he expected her to protest. "He went off searching about ten minutes ago."

"Oh." So he'd shown up after all. Early. And was so anxious to see her he'd gone off to search.

She didn't know whether to be flattered or terrified.

"Maybe I should go . . ." She began to slide off the stool, and Jake's hand came down over hers, holding her in place.

"If you go off looking for him, he'll only be back here trying to find you, and you'll be missing each other all night. Keep your butt planted. He'll find you soon enough."

He released her, and she kept her hand where it was, flattened against the scarred wood of the bar.

"Or were you running away?" he asked her.

"Nooo." She folded the corner of the napkin under her drink, turned it so she could match the other side. "Never crossed my mind."

"That's good." He nodded toward the dance floor, where a cowboy hat bobbed above the sea of heads. "Because I think he would have caught you."

"There you are!" Bobby beamed at her, his round face red and shiny. He'd switched to another Hawaiian shirt, this one printed with multicolored beer bottles, and only bothered to fasten the bottom three buttons. He'd kept the cowboy hat, added a necklace of tiny white shells around the crown to strengthen the theme. "Don't you look purty!"

Wonderful. Because obviously he had *such* good taste, she thought, then quickly pushed it away. She wasn't going to let Tom make her sour on all men. "Thank you," she said, and meant it. There were plenty of women here, and he'd chosen to spend the evening with her, and called her pretty. It wasn't his fault she hadn't gone on a first date in a lifetime. "I'm sorry I was a little late. I just lay down for a moment, and before I knew it—"

"Forget it." He shoved his hat back on his head, exposing a broad forehead gleaming with sweat. "You had a big day. Earned a nap."

"I guess I did," she said. *Oh, clever answer, Ellen. That's exactly why I hate dating.*

"So now you'll have plenty of energy for the night."

She frowned at him. If he thought she'd taken a nap so she'd be ready to—

He lifted his hands, all innocence. "Naw, I didn't mean that, I just—" He shrugged. "I give up. Anythin' that comes out of my mouth is just gonna get me in more trouble. So let's just say I didn't mean anything by it and leave it at that, huh?"

She was used to men who were . . . smoother than he was, no doubt about it. He wasn't her type. But what was her type, anyway? Might as well start figuring it out. And there was a certain straightforwardness about him that she found appealing. "Good enough."

"I hope you ain't been sittin' here by yourself too long. I just thought maybe we got our wires crossed, got the times mixed up or somethin', so I thought I'd better go check."

"Don't worry." The fleet of piña coladas had gotten Jake ahead of the demand for a moment, and he had taken the opportunity to wipe down the bar. "I beat off the slobbering hordes for you. Made sure nobody snatched her away." He tucked the cloth in his waistband. "A tough job, I gotta say. You want something to drink?"

"I don't know." Bobby looked to Ellen, giving her the option. "You want to stay here? I'm not much of a dancer, but . . ."

"No," she said quickly. "Why don't we just go ahead and go to dinner?"

"Dinner'd be great."

She turned to thank Jake. He'd done a good job of distracting her, so that now she only felt like fainting instead of actually bolting. He'd already turned away, handing a pink drink in a martini glass to a lovely blond who had no need at all for a cover-up, and giving her a smile that had the woman preening and tossing her hair over her shoulder.

Well. Apparently his assignment was over.

"You want to take your drink?" Bobby asked.

"No. No, that's okay." She looked up at him, giving him her full attention. She might still feel like a wallflower, but she'd learned a few tricks in all those years of making polite conversation with Tom's coworkers, and one thing was to give your partner your full attention. "Ready?"

"Always."

15

Maybe

SIZZLE had three restaurants, not counting the take-out stand by the beach that handed out quick sandwiches and box lunches for guests who were too busy having fun to take time out for a proper meal. Wouldn't do for the guests to run low on blood sugar at an inopportune time.

There was a buffet by the pool, a barefoot spot nearly as lively as Heat. A casual terrace overlooking the beach, with sand tracked over the stone floor and a live, and very crude, parrot on a perch in the corner.

But Bobby had chosen Moonlight, the smallest and quietest restaurant on the island. This early in the week very few couples had paired up, and so it was nearly empty, only two of the dozen tables filled by the time they arrived.

Unlike most of the other public buildings on Sizzle, the entire structure was enclosed, although tonight the huge sliding glass doors were open to the ripe air. It overlooked the ocean, hovering at the far tip of an arm that enclosed Sizzle's beach, facing away from the complex so one saw only a long stretch of water.

Deep, glossy blue tile covered the floor, and gauzy white fabric draped the ceiling, hanging in sweeping loops that wavered in the breeze. There were candles on the tables, in glass cylinders with sand in the bottoms. A small, tinkling fountain danced in the center of the room. No music; Ellen wondered about that at first, expecting something quiet and classic. But that would be redundant; why cover up the sound of the ocean, the fountain, the wind sifting through the palm fronds?

The hostess had an island accent and mile-long legs. She showed them to a table in the far corner, right up against the open door. Bobby escorted Ellen with his hand on her lower back, light, warm, respectful, and pulled out her chair for her.

"I didn't know men from Texas had such good manners," she said.

He took his own seat, removed his hat, and placed it on the nearest unoccupied chair. Yup, balding. But she didn't really mind. He had a nicely shaped head, a broad forehead. And at least he didn't try to pretend he wasn't, combing hair across places it didn't grow. "Men from Texas have mamas."

"Doesn't everyone?"

"No," he said. "There's mothers, and there's mamas. Mamas got no problem whacking you up against the side of the head if you forget to say *ma'am*."

One couldn't help but look out over that water, she thought. Dusk was falling, drawing shadows under the waves, turning them dark and mysterious. Glitter blazed when light dashed across the tops of the waves, always changing, endlessly fascinating. "It's like you're the only ones in the whole world," she murmured.

"Just about." But he was looking at her instead of the view, his focus unswerving.

After bowls of conch chowder, a simple and quite good grilled fish for her and a bloodred steak for Bobby, and the endless wine their waitress kept pouring into their glasses—*they weren't kidding about that "all liquor included" thing,* she thought hazily, *and they sure weren't stingy*—Ellen was feeling relaxed, and Bobby was spilling his guts.

"We were high school sweethearts." He forked up a huge chunk of coconut cake, held it up in the air while he talked. She glanced down at the platter of sliced tropical fruit she'd chosen. Pretty, virtuous, colorful, and terribly uninspiring compared to the coconut cake she wished she'd ordered.

"Head cheerleader and the captain of the football team?"

"How'd you know?"

"Lucky guess."

His fork circled in the air, the thick coat of icing keeping the cake glued to the utensil. Ellen popped a slice of mango into her mouth. It was sweet, perfectly ripe, and she really wanted that cake.

"I broke up with her. When I went off to A&M. Gonna be big man on campus, you know?" He had the grace to look embarrassed. "I was such an idiot."

"You were eighteen and a football star. Aren't many who keep their head on straight." Her willpower failed. "Mind if I try your cake?"

"Hmm? No, no, of course not. Try away." He put down his fork and slid the plate across the table. "Still, I coulda figured it out sooner. Bet you weren't an idiot at eighteen, were you?"

Oh, Lord. The cake was the best thing she'd put in her mouth in years, and she resented having to talk instead of concentrate on enjoying every last sugar crystal before it melted. "Depends on your definition of an idiot."

"Well, we were apart about six months. Ran around like a fool, goin' through girls like popcorn, and couldn't figure out why I wasn't having as good a time as I shoulda been."

One bite was enough, she tried to convince herself. The second bite was never as good as the first. She had all that beautiful fruit, which was a perfectly sufficient and healthful dessert.

"Funny how that works sometimes." She wondered if Tom ever felt like that, if all those affairs were more fun in his imagination than they were in actuality. It was a comforting thought.

"Then I got hurt."

"Hurt?" One more bite couldn't hurt. Bobby wouldn't notice.

"Blew out my knee in the Oklahoma game. Tore it up completely. Six months of rehab."

"Ouch." There was no way she was going to get through this entire week without putting on a swimsuit. It should have bolstered her willpower. But the cake was right there between them, and wasn't she supposed to be enjoying herself? Having a decadent week?

He shrugged. "Mindy was there when I got out of surgery. Drove me to rehab, brought me chicken soup, the whole ten yards." He glanced down and discovered half his dessert was gone, even though he hadn't eaten a bite. "You can order another one of those, you know."

"I already have dessert."

"So what? You can order as many as you want. It's Sizzle. No limits."

Tempting. And she'd be really embarrassed when she didn't fit into her Bermuda shorts tomorrow. "The calories only count half when you steal it from somebody else's plate. Everybody knows that."

He had that aw-shucks kind of grin that she would have sworn would set her teeth on edge. Instead, she found it kind of endearing. Maybe she was broadening her horizons.

About time.

But she couldn't eat and talk at the same time, so she figured it was better to get him talking again. "That's what friends are for."

"It's more than that. The knee was never the same. Before that, everybody thought I was going pro. But after that . . . well, it's one way to find out who your friends really are, isn't it?" He looked down, caught her in the act of snitching a forkful of frosting, and simply reached over and switched her plate with his. "She stuck with me the whole way. Even tutored me. I hadn't been workin' all that hard in class," he admitted. "Married her the day after we graduated."

Because her mouth was full, she nodded encouragement.

"Which was why it was such a surprise to me when she up and left five years ago." His mouth quivered. "Things were just going good, y'know? It was tough sometimes, getting the business going. I had to work a lot. There wasn't much money. But I'd finally made it. It was time for us to enjoy it, and each other. And she left me for the twenty-eight-year old wannabe actor who sold her coffee every mornin'."

"Oh, Bobby." Sympathy swelled. "I understand what it's like." She patted the back of his hand and didn't object when he took hers. Poor man.

"Do you? It's a lot different, bein' widowed."

"Wi—" Oops. "Loss is loss, Bobby."

He nodded. "And shock is shock, ain't it?"

Of course. His eyes glistened, and she was afraid that he was going to start crying. Not that he didn't have the right—she didn't really *mind* providing a shoulder to cry on—but what was it about her that encouraged guys to break down? It wasn't the emotion she was going for.

Plus she'd probably had enough cake.

"Why don't we go for a walk on the beach?"

* * *

You could not even like the person you were with, Ellen thought, and start feeling romantic after a few minutes of strolling Sizzle's beach at night.

The air was silky warm and smelled like perfume. The moon dashed in and out of clouds, sending flickering streamers of silver across the water. The palms rustled above, and now and then a spray of laughter, a tinkle of music reached them, faint enough that it only made you feel farther away.

"Sounds like everybody's having fun," Bobby said.

"We can go," she said immediately. "If you want."

"I wasn't implyin' they were having more fun than *us*. They're all over there trying to find somebody to walk on the beach with, anyway." He said it with such sincerity that she decided to believe him.

They'd taken off their sandals. Bobby'd taken her hand to help lead her through the path and hadn't let go once they reached the beach. They walked right at the edge; sometimes the sand was soft and warm beneath their feet, sometimes damp, coolly hard-packed. Now and then a particularly big wave slid up to them, sucking the sand from beneath their toes when it rolled back.

"This is nice," Ellen said. They didn't talk much, but he didn't seem to mind. Maybe that was something that came with age as well: the ability to enjoy the silences, to not feel like you had to fill every second with chatter. What did all those details matter, anyway?

They were both alone, and she liked the way her hand felt in his, and for once she was going to let that be good enough.

"Sure is pretty out. Almost as pretty as you." Okay, he wasn't exactly original. But at least he tried.

She wasn't ready when he kissed her. Maybe it was better that way, so she didn't have time to worry about it, didn't have time to prepare.

He swooped right in and planted one on her, catching her with her mouth half-open in surprise.

It wasn't great. But it wasn't bad, either; mostly she was just too surprised to know *what* she felt, and it was over before she had time to figure it out.

He was grinning when he pulled back, a big smile like he'd just recovered a fumble during the playoffs. Nice to think that kissing her could make somebody that happy.

"Let's go to your room. Or mine."

Wow, that was fast.

She'd now been propositioned three times in the past two months, which was more than she'd been hit on in the previous ten years. And all of them had been so quick, a suggestion as simple as ordering a cup of coffee and apparently taking no more consideration. Was this what it was like out there now? What happened to . . . seduction, to working up to things? Back in the day, she didn't remember any guy just flat-out asking; it was something one sidled up to in the heat of the moment, one step at a time, until asking *anything* was the last thing on anybody's mind. You just *did*, because you were too lost in the excitement to say no.

She supposed this way had a certain efficiency to it. Nobody was going to get any mixed signals. Nobody was going to put a lot of effort into something that wasn't going to end up in bed.

But boy, she missed the effort.

She considered his suggestion; it deserved real thought, didn't it, instead of an automatic no? She liked him pretty well. Liked his Southern manners, his big, strong hands. And he liked *her*, a lot; she wasn't so out of practice that she didn't know that. That counted for a fair amount. There were a lot of women floating around Sizzle, some of them a lot more obvious and a lot younger than she was. He was plenty attractive enough to interest one of them. But he'd picked her out, right that first day, and as far as she could tell, his interest hadn't wavered.

But she wasn't wildly in lust with him. She was starting to wonder if that kind of instant hunger just wasn't in her sensual vocabulary.

"Bobby, I . . ."

His face fell.

"No, wait! I wasn't saying no."

"All right, then." He grabbed her hand and started towing her back toward the cottages.

"But I wasn't saying yes, either."

He stopped, planting his feet in the sand. "What *are* you sayin', then?"

"I'm just saying . . ." *Crap.* What was she saying? "I just don't know. I haven't . . . since my husband, I mean. This is difficult for me."

His expression cleared. "Since your husband? Well, then, it's natural you'd be a tad skittish. But I'd be right honored."

"But—"

He leaned toward her, suddenly sure of himself. "I'd take good care of you. I promise."

"I'm sure you would." She really wasn't in the habit of turning people down. Especially not people she didn't want to hurt. Wasn't even sure she really *wanted* to turn him down, not completely. "I think I'd just . . . can't we just see how it goes?"

"Sure. I can be patient." He put out his elbow, and she slipped her arm in. "But I've got to warn you. I do love a challenge. And I'm in the habit of getting what I want."

16

After Midnight

SHE didn't sleep well. It was the stupid nap, she decided around two thirty in the morning. She never napped. Plus the time change, and the strange bed.

And yeah, well, probably the fact that she'd come here to have an affair, and there was an attractive man ready and willing to hop in the sack with her the second she gave the word, and everyone back at home, including her husband, waiting to find out if she did it . . . no wonder she couldn't sleep.

So she gave up and climbed out of bed. Briefly she considered going out just as she was, in the long purple T-shirt she slept in. Who would see her? Anybody who was up was probably thoroughly . . . occupied. Plus she was still better covered than most of the other guests.

But she pulled on a pair of khaki shorts anyway, slid her feet into flip-flops, and slipped outside.

It was quieter now, as if the night muted the sounds. The wind had softened, so the sound of it sighing through the trees was a bare whisper.

She wandered along a path, enjoying the warmth and the silence. There were lights on here and there, low, muted glows in windows swathed in gauzy curtains. She heard a giggle as she passed one, low and throbbing soul music as she strolled by another.

And suddenly she was lonely, a piercing and melancholy wave. The night was far too beautiful to be spent alone. She didn't want to be passing gorgeous nights alone for the rest of her life, but she could see that probability stretching out in front of her, one solitary night after the other.

It would still be a good life. She had people she loved and was groping her way toward good and productive work. She'd travel, get another dog, volunteer. She knew how to make a life.

But it was so much richer to share it with someone you loved, someone who loved you back.

The pool lay ahead, the underwater lights glowing deep blue, outlining its sensually free-form curves, the swim-up bar at the far end empty.

But the pool wasn't. She heard a splash and glanced that way automatically.

At first she thought there was only one person in the water. But there were two, naked, entwined, and moving.

She froze for a moment, openmouthed, too shocked to react. She'd never seen someone else having sex, not live and in the flesh. She'd gone to an X-rated movie once in college, with a whole group, and they'd gotten kicked out about ten minutes in for laughing too loud. Apparently that ruined the mood for the other patrons.

The bodies moved apart, together, the water lapping and swirling, a low and even rhythm that caught and held the attention like the advance and retreat of waves.

Didn't they know that anyone could come across them? Didn't they care?

The moan, a rising keen, mobilized her. If she was any judge, they'd be done soon, and she'd be mortified to be caught gawking. Even if they didn't care. *Especially* if they didn't care. What if they asked her to join them? Jill would bust her bra laughing at the idea of Ellen being propositioned to join a threesome. And Ellen would have to spend the rest of the vacation hiding in her room because she wouldn't risk running into one of them over breakfast.

She took the nearest path and fled toward the light that flickered through the palms.

She stumbled toward Heat. Nobody could be having sex in the bar, could they? It had to be safe.

And if somebody *was* having sex in the bar, she was going to go find that underage pilot and force him to fly her off this island tonight.

The twinkle lights were off. One bare bulb shone over the bar. Several of the flowers on the tables had been pulled from their vases and crushed on the floor—beneath dancing feet, no doubt—so there was perfume in the air, layered beneath the scent of fruit and alcohol.

For a moment she thought the place was empty. But Jake was still there, shirtless, his back to her, swishing glasses in a sink of soapy water. He whistled something light and tuneless.

She hopped up on one of the stools, boat seats fastened on aluminum legs. "You're working late."

He glanced over his shoulder while his hands kept running glasses through the water. "And you're out late. Or early, depending upon your point of view. Disappointing evening?"

"What? Ah . . . oh." He thought she'd . . ."No. I didn't. I mean, *we* didn't. Oh, hell." Why was she trying to explain, anyway? It wasn't any of his business, she shouldn't care, and she wasn't even certain if she'd rather he believed she *had* or she *hadn't*. "Where is everybody? I thought there'd still be a party going on."

"There're still parties going on. Just not here. They're smaller by this time of the night." He turned and dried his hands on a nearby towel. "Can I get you something?"

"You're closed. I just stopped by to . . ." To gather her courage to return to her room, knowing that she might run into Lord only knew what on the way.

"We're never closed for you."

She didn't want to go back yet. Not alone. It was pleasant here, with nobody around, everything calm and hushed. And there was the added bonus that she'd be perfectly content to admire Jake's rear view while he washed the rest of the dishes. "What's your favorite?"

"To make? Probably a Sizzle-tini."

"Did you name that?"

He smiled. "No. But I created it. Goes down smooth, but it packs a helluva kick."

"Hmm." That sounded a little strong. She didn't want to end up in the pool, after all. "What's your favorite to drink?"

He studied her for a minute, as if debating something, and she remembered she must look like hell. She hadn't even run a comb through her hair.

But what difference did it make?

"Okay," he said. "But you have to close your eyes."

"Close my eyes?"

"Can't have you seeing my secrets, now, can I?"

"All right." She obediently closed them. She heard the clink of glasses, the slosh of liquid being poured. She dared to open one eye, peering out through her lashes. He was long and lean; another ten pounds gone, and he'd be too thin. His skin gleamed bronze, and shadows played across the muscles as he moved.

"Shut 'em!"

"Okay, okay," she grumbled. "I *always* get caught not following the rules."

"Obviously you need more practice." His feet scraped against the floor. "Here."

The glass was the size of a basketball, the liquid inside golden and opaque. A deep purple flower drooped from the rim.

"Sorry about the flower," he said. "It was fresh a few hours ago."

"It looks . . . great." It looked like she could drown in it. But at least then she wouldn't have to walk back past the pool. Or get back on that toy that passed for a plane.

"Try it."

Steeling herself for the punch of alcohol, she took a tentative sip and looked up in surprise. "It tastes like pineapple juice."

He grinned. "That's because it is pineapple juice."

"A bartender who doesn't drink?"

"I was nineteen when I came to work here. Place had only

been open three years." He moved back to the sink. "Mind if I work?"

"Of course not. And kick me out when you need to go. I'd hate to hold you up." She tried to imagine him at nineteen. Much the same, she supposed, but paler, smooth-skinned—maybe a zit or two. But missing the lazy confidence that was so much a part of him now; no nineteen-year-old was that at ease with himself. "Bartending in paradise. Dream job for a nineteen-year-old."

"It was." There was a rhythm to his work—dunk, swish, set aside—that said he'd done that thousands of times. "Had a helluva good time, too."

The mother in her had to ask. "Too much?"

"I don't know about *that*." She could hear the smile in his voice. "But after a while it sort of wears off. Plus I got tired of waking up feeling like crap. So I stopped."

"How long ago was that?"

"I don't know. Five years ago, maybe?"

He said it like it was no big deal. He was so relaxed, unhurried. She wondered if it was the island that had done that to him. Or if he'd always been like this and that's what had drawn him here in the first place. "Would you like some help?"

He glanced over his shoulder, his brows lifted in surprise. "You want to help?"

"What? Nobody's offered to help before?"

"Not with the dishes."

"It's about time, then."

He considered. "Letting a customer help clean up the bar? They'd fire me if they found out."

"One of the house rules?" She picked up the flower and twirled it between her thumb and forefinger. "No drinking up the profits, no fraternizing with the guests, no letting the guests behind the bar?"

"We can fraternize with the guests," he said. "In fact, it's downright encouraged."

Encouraged? She didn't think she wanted to know how they did that. Hand out bonuses for how many customers they sent away *happy*? "Oh, come on." She got up and came around the bar. "I've been away from the kids for fifteen whole hours. I've got to clean up after somebody. I'm going into withdrawal."

He chuckled. "I still shouldn't—"

"You get caught every time you break the rules, too?"

"I do not," he said, insulted. "I *never* get caught. Unless I want to."

"Then let me help. You have to be more than ready to go home. You served a zillion people tonight." She grabbed a towel with one hand, a wet glass with another. "I'll dry."

"You're the guest. Suit yourself."

She quickly fell into the rhythm of it, working side by side with Jake in the gentle night. He didn't even have background music on, she realized, surprised; most of the young people she knew lived their lives to a soundtrack.

But his whole working hours were filled with noise: laughter and music and voices. The quiet was probably a nice change.

It was the most fun she'd had since she'd landed, she realized, and wasn't that kind of a sad thing? Jill would be horribly disappointed in her.

But that was exactly what she'd always hated about dating: the tension, the trying to impress, attempting to find the right thing to say. This was so much more relaxing, her only task to make sure the glasses were streak-free, no need to be charming and witty and attentive. No wondering if the person across the table from her found her attractive or if she felt the same about him.

"You sure you don't want a job?" Jake asked. "You're awfully good at that."

"I do want a job, actually. But probably not this one." She'd surveyed her neat rows of clean glasses with satisfaction. "Somehow I don't think Sizzle's the best place to raise teenagers."

"They'd have a good time."

"I'm sure they would." She shuddered at the thought. "I can't imagine what your mother thought when you ran off here at nineteen."

"Honestly? I think she was glad to be rid of me."

"I can tell you're not a parent."

"It's not that she doesn't *like* me." He dunked the last of the glasses in the water, and Ellen couldn't help but be a bit disappointed that they were almost finished. She'd gotten way too used to taking care of people, she reflected; she didn't know what to do when she couldn't help. "But I was kind of wild when I was a teenager."

"Surprise, surprise."

"Hey!" He handed her the last two tumblers. His fingers, slick with soapy water, brushed hers. "I wasn't that bad."

"Mmm-hmm."

He turned to scrub down the bar. "Anyway, I think she figured I'd get in less trouble here than in Philly. No cars to crash, no cops to drag me home."

"Was she right? That you'd get in less trouble here?"

"Depends upon your definition of trouble."

She had little doubt that, by her definition, he'd gotten himself in plenty.

"You want me to do the tables?"

"You really don't have to—"

"Too late." She grabbed a cloth and ran it under the water before moving to the first table.

"You're sure going to have a lot of stories about your wild times on Sizzle," he said.

"I've got six days left." There was a sticky footprint right in the middle of the table, and the scars from a whole lot of high heels.

"If you make the same progress every day that you did on this one, you might be up to cleaning the toilets by day five."

"Hey! Don't knock it if you haven't tried it."

"I'll pass." He lined bottles up behind the bar, replacing those that were almost empty. "Guess what Sizzle used to be called."

"It wasn't always Sizzle?"

"Oh, no. It was originally called Lizard Cay, but the bosses didn't think it sounded hot enough. First thing they did when they bought a scrubby little island was start planting palms and hauling in sand. Second was renaming it."

"You're ruining my romantic notions."

"Weren't they ruined already?"

She straightened, the damp cloth in her hand, and found him watching her seriously, as if her answer mattered.

"Oh. You're not done yet."

Ellen turned. A woman of about twenty-five teetered into Heat, clad in nothing but a sliver of a bikini bottom and a loose, completely sheer shirt that did nothing to hide the breasts that she must have paid a fortune for—and she'd definitely gotten her money's worth. Her heels were so high Ellen couldn't imagine how she'd navigated the path in the dark, her hair was dark and tumbling around her shoulders, and her lip gloss was so shiny it looked as if her mouth had been coated in glass.

"Not yet," Jake said.

"Oh." The woman pursed her lips, then moved toward the bar, into the stronger light, and Ellen wondered where they'd hidden the scars; she couldn't find them, and the shirt sure didn't disguise a thing.

Jake barely glanced at her, as if half-naked women wandering into his bar were an everyday occurrence. And maybe it was, though Ellen couldn't believe very many of them looked like this one.

"She can finish, can't she?" She jerked her chin toward Ellen.

Jake ripped open a cardboard box and started loading bottles of beer into the half refrigerator beneath the stainless back counter. "She doesn't work here."

"Oh." The woman put her hands on her hips and looked Ellen up and down, appraising. She frowned, puzzled, and then sashayed to the end of the bar. As if she thought that, if Jake got a better look at his options, he clearly wouldn't be making such a ridiculous choice. "I was hoping you'd walk me home." She rose to her toes, put her forearms on the bar, and leaned over. It would have given Jake one hell of a view, if he'd bothered to look. "I promise I'll reward you properly for the escort," she purred.

Ellen would sound like an idiot if she'd said something like that, she mused, if she could even get it out without laughing.

Glass clinked as Jake just kept transferring beer to the fridge. "Appreciate the offer," Jake said. "But it's going to take me a while. I couldn't ask you to wait."

"I wouldn't mind," the woman said.

Jake straightened and shut the fridge door, giving the woman an impassive look. "I would."

She must have practiced that pout. That offended walk, too, as she clicked her way across the floor, her round butt jiggling in the bottom that was not technically a thong, but only technically.

Curious, Ellen threw the damp towel over her shoulder and moved to the bar.

"That happen often?" she asked.

"Pretty often." Jake shrugged and started breaking down the box. "Some people who come to Sizzle consider it a personal challenge never to go back to their rooms alone. If they don't like the pickings among the guests, sometimes they come back here to see if they'll have better luck."

Ellen would be willing to wager that most of them weren't quite such an achievement of nature and science, however. She felt bad if her presence had gotten in Jake's way.

"You could have gone." She folded up the towel into a neat square. "I could have finished up."

He slid the box into a narrow space behind the garbage can. "I'm done, anyway. Thanks for the help."

"Done?" she asked in surprise.

"Ellen, if I'd have wanted to go, I'd have gone."

"Oh. That's good." She wondered if it happened so often that the novelty had worn off. She wanted to ask questions, a zillion of them she had no business asking. But she was curious. How often did he go? How did he decide when to, when not to? Did he ever really fall for one, had his heart broken when a guest left? Or did he always look forward to the next arrivals?

"Time to go home." He snagged a shirt from a shelf and shrugged into it, leaving it hanging open. "Thanks for the help."

"Home." They were probably done in the pool by now. Probably. "Um . . . could you show me which way to go?"

"The same way you came."

"Well, actually . . ." He gave her a strange look, surprise and confusion.

She realized in horror that he thought she was angling for him to take her home. As if she'd succeed where Miss DD and Not Afraid to Show It hadn't.

"No! God, no. It's just . . ." She sighed. "There were people in the pool."

"So? You just . . ." Comprehension dawned. "Oh, Charlie hates it when they do that. Now he's going to have to shock the pool tomorrow morning."

He rounded the end of the bar. "Come on. There's another route. I'll walk you home."

"I couldn't ask you to do that. If you'd just point out the path, I'm sure I'll be fine."

"I'm supposed to be taking good care of you, remember?" The skin was paler around his eyes where his sunglasses had shielded it, but his eyes were still that brutal blue. "Besides, there's no guarantee that you won't stumble across somebody that way, either. I promise to cover your eyes if necessary."

"This really is a full-service resort, isn't it?" She fell comfortably in step beside him.

No matter what his mother thought, she decided, he really was a very nice young man.

17

Liftoff

SHE woke up late and starving.

Eleven, her watch said. She blinked and brought it closer to her eyes.

Yup, eleven. She hadn't slept that late since college.

She contemplated rolling over and going back to sleep. It was the best use she could think of for her time on Sizzle. Why run around looking for a lover when you could *sleep*?

But her stomach wasn't cooperating.

Breakfast or lunch. She pondered that pleasant dilemma for a while before she lifted the phone and asked for an omelet. She was ordering hangover food, and she didn't even have a hangover.

She'd just finished her shower when the knock came on the door.

"Oh, good. Food." The young man had dreadlocks that fell to a lovely set of shoulders, a crisp white shirt, and a tray that held a silver dome and a spray of purple orchids. "I am very happy to see you."

"Sizzling nights make for hungry mornings."

"Do they beat you all if you don't work the word *sizzle* into every guest conversation?"

"We get to work here. It's worth sounding like an idiot now and then."

"Is being gorgeous a requirement for working here, too?"

His smile broadened. "It's in the water." He lowered his voice as if sharing a dark secret. "I had no teeth, hair on my back, and the body of a panda when I started."

"I'm never going home."

"I hear that a lot." He held out the tray to her, and it smelled like heaven. "Do you want your breakfast in or out?"

She glanced around the spare room, wondering where she was supposed to eat.

"There's a table beneath the bed. Pops right up," he told her.

"They think of everything, don't they?"

"We try."

Then she caught glimpses of the ocean behind him, the sunshine that poured through the lush leaves overhead. "But I think I'll go with outside."

"Good choice."

There was a tiny veranda in front of the cottage, shaded by twining vines that bloomed with white flowers the size of dimes. He set up her plate, a small pitcher of juice, a snow-white napkin.

Then he reached in his pocket and handed her an envelope. "This e-mail came for you last night—"

"You have e-mail here?" She snatched it with the greed of a chocaholic who'd sighted Godiva. "Internet? Computers? Where? Why didn't anybody tell me?"

"We try not to let the guests know." He adjusted the orchids in a slender silver vase. "It's in the office. It's mostly for staff use. Guests can be reached in care of the resort."

"This is very archaic of you all. What kind of resort doesn't have a business center?"

"A resort that people come to to get away from their regular business." Apparently satisfied with the look of the table, he straightened. "Is there anything else I can do for you?"

"You must get really interesting answers to that question sometimes," she said. "But no, this looks wonderful."

"Have a lovely day."

"I'll do my best."

The e-mail was from Jill, and it was short and to the point.

Two questions:
1) Did you wear the bikini yet?
2) Did you have sex yet?
The answers better be yes by the time you get home. You don't want to know what I'll put you through if the answers are no. And don't even think about lying, because I'll know. You know I'll know.

Dropped by Tom's unexpectedly to check on the kids for you. They're good. Eating way too much pizza and McDonald's, but they'll survive. They said he's been working a lot. I'll just bet he is.

Well, nobody ever accused Jill of being subtle.

She would have loved Sizzle. And she wouldn't have spent her night washing dishes with a bartender, either. Unless she was doing it naked.

Which sounded way better than it should have.

* * *

AT four o'clock, Ellen realized she really didn't know how to be exciting.

After brunch, she'd tried an exercise class. The class was held in an open-air room, the thatched roof held up by silver metal poles. The instructor was certainly fit, in tiny briefs and a strip across her breasts and . . . high heels?

"All right, ladies. Ready to let out your inner vixen?"

Ladies? There were plenty of men in the crowd. No doubt word had gotten around about the instructor.

But then the men all moved to the side of the floor, sitting in chairs they'd dragged from the pool or plopping right down on the ground.

Maybe she'd come to the wrong place. She'd stumbled into some kind of mixer, some game, instead of an exercise class.

"All right, ladies. I'm Angie. I'm from Las Vegas."

The men applauded from the sidelines.

This wasn't looking promising. Ellen exercised wearing as many clothes as she could without being mistaken for an athletic nun. Whenever possible she deliberately chose times when there were few men around, and they were too serious about their workout to notice her.

"You all ready to sweat?" the instructor called out, earning a rousing "Yes," both from the men on the side and the women on the floor.

Ellen didn't belong here, something she was becoming more and more certain of. The other women, even those who didn't look like they spent much time exercising, seemed perfectly comfortable in their tight shorts and cropped tanks. She'd chosen her outfit for comfort: loose nylon shorts that came almost to her knee and an oversize T-shirt that her father had bought her in Branson. It hid what she wanted to hide, she could move in it, and it was safely anonymous.

Except her clothes stood out by virtue of being made of more fabric than a hanky. The other women smiled at the spectators, maneuvering for good visibility. Ellen tried to find the most inconspicuous corner and edged her way there.

They cued the music, something with a heavy bass and a mesmerizing rhythm.

"All right, girls, let's get warmed up."

Angie planted her feet shoulder width apart, rocking her pelvis back and forth in a sinuous movement more suited to a bedroom than an exercise class.

Ellen turned to run. And then the voices flashed inside her head. Jill's: *Cluck cluck cluck*. Tom's: *See? No heat*.

What the hell. One glance at the audience proved that nobody was looking at her, anyway. They were all completely transfixed by Angie.

With good reason. Hips weren't made to move like that.

Ellen tried gamely, bumping back and forth, feeling awkward and graceless.

Crap. She could dance. She just couldn't do *that*.

"Okay, ladies. Now circle!" Angie's hips transcribed a sinuous path. Heck, *Ellen* could hardly keep from looking at her. She didn't blame the men at all. "Forward, side, back, forward."

Okay, this wasn't so bad. Forward, back—no, side. Forward, side, back . . .

If she didn't look at anyone else, if she just listened to the music, she could almost believe she was getting the hang of it.

"Now a little shoulder shimmy, ladies!"

She heard the collective intake of breath from the watching men as Angie's sports bra nearly failed in its duty. Or maybe staying on was the wardrobe malfunction.

What muscles were they supposed to be working? These were not the usual arm circles and crossover right.

Shaking her assets like that was not something she ever imagined doing in public.

Loosen up, Ellen. Juice time.

Ellen could only hope that her voice haunted her children as effectively as Jill's haunted her.

She tried a little shimmy. Nothing terrible happened; her boobs stayed in her bra, and it didn't even hurt. Her shoulders felt looser. She shook again, with more enthusiasm this time. *Look at me, Jill. I'm loosening up.*

"Excellent." Angie sauntered forward, a sultry smile on her face. "Now, ladies, grab your stripper pole and get ready to find your inner temptress." She seized the nearest pole and leaped in the air, her legs scissoring around it, and spun twice. The men erupted into cheers.

This time, Ellen did turn and run.

* * *

SHE took a hike instead, a pleasantly solitary one, along a well-marked path with cute signs shaped like starfish that told her the names of the plants she passed. She did not run into one single copulating couple, and she counted that a major plus.

She spent the rest of the afternoon in her hammock, with a

big fat thriller set on the mean streets of New York. Lots of blood, a creepy killer who met a satisfyingly horrible end.

It was, she thought, pretty much her perfect afternoon. And not at all what she'd come here for.

She didn't *have* to have sex, she reminded herself. But shouldn't she at least be exploring the possibility? She hadn't had sex in four months, not since she'd learned of Tom's affairs. Shouldn't she *miss* it? Was she going to let him take it from her, too?

Obviously he was having plenty of it.

"Well. You look comfortable."

She opened her eyes to find Bobby standing beside her hammock, looking at her like she was the best thing he'd seen all day. "I am," she said. "You got some sun."

"You didn't." He tipped back his cowboy hat. "Don't you want to go back to Minnesota and make everybody jealous that you've been someplace warm?" He grinned. "I checked the weather for you this mornin'. It was ten below in Minneapolis."

"Oh, Lord, get me to the sun."

"That's why I'm here." He put his hands on his hips. He wore a loose A&M T-shirt over a baggy swimsuit printed with orange hibiscus flowers. "How adventurous are you feeling today?"

Adventurous and *Ellen* were not two words that had ever been used in conjunction with each other. It wasn't even something she'd ever *wanted* to be. She'd taken her study abroad in London, for heaven's sake, while her friends ran off to places like Ghana and Istanbul.

And suddenly she felt bad about all those things she'd missed out on. What had she been thinking, being so careful all those years?

She'd been thinking too much, that's what she'd been thinking.

"Damned adventurous," she told him. Right before she fell out of the hammock.

* * *

"PLEASEDONTLETMECRASH, *pleasedontletmecrash, pleasedontletmecrash.*"

Baby steps, she'd told herself at first. She'd put on the bikini, so she could at least tell Jill she'd worn it, but then she'd thrown a big white T-shirt over it. Sun protection wasn't being over-cautious, she consoled herself; it was just good sense.

But then Bobby had taken her to the bay where a long, sleek yellow boat waited.

"Parasailing?" Her throat closed so fast she was afraid she'd squeaked. "You want me to go parasailing?"

"Sure." His face glowed. "Always wanted to."

"You did see me on that airplane, didn't you?"

"Yup." He grew serious. "Confront your fears, Ellen, and face them down. It's the only way to make them smaller instead of lettin' them grow."

Darn. It sounded like something she would have said to her children. In fact, she was pretty sure she had. Nothing like shov-ing her own advice back into her face. "Okay," she said. "But you go first."

It did look kind of fun. At least, Bobby sure seemed to be en-joying it, whooping as he went higher and higher behind the boat.

"You ready to try it?" His name was Matt, and she couldn't tag his background—he could have walked into half of the countries in the world and looked at home. His long dark hair was tied back, his dark blue surf shorts hung low on his narrow hips, and he handled the gear with supreme confidence.

"Tell me the truth," she said. "I'm a mother, so I'll know if you're lying. Have you ever lost one up there?"

"Okay, I'll tell you the truth," he said soberly, and her stom-ach started to churn. "I've never lost anyone who didn't want to be lost."

"That's good." Though she'd almost rather he'd said yes; that'd give her a good excuse. "Are you *sure?*"

"If it'll hold him up"—he nodded at Bobby, who was clearly having the time of his life for all that he looked like a Macy's pa-rade balloon—"I'm pretty sure it'll hold you."

"Okay." She sucked in a deep breath, blew it out slowly. "Okay. Let's do it."

Matt signaled to the boat's driver and hauled Bobby in. It looked easy, a slow drift toward earth, and Bobby was crestfallen when his feet hit the platform.

"Done already?" he asked.

"Man, I gave you twice as long a ride as usual."

"You could go again," Ellen suggested. "Since you obviously hated coming in."

"Oh, no," they said together. "You're getting up there."

The straps cut into her thighs, pressed in all sorts of places that were tender.

"You comfortable?" Matt asked her, tugging on the band that smashed her breasts into something less than an A cup.

"Not a bit, but don't you dare loosen a thing." She wriggled, testing whether there was any chance she was going to slip out of something. "You're sure they're tight enough?"

"I'm sure."

"Don't laugh at me."

"Not laughing. And you're gonna love this."

"You can do it, Ellen," Bobby said encouragingly.

"Okay," Ellen said. "Let's get this over with."

"This is what I live for," Matt said. "Basking in our guests' enthusiasm."

"I'm not shaking in the corner of the boat," Ellen told him. "Enthusiasm's asking a lot of me."

"You're going to love it," he said. "I can always tell."

"Let's do it."

"It'll help if you breathe," he said. "You remember the signals, right?"

She nodded. Not at all, actually. But she remembered the one for *down*, and she figured that was all she was ever going to need.

"Fire her up!"

She felt the breeze against her face, strengthening steadily.

"I don't think it's working," she shouted over the roar of the boat engine. She was *not* too heavy for this, darn it. She was *not*.

Her feet lifted off the platform, so gently she almost didn't feel it at first. Then she slammed her eyes shut and started praying.

Her stomach lifted into her throat.

If she threw up, it was going to be the most embarrassing moment of her life. And there was no way Bobby would *ever* want to have sex with her. Not that she'd decided that she wanted to have sex with him.

The straps were creeping up her butt, wedging her bikini bottom between her cheeks. That really couldn't be a flattering view from below, she realized suddenly. She hadn't taken that into consideration.

It didn't feel as fast as she had expected. It felt more like she was drifting, a lazy float. Matt must be taking it easy on her. She probably wasn't more than twenty feet from the water.

She heard shouting and opened her eyes in reflex.

"Oh my God!"

She was *way* high. Had to be higher than Bobby had been, way to the end of that rope. A rope that now appeared thin and fragile as a thread, stretching in a gentle arc all the way down to the boat, which from this distance looked about three inches long.

She'd make the signal for bringing her down, as soon as she could pry her frozen fingers from around the straps.

She could see Bobby standing on the boat, his feet spread wide. He gave her an enthusiastic, two-handed thumbs-up.

Don't scream. She bit down, hard, and wondered if she should close her eyes again. A gull wheeled by, screeching. And then she looked, really looked, around her.

God, but it was gorgeous. The blue sweep of the sky, the saturated blue green of the ocean. The sun dazzled them both. Other islands dotted the horizon, some big and deep green, others small and sandy. A big sailboat wheeled around one of them, its sails fiercely white.

She was flying. Flying! Imagine that. She'd been so careful to keep her feet on the ground that she'd no idea how it good it felt to let go.

Too soon, Matt started to reel her in. Her feet barely touched down before she started to move.

"Wait!" he said. "I've got to get you unstrapped."

"When can I go again?"

"I take it you liked it?" She was grinning like a fool and didn't care. "Tomorrow, if you want. If the wind stays down."

"Great!" The instant she was free from the contraption she hugged him. He staggered, then laughed and hugged her back.

"Hey! What about me?"

Bobby spread his hands wide, and she launched herself at him. "Thank you for making me do that!"

"For a while there I thought you were going to kill me when you got down."

"For a while I was." Her skin tingled, warm from the sun and the exhilaration. "I can't believe I never tried it before. The kids wanted to, in Cancun. But I thought it was too dangerous."

"In Mexico, it might have been," Matt said. "You didn't have me to take care of things."

"I'll tell everyone. If you want to try it, you just come down here and find Matt."

"You do that." He stowed away the gear, then took over at the boat's controls. "You ready to go home?"

"Nope," she said. "I'm never going home."

"I'll get you a job," he said. "No problem. Can always use another pretty lady around here." He shifted into gear, and the boat took off, skimming over the waves.

Ellen sat high, letting the wind whip her hair, craning her neck to view everything she could. Her mouth tasted of salt from the spray they kicked up, and she grinned all the way in.

Oh, she'd miss her kids soon enough, undoubtedly before her time on Sizzle was up. But she wasn't missing her life, that safe, narrow space she'd lived in for so long.

She could do anything when she got back home.

She could fly.

18

Maybe Not

HER newfound adventurousness was tested the instant her feet hit the beach.

"I'm hungry," Ellen told Bobby. "Would you like to have dinner with me?"

She thought it was brave of her, asking him if he wanted to join her. She didn't think he would say no, not really, but still . . . for Ellen it was a risk. She'd skipped every single Sadie Hawkins dance in high school rather than work up her courage to invite a boy.

"Sure." He'd taken her arm to help her from the boat, and his hand slid down, gliding over bare skin. "How about we have room service in my cottage?"

Her stomach lurched, just like it had the instant before her feet had left the boat's platform.

"I . . . I thought you said you could be patient?"

"This is patient," he said. "I've been patient for hours. We've only got a few more days."

"A few more days," she repeated. If someone was pushing Katie like this, Ellen would advise her to turn and run. "What if I say 'not yet'?"

"Do you know when 'yet' is?"

At least he didn't seem upset by her answer. Not happy, but then she didn't really want him to be happy about her putting him off again. In fact, he should be horribly disappointed. "No, I don't know when 'yet' is."

"Well." He squinted off at the ocean, then blew out a sigh.

Then he leaned over and kissed her, good and hard, until she was breathless. "I guess I'll just have to try and move that 'yet' up a little."

"That's a good answer." Her stomach fluttered. She didn't know why—it could have been passion, could have been fear, could have been nerves. All she knew was she felt alive in a way she hadn't in a very long time. As if there were possibilities all around her, and it was only up to her to choose them.

And there was one big possibility right in front of her, one with strong arms and broad shoulders. He'd given her a gift today in encouraging her to take a chance. And in wanting her. On an island of women who would have said *yes* instead of *not yet*, he'd chosen her, wanted her.

She was flattered. And interested. And it went against a lifetime of caution to just plunge right in.

But sometimes you just had to. Being careful, studying every angle . . . did it really help? Had she made better decisions, protected herself so well? Maybe. But there'd been disaster anyway. Even worse, what had she missed out along the way?

Maybe not much. Maybe a whole lot.

Maybe sometimes, you just had to make the leap. Strap on that parasail, let your feet lift off the earth.

"Bobby?"

"Huh?"

"It's 'yet.'"

* * *

IT didn't take her long to figure out she was too scared to be excited.

Bobby did everything right. Oh, he hustled her down the path to his cottage, but he held her hand firmly the entire way, stopping twice to press her up against a tree and kiss her until her breath was coming fast and her heart was pounding.

His cottage was set farther back from the ocean than hers, tucked into a grove of sea grape trees with orange-flowering vines climbing up the veranda poles.

"Here we go." He unlocked the door, stepped aside for her to enter. There was no hesitancy in his manner, no hint that he was troubled by any nerves or reservations.

In some ways it had been easier with Joe, when he'd been as uncertain as she. But that hadn't worked out the way that either of them had planned, though the end result was an unexpected friendship that they both valued.

It should have been reassuring that it seemed so easy for Bobby. That he knew exactly what to do, what steps to take. But there was something that seemed a little . . . practiced about it.

It was just nerves, Ellen told herself. Of course she had nerves. She hadn't ever expected to find herself in this situation. Had never *liked* this situation, even back when she had expected to be in it.

She took a deep breath and stepped into the cottage.

She focused on the details of his room, letting it fill her mind instead of the doubts. It was a twin of hers, faint shades of watery green breaking up the brisk white.

The bed—*oh, don't look at the bed.*

Of course, she looked at the bed. And the room started to spin. *Don't look at the bed.*

A sleek silver laptop rested on his side table, out of place in the simple room.

"A computer! For shame. I didn't think working was allowed."

"Shh." He put his finger on her mouth, and she jumped. She couldn't get used to the idea that such casual contact was allowed, that he could touch her so freely, that she'd given him that license. "You're not going to tell on me, are you?"

"Maybe," she said, and felt the roughness of his fingers against her lips when they moved. He had big hands, and his natural body temperature had to be a couple of degrees higher than hers.

He lowered his head until his mouth was so close she felt the current of his breath with every word. "I guess I'll have to make certain you're very happy with me, then, so you won't narc me out."

"You'd better." It was the right answer, but instead of sounding seductive, she had to force the words out.

"I'd better go rinse off." He drew his finger down, over her neck, right between her breasts, until it hovered just north of her belly. Ellen went rigid, willing herself not to move. "Don't forget where we were."

"I won't." As if it was possible for her to forget. She was hyperalert, so that each breath was nearly painful. If there were a sudden sound, a sudden move, she'd jump right out of her skin.

She didn't move until she heard him start up the shower. He was singing something—oh, Lord, Rod Stewart, in a surprisingly rich baritone.

Close the windows, she decided. It'd be easier if it was dimmer in the room; it was asking too much of her to have her do this in full light.

And it was probably asking too much of herself for her to relax and enjoy it. It just wasn't her pattern. She hadn't slept with someone new in over twenty years. Of course she was anxious—okay, scared to death. Of course it felt weird. An orgasm was probably not a possibility, no matter how skilled and experienced Bobby was.

It was a good thing she decided to go ahead and do this now. Maybe she'd have some fun by the end of the week.

She went over and closed the shutters, fastening the simple hook and eye, and the room darkened. Went quieter, too; the sound of the sea was barely perceptible.

She looked wildly around the room for something, anything, to keep her from thinking any more. If she thought any more, she was going to pass out. And while in some ways that would be much easier, if she was going to have an affair, she'd like to remember it, one way or the other.

The computer tempted her. Spider Solitaire had gotten her through many a night in the last few months, when she couldn't sleep and was too unsettled to even read.

She smiled, imagining Bobby's reaction if he came out of the shower and found her playing on his computer. He was probably expecting her to be naked, spread out on the bed, waiting for him.

Don't think about that.

She brushed her fingers over the edge of the computer. There was a metal plate attached. Engraved. She leaned over, squinted at it in the dim light.

Robert McCracken. Price Waterhouse. If found, contact . . .

"Hey." Bobby sauntered out of the bedroom, scrubbing at his hair with a towel. He was wearing another one around his waist—thank heaven for small favors; she wasn't ready for him in all his naked glory.

"Who's Robert McCracken?"

"What?" His gaze flicked to the computer and back to her.

"Robert McCracken." She indicated the computer. "The guy whose computer that is."

He lowered the towel and held it fisted at his side. Then he shrugged, too casually. "My partner. We've got a big project kicking off when I get back; I had to go over the plans. My computer crapped out before I left, so he . . ." He trailed off as Ellen shook her head.

"All right." He dropped the towel on the bed and came around the end of it, toward her. "When I'm on Sizzle I always use another name, another hometown."

He was almost naked, and he was standing too close for comfort. She took a step back. "You lie."

"I don't know if I'd call it *lying*." He drew out the word. "Technically, I suppose, but I was just bein' careful. I don't want somebody trackin' me down when I get home." His voice softened. "Not unless I want 'em to."

"Worried about somebody going *Fatal Attraction* on you?"

"Well, yeah." His smile was disarming. She wondered if he practiced. "I'm no Michael Douglas, but . . ." He laid his palm against her neck, rubbing gently. "Wouldn't hurt you to be careful, either."

"I appreciate your concern." *You cheating bastard.* She knocked his hand away. "How stupid do you think I am? You're married."

He opened his mouth—to lie again, she was sure—and then shrugged, as if it was too much bother. "So?"

Violence whipped through her, the adrenaline making her skin burn.

"Price Waterhouse," she said. "An accountant, not a big-time contractor."

"Women don't find accounting all that fascinating."

"Imagine that." If there'd been anything within reach, she would have pitched it at him. "What is it about you football players? This is the second time—" She caught the flash of guilt on his face. "No Texas A&M."

"Miami of Ohio."

"No football."

"I won the regional chess championship."

"Oh, Lord. You're a geek."

"People always expect men my size to play football," he said defensively. "I just go along with them."

"You know what? I would have liked you better as the geek." Did she have a special gift for picking out assholes, or was that all there was out there? "No Dallas."

"Indianapolis—" He frowned. "You are *not* calling my wife."

It hadn't, until right that second, occurred to her. "She deserves to know."

Anger called color to his face, tension to his jaw. "What gives you the right to be so fucking high and mighty? It's not as if you're not married, too."

That stopped her. He'd known she was lying from the first. "It's complicated."

"I'll just bet it is," he said, self-satisfaction making his tone smug, his mouth a smirk.

"And he knows I'm here."

"Really?" Suddenly fascinated, Robert plopped down on the bed, settling in for a chat. "How's that work? I've always wondered. Because if I thought my wife would go along—"

"Arghh!" She snatched up his laptop and sprinted out the door.

19

Technically Speaking

SHE ended up at Heat again.

Her first instinct had been to run back to her cottage and burrow under the covers until it was time to go back to civilization. But what would be the use of that? She'd only be miserable, lonely and angry, and convinced that every man in the world was a philandering jerk.

They weren't *all* jerks. The law of averages said so.

Just most of them.

But moping in her room wasn't going to do any good. She knew herself well enough to know that once she got there, she wouldn't be going out again.

If anything, the bar was livelier than it was the night before. The steamy air, heavy with the threat of rain, trapped the heat of all those dancing bodies, all those lusting people, beneath the tin roof.

There was an open seat at the end of the bar. She took it, watching the dance go around her. Approach and retreat. Overtures, flirtation, rejection. Acceptance.

She couldn't tell if it was just about the juice—the heat. Did they crave excitement, or simply not want to be alone?

Obviously most of them were propelled by a drive that she simply didn't have, and she was no longer sure if that was a good or bad thing. Tom thought she was broken. Jill believed she was pathologically careful. They were the people who knew her best.

"Where's your friend?"

She glanced over her shoulder at Jake. He looked the same as the night before: baggy board shorts, beat-up leather sandals, a tangle of cords around his neck.

"Do you own any real clothes?"

He glanced down at himself. "These aren't real clothes?"

"You know. Shirts, pants, shoes. Things that you can't wear while jumping in the ocean."

"What would be the point?"

"The whole world can't live on the beach, you know."

"Why not?"

Why not, indeed. She struggled for a reason, scowled when she couldn't come up with a good one. "Don't you have work to do?"

"If somebody wants a drink, they'll let me know." He nodded to the line of shot glasses on the bar, a neat double row of neon colors. "This'll keep 'em busy for a while. They'll holler if they want anything else."

A redhead in a fishnet tunic and little else grabbed a glass— one watermelon pink, one lime green—in each hand and, tipping her head back, downed them one after another. She held them aloft in triumph as the half-dozen men around her cheered.

"So. Tell me all your troubles." He planted his palms on the bar, claiming his kingdom, and gave her his complete attention. "You seem to have lost the Sizzle spirit."

"Did I ever have it?" She grabbed the nearest shot glass and held it up to the light. It was an intense, unnatural blue, like blue raspberry Kool-Aid.

"You gonna find it there?" There was no judgment in the question, merely curiosity.

She nodded at the people dancing and laughing under the twinkle lights. "Seems to be working for them."

"Seems to," he agreed, but something in his voice indicated that he was no more convinced than she. "So. Where *is* your friend?"

"He's not my friend." She sniffed at the glass and nearly reeled. "As to where he is, the last time I saw him he was in the swimming pool."

"Uh-oh. You drinking your courage so you can join him?"

"God, no." She sipped at the drink, shuddered at the taste of it, undiluted alcohol mixed with corn syrup. "Actually, I believe he's trying to fish out his computer."

"You going to tell me how that got there?"

"It flew." Better to take it all at once, she decided. Like medicine. She tipped her head back.

No, not better. She pounded at her chest as the liquid burned its way to her stomach.

"You okay?"

"Yes." Then she thought better of it. "No. Give me something to kill the taste. Something that doesn't taste like gasoline mixed with Jell-O."

"I could be insulted by that." He pulled down a mug that must hold a gallon and reached for the soda spigots.

"I don't think your talent as a bartender is the point of those things." She took a careful sip of the drink he set before her and sighed in relief when she realized it was simply Diet Coke. Her one true vice, and she tried not to feel bad about that.

"No. It's not." There were only a couple of shot glasses left, so he reached beneath the bar and started pulling out empty ones, four at a time. "You gonna tell me or not?"

"He's married."

"Yeah." He started pouring rainbow liquids, all from lovely, curved bottles with silver labels that made the shots seem a lot more classy than they tasted.

"You knew?"

"Sure."

She reached across the bar and gave him a whack across his shoulder. "Why didn't you *tell* me?"

"Some women like the bad ones."

Hell. She hadn't a clue what was going on out there in hookup land.

"Me?" she asked. "*I* seem like the kind of woman who has a bad boy complex?"

"I don't know." He nodded at the signal of a man down the

bar, then pulled out two bottles of Kalik and expertly popped the caps. "Lime?" he asked. The man shook his bald head, and Jake sent the beer sliding toward him. "Not really, no. But some people come to Sizzle to shake out of their comfort zone."

Across the dance floor two men nearly came to blows over a shrieking woman in a shrunken coral halter dress. Finally one tossed her over his shoulder and charged into the trees. "They all look damned comfortable to me."

"You really didn't know he was married?" He reached beneath the bar again and placed a platter of sliced fruit and cheese before her.

"What's this?"

"Did you eat dinner?"

"Well, no, but—"

"Then eat."

Her stomach rumbled. She hadn't, until right that minute, realized she was starving. She hadn't eaten since breakfast. They'd brought sandwiches along on the boat, but she'd been too terrified to eat. And dinner . . . well, dinner hadn't happened.

She popped a piece of pineapple in her mouth, pure sweetness in a thin yellow slice. "Why does anybody drink that stuff when you can eat this instead?"

"'Cause you don't get a buzz off of fruit."

"Speak for yourself." She tried a chunk of mango next, and it tasted like sunshine. "No, I really didn't know," she admitted.

He shook his head. "How'd you make it this far without developing any instincts toward self-preservation?"

"I was married."

"Ah." He nodded, as if that made complete sense. "Next time you decide to, ah, make a friend, why don't you run 'em past me first?"

"Oh, yeah, that sounds like a good plan. Let the bartender pick out my 'friends.'" She tried a slice of hard, white cheese, very sharp, with a strong and earthy tang on her tongue.

"Because you've got such good track record doing it yourself."

"Hey!" She tried to work up enough outrage to protest.

Shouldn't she want to protest? But obviously she didn't have the instincts for such things. "It's tricky out there in the single world. Almost worth staying married to avoid it."

"You're still married?"

Someone hollered from the far end of the bar.

"Hang on just a second, would you?" He moved farther down the counter, dumped ice and squeezed limes into an industrial black and chrome blender.

He was very efficient at his job. He never rushed, and there was none of the flashy bottle-spinning you saw in the movies. Nothing unnecessary, nothing that took attention away from the guests. He seemed to be able to manage a dozen things at once: clean the bar, keep the customers happy, sort out three orders being shouted at him at once, and keep a conversation running at the same time.

Even, she thought as she wrapped a thin slice of prosciutto around an orange crescent of melon, *notice when a guest is about to keel over from hunger and feed her.*

He poured a dozen margaritas into salt-rimmed glasses as big as basketballs sliced in half. He ran his cloth over the bar as he strolled back to her. "Okay, where were we? Oh yeah. Still married."

"You don't have to entertain me. I know you're working."

"I like the challenge."

Maybe part of his job was counseling shaky guests. Or maybe it was just an avocation, something to do when bartending got too easy. "Yeah, I'm still married. Technically speaking."

"Technically speaking. What's technically?"

He either really was interested or putting up a mighty good front. Did it matter which? It was good for her to talk it through, sort through all the paths she'd taken to get here and what she might do about it.

"We're separated."

"On the way to divorce?" His hands kept busy as he talked, plopping blue-cheese-stuffed olives into a martini, hanging a twist of lemon peel off the rim of a sidecar.

"I haven't decided yet." The alcohol must have reached her veins. Her joints felt loose, her mood, mellow. "That's part of why I'm here."

"Any conclusions yet?"

"Nope." The food had been a good idea, too. Good enough that the details came out easily, without any anger twisting her up at the same time. It was just another story. "He cheated on me. Repeatedly and enthusiastically. Claimed it was 'just sex.'"

"Sometimes it is."

"Told me I should have an affair, too. So I'd know that's all it was. So I'd understand why he did it."

His brows shot up. "Okay, that's a new one, even to me."

"Is it? He seemed to think it was perfectly reasonable." She spun on her stool, surveying the crowd. Some of the people were familiar now. The striking blond, who Ellen suspected was actually over fifty but had a *very* good plastic surgeon, was never attended by less than two men at least twenty years younger than she. Good for her.

The swaggering, handsome man who looked like he belonged in Vegas had a different woman on his arm every time she saw him. And there was an entire clutch of thirtysomething women who she'd never seen apart, and who didn't seem to have any interest at all in the men who approached them regularly.

"So you came here to choose a lover."

She winced.

"I don't know how you're going to pick one out if you get that look on your face every time the topic comes up," he said.

"It's just that word."

"What's wrong with that word?"

She considered. She did flinch at the term, but she'd never given much thought to why.

"Maybe," she said slowly, "because I don't want to think about it like that. That there's love involved in it. It doesn't seem much like love to me." He was so easy to talk to. Maybe because, unlike everybody else, he didn't really care what she did. It was strangely comforting.

"Okay. A playmate, then."

"God, no. Makes me think about bunny ears and cottontails."

An exuberant conga line had started and was snaking its way across the floor. And the dancers didn't seem too worried about where the people behind them were putting their hands.

"What do you want to call it, then?"

She wasn't at all sure she wanted to call it—him—anything. "Nothing too personal."

"It's usually a kinda personal thing."

"Okay. Not too impersonal, either."

"This is going to be tough." He chuckled. "You want some help?"

She looked over her shoulder at him. His eyes were direct and friendly. "What, exactly, would your help entail?"

"You show me who you like. I'll tell you if he's trouble or not, since you can't seem to tell by yourself, and you can decide what you want to do about it."

"Oh." Of course that's what he meant. And that was *not* a twinge of disappointment she was feeling. "Are you serious?"

"Full-service bartender, that's me."

But he hadn't been a full-service bartender for crochet girl last night. She wondered why.

"Okay," she agreed. "Can't do any worse than I'm doing on my own."

"All right then." He waved his hand toward the dance floor. "Behold the buffet spread. Plenty to choose from, pick as many or few as you want, whatever suits your fancy."

Her fancy hadn't entered into this at all, as far as she could tell. Which was really kind of sad.

She looked at all those men. Handsome and not, outgoing and shy, every age from twenty-five to sixty-five, from all over the country. And all she felt was tired.

"I'll do it," she said. "But I'm going to need a day to recover first."

20

Off the Pedestal

IF she had to stay in this apartment one more second, Kate was going to go stark raving insane.

The whole situation sucked. She didn't know why Dad had to pick an apartment downtown. It had sounded cool at first, living in the city, way up on the eighteenth floor. She had to admit the view kicked ass. But you could only look at the lights so long.

She'd expected it to be exciting. But Dad wouldn't let her go wandering around alone. He wouldn't even let her go *shopping* alone. All her friends had no way to get downtown. She'd asked Dad to drop her off at the mall for the evening, so she could meet up with Merry and Sarah, but he had to go into the office for a few hours, and he didn't want to leave Eric alone.

As if the brat cared whether she was there or not. Okay, brat was too much. He was half-decent as younger brothers went, didn't bug her too much, pretty much left her stuff alone. Most of her friends' brothers were a lot more annoying.

But Christ, she wished he would do something besides play video games once in a while.

The cheap metal blinds clattered as she dropped them and flopped on the couch. "Could you turn the stupid volume off?"

Eric didn't look her way, just pushed a button until the game went quiet.

"Thanks." She watched for a moment. On the screen a guy who looked like Muhammad Ali in a diaper pounded on a girl dressed in topless ninja gear who had boobs the size of watermelons. And what . . . was that a fairy, fluttering over the tree with a face in the corner? The weirdness knew no bounds. "How about a movie?"

"I've got *Howl's Moving Castle*."

"No!" He liked those Japanese anime things. She tried watching with him once—being the good sister—and she couldn't figure out what the hell it was supposed to be about.

That's what was wrong with staying at Dad's. She didn't have her *stuff*. Her books, her own television, all her clothes to try on, her nail polish. Dad said she could bring more things, but then they would be here when she wanted them at home, and there wasn't really room. She had to share a *room* with Eric, which was just insane, and she didn't want all her things lying around just tempting him to snoop.

Besides, she really hadn't figured Dad would be living here that long. Sooner or later he'd be coming home. He had to. Mom was too sad, and things were too weird. She didn't understand why Mom just didn't take him back already; she was obviously miserable without him. It wasn't like being single was any fun at her age.

Dad had said Kate could buy whatever she needed, but then they were right back to that why-she-couldn't-go-shopping-alone thing.

All she had here was her cell phone. But there was nobody to talk to. Merry and Sarah had gone to the movies. Caleb was off with some of his friends. Partying. Drinking too much. But he'd promised her he wouldn't get totally wasted, and that he wouldn't drive, though he'd laughed and kissed her and told her she'd have to make it worth his while if he was going to behave.

He'd been really sweet lately. Hardly pushed her at all. Sometimes, though, she wondered *why* he wasn't pushing her anymore. Was he getting it someplace else?

"You want something to eat?"

They were supposed to wait for Dad to get back, but it was nearly seven. He'd told them he'd be home by six, but you had to always add at least a half an hour to that. There was always one last phone call, one more person sticking his head in his office and asking for a moment.

She understood. He worked hard, made a lot of money, and she was proud of him. Sometimes he took her to work occasions, family picnics or the suite at the Wolves games, and she could see the way the younger men and women who worked for him looked up to him, almost shoving to get a chance to talk to him, desperately trying to impress him.

She just didn't understand why he didn't take that all into account. It was way worse to expect him and then have him show up late than it was to *know* he wasn't coming home until nine or whatever.

"That'd be great!" Eric said. The kid could eat, no doubt about that. It was so unfair; he ate three times as much as she did, and he never gained any weight at all. The last year or so, she had to be really careful if she wanted to fit into her jeans, which sucked the big one.

"Grilled cheese?" Dad's kitchen wasn't as well-stocked as Mom's, but you could usually count on bread and cheese and butter.

"Sounds good."

"You gonna stop long enough to eat?"

His thumbs moved faster, and one of the figures on the screen exploded in a shower of blood. "I'm in the middle of a battle."

"You should—" She stopped when she realized she was starting to sound like Mom. She hated it when Mom wanted her to stop talking on the phone or whatever so they could have a "civilized" dinner. "You want one or two?"

"Two."

Kate got up and padded toward the kitchen. The doorbell chimed. "What the—" She veered off toward the door. She hadn't buzzed anybody in . . . must be somebody at the wrong apartment. She started to unhook the chain, then remembered that she was supposed to be careful. Mom ranted about that all the time, how she couldn't take her safety for granted, *especially* in the city.

She rose to her toes and peeked through the spy hole.

A woman stood right outside. She wore a blue flight attendant's uniform, and she was tapping her foot impatiently.

She *had* to have the wrong door. Kate debated for a minute, wondering if she should just pretend there was nobody home. But the woman buzzed again, and Kate would hate it if somebody just left her standing out in the hall.

With her mother's warnings in her ear, she left the chain attached and opened the door the few inches it allowed.

"Hey, baby, I—" The woman stopped talking and started frowning.

"Can I help you?"

"Well, aren't you a young one?" She nodded as if she expected nothing else. "Figures. You tell Tommy—"

"He's my *father*," Katie said, horrified that anyone could think anything else.

The woman plastered on a smile that anybody could see was fake. "Oh, yeah. You must be Katie."

She knew her name. Huh.

Katie looked her over good. She supposed the woman was kind of pretty, though it obviously took some work to get there. Her hair was highlighted in pale blond, and she really knew how to use makeup. She had hips that made J.Lo look positively skinny, and that polyester skirt wasn't helping. But hey, some guys liked that.

Though Kate had a really hard time connecting that with her dad. This woman was *nothing* like Mom.

But maybe that's what Dad liked about her.

"Can I come in? Talking through this crack's awkward."

Kate wanted to slam the door in her face.

It wasn't as if she didn't know her dad would date eventually. Mom had kicked him out, and why should he be alone? Served her right if he'd found somebody else already.

But this woman was too fake. She just wasn't . . . classy enough.

"I'm not supposed to let strangers in," Katie said.

"I'm hardly a stranger," the woman said. Her smile remained fixed, but her eyes went hard. "Would I have known your name if Tommy hadn't told me?"

Okay, so she wasn't *entirely* stupid.

Katie unhooked the chain and opened the door. If this one was going to stick around for a while—not likely, she was probably just a rebound chick, but Kate might as well play it safe—it would probably be a good idea to be polite to her.

But she didn't back up to let the woman in.

"Tommy here?"

"Nope." Katie crossed her arms. Again with the *Tommy*. Made it sound like Dad was Eric's age.

"Oh." She pursed her lips; she wasn't afraid of the gloss, that's for sure. "Where is he?" she asked, trying hard to sound casual.

Worried if her dad was out with someone else, was she? Well, she *should* worry.

"I'm not sure."

"Hmm." Her gaze flicked down the hall, as if she wasn't sure whether to believe her. "When's he coming home?"

"I don't know that, either."

"Kate? There somebody here?" Eric called from the living room.

"Nobody you need to worry about," Katie called back. "I'll be right there."

The lady cocked out her big-ass hip and stuck her hand on it. "Look, I suppose you don't have any reason to trust me. But really, he'll be glad to see me. We get together almost every time I'm in town. I'm Tricia. Tricia Wilcox."

"He didn't mention you to me."

Lines furrowed between her brows. Deep ones; she could use some Botox. "I suppose he didn't." The fake smile again. "He didn't know I was coming. I'm based in Atlanta, been flying the routes up and down the East Coast lately. I got pulled in to come to Minneapolis at the last minute because somebody's kid got sick—well, I suppose you don't need to know that."

"No, I don't." Hell. She should never have taken off the chain.

"Anyway. Figured I'd surprise him. Celebrate his new apartment."

"Too bad you missed him." She put her hand on the door, hoping the woman would take the hint.

Wait a minute. Katie's mind churned.

She forced her own smile and hoped she faked it better than Tricia did. "You haven't been to his new apartment yet, huh?"

"No." Tricia looked relieved. "Looks nice, huh?" She craned her neck, trying to sneak a peek into the living room.

"It is nice." Kate edged over to block the view. The last thing she wanted was for Eric to get a look at Tricia. "When'd you meet my Dad?"

"Oh, it's been years." Her eyes went dreamy with nostalgia. "Two? Three? I was on the New York to Paris run." She giggled. "Your dad was in 1B."

"Cute. You remembered." She was gonna puke. She felt it push up in her throat, thick and hot. "Well, I gotta get some dinner."

She pushed on the door until it bumped against the toes of Tricia's ugly blue pumps.

"Wait! Can I leave a note?"

"I'll tell him you stopped by. Promise. Bye, Ms. Wilcox."

"Nice to meet you, Katie!" she chirped.

Kate pushed the door shut and fumbled with the chain, whipping it across as soon as she got it in the slot.

Years. Two, three.

Her head throbbed with it. Years. Her dad had been seeing that woman for years.

Blindly, she dashed through the living room.

"Supper ready?" Eric called.

"Not yet." She swallowed against the thickness in her throat. "I'm not feeling too hot. Gonna see if Dad's got some Advil or something."

She bolted into Dad's bedroom and slammed the door behind her.

He didn't make his bed. She tried not to look at it, the stupid beige cover that looked like it belonged in a cheap motel.

The bedside table was fake cherry. She flicked on the lamp, a vanilla ceramic one shaped like a vase.

Her hand shook as she pulled open the drawer.

At first it looked okay. A pile of Kleenex, batteries, some *Breathe Rite* strips—he snored like a bulldog.

Ick. Ick, ick, ick.

She ran for the bathroom, held her hair out of the way as her stomach heaved. But nothing came, even though she started sweating and it hurt like hell.

Okay. Okay. So now she knew why her mom was so lousy to her dad, why she'd kicked him out, and why she looked so sad all the time.

She grabbed her dad's toothbrush so she didn't have to touch anything in that drawer. She used it to push aside a pair of handcuffs, a couple bottles of lube, a dildo the size of a corncob.

There. A big pile of condoms. She grabbed a handful and stuffed them in her pocket.

Then she pulled out her cell phone and hit speed dial number one.

"Caleb? Are you drunk?"

She could hear music in the background, cheers. Giggling, laughter, a crash.

"Wait a minute, let me go to another room."

The background noise grew fainter.

"Okay, baby, go ahead. What is it?"

Kate felt calmer, just hearing Caleb on the other end of the phone.

"How much did you drink?" she asked.

"You checking up on me?" He wasn't mad yet, but he sounded like he was headed that way.

"No. Just wondering if you can drive."

"Drive?"

She spun away from the bed. He'd had women there, lots of them, using that . . . the vomit threatened again. She closed her eyes, thinking of Caleb, his gorgeous face and the way he shuffled along, taking his time. "Yeah. I need you to pick me up at my dad's."

"Thought you had to stay there with your brother."

It wasn't her fault her dad hadn't come home when he said he would. If he had, Eric wouldn't have been left alone. And she wouldn't have met the slutty Wilcox bitch.

And anyway, Eric was old enough to stay in a locked apartment by himself until Dad got there. She'd been babysitting when she was that age, for Christ's sake. All he was going to do was sit there and stare at that stupid game, anyway. He probably wouldn't even notice she was gone if she didn't tell him.

"It's okay," she said. "When can you get here?"

"What's up?"

She sucked in a breath to steady herself. *No turning back now*, she told herself. Why should she? "I'm going to make it worth your while."

21

The Voices of Experience

THERE was another e-mail from Jill the next morning, delivered with her fruit platter and yogurt, and it was only one word: *"Bikini!"*

Be brave, Ellen told herself. *Be brave.*

So she tugged on the bikini, looked down at herself to gauge the level of hideousness, and nearly stripped it right back off.

Her thighs bulged beneath the high-cut legs like overrisen dough in a too-small pan, her belly pooched in the gaping space between bottom and top, and she wasn't at all sure the narrow straps provided nearly enough support for her boobs. Okay, technically speaking, they were too small to sag far, but still. Hoisting them up a notch or two couldn't have hurt.

She figured a look in the mirror would either bolster her confidence—*Hey, you don't look that bad, not for a forty-two-year-old with two kids and a C-section scar*—or knock enough sense in her once and for all that she'd throw the horrid thing away and never be tempted to try such insanity again.

But there was only one small mirror, a framed oval hung above the white pedestal sink in the blue-tiled bathroom. She couldn't see much, just a patch of pale flesh at a time. She rose to her tiptoes, then cursed and dropped back down.

She didn't need to know just how bad she looked, did she? She knew she hadn't morphed into a supermodel overnight.

She threw on an oversize U of M T-shirt, dull gold with a

buck-toothed gopher charging across the front. Wouldn't do to risk sunburn, she reasoned.

And then she gathered her courage to head out for the day.

Blood-curdling shrieks from the beach proved to be caused by a cutthroat volleyball game. Bobby lurked in the front lines, smiling sweetly at the strikingly tall blond across the net from him. Ellen couldn't help but applaud when the Amazon smashed a spike right down on his feet, making him yelp and rub his wounded toes. He scowled at Ellen, then went right back to flirting with the blond.

Ellen decided she needed a break from man-hunting.

So she went snorkeling instead. She caught a ride with a boatful of friendly women. She remembered them laughing together at Heat, turning away all the hopeful men who approached.

It made for the most relaxing day she could imagine. The only man involved was Ryan, an eighteen-year-old from Miami who piloted the boat that shuttled them to a flat, clear bay by a nearby island and handed out sandwiches and bottles whenever one of the women snapped her fingers.

The women were from Boston. They'd all gone to law school together, and they'd come to Sizzle for a weeklong bachelorette party. They welcomed Ellen into the celebration as if they'd known her all along.

So she drifted over the clear water, feeling weightless, unfettered. The fish were gorgeous, and after a quick lesson from Ryan she could recognize the angelfish, a cinnamon clownfish, a huge, slow grouper. Caroline, the bride-to-be, swore she saw a toothy green moray peeking out from the reef, which had Ellen paddling the other way. The sun beamed genially, and Ryan was a complete flirt, which was just absurd enough for them all to enjoy his attention without anybody taking it the slightest bit seriously.

When Ellen grew tired of snorkeling, she lay on the front deck of the boat next to Caroline. Their drinks, bright red, sweet, and potent, sat beside them.

Caroline was thirty-eight, a hotshot litigator who was as

sharp as she was attractive. Deep into her third glass, she regaled Ellen with tales of her first, disastrous marriage.

"I should have known better than to marry an actor." She shielded her eyes with a huge pair of purple sunglasses studded with rhinestones and lay back on a striped towel. "A *theatah* actor, no less. He was *such* an artiste. I didn't care that I made twenty times what he did. He was handsome and articulate and *way* cooler than I was."

"Impossible."

"Thank you." She drew a stripe of oxide down her nose.

"What happened?"

"What do you think? It was the opening night of his new play, I walked into his dressing room with a bottle of champagne under one arm and a fistful of roses, ready to gush, and he was fucking the girl who played *Dumb Blonde Number Three*. Not even very well, I might add."

Ellen choked on her drink. "The acting, or the fucking?"

"Both, now that I think about it." She scraped damp hair off her face. "You know the best thing about going to law school?" Caroline lifted her glass in a toast. "He didn't get one dime of alimony."

"Good for you."

"Yeah. Good for me." She shifted on her towel. "Jeez, it's hot. Hey, Ryan?"

"Yeah?" He paused in the act of dumping Doritos into a plastic bowl printed with surfers.

"You care if I take my top off?"

He reached up and spun his Miami cap backward. "Do I have a shirt on?"

"Nope," Caroline said. "And we do appreciate it."

"So then I guess it would be sexist of me to care if you do the same." He grinned.

"Good." She untied her halter top and balled it up at her side before lying back, as relaxed as if she were still fully dressed. Ellen's T-shirt was damp and sticky with salt water, clinging to her in uncomfortable places.

"Aren't you worried that you're going to . . ." She tried valiantly to ignore her mothering reflex. She made it a full three seconds before she shot a glance at Ryan, who was ripping open a bag of pretzels and didn't seem at all flustered. "Burn?"

"SPF 100," Caroline said, then grinned. "Don't worry, we're not corrupting Ryan. He works at Sizzle. He's seen more naked women than a bouncer at a nudie bar."

"Yup," Ryan said cheerfully. "But that doesn't mean I don't appreciate it, each and every time."

"See?" Caroline flopped over, resting her head on her hands. Caroline'd been burned by her first husband every bit as savagely as Ellen had. And yet here she was, with a tiny chip of a diamond in platinum glinting on her left hand, ready to take the plunge again. "How'd you manage it? Getting . . . out there again. Getting married."

"Taking the leap?" Her expression softened. "I met Scott. He's a math teacher, and he coaches junior high hockey, and he told *me* we needed a prenup."

"And you love him." Ellen couldn't imagine getting all the *stuff* inside her—the anger and hurt and bitterness—to move aside far enough to make room for love. There just wasn't space for something so huge.

"Yeah, I love him." She lifted herself to her elbows, her breasts drooping free. "How about you?"

"How about me what? I already told you about Tom."

"Yeah. But what about the *after Tom*?"

"I don't know. I haven't even . . . I don't think I can . . . Oh, crap."

"You mean you haven't even slept with someone else?" Caroline sat up in shock, as astonished as if Ellen had confessed she'd been born a man. "Why the hell not?"

"I don't know." She really didn't. All the reasons that seemed to make so much sense, all the logic . . . maybe it just all came down to the fact that she was scared. And she was *so* sick of being scared.

"Well, what are you waiting for?"

"I'm waiting for . . . it to feel right?"

"Oh, honey," she said sympathetically, then raised her voice. "Hey, Ryan?'

"No!" Ellen grabbed Caroline's hand in a panicked vice.

"Hey! Oh, no." Caroline burst out laughing. "I'm not going to ask *him*," she said. "You can start breathing again." She eased her hand from Ellen's grip. "Ryan, we really, really need some Doritos over here."

"Coming up." He passed over the bowl.

"Here." Caroline whacked the bowl down on the boat deck. "Eat."

Ellen obligingly popped a chip in her mouth. They were salty, a bit soft from the humidity. "Oh, Lord, these are good."

"Aren't they?" Caroline shoveled in a couple and chewed while she rolled her eyes. "You have to promise to eat most of them. I've got a wedding dress to fit into." Then she sat up and crossed her legs, settling in for a serious lecture. "Now, you listen to me. How long has it been since you've had sex?"

Ellen had to think. "Four months? No, five."

Caroline shook her head sadly. "Glad to know it was memorable."

Ellen crunched another chip so she didn't have to answer.

"Okay, so five months. And how long has it been since you slept with anyone but Tom?"

Ellen wondered when virtue and restraint had become so horribly embarrassing. "My freshman year in college."

"Oh, you poor *thing*." Caroline groped for more chips and scooped out a huge handful. "These are the last ones. Really. Now. How was your first time?"

"The very first one?"

"Yup."

"I've blocked it from my memory to limit the post-traumatic stress syndrome."

"Probably a good strategy." She licked orange dust off her fingers. "Okay, how about the first time with the *next* guy." Her jaw fell open. "It wasn't just Tom, was it?"

"No, it wasn't just Tom." She wasn't going to admit just how few there were, though.

"Thank God. So. That one?"

"Better. But still not great."

"Right." She hollered across the water at the woman who was padding around in circles. "Hey Christie!"

Christie, a robust brunette who practiced tax law and studied belly dancing, popped up, her face half-covered by a mask, and spat out her snorkel. "What?"

"The first time you did it with someone else after you and Mitch got divorced. How was it?"

"It sucked," she said. "Actually, it more than sucked. You want the horrific details?"

"Nope, that'll do."

Christie fit her snorkel back in her mouth and resumed floating.

"You're just going to have to accept it, Ellen. The first time's going to be mediocre at best. You're going to be too damned nervous for it to be anything else. You really should just pick someone and get it over with," she advised. "The sooner you get a bad night or two out of the way, the sooner you can get to the good ones."

It sounded so sensible, eminently reasonable. Caroline had no agenda. She was merely sharing the benefits of her experience, one woman who'd been kicked around to another.

"Maybe," Ellen said. "Maybe."

"But—"

"Here." Ellen shoved the bowl at her. "Button up the arguments, counselor, and eat some chips."

22

So Many Men

THE bridal party invited her to meet them at midnight for a moonlight skinny-dipping excursion. Ellen hadn't exactly agreed, but Caroline insisted they were coming to find her, and the only acceptable excuse would be if she were getting the "second first time" out of the way.

So she kept on her bikini, dropping a gauzy cover-up that stopped four inches above her knees over her head. "Not bad," she said, peering at the tiny mirror. The drapey fabric covered everything she wanted hidden, and she'd lost her winter pallor over the last couple of days, which the white set off nicely.

She reached for flat sandals, and at the last minute grabbed some bronze wedges instead. She *did* have good legs; might as well show them off.

She tried the buffet by the beach, but her stomach was bloated with rum punch and Doritos, and nothing appealed. *Nobody* appealed, either, which was a more serious problem.

Her time on the island was running low. If she was going to do this, it had to be soon. And much as she disliked Caroline's advice, it made a certain sense. It was asking too much for it to be easy. She'd never in her life been swept away by passion, fallen in lust, and had it work flawlessly from the start, every kiss, every touch magic. She'd always had to put some time and effort into it.

Heat was firing up by the time she got there at eight. But her favorite stool was still empty. It occupied the far end of the bar, too distant from the center of the action to be widely coveted. People didn't come to Heat to sit alone and unnoticed.

Nobody but Ellen.

"Hey!" Jake strolled from the other end of the bar, grinning as if he were genuinely happy to see her.

"You've got help tonight." She nodded at the young man at the far end of the counter. He didn't appear old enough to be tending bar, but the three young ladies who fluttered around him seemed delighted by his presence.

"Manuel? He's the new guy. Training him in."

"Are you leaving Sizzle?"

"Me?" Without asking, he squirted Diet Coke into a glass, squeezed in a wedge of lime, and set it before her. "Why would anybody give up this job?"

Why, indeed? It wasn't her thing, wasn't her place. She wasn't cut out for hedonism. But most people probably would have killed for his job, his life. Unfettered, with nothing to do but tend bar and hang out on the beach, the weekly arrival of a brand-new crop of women looking for . . . not love, but a few days of no-strings entertainment.

Tom would have made a deal with the devil for Jake's job.

"Is there a rule that you have to be gorgeous to get hired here?" she asked. If Katie had gotten a look at Manuel, she would have forgotten all about Caleb in a heartbeat. "Where do they *find* you all?"

"Gorgeous." He preened. "You think I'm gorgeous?"

"Oh, stop." She couldn't help but laugh. "You know what you look like."

"Come on." He leaned over the bar, flirting outrageously. "Tell me I'm gorgeous."

"You're gorgeous." She had to stop playing with him. It was the most fun to be had on Sizzle—what was it with her and bartenders, anyway?—but it wouldn't accomplish anything. "Now prove you're more than a pretty face." She waved her arms, the gesture encompassing all the people in the place. "Pick one out for me."

"Excuse me?"

He had a towel looped over his bare shoulder, a baseball cap on backward, and wore cut-off denim shorts that were worn down to a thread. A few months ago, if she passed him on the street, she would have thought: *Hmm, nice-looking fellow. Too bad he's such a slacker.* If she'd noticed him at all.

But she got it now. Understood the appeal of youth and ease and comfortable sexuality. It wasn't for her, wouldn't ever be for her, but she could appreciate it.

"Choose a . . . friend for me. You said you could do it better than I could. So prove it."

"You want me to pick a lover for you."

She flinched. "Well . . ."

"You have to say it," he said, smiling at her discomfort. "Or I won't do it."

The words were stuck in her throat, fishhook barbs that kept them lodged in place.

"If you can't say it," he said, his voice soft and intimate, "you can't *do* it."

"Fine," she snapped, harsher than she intended. The anger was so close to the surface, fueled by Tom and Bobby and all the other asshole men in the world. She was close to letting it take over completely, making her hard and bitter. She'd be protected, but that was all. Unlike Caroline, she'd never again be open enough to be anything more. She could feel the armor congealing around her, thickening, tempering. It could still be cracked, but that wouldn't be true for much longer, not if she didn't do anything about it.

She gentled her voice. "Help me choose a lover."

"Okay." He nodded, as if he'd simply agreed to mix her a drink. It felt momentous to her, as if the earth should heave beneath her feet, the sky should split with lightning. But temporary couples formed weekly around here, dozens of them. It was nothing of particular importance to him, a mildly interesting diversion, a funny story to regale his coworkers with over drinks after the shift ended. "Turn around."

He put his hands on her shoulders and spun her to face the dance floor. His hands were warm, rough enough to be felt through the thin gauze of her tunic. Obviously they weren't the hands of an office worker. "Tell me what you like."

"What?" She wouldn't have pegged him for a voyeuristic streak, buzzed on hearing women's preferences and fetishes. She didn't think she could tell him. Wasn't even sure she knew what hers *were*. And that'd be too mortifying to admit, as well: *I like it in the dark, missionary-style, in a comfy bed with someone I'm married to.*

Oh, yeah, that'd sound exciting. Heck, this was Sizzle; it was probably a lot more scandalizing and unusual here than stories about whips and leather. "I don't think I can do that."

He chuckled, as if he knew exactly what she was thinking. "Not what I meant. Though I'd be more than happy to listen, if that's what works for you."

Lord. She felt heat crawl up her neck, her face; she was glad she faced away from him, so he couldn't see her blush.

"But if we're going to pick you out a good one," he went on, "you've got to give me something to work with. I need to know what you like." He took his hands away, and she was a lot sorrier than she should have been.

She scanned the crowds. There were too many men; she couldn't focus on any one. It was like walking into a department store, being so overwhelmed with the merchandise that they all blurred together and none of them tempted her any more than the rest. It was why she hated shopping. She liked an edited selection. With a handful of presorted choices, she could process and make the correct decision. Throw thirty or forty shirts at her, and none of them looked any good.

"I don't know."

"You don't know?" She heard him working behind her, the clink of glassware and ice, the slosh of liquid being poured. But he didn't sound the least bit distracted. His voice was warm and interested, as if she were his only task for the night. "That's really too bad."

"Too bad?"

"You're old enough to know what you like."

"I don't want to disabuse you of any hopeful expectations, but you don't suddenly figure everything out when you hit forty." She took a sip of her soda, torn between wishing it had a shot of rum in it and being grateful it didn't. This wasn't something she wanted to decide with an alcohol-muddled head; she'd warned her kids about that sort of thing often enough. Alcohol was involved in 60 percent of the new cases of sexually transmitted diseases, after all.

"You're over forty?"

"Bless you." Clearly a lie to placate the customer, but she was grateful for the attempt. "But yes."

"I don't know what your problem is, then," he said. "The day I hit forty, I'm going to wake up with all the answers."

"You let me know how that works out for you."

"I will," he said, as if he had every intention of still knowing her then. Right. "But you're slacking, girl. When you walk down the street, when you're sitting in a café watching the world go by, what kind of guy catches your eye?"

She scanned the crowds. There had to be someone. She knew how to appreciate a handsome man. She was a healthy female.

But appreciating them from a distance, noticing a particularly nice butt, a clean jawline, was far different than contemplating crawling into bed with one of them.

"I like . . ." They all blended together, looked more ordinary en masse than they would individually. "I don't know."

"Okay, that's just pitiful," Jake said, though there was warmth in his voice.

She heard ice clink into the metal shaker behind her. "It is, isn't it? But I'm just not used to thinking that way. I was married a *long* time."

"I thought the saying was 'married, not dead.'"

"Apparently they're a lot more similar than I realized," she said dryly.

He handed two flirtinis to a grandmotherly woman in a hot

pink caftan and a straw hat decorated with paper orchids. "Keep mixing, hon. I'll be back soon."

"Sure thing, Mrs. Lessard."

A man who looked like he'd walked straight out of an Abercrombie ad, perfect abs, deliberately windblown hair, and all, swung by and requested a cranberry juice. He nodded politely at Ellen and went on his way.

"How about him?" Jake asked her. "He your type?"

Sure, Ellen thought. *That* was going to happen. Though she was kind of pleased that Jake had, however briefly, believed she had a shot at a man like that. "Well, really, he's everybody's type, I suppose. But he's too good-looking."

"Too good-looking? That's a flaw?"

"Umm-hmm. No good in bed because he's never had to be; women are halfway to fireworks just looking at him."

"Reeaally?" She'd finally shocked him. He went silent for a while, as the vibrant reggae segued into something soft and sexy. "Am *I* too good-looking?"

She glanced over her shoulder at him, as if seriously appraising him. "Maybe ten years ago you were," she said. "Not now." And then she broke out laughing. "Look at you! You don't know whether to be flattered or insulted."

"You'd better watch it, or I'm cutting you off."

"Please, not that! No Diet Coke, and I become an ugly, ugly creature. You don't want to see it."

He shuddered. "You're right, I don't." He nodded his head at the model look-alike, who had attracted a cluster of twittering females. "So how do you know this? You don't need my help if you know all about what kind of lover a guy's gonna be."

"I have a friend," she said. "Jill. She knows guys. I listen now and then."

"What's she think about your little project?"

"She thinks I've put it off way too long."

"Me, too. Now stop stalling." He indicated the band's drummer, a long-haired, smooth-skinned blond with tattoos up and down each arm and who reminded her vaguely of Eric's friend, Evan—minus the tattoos.

"Too young," she said quickly.

"Okay." He scanned the crowd and nodded to a distinguished sixty-plus-year-old who was twirling a blond a good thirty-five years his junior in a polished tango.

"Too old."

"You're an ageist," he accused her. "You need to broaden your horizons."

"He looks too much like my dad, all right? I couldn't."

"That's a good reason," he allowed. "But this is like trying to find porridge for Goldilocks."

It stung, even though she knew it shouldn't. "I'm not that hard to please." Determined, she took a harder look.

Panic fluttered in her stomach, as if she'd drunk something much harder than soda.

This was an idle conversation, she reminded herself. Just because she pointed at one, it didn't mean she had to get naked in front of him.

She picked the most inoffensive man she could find: around fifty, ruthlessly bald, his scalp glowing neon-pink from a savage sunburn. In a crowd of a hundred middle-aged businessmen, he'd be indistinguishable from half of them. He was attempting to dance and not quite pulling it off but being good-natured about it. He might conceivably like her, and he didn't look like a slimeball.

"You can do better than *that*, Ellen."

"Thank you very much, but maybe I *like* that."

"Yeah, here, just let me wipe the drool off your chin." He made a show of dabbing at her mouth with a napkin. "What do you feel when you look at him?"

"I . . ." What did she feel? She just didn't think that way. When everything she'd felt for months was unpleasant—anger and frustration and despair—it had become easier to simply close off the deeper emotions. Passion had gotten shut off with them. "I feel . . . fine?"

"You're just restraining yourself from jumping him, aren't you?"

Maybe this wasn't such a good idea after all. "Don't you have work to do?"

"Manuel's gotta learn. Now, try again. Take a good look. Who gives you that shaky kick in your stomach? Who makes you *want*?"

Her eyes blurred, the dancing bodies bleeding together, motion and color, an impression of life that left her on the sidelines again. "What am I supposed to want?"

"More," he murmured. "You should want more." His voice, rich and seductive as the ocean, was so soft she barely heard it over the music. *More.* She didn't dare look at him. She wasn't that stupid.

In desperation she pointed to a tall, lanky man alone at a table, staring intently into a tumbler of scotch. Byron could have written about him, with his tumble of dark, shoulder-length curls and narrow, poetic face. "How about that one?"

"Hmm. You like the brooding type? Wouldn't have pegged that one."

Did she? She considered. "I think maybe I do."

"You're not the only one," he said conversationally. "He just sits there and looks depressed, and the women come running, panting to cheer him up. Works like a charm."

"So?" That wasn't a mortal flaw. What man wouldn't fake melancholy if it encouraged women to work so hard to cheer him up?

"So the problem is it carries over. You're going to have to do *all* the work. And I do mean *all*."

She swung around, scowling at him. "How would you know?"

He spread his hands innocently. "Everybody talks to the bartender, Ellen. Everybody."

"You're making that up."

"Hey, go ahead and find out for yourself." Laugh lines crinkled the corners of his eyes. She wondered if he truly was as happy, as easy with himself, as he appeared. "Come back and tell me how it works out, okay?"

"You're enjoying this too much," she said. "But I can't tell if you're having fun because you're reeling out a line, or if you're just amused by my dilemma. And there's no way I can tell until it's too late."

"Maybe it's a little of both," he said. "But we don't get many like you on Sizzle."

"Like me?"

"Yup," he said but didn't elaborate. "You want to try again?"

"Sure." This was stupid, she thought. Surely there had to be men out there that caught her fancy. That she'd look at and immediately wonder what they'd be like in bed.

She'd never been overtly sexual, never as driven by her urges as Jill. But that didn't mean they didn't exist, only that she hadn't indulged them.

She'd felt them, though. She could remember that she used to feel them, the curiosity and hunger that could burst from a glance, a brush in the aisle in the library, the low and rich timbre of a man's voice on the other end of the phone line.

When had it stopped? With her marriage? The first child, the second? She suddenly felt the loss, how her life was less rich for the absence of that emotion. She lived in the middle ground, in the safe and the simple. But she'd gotten the valley, anyway; there should be some recompense. She should get a peak or two, too.

"How about that one?" He was almost too handsome, clean-featured, blond-and-blue. Not really her usual type— she liked them dark, and not quite so sure of themselves—but at a certain point the type was immaterial, and you simply had to appreciate. And he certainly looked like he knew his way around a bedroom. And a woman's body.

"Ah. That's John Belliconti."

"Am I supposed to know who that is?"

"I thought you got TV way up there in the north country."

"Okay, spill." She turned her back to the room. The shark

was grinning over the bar, and Jake's smile was nearly as ferocious. "What is it about me that entertains you so much?"

"I'm not entirely sure."

At his end of the bar Manuel was working hard, flirting with the women, joking with the men, shaking up drinks with each hand. "The boy's learning fast, Jake. Maybe you should be worried."

"Naw. I don't worry."

"Ever?"

He drew his brows together as if pondering. "Not that I can recall. Gave it up for Lent."

"So you're the one."

"You're the one, what?"

"The one I'm making up for in the worrying department. Keeping the cosmic scales in balance."

He leaned toward her, and her breath rushed in. "You should let it go sometime," he said. "See if you like it."

"Don't you think I would if I could?" She sighed and sat back. "So go ahead. Tell me how hopelessly out of touch with popular culture I am. Who's Mr. Tall, Blond, and Handsome? Music, movies, or television?" She turned for another view. He still didn't seem the least bit familiar. But everybody else must know who he was; a small crowd had gathered around him, with the glazed expressions and overeager smiles of those hoping fame might brush a little sparkle their way.

"None of the above," Jake said. "He played third base for the Braves until he blew out his knee in the 2000 playoffs. He's almost as famous for that as that as he is for the women in his life."

"The women."

"He married a playmate, broke the heart of an Academy Award winner. Has seven children by six different women, none of whom he ever married. Last year one of them wanted a raise in her child support. When he said no, she went straight to the papers. Stories of how that duffel bag he carried on the team bus was actually filled with sex toys, how he'd go to a hotel and order two blonds with room service the night before a game. She released a sex tape." Jake sounded amused but not particularly impressed. "If you decide to go for it, you'd better know your tolerance for black latex and handcuffs going in."

"Oh, he sounds like just my type." She grimaced in distaste. "Hey, wait a second. I thought there was no television here."

"There's no TV for the guests," he confided. "There's a satellite dish hooked up to a big-screen in the employee lounge."

"Hey!"

"Gotta keep the worker bees happy."

She kept trying. She pointed out a redhead with a lovely Scottish accent that Jake claimed only came to Sizzle because of the easy access to Jamaican pot; a bookish, bearded professor-type that Jake instructed her to give fair warning if she wanted to go to bed with him, because it took an hour for the Viagra to kick in. The clean-cut, hearty-laughed man with a world-class golfer's tan was actually married to the blond in diamonds with her wrinkles Botoxed into submission and an eye for men twenty years her junior.

After a while she stopped even caring whether she was the least bit attracted to the men she indicated. She chose them simply to hear what story Jake would spin.

Finally she faced him. "So what you're telling me is that *every* man on Sizzle is a deviant."

"Not *every* man," he said. "Just the ones you like."

"If I didn't know better, I'd think you were making this up so I wouldn't go off with someone."

"That could be true." He was mixing coconut milk and rum in a big pitcher, setting out tall glasses packed with ice. She didn't know when he'd started working again. There'd been no pause in the conversation, no indication that she had anything but his full attention. "But why would I do that?"

Why, indeed. The possibilities that occurred to her were impossible. Flattering, thrilling, but impossible.

So she decided to ask. "I don't know. Why?"

"I don't want a guest to go home unhappy," he said. "I particularly don't want *you* to go home unhappy."

"I think that's pretty likely either way." She drained her glass and handed it to him for a refill. "But for once in my life I want to be unhappy because of something I did, instead of something I didn't." Determined, she contemplated the selection again. This time she discarded the obvious, the men who were drooling over the flashy women, even if they clearly didn't have a shot. She tried to look deeper; after all, she wanted whatever man she chose to do the same.

"There!" She pointed to the far corner, to a man who sat alone with a drink the color of cotton candy on the table in front of him. He had the look of a runner, with a lean face and narrow-shouldered physique. His hair was thin and pale, his glasses small and gold-framed. "What about him?"

"Which one?"

"There. In the corner."

"It's kind of a fruity drink," Jake told her, as he piled maraschino cherries into a glass he'd filled with soda.

"Yeah." That was part of what she liked about him. He'd ordered what he liked, not what looked cool. She'd always suspected that Tom detested scotch, but that's what men in his position drank, so that's what Tom ordered.

"And he's kind of a nerd."

"I like nerds."

Jake's hands paused, and then he skewered a pineapple chunk with a purple umbrella and dropped it in the drink with a splash. "Yeah," he said. "I suppose you would."

"Do you know him?"

His face was impassive, absent the warmth that he habitually donned the moment he stepped behind the bar, as much a part of his bartender uniform as his board shorts and his sandals. "I know him."

"And?"

"Name's Mark. He's a high school science teacher from Denver. Been divorced three years and hasn't had a date. His parents gave him the trip as a birthday present because they're desperate for grandchildren."

"He told you all that?"

"His parents did, when they wrote ahead to tell the staff to see if we could encourage him to mingle." He shrugged. "We haven't had much luck."

Better and better. She felt a twist of sympathy, and sipped her pop as she studied him with more interest. He nodded politely as someone came over to borrow a chair, his feet tapping beneath his table in time to the music. His hands, around his drink, were long-fingered, ringless.

"So he's definitely not married," she said. "Sexual perversions of any kind?"

"Not that I know of."

She could be the one who approached the wallflower, she decided. Kindness propelled her in a way that lust never had.

"But that's not necessarily a good thing," Jake continued.

She wiped condensation off the glass with her thumb. "Will he be nice to me, Jake?"

He was silent while he cubed a mango with a knife the size of a machete. "Yeah. He'd be nice to you."

"Then make me two of those drinks he's got, will you?"

"There's no alcohol in them," Jake warned her.

"Good."

"You going over?" He pitched berries and juice into a blender.

"Yes," she said. "He looks lonely."

She stood up and smoothed her tunic. She was just going to make a friend. Nothing to be nervous about, she told herself. And she was pretty certain Mark didn't look like the kind of guy who was automatically going to translate "Hello" into "Let's have sex right this second."

Jake handed her two glasses. They were cold, and her hands were slick around them.

"Go get him, tiger," he told her.

23

The Old College Try

MARK Burley was truly a very nice man. He'd looked up in surprise when she came to his table, as if he'd never considered a woman like her would come over to *him*, and her ego soared.

He was shy. He kept his gaze mostly down, on his folded hands on the table, on his drink, but it flicked up to her regularly, as if he couldn't help but sneak a glance at her, and then just as quickly down again, as if he didn't want to be caught looking.

But he talked if she asked the right questions. His students, his cross-country team; that topic made him light up with obvious pride. He skied, obviously better than she did. He preferred A-Basin, where he worked as a ski patrol on the weekends; she'd driven past it once, when they were staying at Keystone, and she appreciated its stripped-down, serious-skier vibe, even if she didn't dare attempt it herself.

They spent three hours together, and she liked him better all the time. They ate sandwiches on the beach, away from the frantic mating buzz of Sizzle, the music and laughter a distant hum. He pointed out a tropic bird and a black-necked stilt. No expert, he claimed, but he was a bit of an amateur birder.

They tried the trail that wound back behind the main compound, through the center of the island, beneath the swaying palms and casuarinas. She enjoyed the hush, as if they were alone on a deserted island, a place that grew naturally lush instead of the engineered Disney tropics of Sizzle.

He comforted her when bats wheeled overhead and kindly assured her there were no poisonous snakes. But he was more embarrassed than she when they heard grunting ahead that she at first assumed was the sound of wild hogs.

He hustled her back to her cottage, rushing her back down the path as if they'd stumbled across a convention of machete-wielding, hockey-mask-wearing serial killers.

"Here we are!" he said, his voice loud and brisk. "What a nice evening!"

She couldn't help but smile. The more nervous he got, the calmer she became. She didn't stop to consider the fact that her feelings toward him were more companionable than lustful, more compassionate than passionate.

Ellen just knew she felt something, something warm. And that was nice. And that, when it came right down to it, she was awfully tired of sleeping alone.

It would be so pleasant to have someone's arms around her again. To be able to burrow up against a male chest, to smell his neck and let her hand rest on his chest and feel the reassuring beat of his heart. To be able, when the worries and the dreams woke her, to roll up against something solid and real.

"Yes," she said. "I enjoyed it, too."

His head bobbed, his glasses reflecting moonlight. He was much taller than she; when she looked up, she saw the underside of his jaw, the slide of his Adam's apple above his plain blue collar.

He fixed his gaze above her head. "Maybe . . . tomorrow . . ." He swallowed. "Maybe tomorrow we could meet. For breakfast. Or another walk. If you want."

He was really very sweet. And when she went home, she was going to have to make a choice. A marriage, a divorce. Forgive, if not forget, or put Tom behind her and go on with a new life. Shouldn't she know? Shouldn't she see if it could be just sex? Or if she could live in a single world? If sex mattered to her, or if it didn't?

"Or you could stay now," she said, and it was easier than she expected to get the words out.

"Oh." His startled gaze swung to hers. "You're still worried about your daughter and math? Because I could give you some Web sites, some suggestions. I really think that—"

"No." There was a certain power here that she'd never wielded. In being the *chooser*, the one who moved too fast, who shocked and propelled. It was good to realize she could. "I mean, I appreciate it, and yes, I'd like to discuss it further. But not right now." She stepped closer, until her body bumped his, her eyes level with his collarbone, and she heard him gulp.

That's all it took, she marveled. She only had to step close, and she could make him gasp. "I was suggesting that you stay. Tonight. With me."

"You mean—" He didn't want to assume. He didn't want be the one who laid it out there, SEX, if that wasn't what she meant.

"Yes. I do mean."

She lifted up to kiss him, rising all the way to her toes. Their mouths did not fit together well. He seemed frozen, as if he were afraid that, if he moved, if he *breathed*, he might do something to frighten her off.

But she'd never been the one to kiss a man first. She'd always waited, standing on her parents' porch, by her dorm room door, in the front seat of a car. Hinting, maybe, in the way she tilted her head or licked her lips. That waiting was delicious, drawing out the anticipation, the will-he-won't-he, until she thought she might go mad with it.

So she hadn't known this. How equally lovely to not have to wait. To make a move and await his reaction, to feel him shudder when she tilted her head and let her tongue slide along his lower lip.

She pulled back just enough to speak. "Would you like to stay?"

"I—" He grabbed her hand with one of his and reached for the doorknob with the other. He rattled it, shoving it hard. "Key." He thrust out his hand, and she dropped it in, amused and touched when his fingers trembled as he shoved it into the lock.

The door fell open, and he pulled her through, as if he were afraid that she would change her mind if he didn't get her inside fast enough.

He was kissing her before the door shut behind them again. She'd kept the shutters closed during the day, to keep out the sun and keep the interior cool, and so now the room was dark as pitch, unfamiliar.

He had one hand around her waist, his mouth—eager, if not smooth nor expert—against hers, while she heard his hand pat down the wall, looking for the switch.

"Leave it off," she told him.

"But—"

"Off," she said, and pressed closer so he wouldn't protest. Maybe, before she went home, she could add a little light to the proceedings. Right now, if she actually *saw* him, if she had to bare her body to his view, she'd just have to go escape into the night and never be seen again. Heck, she could live in the tangle that passed for jungle on Sizzle. There were coconuts.

"But where's the—" They fell onto the bed, too hard. Pain burst where Ellen bit her tongue, and she heard Mark's *"Oooff"* when her elbow jabbed something vulnerable.

"Are you okay? I didn't—"

"No. I mean, yeah, I'm okay. It's just my side."

"Oh. I thought maybe—"

"No. No, that's working fine," he assured her. "But . . . oh, hell. I'd read my students the riot act if they didn't . . . do you have, uh, condoms? 'Cause if you don't, we can—"

"It's okay." She'd guaranteed Katie that such discussions were a necessary and natural part of the proceedings, completely to be expected. Had even, mostly, believed it. These were modern times, weren't they? Anyone with an ounce of sense understood the prerequisites. *Appreciated* another's responsibility in such matters.

Except she'd horribly underestimated the awkwardness involved. Being swept away in the moment was simply not possible when one had to think about latex, and the practicalities of getting it . . . well, in the proper position. It allowed real life to creep in, and reality with it.

But she couldn't go back to Minnesota without having tried. She'd been *thinking* for months, and she wasn't any closer to an answer than she'd been in October.

"I've got plenty," she said, and felt him jerk against her. "No, I mean . . . shoot. My friend gave them to me, before I left for Sizzle. She even checked my suitcase to make sure I packed them."

He chuckled, and her tension eased. "Mine, too. They gave me a whole sampler box. Thirty-two kinds." Her eyes had gotten adjusted to the dark now, and she could just see his outline in the faint bars of moonlight that sifted through the shutters. "They have a *lot* of faith in me."

"I'm betting Jill counts them when I get back, just to make sure I used some. I should dump them in the ocean before I leave so she'll think I used them all. She'd be so proud of me."

"Maybe you should just leave them for the next guest. Like a Gideon Bible."

Her laughter faded beneath his kiss.

She started out hopeful. She liked the feel of him on top of her, and the smell of his neck—soap, suntan lotion, shaving cream.

He was slow, carefully gentle. That should have been a good thing.

Except it let the thoughts infiltrate her consciousness. She tried to beat them back. Tried to concentrate. There were so many new things; why couldn't she only think of them? His waist was narrow, without an ounce of excess flesh. She could feel the line of his ribs, the lean, ropy length of him. She'd bet he looked great running: focused, easy, determined.

But instead she remembered about her wedding day, her wedding night. About all the hope she'd had, all the dreams.

Unlike many of her friends, she hadn't had cold feet. Not even a frosty toe or two. She'd been so certain she was doing the right thing.

How'd she end up here? In a bed with a man she'd known

only a couple of hours? She'd had no time to get used to anything. No time to become accustomed to the feel of his hands on her breasts before his mouth was there. No time to absorb the press of his hips before he was tugging at her swimsuit bottom. It wasn't that he was rushing. Far from it. It was just that she'd never moved so quickly before. In high school, in college, it had taken weeks, *months*, to work up to this point. All those extended sessions of doing "everything but"—she'd liked them better than the real thing, though she'd never admitted it to anybody, not even Jill, who would have shouted "blasphemy" and instructed her endlessly about what she was doing wrong.

But it had meant that, when she finally had sex with someone, only the final step was a shock. Not every single second, every single touch. They were all alarming, each nerve jolting at the new contact, startling at the fresh sensation. Painful tingles chased over her skin, as if she'd been frostbitten, the pain spreading and sharpening as her skin heated, and frozen nerves warmed to raw life.

Too much, she thought. *Too fast. I can't do this, I can't . . .*

Get it over with. Obviously the Boston crew—the new friends she'd met snorkeling—had been right. It was too much to expect of herself to believe that she could enjoy this.

No, she decided firmly. She *could* enjoy. Pleasure did not necessarily require an orgasm. She would concentrate on the parts she could find satisfaction in, on the things in him she found attractive. It wasn't as if she didn't *like* him.

And as to the rest . . . well, he was a nice man. She only hoped he wasn't terribly perceptive. She hadn't faked it for a long time, but she wanted him to feel good about himself. She could do that for him.

Yeah, she could do this. And she'd have it behind her, this big, honking hurdle that she was making into so much more than just sex. Too much more. That was the problem, wasn't it?

"Are you ready?" he murmured in her ear, his hands gentle on her hips. He was breathing hard, and his skin was as hot as if he'd just come in from an afternoon in the sun.

She opened her mouth to agree. She was *sure* of it.

But instead she started wailing, relentless as a hurricane. "I'm not *ready*!"

"Shit." He sprang away from her as if she'd just burst into flames. "I'm sorry, I'm sorry, what can I—"

"No!" She reached out to him, trying to reassure him through touch, at least until she could stop blubbering long enough to speak, that it wasn't his fault, he hadn't done anything wrong. But he leapt away, as if any contact terrified him.

He got up off the bed, hopping frantically from foot to foot, ready to bolt.

"Wait. Just wait."

"You want me to get someone? I—"

"Wait!" *Get ahold of yourself! You're scaring the poor man to death.* "It's not your—" The sobs caught her again, and she fell back on her Lamaze breathing. Hadn't worked all that great in the middle of transition, but it was pretty effective in less painful situations. She huffed away, while poor Mark jiggled in panic. He got bonus points for not bolting.

"I know this is terrible," she finally managed around hiccups. "Somebody did this to me, once, and I—"

"Somebody did this to you?" The astonishment was enough to jolt him into calm. "A *guy* started crying in the middle of sex? How the hell does that happen?"

She giggled, a wet bubble. "Could you sit down?"

He took a quick step back. "I don't know."

"I'm not crazy, I promise."

Even in the dim light, she could see his disbelief.

"At least not in a way that's scary," she assured him. "That was the worst, I promise."

"But—"

"Please?" His inherent gentlemanliness won out. He sat gingerly on the edge of the bed, the mattress barely dipping beneath his careful weight.

That horrid and mortifying burst of grief dissipated, leaving her sapped of energy, weak and shaky as if she'd just come off a bout of the flu. Wearily she refastened her bikini top and pulled the cover-up over her head before flipping on the bedside lamp.

She had to look like hell. Her eyes were nearly swollen shut, her cheeks were sticky with dried tears.

She faced him head on anyway. Maybe he'd take one look and realize he'd had a lucky escape.

"I'm so, so sorry," she said. "It didn't have anything to do with you. You are *lovely*. But I've been married forever, and I wasn't sure I was ready for this, but everybody *told* me, and I'm . . . it just didn't feel right."

His cheeks puffed as he blew out a breath. "Look, I won't take offense. I promise. But I *have to* know. What'd I do wrong?"

"I swear to you, Mark. It wasn't you." She scooted over beside him on the bed and placed her hand reassuringly over his. "If I lived anywhere within a hundred miles of you, I'd be *begging* to date you."

He looked up hopefully. "You would?"

"Absolutely. No doubt we'd have ended up here eventually, with much better results."

"Really?"

"No question about it." Ellen sighed in relief as he relaxed. "Thank God you believe me. I couldn't stand it if your ego had been irreparably damaged because of my stupidity. I might even have had to have sex with you, just to make sure there was no lasting harm."

"I *am* irreparably damaged," he said quickly. "Can't you tell?" His face fell into the mournful lines of an old beagle's.

She chuckled, wishing that he really did live within dating distance. He was a good guy—not that her judgment in such matters was flawless, far from it, but if he was a jerk, she'd go to a nunnery. "Come on." She gave him a playful shove.

"I'm serious," he said. "Shattered. Probably never be able to have sex again, it's been so traumatic. We'd better do something about it quick, before it has a chance to settle into a real phobia."

"You wouldn't want that. It'd be a . . ." She trailed off. She

knew what Jill would call it, but she didn't know a more delicate term.

"A pity fuck."

She gaped at him until he put his finger beneath her chin to
close her mouth. "Yeah. That."

"And your point is?"

"You wouldn't want that."

"Are you kidding me?" He flopped back on the bed, his arms
spreading wide. He took up the entire width. "I've had sex exactly twice in the last eighteen months. Okay, given the choice,
I'd rather you were mad with lust for me. But if that's not an
option—" He lifted his head and opened one eye. "It's not an
option, right?"

"Umm . . . no."

"Just checking." He dropped his head back and closed his
eyes, comfortably linking his hands over his flat belly. "If the
choices I'm left with are a pity fuck and *no* fuck, I'll take the pity
fuck every time."

"But—" She trailed off, speechless. He was so conversational
about it, completely matter-of-fact. As if the answer were so obvious everyone on earth should have known it. *"Seriously?"*

"Not even a question." He lifted his head again. "Do you
know *anything* about men?"

"I thought so." Okay, so disastrous attempts at sex seemed to
be her pattern. Joe, Mark . . . but she was earning friends out of
the deal. That wasn't bad at all. Maybe even better than sex.

Though obviously Mark wouldn't agree.

"Apparently not as much as I thought."

He pushed the pillow up behind his head, as if he were settling in for the duration. "I suppose you want me to go now."

"It does seem the natural next step."

"Can you do me a favor?"

She narrowed her eyes at him. "It's not sex, is it?"

"If you'll do it, yeah, the favor's sex."

He waited for her answer and then sighed. "Can I stay for a
while? I've got three days left, but if I leave now, and anybody

sees me, it's going to blow my chances with anyone else if they think I'm only good for a few minutes."

She laughed. "Go ahead. Stay as long as you'd like. I wouldn't want to ruin your chances." He really was being awfully good-natured about it. "How about this? I'll get up late tomorrow, and I'll look . . . spent, completely wiped out, and every time I see you the rest of the week, I'll go starry-eyed and sigh longingly. Good?"

"Now you're talking. In fact—" He waved a hand at her, encouraging. "Why don't you go ahead and start moaning? Just in case somebody's listening? Screaming my name a few times wouldn't hurt, either. Make it loud."

She smiled as she shook her head. "You need a wife, Mark."

"I know," he said softly. "But I'm not ready."

24

Just Sex

ELLEN took a shower. Mark took a nap.

She'd forgotten to bring any other clothes into the bathroom with her and didn't want to tiptoe out into the room wrapped only in a towel to fetch them. He'd been a sport, but that would only be cruel to sashay by him, buck naked but for a swatch of terry cloth. So she tugged her bikini and cover-up back on and ran a comb through her hair, leaving it damp.

He was dead asleep, flat on his back, completely sprawled out. What a bed hog; there was no room for anybody else in there. His head was turned to one side, mouth open, and he was snoring loud enough to send the beach crabs scuttling back into the water.

She stood over the bed. So sweet . . . if kids always looked innocent asleep, men looked vulnerable, kind. For a moment she wished she'd been able to do it. Could do it now, curl up beside him and wake him with a kiss, sink into that sleepy kind of lovemaking that took hours. But that kind of sex took people who knew each other well and were long past the urgent, turbulent rush of it.

Besides, it would be unspeakably cruel to get his hopes—and something else as well—up again, only to freak out at the last minute.

But it posed a problem. He looked too comfortable to wake. He'd earned a good night's sleep. But she couldn't crawl in bed with him, not without moving him out of the way. Besides, she was known to snuggle in her sleep. It would be taking unfair advantage of him, asking him to chase her loneliness. She could sleep with him, but she couldn't *sleep* with him? It was just too awkward to consider.

She just wasn't up to Sizzle, though. She didn't want to meet anyone, *see* anyone. She'd given it an honest try, but she was done. If she couldn't have sex with Mark, it simply wasn't to be.

So she left her cottage, wandering aimlessly, away from noise and light and music, veering off as soon as she heard an approaching voice. She sat by the quiet pool for a while, watching the pool light shimmer under water that rippled with each passing breeze, until a giggling threesome showed up, stripped to their skivvies, and dove in.

She ended up on the beach. Always, the beach, choosing a spot near the end of that perfect curve, where she could watch the relentless roll of the waves and allow the sound of the surf to drown out any music or laughter.

The beach was deserted. Kind of stupid, when you thought of it; they built Sizzle here precisely because of this beach, but they'd done such a good job of providing entertainment that everyone forgot about the ocean, at least after sunset.

She plopped down on the sand. It was still warm from the day's sun, but the wind off the water was brisk.

A wave climbed up nearly to her toes before it slipped away. How long had they being doing that? Millions of years? Billions?

She had three more days. Three days to think. When she went home, it needed to be with a decision firmly in mind. This purgatory wasn't working for anyone, not her or Tom or the children. Nothing would change by waiting any longer. She wasn't going to suddenly wake up one day and find that her husband hadn't cheated on her, or that she no longer cared.

She wasn't going to take a lover. That much was clear. She wasn't going to figure out why sex with someone else was so compelling Tom would risk his marriage for it, or know if the sex necessarily mattered that much. Or, if she chose divorce, if she'd ever be able to move beyond it and find pleasure with another man. She might not be as obsessed with sex as Tom, but she wasn't convinced she was ready to give up on it forever, either.

Oh, God.

The tears came again, surprising her so much that when she first tasted the salt, she thought it was the spray from the ocean, for surely she had to have been cried out by now.

It wasn't so violent this time. Her grief was quiet, peaceful, the regretful acceptance that her life would never be as she'd dreamed. It was time to move on, but that meant letting go, and she'd never been good at letting go.

"Hey." Jake dropped beside her, his hip against hers. He made no mention of her tears, asked her no questions, just watched the waves with her as if that had been the plan all along.

His warmth was welcome, his presence soothing, and she felt the emotions dissipate, slipping away with the waves.

"Don't you have work to do?" she asked.

"Trying to get rid of me?" He stretched out his bare, tan legs in front of him, crossing them at the ankles, his battered rubber sandals barely hanging on.

"Trying not to get you fired," she said. "Or is this your primary duty this week? Being my father confessor?"

He slanted an unreadable glance her way. "You have something to confess?"

"Maybe." Experimentally, she stretched out her own legs, just to see. Though Tom was three inches taller than her, her inseam was longer.

Her toes, though, only brushed Jake's ankles. "Maybe not."

"Okay." It was his real gift, this ability to project an openness to listening—to anything, everything—without demanding it. The difference between prying and listening was a narrow but crucial one, and he was always on the right side of it.

She just observed the water for a while, wondering how it never grew boring. It was always the same: water, sand, sky, light. And yet it was never the same, constantly shifting. She could stay right there, absorbing the perpetual evolution, and never long for anything else.

"You don't have to babysit me," she told him. He would stay as long as she worried him, but he certainly had other things to do, other guests to care for. "I'm fine. Really."

"Manuel's got it. He's gotta try it on his own sometime. I've earned a night off."

She turned her head. He inspected the waves intently, the sharp relief of light and shadow caused by the shifting moonlight making him appear older, troubled. This was not the Jake that reigned behind the bar at Sizzle, the man who made the party happen, who lived in paradise and didn't have a care in the world except his next good time.

But nobody had no cares. Nobody. If there was one thing she'd learned in life, that was it. You might get away without cares for a few years. Maybe for a decade, if you were very, very lucky. But nobody skated through without any cares at all.

"Then you should enjoy it," she said. "Instead of spending it with a guest."

"Who said I'm not enjoying it?"

"I'm not going to throw myself in the ocean. I swear."

"That's good. Because I was always a lousy lifeguard. I can't promise to save you."

The clouds unexpectedly shifted away from the moon, sending a burst of silver over the waves, then just as quickly disappeared. Finally he looked her way. "You're not getting rid of me, Ellen."

"What are you doing here?"

"Doing?" He nodded thoughtfully, as if giving his answer serious consideration. "Just sittin' on the beach." He wasn't smiling now, the bright blue of his eyes darkening to dusk. "What about you?"

He didn't really want to hear her problems, she reminded herself. But what the hell; she'd given fair warning and plenty of opportunity to escape. And maybe it would help to talk it through. It wouldn't hurt to get an opinion from an independent observer with no real stake in the outcome.

"I couldn't do it," she told him.

"Couldn't do what?" he asked mildly.

"You know what."

"You make it sound like a duty."

"Maybe that was the problem. It felt like one." Suddenly chilled, she drew her legs up and wrapped her arms around them, dropping her forehead to her knees. "I can't believe I have to go home and tell them."

"Them?"

"My husband. He's going to laugh. Proof that he was right all along, and I just don't get the whole sex thing."

"So don't tell him."

"I'm a really lousy liar. And Jill! Oh, she's going to be so disappointed in me. This was all her idea."

"Hmm."

That was all. No comments, no surprise, just a meditative *"Hmm."*

She lifted her head to find him watching her. She hadn't registered how close he was. She could feel the warmth radiating from him, as if he, too, had absorbed the sun's heat during the day, just like the sand, and now he shared it with her.

"Hmm?"

"Yeah, hmm. Hmm, because it seems to me that you were going to have sex because your husband told you to. Because your friend told you to."

He leaned toward her and put his mouth on hers, and reason fled. Her head reeled, her breath stuttered. And when he drew back, all she could think was *More, more, more.*

"I didn't hear anything about you doing it because you *want* to."

He slid his hand beneath her tunic, resting it against bare skin, and she thought, *Yes.* This was what she wanted, that moment when your skin is hungry with it, desperate, and you want nothing more than the feel of another's body against yours, when the whole world falls away until nothing remains but that stark and powerful point of contact.

"What other reason is there?" he murmured.

He grabbed the hem of her cover-up and crumpled it in his fist, lifting. She raised her arms automatically, and he stripped it off, letting the wind take it. The air was cool on her belly, her chest.

His fingers worked behind her neck, tugging at the tie of her halter top, and she had to bite her lip to keep from shouting, *Hurry, hurry.*

Finally he pulled the strings free. The cups fell to her waist, exposing her naked breasts to the night. He just gazed at her, his eyes as intent as if he never planned to do anything else, or *look* at anything else. She shivered, her skin rippling with chill, while inside, heat spiraled.

And when his palm came and rested on her breast, his thumb moving slowly, she moaned aloud.

He tipped her down to the sand, which was warm and grainy against the bare skin of her back. The sensations overwhelmed her, flooding her nerves until she thought she might be lost in them, unable to find her way back out of the maze. His mouth, his hands, his skin . . . they were all there, a rich bounty.

His fingers traced the edge of her bottom, and she gasped.

Abruptly his hands stilled, and his head came up.

"What—"

"Shh." He sprang to his feet, reaching down to help her up. "Someone's coming."

Then she heard them, too, the crash of footsteps along the path, a slurred but enthusiastic rendition of "Glory Days."

How had she been so careless as to not hear them coming? Apparently her ears had stopped functioning because the rest of her senses were swamped.

She frantically looked around for her cover-up while she groped to pull her halter back up into place. It was gone. "What happened to my top?"

"I took it off."

"What?" She hadn't noticed that, either. "But—"

"No time." He simply scooped her up and carried her into the bay, his speed slowing as he waded deeper until the water rose over her, too.

The ocean came up over her chest just as the singers burst onto the beach. They leaned on each other, laughing, four or five of them, not counting the one who pitched over headfirst and was lying where he fell. The moonlight revealed size and sex but nothing more. Which was a blessing; it saved her from trying to avoid them over breakfast if she couldn't identify them.

A burly man broke free of the group, listing toward the water. Then he bent and scooped something from the sand, holding it over his head with a triumphant *whoop* like he'd just claimed the Stanley Cup.

It was her bikini top.

Defeated, she dropped her head to Jake's shoulder, unable to see any way out of this that didn't end with her exposed and mortified.

Then she caught the smell, drifting beneath the briny tang of the ocean. Not that she had a ton of experience with the stuff, but she *had* lived in the dorm, and that distinctive odor wasn't something you forgot.

She glared at the group and the flicker of firelight that bobbed around the circle. Great. If they were going to get stoned, couldn't it have been with something strong enough so that in the morning they wouldn't remember a thing about tonight? "What now?" she asked Jake.

Silently he shifted her in his arms until she was facing him, and he hooked her legs around his waist. Her bare breasts pressed against his chest, and when he moved his hips, the hard length of him speared severe pleasure through her.

"Jake—"

"Shhh. We'll just wait them out."

She just hung there against him, the water frigid around her, the waves lapping at her torso. He had one hand firmly around her back, and his free hand began to move, cupping one breast, gliding over slick skin.

"Jake." It wasn't a protest this time; his name was a sigh, an encouragement.

"Yeah?" He hummed the question against her neck. His hips moved steadily, and, unable to keep still, she pushed back. The rhythm drove her relentlessly, a mindless blur.

Only a tiny shred of sanity slipped through. "They're going to see . . ."

"So?" His mouth was magic, his hands compelling. "Do you care?"

"But—" It was hard to care about anything except what she might feel next. The guests were far away, on the shore, and it was dark. There was no chance they could see anything but two entwined figures moving rhythmically in the water.

It was the wildest thing she'd ever done. The staggering shock of it sent her heart pounding, made her acutely conscious of every touch.

"Jake—"

"Might as well make good use of the time 'til they leave."

It never occurred to her to protest. The punch of pleasure sent her reeling, unable to do anything but drift along on the current he sent careening through her.

His free hand slid inside her suit bottom, easily, softly, before plunging deep.

"God!" She bit into his shoulder to stifle her cry, clung to him while her body quaked.

She went limp, heavy against him. He was just going to have to do the work of holding her up; she had no strength to help.

"You okay?" he murmured in her ear.

Was she? She mentally checked off the possibilities.

Her body was warm and tingling in the aftershock of brutal pleasure. Yup, the body was okay. Better than okay.

The heart? She wasn't going there. Her heart wasn't involved in this in any way, had nothing to do with it. It had been put in stasis the day she discovered that her husband had betrayed her, and that's where it was staying until it was safe to take it out again.

Her brain . . . her brain was nonfunctional, numb beneath

the flood of sensation, clearly submerged beneath the domination of her body. She'd just had an orgasm, a damn fine one, better than she'd had in years, out in the open air, in the ocean, no more than twenty yards from a group of tipsy partiers, and she couldn't dredge up a reason why that was a bad idea. Which meant her brain had *clearly* abdicated the throne.

Which left her conscience. Now there was the tricky one. She'd just broken her marriage vows, though the technicalities were complicated. They hadn't had intercourse. And her husband had made a complete farce of their marriage vows such a long time ago, she wasn't sure that counted, either—contracts were void when one party failed to live up to the terms of them, weren't they? She'd have to ask her new friend Caroline, the lawyer.

All in all, her conscience was remarkably quiet. Perhaps the body released some sort of neural drug at the moment of orgasm that stilled any such inconveniences, for the only thing she really worried about right now was the *unfairness* of what had just happened, for, while she was thoroughly gratified, Jake had had no such satisfaction.

At least, she was pretty sure. It had all gotten pretty fuzzy there toward the end.

"I think I am," she said, still somewhat surprised to find it was true. Maybe the guilt would come eventually, and she'd pay doubly for its tardy arrival.

Whatever. It had been worth it. "Umm . . . how about you?"

He chuckled softly. "Better than okay."

"But wasn't that a little . . . unequal?"

His hips moved against her, leaving no doubt of it.

"Depends upon your definition of unequal." One hand was beneath her rear, the other drifting soothingly over her back. "Besides, you seem like the kind of woman who'd take it upon herself to balance the scales. Maybe even go above and beyond the call, just to make sure she wasn't unfair." She could hear the smile in his voice. "Feel free to knock yourself out."

"Duly noted." Not yet, though. She was pretty sure that "knocking herself out" was going to require her *moving*, and her limbs were not yet under conscious control. "How long can we stay here?" Forever would be good. Out here, she didn't have to deal with the messy realities of what she'd just done. Real life could stay onshore. Real life wasn't nearly as much fun as this, anyway.

"Long as you want." He kissed the side of her neck, beneath her ear, and she shivered. "Sooner or later the sun will come up, though, and the sunbathers will appear. Snorkelers, too. I'm sure some of them would be pretty happy to find us here. The view beneath the water has to be more interesting than the fish."

She sighed and surrendered to practicality, summoning her energy to turn her head on his shoulder to view the shore.

The fun patrol had grown quiet, lolling against each other on the sand like a pack of tired puppies. Asleep? she wondered. Could she have gotten that lucky?

Of course not. Even as she thought it, one of the women ashore staggered to her feet, tilting distinctly to one side. Her audience cheered lazily while she stripped off her shirt and then bent to wriggle out of her shorts. Unfortunately, she bent too far and tipped right over into the sand.

"Okay," Ellen said reluctantly. "So what are our options?"

He pondered their dilemma for a minute. "I don't suppose you'd go for just walking right past them like it was nothing? I'm pretty sure they wouldn't mind."

"Easy for you to say. You've got your pants on."

"So do you."

"Not the same," she said, wishing once again that a bit more of Jill had rubbed off on her. She would have strutted right out of the waves like Aphrodite and, if the spectators had cheered, which Ellen suspected they would, Jill would have taken a bow worthy of a diva.

"I could take 'em off," Jake suggested. "If it would make you feel better."

"The sacrifices you'd make for me." Yeah, having him naked, too, instead of her just half-naked—that would make her vastly more comfortable.

"I could go get your stuff. Bring it back out to you." His hands were much warmer than the water, as though he carried a fire within, steady and red-hot. "Assuming the guy's willing to give up his prize."

Big assumption. Also assuming he could find her top, her shirt, in the dark.

She tried to imagine standing out here in the water, in the dark, naked except for her bikini bottoms. Shivering, waiting for him to try and roust up her clothes, then find his way out to her again.

"Not sure I like that one, either."

He pondered a minute. "They're not moving now. We could probably walk right by them, and they'd never notice a thing."

"With my luck they'd have a sudden, brief, but extreme moment of clarity for the few seconds while I was creeping past." Then she surrendered to the inevitable. "There's no good way out of this, is there? I'm going to be famous by tomorrow morning. Jill's gonna be so proud of me."

"Do you have shoes on?"

"Shoes?"

"I didn't notice. I was occupied with other things. Sandals, water shoes, whatever—you have any on?"

"Sandals are on the beach with the rest."

"Okay. Don't put your feet down, all right? The coral's sharp."

Shit! She was undoubtedly going to need stitches before this was over. Either that, or she was going to have a close and personal encounter with a jellyfish when it drifted into places she'd *really* rather didn't get stung.

She should have known better, she thought. She *always* paid for even the slightest indiscretion.

But her chest was firm against his, and her body tingled with the aftershocks of pleasure, and she could still feel his mouth against her skin, as if his kiss had been branded there.

He was worth it, she decided. *No matter what, he was worth it.*

"Okay," he said. "We're gonna shift you around, so you're hanging on piggyback."

With the buoyancy of the water it was easily accomplished. It made her feel light, weightless. She looped her arms around his shoulders, her legs around his waist. Her chest, her breasts, lodged securely against his back.

"Comfortable?"

Comfortable wasn't the word that came to mind, no. Alert, astonished, completely out of her comfort zone, balanced on the narrow precipice of something entirely new.

She didn't know what lay ahead, had no bending it her way to ensure it came out right. And for once, she wasn't even going to try.

No, not comfortable. But good. Really good.

"I'm fine."

"Fine?"

"You, Jake? Even you try to fish for compliments?"

"Even me."

She laughed. "Better than fine. Sated. Replete. *Impressed*."

"There you go." He began to move through the ocean, staying at the same depth, choosing a route parallel to the shore. "And here we go."

They followed the curve of the beach, along the spear of land that matched its twin directly across the bay, where Moonlight glowed like a great yacht, its lights reflecting yellow in the water.

He moved easily, a constant pace that neither rushed nor lagged. Waves rose against them, above the curve of her breasts, and sank back to her waist, as if the water itself caressed her. There was a part of her that wished this would never end, that she could simply be carried away by him in the moonlight. But there was also a growing impatience, as the need that seemed so thoroughly satisfied only minutes ago began to swell again.

That would be something else, she thought, if just bumping along against his back made her pop off again. Now *that* would be heat.

But, next time, she'd rather wait for him.

"Where are we going?" she asked.

"You'll find out soon enough."

They rounded the point, and Sizzle vanished. Darkness rimmed the shore ahead; the brilliant half moon drifted in and out of clouds. The only sounds were the roar of the ocean, the wind through the trees. Out of the protection of the bay, the waves kicked higher, wilder, a different, dangerous beast than the mild and playful water that nudged the resort's beach, and her senses thrilled with it.

"We could be the only people on Earth," she murmured, astonished.

"Sounds good to me."

He turned for the shore, letting her slide down as they reached the sand, her wet body slipping easily over his skin, a quick, loose glide.

Then he took her hand, firm and warm. "Follow closely," he said. "There's a path, but it's narrow."

It wasn't far, only a few yards inside the line of the trees. "Wait here," he said.

She could make out little of the simple boxy structure of no grace and less beauty, smaller than a single-stall garage, that lay ahead. A storage shed, perhaps, for sea kayaks and paddle boats and volleyball nets.

A glow suddenly illuminated a small window, and then Jake stood on the front porch, a lantern swinging in his hand, all shadow and golden skin, and her heart started to pound.

"Come on up," he said. "Be careful of the steps."

The structure squatted on stilts a few feet above the tangle of brush, with rough wood stairs and an open porch that ran the length of it. It was made of concrete block, she saw when she reached his side, with two plain front windows squeezing on either side of the centered door, facing a staggeringly gorgeous view of the ocean.

"What's this?" she asked.

He stared at her so long and so seriously that she began to wonder if there was something wrong. "It's where I live."

Inside it was no bigger than her bedroom at home, and it appeared even smaller because the lamplight didn't reach the shadowed corners. The floor was rough-planked wood without so much as a rug to soften it; the concrete walls ugly, slapped with pale beige paint; and the front windows bare. Along one wall ran a stainless counter with a metal sink square in the center. A raggedy curtain of faded blue cloth covered the space beneath, and one lone shelf above that held a pot, a few cans, and a couple of bottles that glittered in the light. There was a small, old fridge with rounded corners, a table that looked like it had been hammered together out of scrap lumber, two cane-back chairs missing most of their cane.

And a mattress, just double-sized, unceremoniously flat on the floor, with pale, crumpled sheets and two limp pillows.

"So." He set the lamp on the counter. He didn't come to her, keeping a safe distance between them as if he were suddenly uncertain. "Here we are. Do you want something to drink?"

"No," she said, and closed the distance between them in an instant.

She kissed him this time, hard, and he seemed as surprised by it as she'd been. She grabbed him and dragged him toward the mattress, and when her heels bumped up against it, she pulled his hands to her breasts and went to work on the knotted drawstring of his board shorts.

Fast. She wanted it fast, and hard, and over before she had a chance to think about it. Just riding the tidal wave of need, letting it sweep her over and drown in it because she didn't know how long it would last, and she didn't want to miss it.

And then he was finally naked, and she had to slow down a minute and press her body against his, feeling him hard against her, and knowing that yes, he wanted her, just as much as she wanted him, and she gasped and pulled him down on top of her.

"Jesus," he said, and lifted his head long enough to gulp air. "We've got to be grown-up about this—"

"Oh, *why*?" She didn't want to be grown-up. She wanted to be reckless and adolescent and stupid with wanting him, all those things she'd never allowed herself to be.

"I . . . oh, *Christ*, that feels good." He put his hand over hers to still her movement, flattening her palm against him. "Hold that thought. Look. I had a checkup six months ago. Clean. I've slept with two women since then, and I used condoms with both of them."

She blinked at him, thinking how gorgeous he was above her, how good his weight felt, before his words sank in. Oh! He probably wanted her to—"I haven't had sex with anyone but my husband since I was nineteen."

"Oh, Jesus. Nothing like putting on the pressure."

"I'm sure you're up to it," she said and squeezed him with her hand, causing his hips to spasm against her. "But he cheated on me. Constantly. I'm kind of amazed that he apparently hasn't caught anything yet." *The goddamn lucky bastard.* "We didn't use—I mean, I had my tubes tied after Eric, and I had no idea . . ." She trailed off as the sheer hazard of it struck her. He could have given her *anything*, just because she'd trusted him.

She shook off the grim reality. She had better things to think of now, and she wouldn't let Tom ruin this, too. "Anyway, I was tested, too. But I'm not completely clear, time-wise, and I suppose it's better if we—"

Damn. She remembered all those condoms Jill had forced upon her, residing uselessly in the bedside drawer in her cottage.

"Taken care of," he said.

"Thank *God*," she said fervently.

Then she didn't say anything for a long time, because her mouth was busy, and she didn't have enough air to do anything but moan. And then finally, one last thing before she was lost completely: "It's just sex, right?"

His body stilled against her, a heartbeat of sharp, wavering tension. "It's just sex," he agreed, and she went under.

25

More Sex

THE night was a heated blur of pleasure, moving in and out of sleep, in and out of sex, no clear demarcation between the two because they were all of a piece.

Finally the bright, strong sun bursting through the uncovered windows woke Ellen for good. She stretched, unhappy to find that she was alone on the rumpled bed, naked and uncovered.

Automatically she grabbed for the sheet and pulled it up, her gaze sweeping the small, spare space. There was a lone bare bulb hanging above her, a pile of snorkeling equipment in one corner, a pale drift of sand across the rough floors.

And, his back to her, clad only in a faded pair of plaid boxers, Jake, clanging and rattling something at the rickety counter.

Okay, so what was the appropriate morning-after conversation? Good morning? Good-bye? Good job?

She settled on the simplest. "Hey." Maybe he'd want her to leave right away. The night was over, time to move on. Wasn't that the usual MO for one-night stands? They hadn't discussed the particulars: was this was a one-night aberration or an until-the-vacation's-over affair?

She devoutly hoped he wasn't kicking her out immediately.

He looked over his shoulder at her. There were pale strips across the top of his feet where his sandals blocked the tan; his hair was a wild mess—she was unaccountably proud that she'd put it in that condition.

His smile was warm and unhurried. "Morning. Eggs?"

Suddenly she was starving. Well, she'd earned that, hadn't she? "Eggs sound fabulous."

He wielded a spatula in one hand like a weapon, and it was all she could do not to drag him back to bed straightaway. But it'd be good have some fuel first. She had a young lover to keep up with.

Lover. The word no longer terrified her. In fact, she rather liked it.

He padded over in his bare feet and bent over to kiss her, warm and slow. "How are you this morning?"

She gave it serious consideration, probing the corners of her conscience for guilt, regrets, recriminations. Surely there had to be *some*. But apparently they were on delayed onset, because she couldn't find a one.

She was happy. It was simple and uncomplicated and totally unexpected.

Her emotions rarely came without conditions or *buts*. So right now, for this brief moment, she was going to let it be.

"I'm great." Her stomach rumbled.

"Better get you fed." Her turned back to the single-burner propane stove. "How do you like your eggs?"

"Any way. Whatever's good."

She watched him for a moment, then realized her dilemma. She was buck naked, and the only stitch of clothes she had in the place was a tiny bikini bottom, which could be anywhere.

"Jake?"

"Hmm?" He whipped a fork in a blue plastic bowl.

"Do you have a . . . shirt, or something?"

"Sure. See the trunk against the far wall? There should be something in there."

The room, which a few moments before had seemed downright snug, suddenly seemed cavernous, when you had to walk across it in broad daylight nude.

She pondered her options.

She could wrap the sheets around her, which would betray her absurd attack of modesty, but at least she'd be covered. Or there was the naked dash, which would make certain things joggle unattractively but would at least be over quickly, hopefully before he caught an unappetizing eyeful.

He dumped the eggs in the pan, then turned around, bracing his hands behind him on the counter.

"You're welcome to help yourself," he told her. Amusement played around his mouth. His riotously *sexy* mouth, which he'd used to such good advantage last night, and heat began to simmer in her belly.

"You're not going to go fetch it for me, are you?"

"Hey, I've got eggs to cook."

"You're not paying a whole lot of attention to the eggs right now."

"Cook better if you let 'em sit for a few minutes first." The amusement widened into open challenge. "Come on, El. There's nothing you're going to flash that I haven't already investigated pretty thoroughly."

Scenes from the night flickered through her mind. He'd been thorough, all right, and the memories weren't doing anything to calm her down. Obviously the "sexual peak of mature women" that Jill was always prattling about had finally decided to make a tardy appearance in Ellen and was all the more ferocious for its late arrival.

She should have made a dash while she could. Now he was waiting for the show.

Yes, there wasn't anything there he hadn't seen last night—and felt, and tasted, and pretty much everything else it was possible to do to a body part. But her body had been veiled in darkness, and Jake's assessment clouded by his, well, *horniness*, a state of affairs that was far different than exposing all her sags and wrinkles in the clear and unforgiving light of day.

But there was no help for it. He wasn't going to be polite. And it would be horribly inhibited—not to mention kind of ridiculous—to admit that she didn't have the guts to stand up naked in front of him, considering that she'd evinced a startling and robust lack of inhibitions last night.

She looked away from him, because she couldn't bear to see the slightest bit of disappointment in his face.

She didn't look bad for forty-two. She wasn't being stupidly humble about it. But he was definitely *not* forty-two, and she'd seen the gorgeous woman who'd approached him in the bar, who undoubtedly would have been more than happy to strut across his floor without a stitch on. Ellen couldn't compete.

So she kept her gaze fixed on the chest when she dropped the sheet and stood up, forcing herself not to rush, while her palms went damp.

It was painfully embarrassing. It was also, to her astonishment, undeniably exciting.

She lifted the lid and dug through the contents. Jake didn't say a word. Obviously the man had nothing to hide, because he didn't seem to care about her pawing through his things.

Not that there was much to investigate. It certainly didn't do much to satisfy her curiosity. A half-dozen swim trunks, all well-used; some boxer shorts, all in as sorry a condition as the ones he wore, clean but so worn that the fabric was sheer; two pairs of cargo shorts, a couple of cut-offs, and a pile of T-shirts. It didn't even fill the small trunk.

She pulled out the top T-shirt, faded, ugly mustard with a *Sam's Surf* logo on the front, a grinning, sunglassed bonefish balanced on a red surfboard. She got it only over her head and was groping for the sleeves when Jake stopped the shirt's progress by the simple method of putting his hands on her waist, leaving her exposed from there down.

"No use in putting that on now," he told her. "I'd just have to take it off again."

He touched her only lightly. It didn't take more. Her body recalled every sensation from the night before, and her skin started to hum just because he was near.

"What about the eggs?"

"I'll make more," he murmured, and walked her back toward the bed.

"Jake?"

"Hmm?"

"Am I a pity fuck?"

"What?"

Shoot. She should have waited; the question stopped his hands in midstroke, and he took his mouth away from beneath her ear, where it was doing quite lovely things.

"I'm just curious," she assured him. "I don't really care either way. I just want to know."

His eyes narrowed, his jaw tightening. She didn't even know he could look like that. In an instant, her easygoing, sexy Jake had transformed into someone edgy, intense, with an anger leashed just beneath the surface.

He grabbed her hand, brought her palm to his hard cock. "Does this *feel* like pity to you?"

She caught her breath. Then she moved her hand, and he pulsed back in response, and she forgot all about questions for a very long time.

* * *

"Okay, now I *am* starving," she said when she could talk again. "And, while I do appreciate the simple rusticity of this place, *please* tell me the facilities aren't in an outhouse."

She was tucked up against his side, her head on his shoulder, her hand against his chest, which rumbled when he chuckled. It was a dilemma. Because she was blissfully comfortable right where she was, and would vastly prefer never to move again.

Unfortunately, her bladder wasn't cooperating.

"See that door over there?" He pointed with his chin to the corner by the fridge, to a wooden, six-panel door with chipped blue paint and a lever handle. "All the modern facilities. Hot water, even."

"Hot water?" Okay, that might be worth moving for. "Can I shower?"

"Sure." He turned his head and pressed his mouth against her temple. Sweet, gentle, and her heart squeezed.

The sex she might, just might, be able to handle.

The tenderness screamed danger.

"Unfortunately," he murmured, "the shower stall's not big enough for two."

"That's all right. No doubt you need some recovery time, anyway."

"You think?" He lifted the sheet so she could take a peek.

"Jeez, how young *are* you?"

"Twenty-three."

Twenty-three.

"Breathe, El, breathe. Kidding. Oh, Lord, you should see your face right now. I'm thirty-one."

She grabbed the nearest pillow and gave him a healthy whack.

"Oh, come on now. It was a joke. And really, don't you feel much better about thirty-one after I started at twenty-three?"

"I'm taking a shower," she said, trying to gather her dignity as she stalked toward the bathroom. This time she didn't even consider covering up. She glanced back before she closed the door behind her, gratified to find his gaze glued to her butt. She gave a little shake, which earned a moan and had him bounding over the bed toward her before she slammed the door shut.

The water felt great, tingling as it pounded over skin that had been sensitized to near pain. Her thighs ached, she was tender in vulnerable areas, and a whisker burn decorated her right breast.

She felt fan-freakin'-tastic.

She used his plain deodorant soap, his herbal shampoo, and laughed to think that, if she hadn't smelled like him already, she soon would. She squeezed a dab of toothpaste on the corner of a rough white washcloth and did the best she could, then tugged on the oversize T-shirt and her bikini bottom, which she'd rescued from where it was decorating the breathing tube of a snorkel.

She was definitely not well-prepared for a fling.

When she left the bathroom, Jake was working at the stove again. Two tumblers of juice, a pair of white plastic plates, and two bent stainless forks rested on the surface of the narrow table. He'd put a flower there, too, something small and orange and fragrant, stuck into an empty beer bottle, and she smiled.

She wrapped her arms around him from behind, marveling that it was so easy to touch him, that she felt so much less awkward than she would have expected. She had no urge to bolt, to run back to safety and forget what had happened the night before.

"Away from me, temptress," he said. "These are the last eggs, and I need sustenance if I'm to keep up with you."

It was a wild exaggeration, but it made her grin anyway, to hear herself described like that.

She released him and wandered around the small room. A gray raincoat hung on a hook by the wall; several pairs of cheap rubber flip-flops piled beside the door. She opened the window, allowing the sound and the smell of the ocean to rush in, and she filled her lungs.

The place couldn't have been more simple. Except for the photos tacked all over the walls. Some black and white, some color, all of the island, but they were anything but the typical tropical happy beach scenes, perfect sunsets, and gloriously blooming flowers.

This showed the other sides of paradise. There was a purple flower, so close up it was at first difficult to recognize as such, the velvety petals and spearing yellow stamen wildly sexual. An old, withered man, skin dark as mahogany, held aloft a dead swordfish, the blood streaming from the gaffe wound the most vivid color in the entire photograph, in sharp relief as the rest faded into haze.

There was a dying palm tree, twisted and uprooted by a brutal storm, shot in murky black and white. A once-pretty blond with red-rimmed eyes, skin peeling from a vicious sunburn, boarded the little shuttle plane with her shirt stained and askew, her shoulders slumping beneath the weight of her unzipped duffel, looking as if, if she'd had one more minute of fun on Sizzle, she would have ended up in a hospital bed.

Pink-beige flesh glistened in an open clamshell. A wild-eyed flamingo stood in the shallows, its neck a graceful curve, while a small crab struggled in its beak. A ripe pineapple rotted against a lush carpet of decomposing leaves, the jet carapaces of the beetles that feasted on it gleaming like polished onyx.

"Who—" And then she saw the camera case, well-worn black leather, hanging by its strap on a hook by the door. "You did these? All of them?"

He shrugged carelessly, but his eyes were guarded. "Guy's gotta have a hobby."

"But they're . . ." She shook her head. *Good* didn't even touch it. "Astonishing. Do you sell them?"

With his spatula he scraped yellow eggs onto the plate. He tossed a box of powdered doughnuts on the table. "Better eat while it's hot."

She sat gingerly, because the chair looked like it might shatter beneath her, and that *would* be embarrassing. Not to mention it looked like it might harbor a splinter or two, and her butt wasn't all that well covered.

His salt was still in the Morton's carton, but his pepper came from a stainless steel mill the size of his forearm. He ground a flurry over his eggs until the yellow was thickly flecked with black.

She popped a forkful of eggs into her mouth and chewed while she studied him. "So," she ventured conversationally. "About the photos."

"It's just for fun," he said, dismissing it as easily as if it were no more important than one of his decrepit rubber sandals.

"That's a shame," she said. "Because they're amazing."

"Thanks," he said, plowing through the eggs, attending to the apparently vital task of keeping up his strength.

She put her hand over the one that held the fork, making him slow down and listen to her. "Seriously amazing."

He paused, studying her face as if he wasn't sure if she was lying to him. Then he picked up a triangle of overdone toast and crunched down. "Glad you like 'em."

Ellen debated. What she was about to do skirted the edge of

the "just sex" rules. Dragging him back to bed was less dangerous than mucking around in his life.

But it would be an absolute shame if he kept work like
that to himself. In fact, if you thought about it the right way,
interfering—encouraging—was the noble thing to do.

"You ever think about selling them? Or at least exhibiting
them?"

"I asked once. They weren't exactly the image Sizzle's going for."

"Those idiots."

"They're right, Ellen."

"Well, yeah, but—" Her urge to defend—not him, of course,
the *work*—was strong, but not so strong she couldn't see the logic.
"Okay, not here. There are lots of other places in the world."

"You want some coffee?"

She shook her head. "I like my caffeine cold." Okay, that was
a clear answer: *Off limits*.

He poured himself a cup, plain white ceramic, then sat down
with his hands wrapped around it. "I was talking to a writer once,
in the bar. He said the minute he sold a book, it stopped being
about writing and started being about publishing. I don't think I
want that to happen. I *like* it being just about the pictures."

It sounded perfectly reasonable, that he'd be afraid of clutter-
ing up something he enjoyed so much with business. It could
even be true.

Or it could be that he was afraid to send his photographs out
to the world. Afraid of rejection, afraid that people wouldn't
like them, afraid that making a living as a photographer wasn't
a practical dream.

Afraid of having anyone see him as something other than a
footloose, irresponsible bartender in paradise. Did he never want
anything more than that? Maybe he didn't. It was not for her to
decide. But it was hard for Ellen to comprehend that someone
would have no dreams, no ambition whatsoever.

None of your business, she reminded herself. This was a three-
day fling, a gloriously physical three-day fling, and nothing more.

She knew better than to make it anything but sex. What good would it do? Even if he did want more than this, more than Sizzle, she couldn't be a part of it. If he suddenly decided to find a life bigger than just the bar, he'd need a woman who'd discover that life with him. Who he could have a family with, if that's what he chose. Not someone who was far beyond discovering life and was well into trying to patch one back together.

"All right," she said. "But they're wonderful, and I love them." She pushed her plate away and looked down at herself. Her nipples showed through the thin, much-washed cotton of the T-shirt, which only covered about two inches of her thighs. She hadn't a brush, so her hair was starting to wave damply. She could maybe beg a cap from him, but the shoes were a problem. She had decent-sized feet for a woman, but his sandals were still at least an inch too long for her, and trekking through the tangle of palmettos in them was a sure way to twist an ankle.

"Well," she said glumly, "I suppose I should prepare myself for the walk of shame."

He looked at her in question, and she waved a hand to take in her getup. "Anybody who gets one look at me's gonna have a pretty good idea what *I* did last night."

"Do you care?"

She winced. "Maybe. A little." It wasn't that she was ashamed, exactly. She *wasn't*. But it was the kind of awkward exposure of matters she considered private that she'd diligently avoided her whole life.

He stood up and held out his hand. "Give me your key, tell me what you want. I'll bring back whatever you need. You can stay here."

Stay here.

It was a thoughtful gesture. And it was so much more than that: *Last night was more than last night; you can stay. And I trust you alone in my place; there are no secrets from you here.*

Something softened in the middle of her chest, and she warned it to toughen up.

It's still just sex. It's just more sex, and aren't you a lucky woman?

"Umm . . . key?" she asked.

It really was unfair, she decided, that she would look like hell after last night, and he only looked more gorgeous.

"Let me guess. It's at the beach."

"You didn't leave me with much, Jake."

"Hey, I'm a thorough guy."

"You are at that," she said in a voice that had him moving toward her, intent darkening his eyes. "Please! A toothbrush, a brush. Maybe a leg razor. Trust me, it's a good plan. You'll appreciate it."

He didn't look entirely convinced. "I'll have to get a master from someone. Do you mind if it's Melody? She might guess. But she won't care."

"It's fine. I like Melody." She pondered for a moment. *What's one more sin?* she decided, and reached for a doughnut. "Besides, she was the one who ordered me to get Jake to take care of me. Wonder if this is what she meant? I'll have to report that you took *extremely* good care of me."

"You'd better stop looking at me like that, if you want any clothes before I have to leave for work."

"Can't help it." She'd only have so much opportunity to look at him; she was taking full advantage of it.

He hesitated just before he stepped out the door. "What do you want me to bring back?"

Now there was a question. How much stuff he brought back had everything to do with how long she planned to stay here. She didn't want to take advantage, didn't want to imply acceptance of an invitation that hadn't been extended.

But he'd asked. He could have just brought her enough to get her out of here without obvious embarrassment.

"Ev—" She swallowed when her voice rose. *Take the chance,* she told herself. *You took one last night, and see how well that worked out.*

But last night she hadn't consciously made a decision. Her body had taken over for her mind, sweeping away any qualms, any ability to call a halt. She'd simply wanted, and when it was offered to her, she took.

This was a decision.

"How about everything?"

His grin was dazzling. "Everything it is."

26

Leaving Paradise

SHE never went back to her cottage.

Instead, she pretended she'd been shipwrecked, the rest of the world thousands of miles away, and she didn't know if she'd ever get back to civilization, with its complications and vows and broken promises.

It was a good thing Jake had taken her at her word and brought everything, including the ridiculous stash of condoms that Jill had given her. But they went through Jake's supply that first afternoon, and even Ellen's was getting low.

When Jake had to work, she read, walked on the beach, floated over the coral reef that rambled only a dozen yards off-shore. He trusted her with his digital camera, which she could hardly believe, and so she snapped a few photos herself. Nothing like his, of course, but none of his pictures were of *him*, and she couldn't resist. Her favorite was when she caught him early one morning on the porch, leaning against a pole, with his sexy morning stubble and his shorts on but unsnapped, his hair uncombed, contemplating the ocean with a coffee cup in his hand. There was not a woman on earth, she thought, who could look at that picture and not want to drag him off to bed. She could still hardly believe that she could—and did, right after she took the photograph.

She subsisted on fruit and peanut butter sandwiches. One night they ate the fresh fish he pulled out of the ocean right in front of their cove and grilled over the fire he built on the beach.

He brought her a case of Diet Coke, bless him, and offered to find anything else she wanted. She couldn't think of a thing.

Often she dozed, her rest deep and dreamless, the kind of restorative sleep she hadn't had in months. Regularly she slept until he returned and woke her, nudging her awake with a kiss, the brush of his hand across her bare belly, and she swam up to consciousness already powerfully aroused, ready for him, and she slid straight from sleep to passion.

He wasn't getting much sleep, though. She felt guilty about that sometimes; he had to go to work, while all she had to do was relax. He swore he didn't mind.

Jake could sleep when she went home. Neither one of them mentioned that prospect, as though, as long as they didn't talk about it, it was far away, an abstraction instead of an impending event.

In some ways the days seemed endless. But she'd never known three days to fly by so fast.

They were very nearly the best of her life. It'd be hard to match the days her children were born, but after that . . . they *shouldn't* be. They couldn't be that important. It was only sheer relaxation and extraordinarily hot sex.

But she was happy, easily so, and it was so simple to let the worries drift away with the days.

Except then it was time to go home.

"Are you sure you don't want me to come to the plane with you?"

She dragged the zipper closed on her brown canvas carry-on and glanced over at him. He was still on the mattress, naked, the sheets puddling low around his hips, his eyes sleepy and warm.

"You stay here," she said. "You didn't get back until nearly three last night. There's no reason for you to get up already."

"There's a reason."

"No." She made a tour of the room, checking to make sure she hadn't left anything important behind. And because she couldn't look at him and not say, *"Yes, please, come with me. Come with me."*

There was a time she would have scoffed at a place like his hut, with its cheap construction and utter lack of elegance. Now she appreciated it. Its simplicity ensured that the house never got in the way of the things that happened in it; it didn't demand much in the way of maintenance, didn't detract from the splendor of the island and the ocean. It never stole attention from more important things.

She'd almost reached the door. She saw the harshly brilliant sun on the ocean, the deserted stretch of pale, clean sand.

She dropped her luggage and ran back to Jake, bending over to kiss him so hard her lips bruised. "Have a good life," she whispered, and lunged for the door.

* * *

"Come on, come on, come *on*."

Ellen was waiting for the shuttle on a concrete slab, the tin roof overhead blocking the strong morning sun. The day was perfect for flying, Melody was there to see them all off safely, but the plane hadn't arrived yet. A connecting flight from the States had been delayed, and they'd waited for those guests in Nassau. Melody had apologized profusely and offered to fetch them anything they wanted in recompense. Surprisingly, nobody took her up on it.

Apparently the party was over.

Three women from Chicago, their faces as red as cooked lobster, save for the white bandit marks around their eyes left by sunglasses, slumped against each other on a slatted bench, dozing, their feet propped against their Vuitton cases.

A tall, thin man, small black glasses perched on his long, sharp nose, had already shifted into work mode. His blue Egyptian cotton shirt was growing damp, though it was tucked neatly into gray tropical-weight wool slacks. His black shoes had a glassy shine, and he was frowning at the sheaf of papers he'd pulled from his briefcase, muttering as he flipped from one to the next. Going straight to a meeting, no doubt.

One of the workers was leaving, too, a young, lovely server

from Atlanta, who'd excitedly told everyone she was off to meet her new niece for the very first time.

"Come *on*," Ellen repeated again, tapping her sandals against the concrete. She was too jittery to sit, too scattered to read. She could only hope that plane came to take her home before she did something irreversibly stupid.

"Still worried about the flight?" Melody asked pleasantly. She held a clipboard in one hand, a handful of glossy brochures in the other, ready to welcome the new arrivals.

"No, actually." She wasn't worried about getting home; she was worried about what was going to happen once she got there.

"Did you enjoy yourself?"

Ellen shot her a sharp glance. It wouldn't be unusual for staff to gossip about guests. She'd worked at a resort in northern Minnesota one summer, not far from her family's cabin, between her sophomore and junior years. The girls who cleaned the cabins knew *everything*, and they had no problem telling everyone else about it. Besides flirting with the caddies and lifeguards, it was the most fun to be had.

But if Melody knew anything, she was wasted on Sizzle; she should be in Hollywood. Her expression was pleasant and strictly professional.

"I did. Very much." And suddenly her eyes burned.

"Oh, dear." Melody scrambled in her pocket for a tissue and thrust it at Ellen. "I guess you're going to miss us."

"No." She sniffed, flapping her hands in front of her face to dry the moisture. "I guess I just missed my kids all of a sudden." And abruptly she did, with a piercing longing that actually hurt. She hadn't been away from them this long in years. Tom had wanted to take her to Italy for their fifteenth wedding anniversary, but Eric had had nearly constant strep infections that winter, and she hadn't wanted to leave him.

"You did pretty well," Melody assured her. "That usually hits most mothers on the fourth day."

"Yes? Well, maybe it should have. Maybe I'd have it out of my system by now."

The kids were fine, she told herself. She would have heard otherwise if they weren't.

Suddenly the hours of travel ahead seemed unbearable. She wanted to be home *now*, to put her arms around her children and hang on. They were her life, always had been, and she needed to be with them.

"Yoo-hoo! El! Over here!"

The Boston crew scooted toward her in bikinis and high heels, multicolored martini glasses in their hands, their eyes shaded by floppy straw hats and sunglasses the size of coasters.

"There you are." Caroline was panting by the time she reached Ellen's side. "Christie *swore* she saw you headed this way, and I didn't want you to leave without saying good-bye."

"Are you coming now?"

"Nope. Two more days." She scrabbled through her big-flowered tote and pulled out a card. "Here," she said, pressing it into Ellen's hand. "Just in case you ever come to Boston. Or you want to come to a wedding."

"Thank you." Shoot. She hadn't even lifted off from Sizzle yet and already guilt was starting to nag her. She thought it might wait until she touched down in Minnesota. "I'm sorry I haven't seen you. The last couple of days—"

"Oh, psshhaw. No worries." But she was grinning, lit up with *I-know-a-secret* glow.

"I know I said I'd meet you that night, but—"

"Not to worry," Christie put in. Her sunglasses swallowed her face, and apparently one drink wasn't enough, because she had one for each hand—one pink, one orange. "'S okay that you started the skinny-dippin' before we got there."

"I didn—" Ellen closed her eyes, concentrated on her breathing so she didn't flip right into hyperventilation. When she opened her eyes again, they were all beaming at her. "You were . . . there?"

"Damn right we were there!" Christie crowed.

"Oh, Lord." Ellen swayed, as she tried to recall how much moonlight there'd been that night, and how far from shore she'd been, how much they could possibly have seen. "I didn't see—"

"Of course you didn't," Caroline said kindly. "You were kind of occupied."

There was no leering. Not even a smirk, and certainly no judgment. Caroline looked more like a mother awaiting her child's report on her first day of school, anxious and proud.

"I—" There was nothing for her to say, no way to pretend it was anything other than it was. She eyed her new friends uneasily. Depending upon how many drinks they'd had already this morning, the next questions could be *very* uncomfortable.

Luckily, the roar of propeller engines drowned out Caroline's words. The wings waggled, as if the plane was waving at them, and veered toward the narrow, rough strip that passed as a runway.

The sleepy girls on the bench staggered to their feet. The businessman scowled impatiently at the plane and shoved papers into his briefcase.

Workers scurried out to pull down the stairs. Melody stationed herself beside the bottom step, her wide, welcoming smile fixed.

As the door opened, new guests popped out, wary heads emerging first like groundhogs checking for sunlight. Fish-belly pale, squinting at the unaccustomed brightness, they stepped gingerly down the stairs.

"Well. We'd better let you go." Caroline tugged her into an unexpected hug. Ellen found herself squeezing back, hanging on to this one last remnant of Sizzle. "Have a good life," Caroline whispered in her ear, then released her.

"I'm damn well gonna try." Though she had no idea what "a good life" meant for her anymore. It was past time to start finding out.

She grabbed her luggage and turned for the plane.

* * *

THE cold smacked her the instant she stepped off the plane in Minneapolis. The gangway was uninsulated, its thin, rattling metal no match for January. The vacationers, worn from sun and fun, huddled into the jackets they pulled from their carry-ons and clattered through it at top speed, into the sterile warmth of the airport.

She hadn't arranged for anyone to meet her. She didn't want them waiting around for her, and now that increased security meant people couldn't even go into a restaurant but were instead relegated to the luggage pickup area, hanging around the airport for a late plane was anything but fun.

She'd grab a cab, dump off her stuff, and zip downtown to pick up the kids.

And then she'd start her list, pros and cons. She and Tom had an appointment with Lauren on Thursday, and by then she needed to make decisions, both about what she intended to reveal to Tom about what had happened on Sizzle and what she was going to do with the rest of her life.

She slumped against the railing of the escalator.

Opposite her, happy travelers chattered as they rode up. They were getting out of here, escaping the cold, the dreary, heading off for skiing or golf. No set-faced businessmen and -women facing a week of work and planes, not on Sunday afternoon.

Her fellow travelers descending were glum. Playtime was over. Tomorrow morning they'd have to pull on work clothes and trudge to the office.

She didn't feel ready to make a decision. Not enough information; she didn't have all the angles researched, couldn't ensure that the next twenty years would run according to plan.

The lined metal steps flattened into the floor. She lifted her eyes, glancing through the double glass doors ahead, and saw Kate.

Kate, serious-faced in puffy down, who gave an awkward wave—*Anybody notice me? Can't get caught looking happy to see my mom*—when she realized Ellen saw her.

Eric stood beside her, somehow older than when she'd left. Still an adolescent, yes, but traces of the boy fading, suggestions of the man peeking through. Kate elbowed him, and he snapped his DS shut and pocketed it, then grinned at his mother, shifting impatiently from foot to foot.

Ellen charged through the door and hooked an arm around each one, dragging them both into her embrace. If it embarrassed them, so be it. A little parental embarrassment now and then was vital to their character.

Tom stood behind them, looking pleased with himself.

"I wasn't expecting you all to be here!"

"We thought we'd surprise you," he said. "It'll be cold out at the taxi stand, and we knew you'd be missing the kids."

"Thanks." She shut her eyes and hugged the kids tighter. Eric smelled of popcorn and the Old Spice deodorant he slathered on after his twice-daily showers; Kate had ditched her usual Stella McCartney perfume; she smelled of mango-scented shampoo, close to the Dragonberry Kids she'd favored at eight.

Ellen steeled herself for when they'd start to pull away. It was no reflection on her parenting if they didn't want to hug her in public.

But surprisingly, Katie hung on, gripping around Ellen's neck like she used to when she'd been awakened by a nightmare, and Ellen had come running at her cries.

"I'm glad you're home, Mom."

"Kate?" When the hug ended, Ellen tried to peer into her face, all her Mom instincts on orange alert. But Katie had her head down, corn-silk hair shielding her expression.

Then her cell thumped with Timbaland. She pulled it out of her purse and turned away to mumble in it.

"Ready to go?" Tom had already snagged her suitcase from the carousel and held it in one leather-gloved hand and he'd slung her carry-on over his shoulder. "They unloaded fast today."

"You don't have to carry all that," she said as she fell into step beside him, the kids trailing behind.

"No problem."

An insidious tapeworm of guilt wound its way through Ellen's stomach.

There it is. Her conscience had stayed mute longer than she'd expected.

If only Tom hadn't shown up to fetch her. She could curse him as she froze her ass off at the taxi stand.

But he could be thoughtful. She'd managed to block that quality from her consciousness completely and didn't appreciate the reminder.

One for the good side of the list. Damn it.

"How'd it go?"

He pursed his lips, as if giving it serious consideration. She'd expected a breezy "Great!" reminding her that *he* had no trouble handling the children in her absence.

"Okay, I guess. Eric didn't say much. Kate broke curfew. We'll have to talk about that."

"You didn't ground her?"

"Figured I'd better talk to you first, since you're the one who'll have to enforce it."

Ellen shot him a shocked look. He strode comfortably along beside her, matching his speed to hers, while Kate cruised ahead with her phone to her ear and Eric bopped along behind, inspecting the magazines at every stand they passed, his iPod headphones in his ear.

"Thank you," she told him. "For this, and that, too."

"Sure." The automatic doors to the parking ramp rolled open in front of them. "It's harder than I thought."

She wasn't sure what he meant: raising the children, being separated, the state of their marriage. Just being a grown-up, maybe. She was finding it a lot harder than it had looked from the front end, when adulthood, with its independence and choices, had seemed like heaven compared to the constriction and duties of high school.

"Yeah," she said. "It's harder than I thought."

27

Choices

TODAY the tea was green jasmine, the background track a haunting Eastern flute, and Lauren's suit a rich chocolate tweed. She crossed her legs, clad—undoubtedly to Tom's dismay—in gleaming brown boots up to her knees, with heels that should have been registered as lethal weapons.

"So," Lauren said, her pen hovering over her notepad. "Was it just sex?"

The question caught Ellen by surprise. It shouldn't have; that had been the whole point of the little experiment, hadn't it? "Of course it was," she answered automatically, the lie bitter in her mouth. She'd tried, she really had, to make it nothing more. But obviously she just wasn't built that way.

Or maybe it was simply impossible for Jake to be *just* anything. She should have chosen someone less . . . that was it. Just someone *less*. Then maybe she'd be able to sleep without expecting to find him next to her when she awoke.

It had been such a brief interlude. It had never been intended to be anything more. But he'd somehow imprinted on her in that brief time, her skin holding the sensation of his touch, in her mind a clear picture of his smile. She wondered if it would simply fade, or if it would have to be overwritten with other sensations, other memories, or if he would simply be with her forever.

"And what did you learn?" Lauren asked.

Ellen's gaze flicked toward her husband.

He sat back in his chair, his legs wide, claiming his space, sipping from the coffee he'd picked up at the Starbuck's in the lobby. Tea just didn't have enough kick for him.

He'd taken the afternoon off, which was unusual enough to put Ellen on alert, and so he was in casual clothes, plain khakis and a mossy green sweater that showed off his eyes. He looked handsome, comfortable, completely undisturbed by the fact that his wife had just confessed her affair.

It only served to remind her how little she could read him. More than twenty *years*, and she had no idea if he was jealous that she'd slept with someone else, pleased that she'd followed his orders, or merely titillated by the whole thing. Every possibility seemed unpleasant.

But hedging the truth to their counselor didn't seem productive. "It was easier than I thought," she said slowly.

"Easier, how?" Lauren prompted.

"I get the—" She paused, attempting to sort through the lunatic jumble of emotions. "I get the excitement of it. How someone could get swept away by it. How it's possible to not *think* for a while, or just not to care if you do."

Tom shifted in his chair, his brows lifting.

"You seem surprised," she said. "I thought that was what you wanted."

"It is. I just—" He stopped abruptly, as if sensing danger ahead.

"You just didn't think I had it in me, did you?"

Stalling, he gulped his coffee as if it were the only thing between him and instant death.

"What step do you envision next?" Lauren asked.

Next was exactly what she'd been trying to ignore. *Next* haunted her, reminded her that it would come whether she wanted it to or not. Mocked her with its inevitably and unpredictability.

"I don't know."

"You don't know." Tom's sigh was pure exasperation. "What else can we do? It's been months. I can't keep on like this, Ellen. You have to decide."

"I can't—" Her hands shook. She felt she was playing *Let's Make a Deal* with her life, the dingy cloth curtains lined up before her, but there weren't any cute prizes behind them. There was only her future, potential disaster lurking behind each one, and no hints as to the one with the jackpot. Tom wanted her to pick blind and live with the consequences. "I have to be sure, and I don't *know* . . ."

"No one ever does," Lauren said kindly. "You want guarantees, and life simply doesn't offer them. You can only make decisions on the best available information, which is never complete, and then adjust course as events warrant."

"I *hate* that!"

"Of course you do." Lauren put down her tea and leaned forward. "Who wouldn't prefer a guarantee, if one were possible? But it simply isn't."

Ellen fought the urge to bolt out of that serene room, away from her faithless husband and uncertainty. She'd find a deserted island, someplace just like Sizzle but without any *men* on it, and she'd just drift, and nobody'd ask her to decide anything until she'd considered every possible angle.

"But you're not only looking for guarantees," Lauren continued, "you're expecting absolutes, which is not necessary. A decision is not irrevocable, and it's not always all-or-nothing."

Ellen exchanged a quick, puzzled glance with Tom.

"I'm not quite clear on what you're suggesting," Tom said.

"Let's say Ellen decides to give your marriage another try today. That does not mean that if, down the road, she uncovers further information, she cannot change her mind. As can you."

"I don't think I can go through this again," Ellen said. She would rather end it right now than have to struggle through the same old misery, the same scary choices, one more time.

"It wouldn't be the *same*, Ellen. That's the whole point. It would merely be an adjustment in light of further discoveries. It is what we all do on a daily basis."

In some ways that made sense. The heavy weight of finality

was keeping her stuck, unable to move forward or back, terrified of making the wrong choice. But if she didn't move, nothing would change. She would learn nothing new, have no better information in a month or a year than she did right at this instant.

"Okay, I get it. Ellen, what do you think?" Tom deferred to her, but he looked supremely confident, as if he were negotiating a contract he already knew he had in the bag.

The simple truth of it was she could not walk away from her marriage until she knew, without any doubt, that she had done everything possible to salvage it. When she envisioned her future, she'd always seen herself and Tom. Walking Katie down the aisle, beaming with pride, finding their own meaning in their daughter's vows. Opening their home to grandchildren, big family celebrations centering around the two of them. Trotting the world together until neither one of them could trot anymore, and then reveling in the memories of a long and full life together.

There had to be some value in overcoming the bumps along the way. In forgiveness, if she could just bring herself to do it.

"I *do* want to try again," she said. "But I don't know if I can."

"So how long am I supposed to wait?" Tom asked, impatience sharpening his tone. "How many hoops do you want me to jump through to prove myself?"

"The fear is freezing you," Lauren said, "and it is not productive. But you find it overwhelming, Ellen, because you are still seeing the decision as either/or. You don't have to say yes today and have him move back in tomorrow. You could make the decision to give your marriage another attempt, but begin with dating."

"Dating?" Tom sounded about as thrilled as if Lauren had just suggested he trade in his cherished BMW for a rusty Chevy Nova.

"Dating will allow Ellen to become accustomed to the idea of the two of you together again. To learn to *trust* again, which is the crux of the problem. And encourage both of you to rediscover what it was that brought you together in the first place."

In some ways Ellen was inclined to Tom's position. What was

the point? Either they were going to get back together or they weren't. There wasn't anything she could learn over dinner that would make any difference.

"It is a commitment between the two of you that you have begun that journey back toward a complete and fulfilling marriage."

"But—" Tom's knee jiggled. "Is there . . ."

"Sex?" Lauren raised one perfectly arched brow. "No. No completion, in any case, not at first. It has always been my position that sex is about far more than intercourse."

"Oh, come on."

"There should be a mutually agreed-upon endpoint. I often suggest a month."

She could do that, Ellen thought. It would give her time. Time to be certain, and yet there was a deadline for when she *had* to know. This would not drag out endlessly.

"I like it," Ellen said and turned to face her husband. "But, since apparently I was not distinctly clear on these points previously, there are some ground rules."

Tom came within a split second of rolling his eyes.

"While we are dating, and *particularly* once we begin sleeping together again—"

"Are we going to sleep together again?" he put in sharply.

"I—" That was the logical conclusion of salvaging their marriage, she supposed. And she had already decided she could not live with herself if she didn't give it one more honest attempt. She'd invested too much to give up easily. "Since we're going to give it another try, that's part of the program, isn't it?"

His smile was completely self-assured. He was getting what he wanted. His family back, and sex, and that—along with an outrageous salary—that was pretty much everything that he wanted out of life.

She wondered when he'd gotten so sure of himself. He looked like he believed that, once she'd climbed in bed with him again, the idea of her wanting to divorce him would be inconceivable.

And she . . . she couldn't summon up a vision of the two of them together again. Strange. It wasn't as if she didn't have a brain full of memories, didn't know every inch of his body, didn't remember with absolute precision how they fit together.

But it seemed like those were other people entirely. She couldn't look at him today and imagine him in bed with her.

"So here are the rules."

"Rules?" Tom shot a glance toward Lauren, as if expecting her to interfere. "She gets to make rules?"

"Let's listen to them first, shall we?" Lauren said.

"You can consider them expectations, if it bothers you less than rules," Ellen told him. "Maybe even *vows*." Okay, that came out snide, but she couldn't help it. "While we are dating, while we are sleeping together, while we are in any way, shape, or form, attempting to continue our marriage, you are not allowed to have sex with another woman."

She waited for his objection. When none came, she continued: "Sex, despite what a former president and a couple of rock stars think, is not limited to genital intercourse. This agreement covers oral sex, mutual masturbation, dry humping, and"—she paused for breath, steeling herself to get the words out, knowing the Ellen of a year ago could never have said them—"the ever-popular titty fuck. And pretty much anything else that involves another living human besides you and me." She bared her teeth at him. "You can keep your hand. And any inflatables you're fond of."

He stared at her, openmouthed, as if she'd morphed into an ogre right in front of him, and she couldn't help but chuckle.

Finally he said, "You sound like you've been hanging out with lawyers. Foul-mouthed ones at that."

"Actually, I have." She was quite proud of herself. She'd laid out all her points without a single stutter or blush. "Agreed?"

"I—"

"You'd better be sure, Tom. This is your last chance. *Our* last chance."

He pondered it longer than she would have liked. Oh, she wanted him to take his answer seriously, but shouldn't he have known already? The fact that sleeping around was not going to be part of his future if he remained married to her should have occurred to him at some point before now.

"I agree," he said finally.

"That's good." Her stomach pitched, as if she'd just jumped off a cliff. "I agree, too."

His mouth twitched, as if the idea of her doing those things with someone else was ludicrous.

"I hope you mean it," Ellen went on. "Because you'd probably prefer to keep all your parts attached." She sipped her tea calmly, but her smile was pure evil. "Just so we're clear up front."

*   *   *

THE e-mail came on Friday, from Jake@sizzle.com.

How like him, she thought. No clever names, no ego-booster monikers, as simple as that.

The message was very much like him, too. No extraneous words, just a file attachment and the note: *"You can open it. It's safe."*

Her fingers hovered over the keys, hesitating, as if she touched the keyboard, she'd set something into motion, as irrevocable as touching him had been.

They'd made no plans to stay in contact. She hadn't given him her e-mail, her phone number. Though it wasn't any great trick for him to get them; the office certainly had them.

But it had never occurred to her that he would go to the trouble. There was no reason to do so.

The topic of the future had never come up between them. Why should it? It was perfectly obvious to them both that there wasn't any. Their lives ran along vastly different paths; their goals and plans couldn't be more divergent.

The next batch of guests began to arrive the day she'd left Sizzle. And Jake would be there, charming them all, king and jester combined of his little fiefdom, and surely there'd be another woman or two to catch his eye.

She liked him. They got along well out of bed and famously

in it. She was modest about her appeal, but she wasn't stupid. He'd enjoyed it as much as she had, which was about as much as it was humanly possible to enjoy something and not fry a few critical nerve endings in the process.

But that was all. It had to be.

She gripped the mouse, moved the pointer over the paper clip that signaled the attachment, and her stomach did that shaky lurch, the same jittery burst of lust and excitement that warmed it every time he kissed her, even that last time, even after he'd kissed her what seemed like nonstop for three days and nights.

She closed her eyes and smelled the beach. Smelled paradise.

She let go of the mouse, and her forefinger hesitated over the delete key.

It would be the smart choice. Gone, along with his address, if not her curiosity.

She and Tom were going on with their marriage. Tonight was a critical first step.

"Shit!" She was going overboard on the cursing lately, as if she was making up for lost time. She was going to have to start clamping down on the habit before she began cutting loose around the kids.

Instead, she closed down her Outlook and went off to get ready for her date with her husband.

28

First Times

DATING at forty-two was vastly different than dating at twenty. And dating the man you'd been married to for twenty years was . . . well, it was just downright weird.

He escorted her politely to her—their?—front door, taking her elbow to make sure she didn't slip on the slick sidewalk. After two days of snow they were having a warm spell—twenty-five counted as balmy in January—and it turned the air damp and soft. The snow was still clean, sparkling like crushed glass wherever the light fell on it, and the sky was gray with thick clouds that allowed only the faint outline of the moon to glow through.

"Well." She'd left the front light on, and the rest of the house was dark but for the weak blue glow of a video screen from Eric's window. She hoped he hadn't played nonstop since she'd left. She really should tighten the rules on daily game time, but he brought home straight As, and it was hard to come down on him. She'd go back to molding his young mind after all the trauma of the broken home—or nearly broken home—was behind them.

"Well," Tom echoed. His hands were respectfully in his pockets, his gray coat open.

"I'll see you . . . sometime." She reached into her purse for her keys.

"On our first date you didn't let me get to first base," Tom said. "Do the same rules apply now?"

"You remember?" A lot had faded over the years, but not

their first date. She remembered exactly what he wore: pressed khakis and a blue button-down, which had stuck out like an army uniform when half the students lived in scrubs or sweats. She'd been flattered that he'd made the effort for her. Abused tennis shoes on his feet, because he hadn't owned any good shoes back then.

"Of course I remember." He'd dressed up tonight, too, but his clothes probably cost about as much as a quarter's tuition had when they were in college. Black cashmere sweater, gray wool pants with an elegant drape, black loafers polished by someone who was a pro at it.

"Sure you do," she scoffed.

"Mmm-hmm. We went to *Trading Places* at the campus cinema, and you wouldn't look at me for five whole minutes after Jamie Curtis took off her top. I dribbled Dr Pepper on my shirt and tried to hide it, and you were nice enough to pretend not to notice. I wanted to take you out for pizza afterward, but I only had five bucks and was too embarrassed to tell you. You made me drop you at the door to the dorm, and your hair was cut to right here"—he lightly touched the side of her jaw—"and you had dangly silver earrings that swung below the fringe, and all night long I kept forgetting what I planned to say, because I couldn't stop looking at your neck."

She stared at him.

Tom was not romantic. His presents were either casual—the automatic roses, the obligatory perfume—or outlandish, from the best jeweler in town, when he was feeling guilty. He didn't send her sweet notes or call her in the middle of the day "just because."

Never in a million years would she have thought he remembered their first date in such detail. Not before he started cheating on her, and certainly not now.

"And I punched a tree on the way home because I hadn't gotten to kiss you," he said.

"You said you hurt your hand playing touch football."

"I could hardly tell you the truth, could I?"

"It wasn't my fault," she said. "You didn't try."

"Don't remind me." He made a face, still aggravated by the hesitant boy he'd been. "Are you saying you would have *let* me, if I'd had enough balls to try?"

She'd gone back to their dorm room and asked Jill what she'd done wrong, because she'd sent out every signal she knew, and he hadn't tried to kiss her. "Sure."

"Oh, don't tell me *that*."

"You made up for it later."

"That I did." He grinned. "So what about tonight? What are the ground rules?"

She had less than a month before she had to know, one way or the other. It was probably time to get started.

"If I told you, that'd take all the adventure out of it, wouldn't it?"

He'd kissed her on the second date, halfway through, right in the middle of the football game. Because he couldn't wait any longer, he'd told her later. He'd been hesitant, so quick he'd nearly missed, and he'd tasted of popcorn.

He wasn't shy anymore. Now he was sure, and firm, and flavored with the scotch he'd had after dinner. And maybe a little too practiced, if one was going to be picky about it.

He pulled back slowly, smiling as he did so, his breath smoking the air.

"Well," she said again, and turned for the door. "I'll see you—"

"Next Friday. I'll see you next Friday."

Like she was a teenager again, she peeked out the window to watch him leave. He strolled down the walkway, hands in his pockets, a bounce in his step, and beeped open the locks on his car.

The dome light came on as he opened the door, faded as he settled in. The engine eased to life, and Tom bent forward.

Fiddling with the stereo. Tom never drove away until he'd found the music he wanted. It used to drive her nuts. She could never understand why, when they were all ready to go, he couldn't futz through the channels when they were under way.

His tires spun, throwing up a small geyser of snow. No traction; should've gotten all-wheel drive, just like she'd suggested, but he'd wanted the 750iL, and Tom always got he wanted, sooner or later.

She hung up her coat and made her usual pass through the house. Check the locks, put the glasses the kids had left by the sink in the dishwasher, lift the phone to see if anyone had left a message, shut off the bathroom light that Eric had left burning.

He was asleep after all, sprawled across his bed in his boxers and T-shirt, which made him look all the skinnier. His ribs bumped against the white cotton like they were corrugated, and his shoulders looked sharp enough to cut steel.

His sheets were tangled at the foot of the bed, their usual spot, because Eric couldn't stay still while he slept. He tossed and turned and spun all night long, as if he'd taken the monsters from his video games to bed with him and battled them through the night. She often speculated that was why he stayed so thin, burning off the thousands of calories he'd consumed during the day in fighting his dream demons.

She picked up a pair of socks with bottoms so dark it looked as if he'd tramped through mud without shoes and tossed them in the hamper, along with a damp towel he'd left in a heap by the bed. She navigated the maze of stacked books and sneakers, avoiding the tangle of cords and a healthy pile of game cartridges. On his dresser his hermit crab clattered its way across the bottom of its aquarium. Next to it the television was on mute, and a hard-bodied infomercial queen in a black leotard strapped herself into an exercise machine that looked like it belonged in a dungeon. Ellen clicked it off.

She passed Katie's door on the way to her own. Undoubtedly she was still out with Caleb. It was only eleven thirty, her curfew was at twelve, and she never made it with more than a quarter minute to spare. Ellen figured she must synchronize her watch just before she left the house, so she didn't waste one precious second with Caleb by getting in too early.

Katie'd been unusually quiet since Ellen had returned from the Bahamas. Two nights, she'd even come down to do her homework in the family room next to Ellen instead of locked away in her room as usual, not to be disturbed upon threat of death. Last night she'd even stayed at the table while Eric wolfed down his dessert rather than mumbling a feeble excuse and bolting the instant she could get away with it.

She hadn't exactly been warm. But she hadn't been her usually snarky self, either, which was an improvement. Ellen had hopes that perhaps she was outgrowing her adolescent tempers.

Or maybe she just missed Ellen. A mother had a right to comfort herself with such delusions.

But Ellen heard music as she passed, faint, as if it were leaking out from headphones.

Probably left her stuff on again. When Caleb honked, Kate went running, leaving her lights on, her computer fired up, her phone in midconversation, discarded outfits strewn in her wake like a garage sale hit by a tornado.

Ellen opened the door to shut everything down. On the bed, Katie's head whipped toward the sudden light.

Oops. Ellen knew better than to go into Katie's room uninvited. She'd be lucky if she saw a smile from her for a week.

"Sorry, hon, I didn't know you were—" Katie's eyes were wide and watery, her expression pure misery. "Oh, sweetheart."

Ellen rushed to her side and put her hand on Katie's forehead. Warm. Not horribly so, but definitely warm.

She flicked on the bedside lamp to get a better look. Katie flinched and rolled her head away. "Katie, I'm sorry, I just—" Ellen lifted off the headphones, which got her daughter's attention, and also earned her a glare that should have sliced her in two. Now *there* was the Katie she knew and loved.

"Sorry, sweetheart," Ellen said softly. "Let me just go get a thermometer, take your temp, and we'll see what we can do to dope you up."

"Not sick." Katie burrowed under her covers, until all that was visible was her moist forehead and a tangle of stringy blond hair.

"You're home in bed at eleven thirty on a Friday night. Of course you're sick."

"Go away."

"You're warm. The thermometer's in the bathroom, I'll be right back."

Her sigh was equal parts exasperation and condescension. She flopped her arms down to her sides, bringing her covers across her chest. "I don't have a *fever*, Mom. I'm in bed, under the covers. Of *course* I feel warm."

"If you'll just let me make sure—"

"Damn it, Mom, I'm *not sick*."

Wow. For all the attitude Katie'd grown with her breasts, all the you-are-just-too-clueless-to-be-real irritation she wore as frequently as her leather jacket, she'd never sworn at Ellen before.

Ellen found an empty spot at the edge of the bed and eased down, careful not to encroach too much on Katie's territory.

"What's going on, Katie?" Sick kids, unhappy kids . . . they were the worst. They never understood that when you said, "I wish it was me," you really meant it. Ellen hated the helplessness of it, and so she just kept fluttering around, trying to help, until she started to annoy them.

Katie stared up at the ceiling. She had on an old flannel shirt of Tom's, sleeves rolled up and flopping around her elbows, and her nose was red.

"Did you have a fight with Caleb? Is that what's wrong?"

Katie's mouth thinned, as if she'd pressed her lips together to keep the words inside—God forbid she confide in her *mother*—but the corners trembled.

Ellen tried again. "Is that why you're home so early?"

Katie thumped her arms on the bed in frustration, then blew out a breath. "It's just my period, that's all."

"Oh." Ellen dared to brush her fingers over Katie's forehead, smoothing away a fine strand of hair. "I'll get you some Advil, a heating pad. You want some tea? Hot chocolate?"

"No." Kate shook her head, a slow, tired roll from side to side. "It's not that bad."

"Must be pretty bad if you told Caleb to bring you home early."

Katie grabbed Chester, her stuffed purple gorilla, and hugged him close.

While Ellen waited for an answer, she took in Katie's room. She wasn't in there much anymore; Katie'd made it clear that parents were no more welcome than younger brothers. Ellen finally decided it was easier on her, as well; she couldn't be mad about clothes that weren't put away if she didn't *see* them.

There were plenty, in bright-colored piles on the desk chair, the beanbag, the floor. Bottles and hair appliances took up every inch of space on her dresser, and shiny beads looped over the corners of the mirror, which had photos of Kate and her friends, Kate and Caleb, stuck all around the edges.

Right above her bed was taped a poster of a seriously muscled young man in dreadlocks. If his jeans sagged any lower, they were going to show if that substantial bulge in his pants was real. In its place Katie used to have a safe, pretty landscape with rainbows. Ellen was grateful his tattoos were pretty much illegible.

Kate had taken down her curtains and draped sari fabric over the windows. The wall was papered with movie posters: *Fight Club*, *The Lord of the Rings*, *Donnie Darko*, *Brokeback Mountain*.

It wasn't the room that Ellen had designed for her so carefully. The lavender color she'd spent three days painting was nearly obliterated by the posters and a giant corkboard that held a flurry of photos and ads torn from magazines.

Kate, Ellen thought. Not Katie anymore, and she was just going to have to get used to it.

"Kate? What happened?"

"I told you. I had my period, and so Caleb brought me home."

"But you said it wasn't that bad . . ."

Kate's head flopped toward Ellen, eyes wide with guilt and defiance, mouth mutinous, and knowledge iced Ellen's veins. "Oh."

Shit. Shit, shit, shit. She'd known this would happen, sooner or later. She'd been banking on later. Later, when Kate was off at college and Ellen could pretend it wasn't happening. Later, when

Ellen had had years to work up to the idea, so maybe it no longer made her feel as if she were suffering from morning sickness, round three.

I'm not ready. Oh, God, I'm not ready.

But whether or not she was ready was immaterial, wasn't it? Right now it was all about Kate.

"He brought you home," Ellen said, her voice held even as her stomach pitched and rolled like she was on a ship in a grade-five hurricane, "because you had your period, so you didn't want to sleep with him tonight."

For a moment Ellen thought Kate would burst into tears. Her eyes swam, her mouth wavered, and her arms drew tight around her gorilla until Ellen thought the cheap fake fur would burst, spilling out its cotton guts.

"So?" Kate said, an unconvincing snarl of defiance. "So what if he did?"

"Oh, Kate." *Careful. Don't blow this one, Ellen.* She fixated on the brooding rapper above the bed, all sneering sexuality and abs that looked like they'd been chiseled. *Fifteen. You'd do a fifteen-year-old, too, wouldn't you?*

"Mom?" Kate asked, when the silence stretched into minutes.

"Give me a second, Kate. I'm going to attempt the sane, supportive Mom thing, but I've got to get myself together first. Because right now I'm wondering if any jury in the world would convict me if I shot Caleb. I'm thinking, as long as they're all parents, I'm getting off."

"Mom!" Kate rolled her eyes. "You can't *shoot* him. You don't even know how to shoot."

"Yeah, but I'm highly motivated. Joe'll let me borrow his gun. And really, I promise I won't shoot him anyplace *important*." She indulged the fantasy for a brief but happy moment. "There, was that a smile?"

"No." But Kate's death grip on the gorilla had relaxed.

Her little girl. Oh, she looked like she belonged in *Playboy*, but in Ellen's head she was still feeding "tea" to her stuffed animals. She wondered what happened to them all; Chester was the only one in sight, but Ellen figured the two dozen or so that used to crowd her bed until there was barely room for Katie were safely tucked away in the closet. There'd be plenty of room, because there certainly weren't any clothes in there; they were all on the floor.

"Katie," Ellen said gently, "were you safe?"

Color crept into Kate's bone-white cheeks. Ellen felt the heat crawl into her own face as well. She'd never had any trouble spouting off the relevant statistics and warnings, but talking about specifics with her daughter, reality instead of possibility, was considerably more awkward.

"I told you I had my period."

"I know." Ellen ventured to slide her hand over Katie's, half-expecting her to shake it off. "Babies aren't the only things to worry about, honey."

Kate sighed. "You want to know? Fine. Caleb used a condom, and I used a spermicide, too. Good enough, or you want to know the brands?"

"That's okay," Ellen said, caught between tears and laughter, knowing either one would be a disaster. "Not exactly romantic, is it? But I'm proud of you."

Kate slanted her a surprised look. "I didn't expect to hear *that* tonight. Figured I was grounded for at least a month."

"Hey, that could still happen. But I'm glad you had the sense to be careful. A lot of girls don't." *And I'm pretty sure Caleb doesn't,* she didn't say. She wanted to, but Kate was talking, and pointing out Caleb's shortcoming was guaranteed to shut her up.

"Well, you're right. It wasn't romantic." Her lip curled in disgust.

"Kate." Ellen scooted closer. She couldn't believe what she was about to say. A treacherous, protective part of her hoped that Kate's experience was horrid, unpleasant enough to scare her off of sex for another decade.

But if Kate was going to be grown up about this, Ellen could, too.

"You know, if it wasn't much good the first time, it does get—"

"Who said it wasn't good?" She scowled.

"Umm . . . well, *usually* . . ."

"No, it was pretty good." She plucked at the gorilla's small, half circle of an ear until a shred of acrylic fur came off in her fingers.

What now? Ellen wondered. It seemed as if there should be more to this conversation. Some wisdom she could impart, some gentle advice that would encourage Kate to be cautious, to go forward slowly, but at the same time wouldn't make her feel ashamed of what she'd done.

She wanted Kate to have a healthy attitude toward her body and the pleasure it could provide, and a satisfying and fulfilling sex life.

She just hadn't wanted it yet.

"Mom?"

"Yes?"

"Dad cheated on you, didn't he?"

That caught her up short. "What?"

Kate eyed her while she rubbed the satin lining of the gorilla's ear between her fingers, the way when she was small she used to stroke the satin edging of her blanket to soothe herself to sleep.

"That's why you kicked him out. That's why you're so mad at him. He cheated on you."

Ellen had expected this topic to arise sooner or later. Kate was too smart and too curious not to consider the possibility.

Part of her wanted to start spilling immediately, spewing blame where it belonged. *Yes, all the time; it's all his fault.*

But was that what was best for Katie, or merely what was best for her? She didn't know. She was afraid that finding out her father, whom she'd idolized so much, was not all that admirable would make Kate mistrustful of all men. She wanted Kate careful, but she didn't want her hardened, too guarded to ever trust completely.

"Umm . . . can't this wait?"

"No." Kate flopped on her side, propping her head up on her hand. "This woman showed up at Dad's door when I was there. I'm not stupid."

"I never thought you were, hon." She tweaked her nose, which Katie immediately wrinkled in response. "Sometimes it'd be a whole lot easier if you were."

So this was it, Ellen thought. No more time to weigh what to reveal and what to hold back. When it came right down to it, she didn't want to lie to Kate. Kate had been honest with her tonight; she deserved the same respect.

Ellen ran a shaky hand through her hair. "Yeah. Okay, he cheated."

Kate's eyes narrowed to angry slits. "I *knew* she looked like a slut."

"Kate!"

"She did," she repeated, her voice vibrating with fury, her face hard.

Not a coincidence, Ellen thought, that this had come up tonight. So here was the reason; she'd been angry at her father, and she'd gone out and done something she knew he'd hate.

"Did he do it a lot?"

Ellen tipped her head back to stare at the ceiling, with its cheap constellation of plastic stars that Tom had put up there to encourage Kate to dream of them. "Jeez, Kate, you're asking a lot of me. Can't we stick to one awkward and painful discussion at a time?"

"Sure thing, Mom. I pick you and Dad."

"Nice try, girl." Ellen blew out a breath and returned her attention to her daughter. Her beautiful daughter, who looked tough and mature and sophisticated, and who had such a tender heart.

"Kate." Ellen couldn't help but touch her cheek, which was as downy as a baby's. No acne for Kate; that curse was going to Eric. "You know, if you—with Caleb—if you didn't *want* to—"

"Of course I wanted to," Kate put in quickly.

Ellen groped her way toward the words, desperately conscious that this was important, that she needed to get it *right*.

"I know, but . . . that's really the only reason to do something like that. Because you really, really want to."

Kate's eyebrows shot up. "You think I should have sex whenever I want to?"

"No!" Lord. This wasn't coming out right at all. "No. There are a zillion reasons *not* to have sex, even if you want to really badly. But there's no other good reason *to*." She paused, decided it was time to lighten it up. "Except procreation. As happy as I am that you were careful, at the appropriate time, you *are* required to reproduce. I need grandchildren. I don't care how you get them—grow them yourself, adopt, marry into them. But I need them eventually, or you're out of the will."

"*Mo-om.*" Kate said, with the fond exasperation Ellen was accustomed to, and Ellen smiled. It was going to be okay. Maybe.

"Or if you want to be a modern-day Mata Hari. You want to save the world, I might make an exception."

Kate giggled. "You think I'm worth saving the world?"

Ellen's heart turned over. Kate spoke lightly, only kidding, but Ellen heard the vulnerability beneath it. "Oh, baby. You're worth everything."

Kate snorted. "Yeah, you're just a *little* biased."

"Just a little."

Kate's eyes still looked wounded, deep purple bruises in the light.

"So what's really the matter, if it's what you wanted?"

Kate shrugged, a good but unconvincing show of casualness. "It wasn't the . . . it wasn't *that*. It was the . . . after, I thought it would bring us closer. That it'd be . . . I dunno, I know it's stupid, but . . ."

"Romantic."

"Yeah, romantic. Silly, huh?"

"No, sweetie. It's not silly at all." She'd thought she was going to get through this without crying. But it was starting to look like a really close call. "You know, just because you had sex once—that doesn't mean you have to do it again."

"Yeah. I'm never having sex again."

"Thank God."

Kate's eyes widened in alarm, as if her mother had taken her sarcasm as a promise.

"No, no. I'm just saying that it's up to you. It's *always* up to you. Whether it's tomorrow, whether it's ten years from now, whether it's never again. Nobody gets to decide it but you."

"Yeah, Caleb's gonna *love* that."

"So?"

She rolled her eyes again, as if the answer was too obvious to be even considered.

"No, seriously. If he's gonna be angry about something like that, if he's not going to be respectful of your feelings about something this important, isn't that something you want to know now?"

Kate dropped her eyes to her gorilla's head, tucked up against her shoulder, clearly cutting off the topic. Ellen wanted to say more, to impress how important it was, but she knew that pushing too hard was going to get the opposite response. She could only hope she'd planted the seed, and that Kate's usual good sense would do the rest.

"Mom?" Kate said softly, muffled against the raggedy stuffed critter. "You gonna tell Dad?"

"Oh, hon." Her poor, wounded, angry daughter. She'd done this on impulse, driven by hurt, and now she wasn't at all sure she wanted him to know. Maybe wasn't quite ready to give up being his perfect little girl after all. "I don't know."

And wasn't that the truth? Forty-two years old, and she didn't really know much at all.

29

Friends and Lovers

JILL's firm was a one-stop shop, combining advertising, public relations, branding, and even the occasional product development to capitalize on trends all under one roof.

The roof was a big one, the top two floors of a sprawling former door factory in Minneapolis's warehouse district. The décor featured soaring industrial-chic ceilings crossed with bare metal pipes, battered brick walls, the few interior dividers painted the saturated colors of Skittles candy and punctuated with art that looked like it had been blown up from comic books. A gleaming beast of a Harley-Davidson was parked in the two-story lobby like a sculpture, a foosball table held a place of honor in the center of the huge open main room, and a mirrored yoga studio—free class twice a day—bordered the break room, which was stocked with sparkling water, juice, protein bars, and a cappuccino machine that cost more than Ellen's van and was undoubtedly harder to maintain.

Ellen diplomatically refrained from mentioning that it looked like every other "creative" company in town, original only when compared to places like law firms and banks.

Monday morning, she breezed by the receptionist who held court over the metal and glass table that faced the rickety cage elevators, which they'd kept because of their "character," which was apparently more important than safety.

"Hi," she said. She waved but didn't stop. Olga, who was delicately and classically beautiful despite her purple, half-shaved hair and the blaze tattoos that streamed out from each eye, was a lovely girl, but if Ellen paused, Olga would inspect Ellen's eyelids and fingernails and start diagnosing her nutritional deficiencies. Then Ellen wouldn't be able to wallow in the French fries that she had every intention of ordering with her burger for lunch.

She wound her way through the maze of desks; cubicle walls "blocked flow," the head of the firm believed, which made the place lively but distinctly noisy. She turned left at a fiberglass dancing Snoopy dressed like a hockey player and snagged a homemade caramel from Mario, who served as Jill's assistant during the day and played in an emo band at night.

The senior staff had revolted three years ago and demanded actual offices when they'd moved into the space. Flow, shmoe, Jill had insisted; she needed privacy. She'd been firmly backed by their operations manager, though Jill had always theorized that he wanted walls so he could watch porn during his coffee break with no one the wiser.

What he failed to realize was that, around here, nobody would have cared. Unless you hogged the URL of a really good site.

Jill was pacing when Ellen entered her office, her phone to her ear. She waved Ellen in and indicated the nearest chair, then went back to politely reaming out whoever was on the other end of the line. Apparently the person on the phone had failed to understand that "finished by Monday" actually meant he was supposed to be finished by Monday.

In stark contrast to the rest of the space, Jill's office was serene and spare, in pale woods and delicate shades of cream. The pale green spear of an orchid stalk, its flowers a fragile white, sat in a crackled white ceramic pot on the windowsill. And what a windowsill it was: thick gray concrete that was only a foot off the floor because the rest of the wall was completely taken up with a view of the river. The glass was multipaned and old, smeared with the grime of decades, but you could still see bridges arching over the Mississippi, smokestacks spewing thick gray clouds on the far side, the sleek glint of all the new condominiums spearing toward a brilliant, icy blue sky.

Ellen had never figured out if Jill had decorated her space monochromatically so it wouldn't look anything like the rest of the office or because the pale background made Jill herself look all the more vivid and powerful.

"How do people like that manage to keep their jobs?" Jill slammed down the receiver, her red fingernails flashing in the sun like drops of blood. Her sweater was red, too, which should have clashed with her hair but somehow didn't, and she was wearing a black-and-white checked skirt that hugged her hips and flared around her knees. She stood out in the neutral space like a cardinal in snow, impossible not to watch.

"So," she said, coming around her desk, a thick glass oval balanced on steel legs, and perched her hip on the edge. "How was the date?"

"It was weird."

Jill swung her foot, so that her sleek, patent red peep-toed pump with its four-inch heel dangled by one toe. "Weird, how?"

"I don't know." Ellen blew out a breath. "We didn't know what to talk about. Weren't supposed to talk about the kids, our marriage, all that stuff. But all the usual first date topics, families, hobbies, what you did when you were five . . . we *know* all that already."

"So what'd you talk about? Sexual preferences?"

"Movies. We talked about movies." She contemplated her booted toes. "That's not really what I want to talk about, though." She lifted her eyes to the window. Cars streamed over the stone bridge. A crane swung a wrecking ball, smashing another old building, making way for the new. "Kate slept with Caleb."

She heard the click of heels on polished maple as Jill stood up. "You want him dead, or you just want me to maim him?"

She could always count on Jill to get to the heart of the matter. "I'll let you know." She swung her gaze around. Jill stood with her feet spread wide, her arms at her side, a badger in four hundred dollar shoes snarling for a fight.

"Sure?"

"I'm sure." Ellen sighed, wishing the answer could be otherwise. Satisfying, maybe, but not productive. "Besides, *you* slept with Jimmy MacGregor when you were fifteen, and you turned out okay."

"Despite, not because. But I wasn't nearly as together as Kate is, either."

"I don't know about that. You've always been together." The sunshine warmed her, a gentle heat that reminded her of Sizzle. "Ready for lunch?"

Jill grabbed a thick manila envelope from the pile on the top of her desk. "Let me run this down the hall, and then we'll go. You got a craving for anything special?"

"Beef, cheese, and grease."

"Wow, you *did* have a rough weekend." She waggled the folder. "Be right back, and we'll go have a couple of Juicy Lucys. Each."

Ellen relaxed back into the chair. "Right back," when said by Jill, could mean anything between two minutes and sixty, depending upon how many people snagged her in the hall with assorted problems.

Wearily she let her eyelids drift down. She hadn't gotten much sleep the last few nights. Her brain simply refused to shut down. But that friendly swath of sunshine drifted through the checkerboard windows, and the background music was something that a masseuse might play while she was kneading out your stress.

"Hey."

Damn. Ellen struggled up out of a groggy fog, prying open the lids that felt as if they weighed a couple of pounds apiece.

The man at the door was handsome, blond and blue-eyed, wearing a distressed charcoal gray blazer over a Gnarls Barkley T-shirt and loose-fitting jeans that were either two decades old or brand-new and outlandishly expensive. Ellen couldn't help but smile. The amount of effort put into appearing hip around here was staggering; she wondered sometimes how they had any energy left for their clients. Thank God she didn't work here.

He waited expectantly, his hand on the frame. "You conscious enough for a question yet?"

She scrubbed her palms over her face, trying to wipe away the fatigue. "Go ahead."

"Jill around?"

There was something familiar about him, with his blue, blue eyes and the thumb-deep cleft in his chin. He should have been posing for ads, rather than creating them, but she just couldn't place him.

"She just went down the hall. She'll be back soon."

"Really soon, or Jill soon?"

"Your guess is as good as mine."

"Great." He relaxed, leaning against the doorframe. "I'm Andrew McMillan, by the way."

"Ellen." She stood, extending her hand. "Jill's friend."

He shook her hand, brisk and firm, then glanced down the hall when a young girl's giggle bubbled. "We're supposed to meet at one, but my wife brought my kids down for lunch. I was hoping to push it back an hour." He grinned. "My four-year-old's got the toy department on her very determined mind, but once she gets there, she can never make it up."

"Daddy!" A blond rocket hurtled herself down the hall, leaped into his arms without a second's hesitation that she'd be caught. A second later a toddler came tripping along, as fast as his sturdy legs could churn, saved from pitching face-first to the floor by running into father's leg first.

Andrew chuckled.

"I'll tell her," Ellen said.

"Hmm? Oh." When he turned his head, the two little heads followed. "Thanks."

"They look like you," she said. "Right down to the dimples in their chins."

"Yeah, poor things didn't get a bit of their mother."

On cue, a stylish brunette rushed up. "Sorry, Andy, they couldn't wait."

"No problem." Andrew shifted his giggling daughter around to cling to his back like a monkey, then lifted his son, grinning before he buried his face in his neck, the raspberry he blew there causing merry shrieks from the toddler.

The family moved away and left Ellen staring thoughtfully at the open door.

"El?"

Seconds or hours passed, she couldn't have said which. She came out of her daze to find Jill in the doorway, shrugging into the long non-kid-friendly cream coat she'd bought before Josh, one of the few remnants of her former life she still used regularly.

"What's up? You look a million miles away."

"Yeah." Ellen stood up and tried to shake off the fog that pressed her down, weighing her shoulders as if someone had tossed a leaden blanket over them. "Andrew . . . Andrew something stopped by. Wanted to move your meeting back."

"The Zephyr account. Did you tell him yes?" She picked up her purse, a three-foot square tote of shiny red leather in a reptilian print with silver buckles that looked like they'd been stolen from a harness.

"Yeah. He had his kids with him." Her knees wobbled, and she put her hand on the back of the chair. "Cute kids."

Color seeped from Jill's face, making the sweep of bright blush on her cheeks, the glassy scarlet gloss on her lips, stand out as if they'd been painted on canvas. "They are, aren't they?" she agreed lightly.

"Does he know, Jill?"

"Know what?" Too casually, she moved things around her credenza, shifting a twisted spear of opalescent glass that served as a paperweight, the sleek race car model that belonged to an account she'd worked on. She fingered her awards, five of them, cheaply burnished gold trophies on fake cherry bases.

"Don't, Jill. Just don't." *Because I can't stand it if you lie to me, too.*

A shudder ran through Jill. Then her shoulders squared, and

she turned slowly, her eyes glittering, her mouth set. "Yes. He knows Josh is his son."

Anger and hurt erupted, roaring in her ears, blurring her vision. "How *could* you?"

How could you do that? How could you keep something like this from me, how could you lie to my face, how could you cheat?

"I didn't mean—"

But Ellen had already turned for the door. There was nothing to say, no excuse that would make it okay.

I should have known, she told herself. *Nothing in my life is what I believed it was. I should have suspected this, too.*

"Ellen!" Jill's voice wavered, desperation cracking through. "Listen to me, El, I—"

"Listen to you?" She spun, all the fury toward all those women that had slept with her husband, *knowing* that he was married, knowing that he had a family, the rage that had never had an outlet, that had churned uselessly inside her for all those months, cycloned in, twisting tighter, focusing on Jill. "What are you going to say? That you didn't cheat, that you didn't lie, that you didn't *do* it? Kind of hard to say that, Jill, when you only have to look at Josh to know otherwise."

Her eyes hardened, green ice that glittered with their own anger. "It's not that simple, El. It's *never* been as simple as you think."

Heat throbbed in Ellen's chest so strongly she wondered if that's what happened to those people who supposedly spontaneously combusted. They'd just gotten so *mad* they burst into flames.

"You *whore*."

This time, when she left, Jill let her go.

* * *

AFTERWARD, she couldn't have said how she got home.

She sat in the warm cocoon of her minivan, her family car chosen for safety and comfort, as the automatic garage door eased shut behind her, and lowered her forehead to the steering wheel.

She had not one memory of driving home. Her arms had turned the wheel, her foot had accelerated and braked, her eyes had scanned for cars ahead. They must have. She'd made it here. But none of those things had swum up to the surface of her consciousness.

She was numb. As if the events of the last months had drained her reserves to drought level, and this one had finally sucked her dry. She'd used up all her emotions.

Maybe numb was good, she thought. It hurt less.

She stayed there in that still, quiet darkness where no one would ever look for her, until the cold stole into the car, overwhelming the heat she'd blasted on high all the way home. Her fingers grew cold around the plastic, fake-wood steering wheel, and a permanent furrow must have been dented into her hard, stupid head.

Stupid! The two people she thought she understood best in the world, and she hadn't known them at all.

With her bones aching as if she'd been beaten senseless the day before, she eased out of the car, shuffled across the concrete floor, and into the house.

She blinked when she entered. Sunlight spilled through the windows. Somehow she'd forgotten it was midday, that it was bright and sunny outside, and that her windows would allow that sun into the house.

Still freezing, she left her coat on and made her way down the short hall to the kitchen.

It looked ordinary. She'd left banana bread cooling on the counter, the beginnings of a grocery list scribbled on the back of an envelope beside it. Eric's knit hat was hooked over the back of his chair; he'd gone off to school without it again.

The counter held her up as she wondered what to do next.

Something she could control. Something productive.

There were bills to pay. Always bills to pay. She moved to the desk that she'd built into a corner of the kitchen, with the big, sleek flat-screen monitor that Eric insisted was necessary.

The kids hadn't liked that she wanted this computer, the big one with Internet access, in the kitchen. Didn't want her looking over their shoulder, which was, of course, precisely the point.

Still on autopilot, she clicked open her e-mail program and watched the messages pile up. *Sick of Dating? . . . Your check is still waiting! . . . Want to cum like a porn star?*

Crap, all of it.

Once she deep-sixed all the spam, the only unread message left was the message from Jake, which might as well have been in neon with blinking lights around it for as much as it stood out and took up space in her mind.

What the hell.

She double-clicked the little paper clip icon, and the file opened, dark and violent color blooming across her screen.

It was the beach. *Their* beach, the one in front of his bungalow, a perfect, deserted curve of sand and sea.

But this photo would never end up on a travel brochure.

A storm rolled in from the sea, thunderclouds stacked like thick, dangerous smoke on the horizon, with a wild flash of lightning bursting within. The waves were higher than she'd ever seen them, brawny things with white foam edging the tops like bared teeth, roaring their way to crush the defenseless shoreline. At the edges of the screen, palms bent sideways, whipped by a fierce wind, vulnerable and exposed against a remorseless storm.

The protective shell inside her burst, the numbness shattered, emotions rushing through.

She hit *Reply* and began to write.

30

Just Sex, Take Two

"ELLEN! What the hell is this!"

Ellen, who'd been standing in front of the full-length mirror in her bedroom, trying to decide exactly what was the appropriate clothing to wear on the night you planned to sleep with your husband for the first time in almost six months, contemplating her fourth outfit of the night, came running when she heard Tom holler.

She got far enough down the stairs to see what was up before she started laughing.

"Ellen? What the hell is this?"

She should interfere. She knew it but couldn't bring herself to do it.

"That's Tucker," she told him.

Tom had dressed up for the night, too, in a dark blue suit that reeked of money, and his face was sheer horror.

"What the hell is a Tucker?"

"He's a dog, of course."

She took pity on him, got a good grip on the dog's wide red collar, and hauled him off.

"Tell me you're dog-sitting for a friend," Tom said, trying with only limited success to brush off the pale gray tufts of hair that covered his suit like a cotton plant had exploded on him.

"I'm dog-sitting for a friend," she said obligingly. "But the friend is me."

Tucker wriggled against her side, and her straight black skirt went the way of Tom's suit.

"What *is* he?"

"Mine." Tucker's copious fur supply hinted at husky ancestry; his generous saliva production spoke of a healthy dash of something big and slobbery, Rottweiler or boxer perhaps; the rest was anybody's guess. What he really was, however, was 102 pounds of pure affection, which he lavished on any and all that came within reach.

He flopped down at Ellen's feet. The jumping was special effort for new arrivals; at any other time, he'd rather sit than stand—hence the 102 pounds—and now settled happily into licking Ellen's ankles.

"We got him from a rescue org on Wednesday," she said. "Isn't he great? Needs a little training."

"Just a little."

"You're my good boy, Tucker, aren't you?" She reached down to scratch behind his floppy ears, which were bigger than Ellen's hands, and his tail thumped like a bass drum.

"Why'd you get another dog?"

"Because I missed having one," she said. Their retriever had died two days after she'd called Tom's hotel room. The emergency surgery had repaired the bloat, but the damage had been too great. In the rush of everything that had happened since then, getting another dog hadn't been a priority. She'd waited too long. "Eric and Kate, too. We picked him out together."

"Shouldn't that have been something we discussed as a family? We could have gone to a breeder, gotten something with good bloodlines."

"Yeah, we could have." Except she hadn't wanted to. She couldn't care less about bloodlines; she wanted a big, floppy, gleeful family dog that needed people to love him, and that's exactly what she'd gotten.

She supposed Tom had a point. Just a teeny one. If he were to move back in soon—and that was the plan, wasn't it?—he'd have to live with the dog, too. But he worked a lot, traveled a lot, and dog care had always fallen mostly on her shoulders, hers and the kids, and so she figured she had a right to get the dog she wanted.

"Sometimes," she told him, "if something feels right, you just have to act."

Tucker rolled over, paws the size of soup bowls waving in the air, and sneezed.

"I'm glad he makes you happy." Tom didn't sound happy, though, and he was still staring glumly at his suit, which despite his best efforts now looked as if it were made of angora.

"If you hadn't just barged in, I would have been able to grab him before he got all over you."

"We're not going over that again, are we? Do I still have to wait at the door?"

She was going to have to get over this, Ellen thought. Sooner or later, she had to let it go and treat him like her husband instead of somebody who'd really, really pissed her off.

"No," she said. "You don't have to wait at the door anymore."

He took in the empty living room, the unusual quiet in the house. "Where are the kids?"

"Eric's at the basketball game. He's staying over at Zach's," she said. "Kate's babysitting. She'll be home at midnight or so."

"Really? The house is empty?" he asked speculatively, glancing up the stairs toward the bedroom. Ellen felt the jitters kick in, the ones she'd been holding at bay all week by adopting a dog and cleaning the basement and repainting her bathroom.

"How easy do you think I am? You have to buy me dinner first."

He grinned in anticipation. "Ready to go?"

"Just let me get the lint brush."

* * *

HE took her to Murray's, the old and clubby steakhouse where he'd proposed. Heck, Ellen thought, half of Minneapolis had probably been proposed to at Murray's; there were two men on bended knee tonight, two joyfully sobbing women who'd said yes.

Ellen couldn't help but think how young they were, how little they foresaw what awaited them, how absolutely certain they were they were taking the correct step.

She knew that's how they felt, because that's exactly how she'd felt.

Now, twenty-one years later, older if not much wiser, she was considerably less convinced that this was the right step. Unsure if there even *was* such a thing as a right step anymore.

Tom did everything right. He had roses awaiting her in the car, *Dom* preordered, chilling in an ice bucket before they reached the table. His attention never wavered from her the entire evening. He didn't appear to notice when a striking blond in a micro-mini strolled right by with a beast of a man that Ellen pegged as an offensive lineman for the Vikings. His Treo didn't ring once, which meant he had shut it off, which was an occurrence rarer than snow in June.

The only blip in the evening was while they were awaiting dessert. That's when he started to plan the best time for him to move home.

"I've got the apartment leased through April," he said. "But I've a day off next week, for Presidents' Day. Might be a good time to move the bulk of my things home."

Next week. She reached for her champagne glass and gulped it down. "Don't you think we're getting ahead of ourselves?"

He leaned back and murmured his thanks while the waitress placed a thick slab of cheesecake before him. "What's the point of waiting? We've dragged this out long enough, Ellen. I'd like to get our life started again."

Reasonable. Logical. Terrifying.

"I just want to make sure the kids are okay with it. It's been a lot of upheaval for them already this winter."

"What's up with Kate, anyway?" He nodded yes for coffee and forked up a piece of his cake. "She's been—" He waved his fork in the air. "I don't know. Distant?"

Delaying, she shoveled in a big bite of flourless chocolate torte and held up a finger while she chewed. And pondered.

Not the time, not the place, she decided, and shrugged. "She's fifteen."

"She is that. And how the hell did that happen?"

"I don't know." They'd packed a helluva lot into those years since he'd gotten down on one knee right in this room. He'd been too nervous to get the words out and so just thrust the ring at her. She'd said yes anyway.

"Ready to go home?" he asked as he pulled out his credit card and waved to their server.

Ready was probably too much to hope for. "Home?"

"Seems appropriate, doesn't it?" He toyed with her fingers, then reached up to stroke the inside of her wrist. "Start our marriage over in our marriage bed?"

"I—" Something inside her balked, and she didn't dare examine it too closely. "If I'm worried about Kate walking in the middle of things, well—"

"Say no more." He glanced at the check, slid his credit card into the pocket, and handed the black leather folder back to their waitress. "A hotel?"

She shuddered. *Tom* and *hotels* did not have good associations for her, not anymore.

"How about your place?" she suggested.

He sat back in surprise. "Are you sure?"

I'm not sure of anything. "Yes."

He held her hand as they drove through the streets of Minneapolis, a quick, straight shot to his apartment, which didn't take nearly long enough for Ellen's peace of mind. Her tension notched higher with every block until she was squeezing his hand with as much force as she had during the painful throes of childbirth.

He kissed her in the elevator. And again, before he opened the door and led her into the blandly decorated living room.

"Wait here," he murmured.

He brought wine, a fragrant and robust red, and she sipped, hoping to settle her nerves and her stomach, while he went to his sound system.

She stopped drinking when the music began.

"Air Supply?"

"Yup," he said. "And you had no idea how much trouble I had tracking down this album."

He came to her and set her wine aside, then took her hand to bring her up against him.

"Keep on lovin' you . . ."

"Gads. I can't believe we liked this."

"It can be excused," he murmured, and started to sway slowly with the music. "We were young."

Would that all the mistakes she'd made could be summed up just that simply: *We were young.*

He led her to the bedroom, and she froze halfway in, her eyes focused on the bed. It was motel-sterile, a plain quilted beige spread and unadorned white sheets.

"You made the bed," she said. "I didn't think you knew how."

"For you. Just in case."

But all she could think of was how many women he might have brought there.

They shouldn't have come here after all. Should have waited until there were no children home, and they could be there without danger of interruption.

But the month was over. Her time was up.

She pushed her nerves away and reached for her husband.

It was good. She shouldn't have been as surprised as she was.

Tom knew her. Knew her body, where all the tender spots were, how she liked to be touched, what rhythm made her moan. He was a determined and focused man when he wanted to be, and he wanted to be tonight.

He was clearly intent on pleasing her, using all his skill, every trick he'd learned, remembering every single thing she liked.

There was only one ragged moment, when he braced himself over her in the dark.

"Wait," she murmured, putting her hands on his chest to slow him.

"What?" His hands slid between them, touching her intimately. "You're ready, El. I *know* you're ready."

"You need to—" Her breath caught, held, when he stroked her. "Put something on. You need to put something on."

His hips went still. "You're not serious."

"Yes." She sought his gaze. "I'm serious."

He frowned. "But—"

Ellen tensed. If he said no, challenged her for not trusting him, complained in any way—that would be it for her, all the answers she needed in his refusal.

Finally he nodded. "Okay," he said, and rolled off her to slide out the drawer in the bedside table.

Ellen came three times, brisk and sharp, before Tom came once. She couldn't have asked for more.

But when he went limp against her, holding her close, murmuring soft, complimentary words in her ear, she couldn't shake the feeling that it was just sex.

31

A Little Help for Your Friends

"WHAT'S wrong?"

It was a few minutes past midnight when Tom roused from a sated sleep to find Ellen fumbling into her clothes.

"Nothing's wrong," she said. "It's just time for me to go home."

"Home?" he repeated, as if he didn't understand the word. "Why do you want to go home?"

"It's getting late." She hooked her bra over her stomach and spun it around to slide her arms into the straps. "I've got to let Tucker out."

"Tucker?" He rubbed at bleary eyes. "Oh, the dog."

"Yes. The dog."

"Can't Kate do it?"

"If she's home." Ellen pulled her thin silk sweater over her head and tugged it down to her waist. "Which is the other reason I need to go. To make sure she's home."

"Call." He held out his hand to her. "Stay."

"And make sure Caleb isn't."

"Got it. Home." He rolled out of bed and reached for the pair of boxers on the side chair. "Can I stay, then?"

She bent down to shove her feet into her pumps so he wouldn't see her face as she answered. "Not yet, Tom." Not until she could plot out the best way to tell the kids. How to explain to Kate that it was the right decision to give her father another chance, but *not* the right decision for Kate to keep giving one to Caleb. "Let's not push things, okay?"

He grabbed her as she was stepping into her skirt, bringing her up against him so their bare legs tangled together. "But it was good, right?"

It was *something*. But it was going to take her a while to figure out exactly what. "Yeah," she said. "It was good."

* * *

HER cell phone rang as she was mincing basil for spaghetti sauce. She flipped it open and tucked it between her ear and shoulder as she scraped herbs from the cutting board into the sauce.

"Hello?"

"El?"

She put down the board and her knife and clutched the phone. "Jake? Where are you?"

Background noise streamed through the receiver: the hubbub of conversations, an amplified voice making an announcement, the wail of a crying baby.

"Jake?"

"Hang on, let me see if I can find someplace quiet."

Her heartbeat accelerated while she waited.

It was a rare day she didn't get an e-mail from him. Something simple, a brief story about the 300-pound guy who decided to do a Coyote Ugly–style dance on the bar; a tale about the Hollywood agent who'd shown up, took one look at Melody, and fallen head over heels in love, and had his private plane fly fifty dozen roses to her the next week; and photos, dozens of them, until she felt she was there and knew the island better than she had when she was standing on the sand.

But nothing more. Nothing important, nothing personal. Nothing that would spur Ellen's guilt at their continued interaction to override her pleasure in it.

He'd never called her. Until now.

"Jake?" she asked again.

"I'm in the Miami airport," he said, sounding distant, his voice tinny. "Waiting for a flight."

"What—"

"It's my mom," he said, all in a rush, as if he had to say it quickly to be able to get it out at all. "It's my mom, El. My mom died."

"Oh, no." Her fingers tightened around the phone. "I'm so sorry."

"I'm on my way home to Philly." She heard him swallow, the shudder of grief in his voice. "Her funeral—" He gulped. "Her funeral's in two days."

"I'm so sorry," she repeated. She heard a *blurp* and turned to find that a thick bubble of sauce had burst, spewing red all over her clean black stove and gleaming granite counter. "Shoot, Jake, hang on—"

"It's okay, you're busy. I just wanted to . . . hell, I don't know what I wanted to do."

"Don't hang up." She slid the pot to an unlit burner, then turned the dial to *Off*. "It's fine. I'm not going to blow up the kitchen now."

"Yeah, well." He went quiet as another announcement blasted in the background. "They're calling my flight."

Shit.

She felt the pressure of inadequate time, the limitations of comfort sent through the air by electronic signal.

If she could touch him, maybe she could console him. His e-mails had been one of the bright spots in her days; he'd listened to her, filled a little bit of the yawning gap in her life that Jill's absence had cut.

And now he needed her. He had to, or he wouldn't have called her.

"Do you want me to come?"

"What? To Philly?"

"Yes. To Philly."

"I couldn't ask you to do that."

"You didn't ask, did you?"

She heard his breathing through the phone, harsh and labored. "It'd be weird. My family's . . . I'm not their favorite person, you know? And they wouldn't take it easier on you. And it has to be hard for you to get away on such short notice."

But he hadn't said he didn't want her there.

"If it'd be awkward with your family, they wouldn't have to see me. I'll just . . . stay in the hotel. Give you someplace to hide out."

"But . . ." His voice faded out, came back shattered. "El, I was going to visit her this summer. I swear I was going to go see her."

And just like that, her decision was made. "Let me make some calls, see what I can arrange. If I don't get back to you before you get on the plane, check your messages when you get off, okay?"

"You're coming anyway?"

"I'm coming."

*   *   *

IT was after eleven the next night before her plane reached Philadelphia, pushing midnight before she checked into her very simple hotel on the east side of the city, where it bumped into the suburbs that marched into New Jersey.

She'd called Jake from the taxi. He sounded exhausted, his voice thin. She wanted to go him, to help in any way she could. But having a forty-two-year-old married stranger descend on his family home in the middle of the night before his mother's funeral didn't seem like the best plan.

The knock came as she was scrubbing her face.

She padded over to the door in her robe, peeked quickly through the hole, opened the door, and opened her arms.

He went straight into them, leaning his full weight against her as if she was the only thing holding him up. She felt him shudder, his cheek cold from outside.

"Hey," she said, and kept her arm around his back to guide him into the room.

"El?" His skin was gray beneath his tan, his lids swollen and pouchy. "Thanks for coming."

"What are friends for?"

The room, with its basic industrial beige carpet and only one chair, an uncomfortable orange vinyl one stuck in a corner next to the pressboard dresser, offered no other logical place to sit except the bed.

She hesitated only a moment before leading him to it, though she left it made and scooted over to make room.

He sat down next to her, swathed in an old gray Eagles sweatshirt, a faded pair of enormous sweatpants that had to belong to his brother. He stretched out and lowered his head to rest on her shoulder. He still wore his flip-flops, but with thick white socks underneath in deference to the weather, the toe piece tucking the sock into a V.

He didn't have Philadelphia clothes, she decided. The sweatshirt had probably been left behind in his old room. It smelled musty, the odor mixing with the scent of cold and shampoo off his hair.

"How are you?"

She felt him shake his head. "Not yet," he said thickly. "Talk to me. Tell me about your kids. Home. Who's watching them?"

"My mom. I told her a friend had a death in the family, and she ran down to stay with the kids and the dog, bless her heart."

"Moms are good like that," he said.

"They are," she agreed, and her heart squeezed.

Traffic rumbled by on the highway just outside. Through the thin curtains she could see the red orange glow of the neon sign of the pancake house across the street, while she waited to see if he was ready to talk about it yet.

But he said nothing.

"Are you hungry?" she asked. "They're open all night over there."

"No. I couldn't eat." He shook his head. "The neighbors have been bringing food all day, brownies, lasagna, garlic bread, cookies. I could barely look at it without feeling sick. In a week or two I'm going to be really sorry I missed it."

"Okay. Let me know if you change your mind." It was a normal human reaction in the face of crisis: feed 'em up, just in case. She'd try again to talk him into eating later; maybe she could at least get some soup in him.

"What'd you tell your husband, El?"

Her hand rubbed his shoulder, seemingly of its own accord; her body was just so used to touching him. "I told him the same thing I told my mother."

His labored breathing was slowing down, going easy and deep. "Not that it was me, though."

"No reason to. You *are* a friend." She'd struggled with her conscience only briefly on that point, pondering the difference between a physical affair and an emotional one.

But there was no emotional affair. Their regular correspondence was certainly friendly, but they'd never edged over into delicate areas. There were no breathless compliments, no soulful outpourings, nothing she wouldn't have written to a female friend. The fact that she'd once had an affair with him was a separate issue entirely.

And besides, she hadn't made Tom fire his executive assistant, Heather, who, now that she'd put a few clues together, she was convinced he'd slept with.

"Will you tell him if he asks?"

"Yes," she said, and meant it. She could omit, but she couldn't *lie*. Still, it was better to get things clear between Jake and her. "I'm glad I'm here. But we can't . . . I mean—"

"I know, El. It's okay." It was so easy. He didn't take offense, didn't push, and he didn't make her feel stupid for having raised the topic under such difficult circumstances, even though in truth, having sex with her was probably the last thing on his mind.

"So tell me how it's going."

"About like I expected." He stiffened. "My older brother thinks I broke Mom's heart because I'm such a slacker. He's probably wrong. My sister thinks I broke her heart because I haven't been home for two and a half years. She's probably right."

"People say a lot of things they don't mean when they're hurting."

"I know." His arm looped comfortably around her waist, his leg pressing lightly against hers. "About the only ones who are happy to see me are my niece and nephew. They think I'm awe-some, because I'm the only one who'll actually play Sorry with them anytime they ask."

"How old are they?"

"Four and six. They're so much fun, Ellen. I made a mistake in staying away so long and not seeing them grow."

"That's such a great age," she said, lost in nostalgia. "You can see them every day and still feel like you missed them grow, though. It goes so fast."

"They're so cute." With his head on her shoulder, his mouth hovered at her collarbone, and she could feel the wash of warm breath over her skin where the neckline of her robe bared it. She didn't allow herself to think of what it would feel like if he moved closer. This was about comfort and friendship. It couldn't be more.

"I can't wait for grandchildren," she said. "I miss having lit-tle ones around."

"Was it raising more you objected to?" he asked. "Or just growing them yourself?"

She stilled, inside and outside.

"I don't know," she said at last. "I never thought about it much. Why do you ask?"

She felt him shrug against her. "Curiosity."

His limbs were growing heavy, as if he were on the verge of drifting off. His voice gentled.

"I was going to come and see her this year. I swear I was. She was only sixty-eight, and she seemed so strong. I thought I had plenty of time." He swallowed thickly. "I thought I had plenty of time."

"We always do."

Regret rolled off him like heat, and there was so little she could do but hold him. "Are you staying here tonight?"

"Do you mind?"

"Of course not." If it helped to be here, instead of the house he'd grown up in, where the memories pressed close and re-morse lurked in every corner, she was glad of it. "Hungry yet?"

"No. Not yet."

He fell silent. Nothing else to say, she thought, and she didn't want to push. He had to know she'd listen if he needed to talk, just as he'd always listened to her. But sometimes even talking was too much effort. *Thinking* was too much effort.

"You want to watch a movie?"

He lifted his head, his brows drawing together as he thought about it. "Yeah," he said in some surprise. "I do."

She reached for the controls and cycled through the offerings. "Oh! *Major League*. Perfect." Not a single touching moment in it.

"*Major League?*"

"You've never watched it? For shame. A huge, gaping hole in your popular culture education."

So they watched. And he even laughed once or twice, rusty-sounding and hesitant, but real. When he drifted off to sleep halfway into *Ferris Bueller*, she watched over him and thought how life always got you, one way the other. Nobody got off easy.

And sometimes the only thing that got you through was not having to go through it all alone.

32

Wine and Cookies

"Mom?"

"Just a sec." Ellen slid a lasagna into the oven and looked up. Eric stood in the archway that led from the kitchen to the family room, a PSP in one hand, one earbud from his iPod in his left ear, the other one dangling from its wire, and he looked worried. No surprise; he'd inherited her worrying gene, poor kid.

"Have you watched the news today?"

"You know I never watch the news if I can help it." It was the worrying thing; watching the news added enormously to her already substantial list, to the point that she never did anything else. If something happened that she really *had* to know, no doubt someone would tell her. She opened the dishwasher and slid in the cutting board.

"I was watching the game, and—"

She paused, holding the dirty skillet she used to sauté sausage and garlic. "You were playing a video game, listening to music, *and* watching TV at the same time? Isn't that an overload of electronic input, even for you?"

"Mom."

"That can't be good—"

"Mom," he said in exasperation, and then he spoke, carefully enough to put her on alert. "You know how, in between periods, they do a short news bit? There was this thing about a cop getting hurt, and I think it's your—"

The skillet hit the sink with a loud clang, and she rushed to the TV. But by the time she got there, the weatherman was talking about the blizzard expected over the weekend.

"Dammit!" She rounded on Eric. "Was it a shoot-out? Is he—" The words caught in her throat, and she couldn't make them come out.

"Mom, easy." He patted her awkwardly on the arm. "He's not dead. At least, I don't think—" He gulped. "I think he got hit by a car."

"Oh." She flapped her hands because she didn't know what to do, didn't know what to *think*. "I should call, I should . . ." There had to be something that she should be doing. She just couldn't figure out what it was. "Think, Eric. What exactly did they say?"

"Mom." He put his hand on her back, and she thought how weird it was, that he was the one trying to take care of her. "We'll go online, okay? Figure out what really happened." He sat her in a kitchen chair while he went to the computer desk, his fingers flying—he was so much faster than she was—while he called up the front page of the local paper. She saw him scanning, frowning, before he turned to her.

"Okay," he said. "Here's the deal. It happened last night, and he wasn't even on duty. He stopped on 394, just past the tunnel, to help some old lady change a tire, and he got hit by a car. They took him to Hennepin County, and he's listed as stable, but it doesn't say much more than that."

"Stable," she repeated. Stable was good, wasn't it?

She got to her feet. "I'm going to make a phone call."

*   *   *

THEY wouldn't tell her anything at the hospital. Wouldn't tell her anything at the station, either, just referred her to their information officer, who reeled off a practiced statement that didn't tell her a damn thing more than the article had.

Finally, in desperation, she dialed his cell phone.

"Hello?" The woman's voice was shaky, unfamiliar.

"Ah . . . I'm looking for—"

"Now's not a good time—"

Ellen took a stab. "Cindy?"

A good five seconds passed before she said anything. "Yes, this is Cindy. Who are you?"

"It's Ellen. Ellen Markham, I don't know if you know who I am, but—"

"Oh, Ellen." She sounded relieved. "Of course I know who you are."

"I'm sorry to bother you, but . . . they wouldn't tell me anything. I just found out. How is he?"

"Ellen." She heard Cindy suck in a big breath, blow it out again. "He's okay. I guess he's okay. He was changing a tire. Stupid; should have called a tow truck, but the lady was on the way to see her grandkids, and . . . well, you know how he is."

"Yes." Okay. She'd said okay. Ellen's heartbeat, which had been at least double its normal rate, started easing down.

"They were off to the side, should have been far enough, but some idiot . . . he'd been drinking, he's in custody, we're lucky it wasn't worse."

"Lucky." The difference between lucky and unlucky was so narrow. A few inches, a few seconds, between okay and tragedy.

"He's pretty bruised," Cindy went on, now briskly efficient, moving into nurse mode. "Broke an arm, cracked a couple of ribs, but there wasn't any internal bleeding. Won't be working for a while, which isn't making him happy. But he'll be okay."

"Can I see him?"

"Sure," Cindy said. "But half the force has been in and out of here all day long, and he's sleeping now. I think they're going to send him home in the morning. I'm sure he'd love to see you then."

"All right." There was a part of her that wanted to hop in the car and go screeching down there right now, a part that wasn't going to be convinced until she saw him with her own two eyes. "Will you call me? If anything . . ."

"I'll call you," Cindy promised immediately. "I should have, last night when they brought him in. I just wasn't thinking . . . well, I just wasn't thinking."

"That's all right." And understandable. "At least this way I didn't have long to worry. He was okay by the time I found out."

Cindy's laugh was rueful. "Yeah, that would have been nice."

* * *

CINDY, bless her, called as soon as she got Joe back to his apartment. A half an hour later, Ellen was at the door, juggling a full grocery bag in one arm, a huge, soft cooler tucked under the other, knocking on the door with her toe.

"Wow," Cindy said as she opened the door. "Let me take that."

Ellen gladly surrendered the bag. "When I'm worried, I cook," she said and stepped in.

Cindy put the bag down on the tiny dinette table and put her hand on her hip while the women appraised each other.

When Joe had said *gorgeous*, Ellen had figured that was love talking. But he hadn't exaggerated a bit. She had to be nearing six feet, her black hair cropped tight to her head, with cheekbones that belonged on the cover of *Vogue*. She had on a ragged pair of jeans that were a size too large, an old fisherman's sweater that was unraveling, and not a swipe of makeup, and she still looked like she could head down a runway.

"Okay, now that that's over with," Cindy said. "Damn it. You're prettier than I thought you'd be."

"Thank you," Ellen said, smiling. She'd been prepared not to like her; what kind of a woman would divorce Joe? But Cindy's smile was full of warmth, and she'd welcomed her ex-husband's female friend without making the slightest attempt to scare her off with her beauty.

"He's in bed," Cindy said. "I don't know if he's asleep or not."

"How'd you manage that?" Ellen would have bet that Joe would have bolted for the precinct the instant he'd been sprung from the hospital.

"Drugs," Cindy admitted. "Really, really good drugs."

"Some of that stuff should go in the fridge." Ellen dropped the cooler on the table with a relieved sigh.

"I'll do it. You go ahead and go see him."

He was asleep after all, cuddled under a blue blanket, only his head and a bare arm poking out. He didn't look as bad as she expected; there was a bruise on his shoulder, a neat row of stitches under his chin, but his color was good.

"Hey," he said, his eyes fluttering open.

"I thought you were asleep."

"Kinda." His voice was slow, sleepy, and she couldn't help but smile. She'd bet there were very, very few people in the world who ever saw this side of Joe Marcioni, and she felt privileged to be one of them.

"Had a bit of an adventure, did you?"

"S'nothing," he slurred. "Way to get the ladies to make a fuss over me."

"Yeah, well." Carefully, she brushed his cheek. "Wouldn't do to wreck your pretty face, would it?" He really was okay, she thought, and for the first time really believed it. Thank God. "I just wanted to check on it. You go back to sleep."

"Naw." He rolled his head toward the door to find Cindy standing there, smiling at them. "My two favorite girls. Lucky me." He tried to fold down the blanket, swore when the cast prevented his right arm from performing as ordered, then flapped at the covers with his left. "Get in. Either side. Luckiest man on Earth."

Cindy laughed indulgently. "In your dreams."

"Thazza plan."

There weren't many women, Ellen reflected, that could listen to her husband, ex or otherwise, invite another woman in his bed and not be upset about it, good drugs or not. Which only went to prove how good a job Joe had done of convincing her how much he loved her.

Cindy Marcioni was a lucky woman, and Ellen only hoped she had the sense to appreciate how much.

Joe's head lolled toward Ellen. "You bring food?"

"All kinds," she assured him. "You can eat for weeks."

"Thass good," he murmured, his eyelids drifting down. "She's really sexy, but she can't cook for shit."

"You're welcome," Ellen said, but he was slipping off already. "Well." She straightened. "I suppose I should go."

Cindy nodded. "You don't have to," she ventured.

"If you don't mind—" Cindy crumpled. Her shoulders sagged, her lips trembled.

Ellen hustled her to the couch, and Cindy dropped into it as if she'd been on her feet for a week.

"Do you have to work tonight?" Ellen asked her.

Cindy blinked up at her, as if the question hadn't registered. "What?"

"Do you have to work tonight?"

"No. My next shift's Thursday."

"Okay. Hang on." She found a bottle of Pinot, filled a glass to the brim for Cindy, giving herself a restrained splash, and dug out the bag of oatmeal-bittersweet chunk cookies.

"Here we go." She handed Cindy a glass, which she downed half of before Ellen settled herself on the couch.

Ellen decided it would be better to ease into things. "How'd your parents meet?"

"Hmm?" Cindy raised her brows in surprise, then shrugged as if to say, *Why not*? "My mother was in the Peace Corps. Mali. She brought my dad home as a souvenir of Africa."

"Are they still together?"

"Oh, yes," Cindy said, "off to Phoenix for the winter like good little snowbirds."

Ellen took a sip. Not bad. "It couldn't have been easy for them."

"I suppose not," Cindy said thoughtfully, as if she'd never considered it much before. "But it seemed easy to me, as I was growing up."

"They must love each other a lot."

"Yes." She drained the rest of her wine and stared into the empty glass as if she didn't know where the rest had gone. "They do."

"Here." Ellen refilled Cindy's glass, resisted giving any more to herself, but gave in to the lure of the cookies, which was, she figured, the lesser of two evils. At least when there was driving involved.

"Thanks." Cindy leaned back, closing her eyes, and sighed.

"Did you get *any* sleep last night?"

"Not really," she said without opening her eyes. "I was on duty when they brought him in." She shivered. "I've had that nightmare since I met him. That I'd be in the emergency room when they brought him in."

"I bet you figured he'd be shot, though."

Cindy brought her head up to glare at Ellen.

"Was it any easier?" Ellen asked lightly.

"Was *what* any easier?"

"You've been divorced a while." Ellen took another bite of cookie before she continued. "Was it any easier now than it would have been a year ago?"

Cindy didn't answer, just gulped her wine and went back to resting her eyes.

"That must be a scary place to work," Ellen said conversationally.

"Hmm?" Tension seeped visibly from her. If Ellen was a kinder and more sympathetic woman, she'd let her off the hook. But life was too short and Joe meant too much to her for her not to make the attempt. "Not really."

"Oh, come on. It's Hennepin County! Overdoses, psych patients."

"We've got good security."

"Still, must be exciting."

Cindy gave a slight shrug. "And rewarding."

"Of course, rewarding." Nope, she decided. One cookie was all she was allowed today. "Diseases I've never heard of, spread in all kinds of nasty ways. Don't you worry about catching something?"

"I'm very good at my job."

"I'm sure Joe worries about you, though."

Cindy only bothered to open one eye, but the glare was still effective. "You're not that subtle, you know."

"Sorry. I've got teenagers. Subtle doesn't work on them."

"Why are you trying so hard?" Cindy asked, sounding genuinely curious.

"Maybe I'm just a sucker for happy endings."

"Maybe." Cindy sat up, refilled her own glass, and poured a healthy dose into Ellen's. "And maybe you love him a little bit yourself?" she said. Her smile was warm, her voice soft.

"And maybe," Ellen agreed, "I love him a little bit, too."

33

Now or Never

ELLEN slogged through the rest of February, a gray and weary month of oppressive skies and dreary weather. The temperatures were higher than January, but the moisture in the air made it feel colder, with a chill that seeped into the bones and sank its claws deep.

Kate and Caleb broke up twice but reconciled almost immediately—but not before the entire household had to endure nights of the drama of a heartbroken fifteen-year-old. Ellen hoped that next time, Katie would either marry him or kill him, just to get it over with and put the rest of them out of their misery.

Tom tried to be patient and failed miserably. He just couldn't understand why, now that they were sleeping together, he couldn't move back in and get on with it. What was Ellen waiting for?

What *was* she waiting for? There wasn't going to be any great sign from above to assure her she was doing the right thing.

Ellen and Tom spent three more nights together. Already she could feel them falling into the same old patterns. It was so easy to do the familiar things they'd done a thousand times before. Efficient, satisfying. But also, she was afraid, part of what had sent Tom in search of new excitement.

Yes, she decided one gloomy Thursday, when Kate was out and Eric was shut in his room playing a game and she found herself sitting alone in the family room, watching a sappy movie on Lifetime and blubbering. Tucker cuddled up and licked her face, trying to cheer her up. He was a good dog, the best dog in the world, but in the end he was still a dog.

What was she waiting for? Nothing.

If she was going to do it, she might was well do it right.

She told Eric she was going to Dad's—he was too engrossed to ask any questions—before she called Katie to make sure she'd be home soon and to tell her not to worry if she was out late.

Then she dug far into the back of her lingerie drawer, pulling out a matching set in sheer black lace that Tom had given her one Valentine's Day and she'd never worn.

Corset, skimpy panties, garter belt, stockings, the full sex-in-a-kit complement. She remembered why she hadn't worn them: the lace was scratchy, and the panties were prone to a world-class wedgie. But sometimes sacrifices had to be made, and she didn't plan on having them on that long, anyway.

It was too cold for sandals but she owned a pair of sky-high black pumps she'd rarely worn.

Standing in the middle of her room all tarted up, her hands icy and slick with sweat, she wondered just how far she could go.

But if she couldn't go all the way, it was better to find out now.

She threw her coat straight over the underwear, double-checking the knot on the belt to make sure it wasn't coming open before she was ready. Then she grabbed her car keys, the key to his apartment that Tom gave Eric, and climbed into her minivan.

Her hands cramped around the steering wheel as she crept through the darkened streets, sliding around corners in the slush, nearly having a heart attack when she thought she was going to skid right into a fire hydrant.

That'd be an eye-opener for the paramedics. An overaged stripper in a minivan.

She stood outside Tom's door for a long moment, giving herself an inspirational pre–hot sex pep talk that unfortunately sounded a lot more like the Gipper than Mae West.

There was a fair chance he wasn't even home from work yet.

That'd be okay, too, she decided. She'd wait for him in bed, tell him he could move home anytime, and then they'd celebrate.

Surprise was a good thing in a marriage, wasn't it? That's what all the magazines claimed.

The lock snicked open, and she went in, closing it behind her. There were no lights in the living room, only the soft glow of the over-stove bulb in the kitchen and the yellow smolder of the city lights through the uncovered windows.

No, he wasn't home. Her heels clicked on the linoleum as she headed for the bedroom, froze in midstep when she heard the sound, a low, husky groan that cut off abruptly, followed by a high-pitched giggle.

Leave, she told herself. *Just leave, and forget all about it. Forget everything.*

But her feet moved of their own accord, carrying her toward the bedroom.

The cheap bedside lamp was on low, a pink bra trailing over the shade. Clothing cluttered the floor, and there was a brace of bottles and used Kleenex on the table.

It was just enough light to illuminate Tom's big white ass, bobbing up and down on the bed like a fishing float on Lake Minnetonka while he grunted like an old hog.

Damn him. Damn, damn, damn.

Afterward she'd be surprised that it never occurred to her to simply slink back out the way she came. They'd never have known she was there. A year ago, that's surely what she would have done, mortified and hurt.

This time she was just plain mad, and instead of creeping off with her tail between her legs, she looked around. His big, heavy Johnston & Murphy oxfords lay discarded on the floor at her feet, next to a pile of smelly black socks and a really tacky thong. She picked one up, took careful aim, and let fly.

"Ow!"

It caught him square on the butt with a satisfying *thwack.* Tom flopped over like a landed fish, and horror flashed over his face. "Ellen!"

The redhead with a few miles on her sat up, and Ellen noted with some satisfaction that, once she hit vertical, her boobs slid down nearly to her navel. "Baby, what's going on—"

"I hope he suited up," Ellen told her, then rounded on Tom. "You gave me herpes, you son of a bitch!" She wanted Red furious, too, as furious as she was, and she suspected the information that Tom was married wasn't bad enough to do it.

Horror morphed instantly into confusion. "What the hell are you talking about?"

The woman scuttled away from Tom like a scalded crab, dragging the sheet with her, and held it ineffectually in between her breasts as she stood helplessly by the side of the bed. "What's she talking about? You swore to me you were clean!"

"Yeah, well, he does a lot of swearing, sweetheart," Ellen said. And promising, and vowing, and none if it meant a damn thing.

"Wait a second, wait a second." Shaking his head as if he could force things to start making sense, he grabbed for a pillow and used it to shield his crotch.

"Don't know why you're bothering with that," Ellen said. "It's not like it's any news to us. Right, hon?"

"What the hell is going on!" the woman shrieked. "Tommy?"

"She's just my wife, Mel," Tom said, and Ellen wondered if he'd always been that stupid, or if it only happened when his dick was hogging all the blood flow.

"Wife?" Ellen flinched at the rising shriek, expecting glass to start popping any second. "You said she didn't care!"

"If I were his wife," Ellen said reasonably, "would I just be standing here talking to you, kindly warning against social diseases?"

The wheels in Mel's head turned slowly, but they did turn. "So help me, Tommy, if you gave me somethin'—"

"Here." Ellen tossed the key toward the bed. "I won't be needing this."

"*She* got a *key*?"

Mel's fuck-me pumps proved considerably more damaging

missiles than Tom's cap-toes had, and Mel, once she started hurling, had a surprisingly effective pitching arm.

Ellen heard his yelps all the way out of the apartment.

As she headed for the elevator she wondered if it was too late to call her lawyer.

Right after she pitched the lingerie in the trash for good.

34

Who Do You Turn To?

THE harsh ring of the phone shot Ellen out of sleep as if she'd been hurled from a slingshot.

"'Lo?"

"El?" The voice was low, thick with tears, so unlike her usual one that it took a while to penetrate.

"Jill?"

"It's Josh." Jill was someplace where there were other people: Ellen heard clattering in the background, the hum of voices. "Oh, El, he couldn't breathe. He couldn't breathe."

Ellen was already on her feet. "Where are you?"

"The emergency room at Children's."

"Hang on, Jill. I'm on my way."

She left on the T-shirt she'd slept in, yanked on the first pair of sweatpants she could find. No underwear, no socks—they both took too long. She paused in her headlong rush only long enough to wake Kate, tell her where she was going, and promise she'd call as soon as she knew anything. Shove her bare feet into boots; grab a coat, keys, cell phone, and out the door.

She'd turned onto the highway, heading east, before she even looked at the clock. Three thirty. It was still above thirty, which had turned the snow to slush. The streets were hauntingly empty, the sky dark and starless. She clutched the steering wheel as if it alone could save him, pointed the car toward the hospital, and floored it. If she got stopped for speeding, so be it. They could escort her in.

The parking lot outside the emergency room was almost full. Every car marked another worried family, another tragedy.

She bolted into the waiting room, got caught up short by the locked doors and the guard in blue before them.

"Jill Lewis . . . her son . . ."

"Take it easy, ma'am. He's in the best of hands." The receptionist behind a Plexiglas shield turned to her keyboard and clicked a few keys. "Who are you looking for?"

"Josh Lewis. His mom's Jill, I don't know when they brought him in. Is he okay?"

"Let me see." The receptionist, her hundreds of bead-ended braids falling forward as she bent over her screen, was rock-solid calm. Frantic people nearly vaulting over her counter to make the computers run faster were probably standard fare for her. "Okay, they're still here in emergency." She looked up, her eyes kind. "That's good. He's not in surgery, and they haven't admitted him yet. Just let me go see if it's okay if you go back. Are you family?"

"Yes," she lied without a blink.

It was probably only thirty seconds before the receptionist returned; it felt like thirty hours. "Okay, you can go on back." She buzzed the door open. "Come in. Down the hall, third room on your right."

Ellen ran down the linoleum-floored hallway, the smell of antiseptic strong in her nose. She could hear a child screaming in one room, the beep of monitors in the next.

The room was small, the metal crib square in the center. The front wall was glass, with sliding doors open wide and a plain white curtain that could be drawn to block the view. The other walls were crowded with cabinets and banks of scary-looking equipment. Hooks and cords dangled from the acoustic tile ceiling.

At first glance Ellen thought she'd gotten the wrong room, because it appeared empty.

Jill huddled on a small blue vinyl chair in the corner, tucked almost behind the bulk of the curtain. She was white as the fabric behind her, her eyes wide with shock, her arms wrapped around her middle. She wore only her pajamas, a plain white cotton camisole and flannel pull-ons, her feet in white socks that were soaked through and black on the bottom.

"Jill? Where is he?"

Jill's head swiveled slowly, as if she were moving underwater. "Hmm?"

"Josh." Ellen dropped to her knees beside the chair and grabbed Jill's hand. "Where is he?"

"X—" She licked lips that were chapped and splitting. "X-ray. His chest."

"What happened, Jill?"

"Croup." She shivered, her hands as cold as if she'd plunged them into the melting snow outside. Ellen pulled off her coat and threw it around Jill's shoulders. "They think. Just croup." She started to shake, and Ellen helplessly rubbed her upper arms, trying to warm her. "They make it sound—the baby books, in the books they make it sound like no big deal. Just a funny cough, keep calm, no problem. But he turned blue." She brought a shaking hand to her mouth. "Around his mouth, his nose. He turned blue."

"But he's okay, right?"

"They think so." Someone pushed a cart down the hall, the clatter making Jill flinch. "They *think*, El."

Think was never assurance enough for a mother. But Jill needed assurance. "They're never going to give you a hundred percent, Jill. That's just how it goes. But you got him here, you're in the right place. He's going to be fine." *Please, God. Please.*

Jill nodded weakly. "Yeah. Thanks, El." She looked down at Ellen, who was still squatting by the chair. "You came."

"Of course I came." It had never occurred to her to do anything else. And she'd known, every second of the drive, that if she'd been the one who'd called, Jill would have come running, no questions asked, no matter what.

"We can't use our cell phones here. I couldn't remember . . . the only number I could remember was yours."

"Do you want me to call your mom?"

Jill shook her head. "Not until we know . . . something. It'd only upset her."

A tiny woman in scrubs, who didn't look old enough to be babysitting, much less be responsible for seriously ill children, bustled into the room with Josh in her arms. His head rested on her shoulder, his eyes at half-mast, and his face was red as if he'd been crying.

Jill shot to her feet. "Is he—"

"Oh, he's fine," the nurse said. "He was a trouper."

"The X-ray, did they find anything?"

"The doctor'll be in to talk to you about it shortly."

She eased Josh down to the mattress and tucked a blanket around him. He looked so tiny there, listless, drained of his usual energy. Ellen creaked to her feet, her cramped legs protesting being too long in that position. She and Jill took up a place on each side of Josh as the nurse clamped an oxygen monitor on his tiny finger.

"His temps only ninety-nine point six," she said. "And see? His oxygen's up to ninety-nine. He didn't like the X-ray much though, poor guy."

Josh gazed at his mother through exhausted, half-closed eyes and managed a gummy grin. Jill choked back a sob, which made his face pinch up in consternation.

"Hey, fella." Ellen rubbed her hand over the soft down of his head.

The nurse paused at the door. "You need another chair in here?"

"If it's not too much trouble."

"And you are?"

Jill's eyes met Ellen's over the crib. "She's my best friend," Jill said.

"Shh." Ellen winced and shot a worried glance at the nurse. "You're supposed to say I'm your sister."

"Close enough. I won't tell if you won't." The nurse's shoes squeaked as she went into the next room and returned bearing another chair. "Here you go. Five, ten minutes, the doctor'll be back. The call button's right there. Push it if you need anything."

They sat down, eyes never wavering from Josh, as if, if they watched him closely enough, it would ensure that there was nothing really wrong. Ellen stroked his chubby leg, which felt healthy and solid and warm. Jill tucked her finger into his fist, and Josh drifted off, blissfully unaware of all the drama he'd caused.

"I'm sorry, El," Jill said quietly. "Really sorry."

"Don't think anything of it. I'm glad you called. Would have been ticked if you hadn't."

"That's not what I meant." Her thumb bumped over the back of Josh's hand, back and forth, as if she couldn't get enough of touching him. "About Josh. About his father. I'm sorry."

"Me, too." Josh coughed, a harsh, deep bark, and they both sprang up immediately, Jill's finger hovering over the call button. But he settled down immediately, the episode barely interrupting his nap.

"I think it bothers me more than him," Jill said.

"It won't be the last time for that, either," Ellen told her. "And I *am* sorry. That I . . . I should have at least listened. I owed you that much."

"True. You did." Jill managed a weak smile. "But you came tonight. That's what matters."

"I'm still not sure what I was mostly mad about. That you hid something like that from me, or that you'd . . . it got all kind of mixed up together inside me, that and everything with Tom, and it . . . I was just so *furious*."

"I know." Jill gazed down at her son, and her smile grew wider. "You want to know the worst part? The truth is—" She leaned over the bar and lifted his hand, pressing a quick, soft kiss on his fist. "I still don't even know if I did it on purpose or not."

"What?"

"We had a party. A dinner, in Chicago, to celebrate winning the Morrissey account."

"I remember that."

"Yeah. We had a *lot* of wine, and our hotel rooms were right next to each other, and . . . I told myself it was just one stupid mistake, for both of us. An accident that neither of us intended. Never happen again."

Jill glanced toward the monitors, the automatic check she took every few seconds. The monitor blinked reassuringly, a steady heartbeat, good oxygen levels.

Her eyes shimmered. "But you saw his kids, Ellen. They come into the office every now and then, and they're so *cute*, and so sweet, and smart, and I . . . I wanted one. Maybe I did it on purpose."

"So what if you did? I'm pretty sure you didn't knock him down and steal his sperm."

"Yeah, well . . ." Guilt overwrote the fatigue on her face. "You know that if I make up my mind—"

"You can seduce any man in the civilized or uncivilized world? Please. He's a grown-up, and well, you're kind of a shrimp. I'd wager he could have fought you off." Even in his sleep Josh had managed to find his fist and was sucking half-heartedly, in and out of dreams. "And anyway, look at him! What difference does it make now? He's here, and that's the only thing that really matters."

For the first time tonight the tension drained from Jill. "If anybody got a gander at either one of us right now, they'd think we'd never be able to seduce anybody."

Ellen ran a hand over her hair, which was snarled up as if she'd been riding in a convertible for hours, and tugged at the torn hem of the shirt she'd stolen when her daughter had decided it was too faded to wear. "Speak for yourself, Lewis. I had to fight off two handsome interns just to get in here."

"Well, looks like things are going better in here." The doctor was spectacularly gorgeous, and if she claimed to be thirty she was lying by at least a couple of years. Her scrubs were hopelessly wrinkled, the stethoscope around her neck askew, and her dark, shiny hair falling out of its ponytail. There was an ugly yellow splotch Ellen preferred not to speculate about on the pocket of her white coat.

"Ellen, this is Dr. Subramani."

She walked to the light box on the wall, slid in the X-ray she carried, and flicked it on. "Looks good. See?" She pointed at the center of the X-ray, where Ellen could identify ribs but not much else. "Everything's clear. No pneumonia."

"That's good, right?"

"Yes." She clicked off the light and turned to face them, jamming her hands into her coat pockets. "We're going to admit him, Ms. Lewis. Just for the night, to be extra safe. We took a few cultures that won't be back until morning, but I don't expect to find anything. His temperature's not that high. I'm convinced it was just croup, just an unusually nasty case of it. You did the right thing by bringing him in."

Tension drained so visibly from Jill that Ellen thought she might crumple to the floor. "So he's fine?"

"Oh, yes. We gave him some meds to open up his breathing. I'm going to order a humidified oxygen tent for the night, just so he can get some sleep. And you, too. If everything goes according to plan, you can probably take him home tomorrow."

"I wouldn't want to rush it," Jill said firmly. Here, in the hospital, he was safe. The instant she took him out of the door she was going to start worrying again.

Welcome to motherhood, Ellen thought.

"We won't," Dr. Subramani assured her. "Any questions?"

"I don't know," Jill said. "I can't think."

"Let me know if you think of anything." The doctor headed for the door. "The nurse'll come when his room is ready."

Jill collapsed in her chair.

"I thought for a while there that they were going to have to check *you* in," Ellen told her.

"Yeah, me too." She slumped back, stretching her legs out in front of her. "You don't have to stay," she said, getting the formalities out of the way.

"Yes I do," Ellen answered, as they'd both expected. "You want food? Coffee?"

"Naw." She linked her hands across her belly and yawned. "So. Catch me up. How's your marriage?"

"Over."

Jill's brows shot toward the scarlet bird's nest of her hair. "Just like that?"

"Just like that."

"Let me guess. He cheated on you again?"

"How'd you know?" Jill didn't appear the least bit surprised, as if she'd expected it all along. Maybe, unconsciously, Ellen had, too, which is why she hadn't been destroyed this time, only seriously pissed off. "Caught him ass-naked, in the act."

"Right in the middle of it?" That brought her up straight, her eyes lit with interest. "What'd you do?"

"Threw a shoe at him."

"Good, good."

"Made the *lady* with him think he had herpes."

"Better." She tapped her finger against her chin, and Ellen could almost see the clever, evil wheels turning in her head. "You think that's enough?"

"God, no." After all the work they'd done, all the counseling, all his promises . . . he couldn't even make it a month, the sorry son of a bitch.

"Well." Jill nodded. "I'm sorry it's over, El. But I'm glad it's over."

"Yeah," Ellen said. "Me, too."

35

The End

At ten thirty at night the lobby of Tom's office building was hushed, the lights low, the escalators turned off. A security guard was nodding at his station, nearly hidden by a flower arrangement as big as a Volkswagon.

Ellen's tennis shoes, wet from the snow, squeaked on the polished granite tile as she made her way across the broad, wide space and roused the guard, who looked none too happy to have his nap interrupted.

"Working late, aren't you, ma'am?"

"Sometimes you just gotta do what it takes."

"Where to?"

"J. B. Halloran Trust."

"Here you go." He turned the appropriate clipboard toward her, and she scrawled her name, right beneath her husband's.

She jabbed the elevator button, hit it again ten seconds later when the car didn't arrive.

Jill had called half an hour ago, her voice jittery with excitement, told her to get her butt down to Tom's office, and hung up before Ellen could ask any questions.

What the hell was she doing in Tom's office at almost midnight? At first she figured Jill was on a clandestine mission, looking for leverage Ellen could use in the divorce case, and she'd called because she'd found something good.

But Tom's name had been in the ledger, so obviously he was

there, too, as late as it was. She couldn't imagine what they both were doing there; she only hoped there wasn't blood involved.

The doors closed quietly behind her, and her stomach pitched as the elevator shot upward. There were mirrors on the walls, and she barely recognized herself. Oh, all the same pieces, the plain brown hair and regular features, her ski jacket over her sweater, old jeans. Nothing different.

Except her whole life was different.

Jill was waiting for her in the lobby of Tom's firm, lounging in one of the black leather chairs with one bare leg hooked comfortably over the armrest.

"What did you do?!"

"You'll see." Jill stood up, balancing on precarious heels. Her hair was spiky, her makeup shimmery and glamorous, her skirt short enough to be illegal in twelve states.

"You look like a hooker."

"I do, don't I?" Jill preened. "An expensive one, I hope."

"Jill, what the hell—"

"Just go to Tom's office. You'll find out soon enough." She sashayed over to the elevator with a skill Ellen could only admire, and pushed the button for the lobby. "Make him suffer," she instructed as the shiny, sleek doors cruised shut.

Deep breath. Another.

The door was open, the light on.

"Ellen. What the fuck?"

Oh, heavens.

Jill had left him buck naked, sitting in one of the straight-backed chairs from the conference room, his hands cuffed behind him and his legs spread, his ankles secured to the legs with his red-striped tie. "Let me out!"

"Umm . . ." She didn't know whether to laugh or cry.

"Ellen, what the *hell*—"

"What the hell, indeed? Seems pretty obvious to me." Anger rose swiftly, because it was already so close to the surface.

This was what he'd ruined their lives for? Because playing sex games with women other than her was so exciting he couldn't resist. He'd broken every promise, every vow, over and over again. It had been obvious when she'd walked into his apartment in her ridiculous seduction getup and found him in bed. He'd made a fool of her all over again, and she could never forgive him for that.

Even worse, he was here in this predicament because he'd wanted to sleep with *Jill*, the one woman on earth who should have been off-limits to him. If he had one shred of respect for Ellen, he would never have done that to her. Ellen would rather have had him sleep with her sister than with Jill.

But it was now perfectly obvious that it had nothing to do with her. Where Tom and his recreation was concerned, his wife didn't enter into the equation at all.

"What do you want?" Tom wriggled futilely against his bonds. "I'll do anything."

She looked him up and down. After the long winter his skin was fish-belly white, and his body showed the toll of too many business dinners and the copious wine that went with them. The position Jill had left him in was anything but flattering, his knees wide, his shoulders slumping. He wore nothing but his black socks, which only made the rest of him look all the more ridiculously bare.

And, sadly, his dick was still at half-mast, proving once again exactly what called the shots. She wondered what it would be like to be so at the mercy of a body part that apparently had little connection whatsoever to his brain.

She tapped her fingers against her cheek as if she was giving his question serious consideration. "Actually, I'm getting what I want right now," she told him.

"Look, El, you've had your jollies. Ha, ha, ha. But you've got to let me out."

"No, I don't *got* to do anything."

"You want me to beg? Okay, fine. I'll beg." His face flushed red, on the way to maroon. "I *can't* be found like this tomorrow."

"I guess you'd better hope that assistant of yours gets here early, then. At least there's nothing here she hasn't seen before."

Ah, so it was guilt that shut him up at last. "I *knew* it," she said. "You son of a bitch."

And suddenly she was tired of playing with him. She'd tell him about Kate, that his beloved princess had slept with her degenerate boyfriend, and it was all his fault. It would be the one thing she could do to him that really hurt long after tonight's embarrassment faded.

Then he'd finally have gotten what he deserved, have some taste of the mortification and misery he'd caused her, and she could finally put this behind her once and for all.

She opened her mouth to tell him.

He looked pitiful, she thought, stripped bare and handcuffed, his small pouch of a belly magnified by the slouch of his shoulders, bulging soft and vulnerable over his thighs. In another twenty years, was he still going to be doing the same thing, only old and wrinkled and fat, desperately chasing ass, begging some woman, any woman, to sleep with him?

It sounded awfully lonely.

She waited for the surge of triumph, the satisfaction of knowing he'd be getting precisely what he deserved.

And found . . . nothing. She just didn't care anymore.

"I'm done." She grinned. "I'm *done*!"

"What the hell are you so happy about?" he snarled.

"Oh, stop whining." She pulled over a chair to face him, three feet away, and plopped into it. "Don't worry. I'll let you out. But first we're gonna have a chat."

He drew back his head, as if she were too close for comfort and he was afraid she would start swinging.

"Okay. Now then." She made herself comfortable, leaning back and crossing her leg at the ankle. "Tom, when this whole thing started . . . what did you really *think* was going to happen?"

His face fell into the sulky lines that she recognized from their son, when he'd gotten caught doing something brainless and wanted to blame it on someone else, though thankfully he didn't use it much. Yet.

"I don't know," he said unconvincingly.

"Hmm." He'd had *something* in mind, obviously. She had a sudden flash of Bobby sitting on his bed in Sizzle, and how fascinated he'd been when she'd said her husband knew she was there. "You didn't think I was going to *like* it, did you? That we were going to have an open marriage?"

His chin lowered until it nearly met his chest, the flesh beneath folding up into accordion pleats, and he refused to look at her.

"You did!" She laughed. "And here I was feeling bad because I was married to you all those years and didn't know you at all. But you didn't know *me* at all, either, if you thought I was suddenly going to embrace my inner slut."

He shrugged. "It could happen."

"No, it couldn't." She dragged her chair closer, drawing his attention. "Not me."

"It could if you'd just *relax*," he said sullenly. "It doesn't have to mean anything."

"No, it doesn't," she agreed, and he met her gaze in surprise. "But I *want* it to." She did. It was her choice, every bit as much as others made another one. She *wanted* it to mean something. There were so few things in life that were allowed to remain special and meaningful. She didn't want this one stripped from her, too.

The harsh fluorescent lights picked out all his bags and wrinkles, and, without the veneer of polish and sophistication provided by his suits, she could envision the man he'd fade into as easily as the one he'd grown from.

"Aren't you worried?" she asked, genuinely curious. "About twenty years down the road, thirty? About whether you'll be lonely?"

His mouth firmed. "There'll always be women," he told her. "As long as I'm a functioning male, and I've still got that wallet over there"—he pointed with his chin at the wallet resting on his desk next to his cell phone—"there'll be women. They might not be as pretty, and they might not pretend quite as well that they're after something besides my money, but there'll be women."

She sat back, pondering the harsh truth of it. He was right, damn the unfairness. The ratios only skewed further in his favor as he aged. A well-groomed, healthy, and financially stable man would always have options.

She hoped, with genuine and surprising charity, that it would be enough for him.

She nodded. "Okay, then, on to the future. I'd rather not drag out the divorce. I'm not going to be unreasonable, but I can warn you right now that there are going to have to be some changes."

"Yeah." He shifted uncomfortably, wincing as he peeled the damp skin of his thighs off the chair seat. "I've been thinking. You know those new townhouses going up right off Highway 100? One of those might be good for me."

"That's an excellent idea," she said. "I think the kids could even get off the school bus there. Which is good, because you're going to have to take over more of the kid herding. I'm going back to school, and then to work."

"School?" He wriggled his shoulders. "Can you unlock me now? I'm starting to stiffen up."

"Soon enough," she said. She might not hate him anymore, but that didn't mean she'd moved completely on to forgive and forget. "As to the school, I'm going back to get certified as a financial planner. I'll specialize in newly single women, divorced or widowed, and women who want to make sure they're not going to be in deep shit if they end *up* newly single."

His surprise registered on his face. "You'll be good at that."

"Yes. Yes, I will," she said and didn't have a single doubt.

She stood and bent down behind him, inspecting the black handcuffs trimmed in neon pink fur. "Oh, one more thing. You're going to need to be in charge on Memorial Day weekend. I'm going to Vegas."

"*Vegas?*" he said in complete disbelief. It took her a while to find the button hidden in the cheap fur, but all it took was a push before they clicked open. Tom brought his wrists in front of him, circling them around to loosen them up. "What the hell are you going to Vegas for?"

"I'm going to be best man at a cop's wedding," she told him and headed for the door.

"Hey, wait a second!"

She turned. He stood in the middle of his expensively conservative office, still naked but for his socks, a handcuff dangling from one wrist, his face red and eyes wide with disbelief, and she had to bite the inside of her cheek to keep from laughing.

"What about my clothes?"

"What about them? Jill must have left them around here somewhere."

"No, she didn't." He frowned. "She took them with her."

"Well, she didn't have them when I saw her in the lobby." That was Jill, she thought, always one step ahead of everybody, including Ellen. "They could be anywhere."

"You've got to help me find them," he said, panic creeping in.

"No, I don't," she said and walked out of his office. "Good-bye, Tom."

36

A Beginning

MARCH both came in and went out like a lamb. Apparently she'd abdicated the teeth to April. Easter had been celebrated with a record-breaking blizzard, heavy snow that punished the buds that had dared to chance an early arrival.

The doorbell rang on a cold and quiet afternoon, when everyone with any sense had holed up, trying to decide if they really had to shovel or if the sun would show up and do the job for them first.

But the kids had school anyway; not canceling school for anything short of a disaster that required calling in the National Guard was a point of pride. They'd refused to bundle up, both of them—that was a point of pride, too—and slogged through the mush to the bus stop.

Ellen spent a lovely afternoon making chocolate chip cookies. She'd greet the kids with them and hot chocolate; it wouldn't be much longer that cookies when they got home from school fixed everything. Her kitchen was warm and smelled like heaven, and Ellen had allowed herself to eat three, with milk, right out of the oven, before putting a few dozen aside. Jill and Josh'd be over later, if the weather cooperated; Eric was forever bringing home stray boys; and Jamie, the five-year-old next door, would be out making snowmen soon enough.

When the doorbell rang, she figured it was Jamie. He had a sixth sense about when Ellen was baking. She slung a dish towel over her shoulder. When Tucker, who typically shadowed her heels all day long, didn't move, she turned to find him with his head on his paws but his eyes on the counter where a rack of cookies were cooling.

"Behave," she told him and headed for the front of the house.

She peeked through the sidelights, then scrambled to yank the door open.

"Jake?"

He stood in snow up to his shins, wearing what looked like at least four T-shirts layered on top of each other, with a thin, ridiculously insufficient windbreaker over them all. His hands plunged deep into the pockets, as if they'd be warmer if he could just get them down far enough.

His black camera bag was slung over one shoulder, an army green duffel over the other, and he shifted from foot to foot, revealing sopping-wet sweat socks and those stupid rubber sandals. Only his head was dressed for the weather, in a purple Elmer Fudd hat lined with bright gold fleece that he must have bought at the airport.

He was the best thing she'd ever laid eyes on.

"Hey," he said, and gave her a wave. "I sold a photo."

"That's great!" she said and waited for the rest.

He sucked in a deep breath, blew it out again so it condensed into a thick fog in front of his face. His eyes, intent, determined, met hers and looked deep.

"Do you have to know," he said slowly, "how it ends, before you even let it begin?"

She didn't even have to think about it.

"No," she answered. She reached out her hand and drew him into the house.